Martian Walker

and Other Stories

Disclaimer:
The stories in this volume are works of science fiction. No character in this story is taken from real life. Any resemblance of a character to any person or persons living or dead is accidental and unintentional. Any resemblance of a commercial trade name to a real-world trademark is likewise accidental and is in no way intended to portray any link to the company holding that trademark. The author, their agents and publishers cannot be held responsible for any claim otherwise and take no responsibility for any such coincidence.

This book written in Palatino Linotype, using Office 365™.
Book and story titles use Eras Demi ITC. Chapter headings use Calibri.
Cover by Miblart (https://miblart.com/services/book-cover-design)

Title: Martian Walker and Other Stories
Author: Alan M. Atkinson (1970—)
Subjects: Science Fiction, Transhumanism, Social Issues, War, Crime.

First Printing: 2025

Printed and distributed by IngramSpark™ (www.ingramspark.com)

ISBN: 978-1-7638780-2-0

Alan M. Atkinson
Words on Paper (Ink)
Townsville, QLD 4810
words.on.paper.ink@gmail.com

This book is dedicated to the brave soldiers and citizens of Ukraine, and their fight against tyranny and fascism.

Слава Україні!

Foreword

I wrote these stories over a matter of months and even years, posting them a bit at a time onto Reddit. Quite often, when I started them, I wasn't sure how they'd end up. In that, I was pleasantly surprised.

They run the gamut of humans in a universe without aliens (though one of the humans is pretty alien), humans helping aliens, aliens helping humans, and humans fighting aliens; all showcasing the importance of teamwork.

I've done my best to present the aliens (and the humans!) as more than just two-dimensional cardboard cutout characters, there to either oppose the protagonists or save the day dramatically.

Quite often, as in real life, the conflict isn't even the point of the story.

I hope you enjoy reading them as much as I enjoyed writing them.

Alan M. Atkinson

September, 2025

Contents

Martian Walker

Chapter 1: Debut

This was it.

This was the big day.

This was the first time she would be going outside for real.

Mik could feel her heart beating faster as she breathed deeper, trying to calm herself. At this rate, Professor Ibrahim would call the test off because she was 'too agitated' or something.

Sixteen years.

Sixteen years to get to this point.

Sixteen years of growing up and being the same as everyone else, or at least similar. Everyone knew who she was, but nobody treated her any differently. There was always that back-of-the-mind awareness of *what* she was, but Ibrahim had never countenanced any discriminatory behaviour toward her.

The only incident of any sort like that had been about six months ago when they'd had a new security guard in the facility, a transfer from Burroughs, who'd pointed through a lab window at her and said, '*What the hell is that?*'.

At least, that was her best bet on what he'd said. Among other things, Professor Ibrahim had been getting her to learn lip-reading, because not everyone always had a working radio outside. It didn't matter anyway; he'd been hustled into Ibrahim's office and was gone within the day.

She knew she looked different. Her skin was dark, but not like the dark-toned staff of the Research Complex: hers was a dusty grey. If she wanted, it could go all the way to black, to improve her pseudo-photosynthesis. In strong sunlight (well, as strong as it got on Mars) the calculations said she could go all day on a pony bottle. And as a backup, her body automatically stored excess oxygen in a modified liver.

Her hair was weird, too. She didn't have eyelashes or eyebrows, but she had a kind of mohawk, silvery in colour and about three centimetres high, just on the top of her head. Professor Ibrahim said that it was a placeholder for a bio-metallic radio antenna for later versions. Mik didn't care. She thought it was pretty.

She supposed her eyes were the strangest thing about her. She'd been gengineered to be able to take low-pressure and micro-pressure environments, neither of which are kind to the human eyeball. So, it was either change the eye or protect it more. They hadn't wanted to reinvent the wheel, so she'd ended up with what amounted to a permanent nictitating membrane that could darken to protect her eyes. Her eye was so close to it that she could see through it easily, but other people could only see a blank white orb.

She'd been outside many times before, but always in an EVA suit like everyone else. Occasionally she'd been tempted to open the faceplate and have a sniff, but Professor Ibrahim had a checklist. And if she knew anything about the Professor, his checklists had to be all filled out before anyone went any further.

Her enhanced sinusoidal cavities warned her of a slight pressure change, and she turned her head as Ibrahim himself entered the room. She wanted to giggle with excitement, but Professor Ibrahim was boring when he was in scientist mode. "Hi," she said, gesturing at the triple-paned observation window showing the Martian landscape outside, with the distant striated cliff-face climbing kilometres into the air. A wisp of fines—micrometre-scale Martian dust—went by. "The weather looks nice."

Ibrahim, a little overweight, his salt-and-pepper beard neatly trimmed to fit inside a standard breathing mask, nodded solemnly. "That is why I chose today for your first outside test, Mik. I don't want anything untoward happening. I don't want surprises. I want this test to be boring."

Mik was tempted to roll her eyes (not that he'd see) and make some kind of smartass remark, but Professor Ibrahim had shown over and over that he cared for her. In fact, a chance remark had led her to understand that he was one of her half-dozen original gene donors. She didn't know who the others were, but she was happy knowing that Ibrahim was someone she could think of as her father. He'd always been there for her birthdays, with a present in hand. Oddly enough for someone who didn't like surprises, he always neatly wrapped them first.

"Don't worry, Professor," she assured him. "I've read the briefing papers several times. I have a series of tasks to carry out, and you need to record me doing it. We need to prove that Project Martian Walker—me—is a success. And then maybe Void Walkers, in about fifty years."

Ibrahim snorted in rare amusement. "I rather think you have been reading ahead, young Mik. Truth be told, your genome is good for the Void Walker prototype. Your skin is vacuum-capable, and your heat-exchange systems already allow you to survive in direct sunlight and total shade. All you're missing is the radio itself."

"Because you're still working on the engineering of a totally biological radio," Mik said. "It's got to work right the first time, every time, because it's not something an engineer can just pull out and fix. So … error-correction safeguards?"

His shaggy eyebrows rose as he nodded in acknowledgement. "You *are* paying attention. Good. You are ready?"

She glanced down at herself: t-shirt, jeans, construction boots. "I'm taking air out there with me?"

"Yes." Ibrahim nodded again. "As a backup only."

"Copy that." She couldn't imagine a situation where she'd need it, at least on a first test, but that was the point of having tests in the first place. Taking up a pony bottle from the rack beside Airlock Three, she tapped the gauge to ensure that the needle was reading true, then shrugged into the strap so it hung back over her left shoulder, out of the way. The transparent breather mask, made to cover her mouth and nose only, went down in front of her. "Okay, I'm ready."

"Not quite." He handed her a radio earpiece. "You will need to be able to hear me."

"Ah, yeah. Good point." The Martian atmosphere was notoriously bad at transmitting sound, especially in the higher registers. She'd been deliberately engineered to be good at hearing low-pitched sounds, but not everyone had a voice like a bass horn.

Fitting the earpiece into place, she ensured that it had a firm contact with her mastoid bone. Tests had established that she'd be able to hear quite well through it, so long as it didn't get jolted loose.

"Very well. Begin recording. Professor Benjamin Ibrahim and Mik Wallace going out onto the Martian surface, for initial unprotected atmospheric pressure testing. Base emergency response has been notified and is monitoring." He pulled the loose hood up over his face, then sealed the faceplate shut. His voice continued, a little more echoey than before. "Opening Airlock Three."

The heavy door to Three rumbled aside. While the pressure differential was so minor that a simple plastic membrane could hold in the air required to keep humans alive, the base had been built by people who thought the same way as Ibrahim. And besides, Mik had seen videos of the occasional dust storms eroding away plastic like water eating away ice.

It probably wouldn't do the same to exposed skin, but she didn't want to take the chance. If there was a dust storm warning, she would need to either find cover or get inside. There was no third option, even if 'cover' meant digging a hole and burying herself.

"Entering Airlock Three," Mik said as she stepped in and made way for the man who had been her mentor for as long as she could remember. "Professor Ibrahim is with me."

Ibrahim nodded to her, his slight smile visible through the EVA suit faceplate. "Cycling Airlock Three," he concluded. There was a manual wheel for doing just this in case of power failure, but it was easier to press a button, which he did. The door rumbled shut behind them.

Mik had been tested on her response to changing air pressures under laboratory conditions and had passed on all counts. According to Professor Ibrahim, humans suffered ear and sinus pain when subjected to even minor but abrupt pressure changes. Mik's sinusoidal channels had been redesigned so that this simply did not happen.

She did, however, have a precise sense of what the air pressure was at any time. Her vestibular systems had been upgraded at the same time, to allow her to orient herself rapidly in a micro-gravity environment. This was something she probably would never make use of, but her genetic descendants would certainly be able to work with.

The Valles Marineris Research Complex was lower in elevation than most of Mars, so it had an outside air pressure of about nine hundred to a thousand pascals. Mik had learned that Earth boasted over a hundred kilopascals, which she thought was just showing off. After all, the Valles facility got by on sixty kPa, though there was a higher partial pressure of oxygen to make up for it. She figured that if she ever visited Earth, she'd be able to survive on about one breath an hour with the rest coming from ambient light, and that was if she didn't have access to direct sunlight.

She *did* want to visit Earth one day. One of her birthday presents from Professor Ibrahim had been an electronic frame featuring a series of still shots of the most beautiful and iconic locations on Earth, and there had been so many of them. Also, so many *people*. Mik only knew a dozen people well, and thirty more in passing, and she could count more than that in just one picture of Times Square in New York. But she knew for a fact that not one of them could do what she was about to.

'Airlock Three Cycling … Airlock Three Cycling …'

As the mechanical voice sounded and yellow lights began to flash, pumps started up, drawing precious air from within the lock. Mik felt the pressure dropping around her, and her body systems reacting and shifting in response. Sphincters closed at the back of her throat and elsewhere, locking her body down against the pressure drop; muscular bands around her torso increased their tension to prevent bloating.

The pressure gauge on the inside of the airlock wound down the scale, and she matched it with her own internal measurement. *Fifty kPa … forty-five … thirty-eight … thirty-one … twenty-six … nineteen …*

At the same time, Professor Ibrahim's suit inflated as if by magic. In fact, it was on forty kPa and a higher oh-two partial pressure again. This would give him a far better chance at surviving a suit puncture in the Martian environment.

The pressure gauge bottomed out at eleven hundred pascals, which impressed Mik slightly; normally, it was lower. The outer door rumbled aside, the vibration barely audible in the rarefied air, though palpable via the soles of her feet. At this point, any unprotected baseline human in her situation would be shoving the air mask over their face with hands that refused to work properly, because the temperature outside was a steady seventy below zero Celsius. Which, as far as she was concerned, was a nice spring day on Mars.

Ibrahim stepped out first, and Mik joined him. She pushed her skin to near-vantablack levels, both for heat absorption and to improve her pseudo-photosynthesis, then looked up at the sun. Thanks to the photochromic nature of the membrane covering her eyes, she was able to observe it directly without damaging her retinas.

Pulling the mask onto her face, she hooked it into place, then opened her throat sphincter and gave herself a single breath of air before turning the bottle off again. "Hm," she mused. "I think there's some high-level dust there. We might be due for a storm."

Turning to her, Professor Ibrahim pointed at the pony bottle. No … at the small radio transmitter mounted in the mask, which she'd neglected to switch on. Her skin was not made to flush, or she would have. Less than a minute out on the surface, and she'd already pulled a rookie move. Of *course* he couldn't hear her in this atmosphere.

She flicked the switch. "Sorry. I was just saying we might be due for a storm. There's some dust against the sun."

"I won't argue with you on that," he said. *"We just won't get too far away. Are you experiencing any discomfort?"*

After taking a moment for a self-check, she shook her head. "None at all. I don't feel like I'm outside my comfort zone with either temperature or pressure. Atmosphere's not a great conductor, though. Should I pick up a rock?"

"Be careful," he warned her.

Well, that wasn't a no. Leaning down, she picked up a chunk of Martian gravel, a few centimetres across. As she cautiously closed her fingers over it, she catalogued the sensations. "It's cold, I can feel that much," she noted. "Not so cold that it's painful. It's just … well, cold." Unlike her pressure sense, the skin was not a very precise thermometer. "I can feel the texture of it, so my tactile sense is unimpaired."

Tossing it into the air so it fell back down at the standard three point seven metres per second squared, she caught it on the back of her clenched fist. Then she flicked it off with her other hand, sending it flying a few metres before it landed on the ground and became one with the rest of the Martian regolith.

"So far, so good." She could see his smile through the suit's faceplate. *"You're doing very well, Mik. I'm proud of you."*

"Hey, I've barely started." She set the pony bottle to scavenge, then closed off her throat sphincter and took the mask off. Spreading her arms wide, she turned in a circle. She smirked at the far distant cliffs before sticking her tongue out at them. There wasn't enough air to taste anything; it merely felt chilled as the little saliva left on it evaporated.

"What was that for?" asked Ibrahim, pulling an electronic pad from a leg pocket and starting it up.

Mik put the mask back on. She was starting to get a slight case of drymouth. Maybe she'd bring out a canteen next time. "Those cliffs are what, six kilometres tall?"

"In places, yes. Why do you ask?"

She grinned. "Someday I'm gonna free-climb them from bottom to top. Because I can."

"Just because Mars has a lower gravity than Earth doesn't mean a fall from even one kilometre won't kill you," Ibrahim reminded her. *"Now, I believe we had tasks to complete."*

"Let's do this." Mik pretended to crack her knuckles. It never worked, because the people who'd engineered her had made sure she'd never get the bends, but she pretended anyway. Then she flicked a switch on the outside of her breathing mask, to activate the built-in digital recorder. "Mik Wallace, test one, ready."

Looking around as Professor Ibrahim read off the first task of the test, she felt a swell of pride. This was Mars, and she was standing unprotected on its surface. It was *her* kind who would explore it more thoroughly than unmodified humans ever could, and *her* kind who would ensure safety for the colonists until the planet was successfully terraformed.

And then, as the Martian Walker was upgraded to the Void Walker, it would be the descendants of her genome that would spread out through the Solar System, opening the way for their progenitors. Shoulder to shoulder, humans all.

And it starts here, with me. Mik Wallace, sixteen years old and a total badass.

She couldn't wait to get started.

Chapter 2: New Friends

The spaceship spun in the void, reaction mass jetting uncontrollably from its ruptured tanks. It was caught in the gravity well of the huge blue and white planet that loomed ahead. Mik muttered swearwords that she shouldn't have known as she wrestled with the controls.

With a loud BANG that reverberated out of the speakers, the ship broke apart and began to drift to its inevitable fate. The tanks, now separated, spiralled off into the distance, still spraying fuel. Across the screen marched the words of doom: **STRUCTURAL INTEGRITY LOST. UNPROTECTED ATMOSPHERIC RE-ENTRY IMMINENT. CHANCE OF SURVIVAL <0.000001%**

"Yeah, yeah, don't tell me the odds," she muttered as she got up and headed over to the mini-fridge in the corner where she kept her drinks and snacks. Ibrahim gave her a fairly wide latitude in her choices, though he made sure to keep her supplied with candy laced with the dietary supplements her body needed to maintain her more unusual modifications. She took out one of these now, along with a soda, and headed back to her computer setup. Activating a playback, she sat back with her snacks while watching to see where she'd gone wrong.

It was halfway through when Professor Ibrahim rapped on the doorframe with his knuckles. She paused the recording and looked around. "Come in," she said, pushing her chair out so it revolved in a half-circle before coming to a halt. "What's up?"

"I came to tell you that the Connaughts are arriving in about thirty minutes." Ibrahim paused. "They have their daughter with them."

Playback forgotten, Mik bolted to her feet. "Now? They're showing up *now*? I thought they weren't due until next week!"

"They weren't," the Professor agreed, a smile appearing on his face as he watched her dart over to the nook where she kept her clothing. "There was trouble in Burroughs, so they left earlier than intended."

Mik paused while rummaging through her garments and looked over her shoulder. "Trouble? What sort of trouble?"

Ibrahim sighed, his bushy eyebrows drawing together. "It would take too long to go into now, but the political tone of the whole Hellas Basin area is becoming … problematic."

That didn't sound good. Professor Ibrahim paid as little attention as possible to politics, and the last thing he had referred to as 'problematic'—a malfunctioning atmosphere recycler—had needed to be torn down almost to the frame and rebuilt from scratch. For him to be concerned about the situation in Hellas showed how serious it was.

Fortunately, Hellas Basin was Hellas Basin, and Valles Marineris was Valles Marineris. Built into the eastern slope of Hellas, Burroughs was a good nine thousand kilometres east of the Valles Marineris Research Complex; nearly halfway around the planet, in fact. Mik decided not to worry about it, and right then she had bigger problems. "Professor? What should I wear?"

He made a *how would I know?* gesture. "I myself intend to wear an EVA suit. What you wear is your business. If I had any sort of skill in that area, I would've been married years ago."

'Incoming shuttle,' announced the base computer. **'ETA twenty minutes.'**

"Ah. I must go and suit up so I can meet them." He bent an avuncular gaze upon her. "I will meet you at the airlock."

As he closed the light plastic folding door behind him, Mik dived back into the clothing nook. She had outfits that were odd and eclectic, basic and hard-wearing, or simply comfortable. What was the right thing to wear when meeting new people for the first time? It wasn't as though she made a *practice* of this sort of thing!

"Call Kathy," she said out loud.

'Calling ... Kathy.'

A moment later, there was a gentle chime, indicating that Kathy was connected. She was about twenty years older than Mik, with a motherly air and a swathe of PhDs. Mik liked her a lot, and often went to her for advice about anything Ibrahim couldn't (or wouldn't) explain to her.

"Hi, Mik," she said. "*What's up? I would've thought you'd be going to meet the shuttle with His Professorship.*"

"I *am*." Mik tried not to let her frustration bleed into her voice, but it wasn't easy. "I mean, I'm going to be. But I don't know what to *wear*!"

"*Ah, of course.*" Kathy chuckled gently. "*The age-old problem. To dress up or dress down. What sort of impression do you want to make?*"

"I want them to like me," Mik said immediately. Belatedly, she added, "and respect me."

"*Good intentions. I like it.*" Kathy paused for a moment. "*I would suggest something bright, with something drab over the top. Such as the clothing you wore on your first outing, along with a coat of some sort in black or dark grey.*"

"But I don't need a coat." Mik wasn't sure why Kathy had suggested that. There wasn't a non-EVA garment on Mars that would save *anyone* from the temperatures out there.

"*It's not about **needing** a coat. It's about **wearing** it. It'll give you more of an adult look and enlarge your silhouette. You're very slender by Earth standards; in a t-shirt, you're almost waifish. We don't want that unless it's* *your aim to make them see you as a damsel to be rescued."*

"Okay, thanks. And should I wear boots or sneakers?" She made a private bet with herself that Kathy would suggest sneakers. They were colourful and comfortable.

"The boots, I would say. It tells everyone you're someone to be taken seriously."

And that was why she shouldn't make assumptions. "Okay, good point. Thanks, Kathy!"

"You're welcome, kid. Have fun."

"I'll try. End call."

'Call ... ended.'

Locating the clothing Kathy had suggested, Mik changed into them, then pulled out a charcoal-grey long-coat that she'd worn as part of a 1940s-era noir private investigator costume the last time they'd decided to celebrate Halloween. Briefly, she considered the fedora that had come as part of it, but decided that it would push the image just a little too far. The work boots went on last.

On the way to the airlock, she decided to forgo the pony bottle—they'd established that she could last hours on her internal storage—but she pushed the earpiece into place as a matter of course.

When she met up with the suited-up Professor Ibrahim, he looked over her outfit and nodded consideringly. "Yes. That will suffice, I believe."

"You think so?" Mik hadn't been this nervous the first time she'd been tested on low pressure atmospheres. "I don't want them to think I'm an idiot or something."

Ibrahim granted her one of his rare smiles. "My dear Mik, you are far from being an idiot. We both know your IQ, EQ and social awareness indices are well above average. Just be yourself. I have known Kyle and Diamantina for years, and young Dani is reportedly a bright child."

That helped a little, though it still felt as though she had an out-of-control rock-hopper in her guts, spinning around and around with a fuel leak like the ship in the game she'd been playing. "Yeah, but how old is she? Five? Ten? Twenty?" She had zero face-to-face experience with other children of any age, and the only other people she'd related with at all were effectively parental figures. *Am I going to have to babysit? I don't know how to do that.*

"To be absolutely honest, I have very little idea," Professor Ibrahim confessed. "But we shall find out soon." He secured his faceplate and slapped the airlock button to open it. They entered, and Mik pressed the cycle button.

'Airlock Two cycling ... Airlock Two cycling ...'

As with every other time they'd done this, Ibrahim's suit inflated as the air pressure dropped. Mik felt her sphincters lock shut and the muscle bands tighten up as her body went to low-pressure mode. She was also getting better at gauging the pressure shift, down to tens of pascals.

Out of the airlock they stepped and Mik looked around. There was a little breeze that she could see, though the air pressure was so low that even a gale was barely noticeable unless it was a dust storm. Having invisible fines impact an EVA suit at sandblaster speeds was a good way to get dead out on the surface. Fortunately, the only loose fines she could see were being whipped up into tenuous dust devils that skittered across the landscape, kilometres away.

A spark of light caught her eye, and she glanced up to see the shuttle incoming. Rocket-powered, of course; there wouldn't be sufficient free oxygen in the Martian atmosphere to run an air-breathing engine for decades to come, perhaps a century or more.

It had finished the parabolic arc part of its flight then flipped around for the landing approach, which would make use of its main engine. Mik had done the same herself on her simulator games a hundred times. It was harder than it looked, especially when the gyros failed halfway down.

Ibrahim gestured forward and she nodded; they set out toward the flattened section of rock which had been set aside for shuttle landings. There was a series of low walls around the shuttle pad, and they paused behind one of them until the vessel was all the way down. The final *clunk* of contact and the long hum of ship systems winding down wasn't directly audible, but she felt it easily enough through her feet. Tilting her head sideways, she walked around the end of the wall with Ibrahim following behind.

She didn't know what to do with her hands, so she stuck them in the pockets of her long-coat as she and the Professor approached the shuttle. Three figures wearing EVA suits were exiting the main hatch of the shuttle; two were adult-sized, while one was definitely a kid. A little shorter than her one-seventy-eight centimetres, if she was estimating correctly, but somewhat stockier.

The breeze was starting to pick up now. It was still barely enough to stir the dust, but Mik could also feel a gradual drop in air pressure, a sure indication that something was coming. As she and Ibrahim waited for the three to clear the shuttle with their luggage, her long-coat flapped slightly, then she felt the first tickle of fines on her cheek. She glanced up then, and spotted the tell-tale scudding of dust across the sun. Touching Professor Ibrahim's arm, she made the hand-signs for '*dust storm incoming'.*

He nodded and keyed his radio. *"If we can hurry things up slightly, this would be good. It appears that a dust storm is imminent."*

Another voice came across the radio channel. It sounded harried, which didn't surprise Mik. *"Crap dammit. Roger that on the dust storm. They promised me blind I'd have another hour's leeway. How you doing with that luggage back there?"*

Mik wasn't keyed into the channel the shuttle crew were using, but it didn't seem to matter. Two more pieces of luggage were thrown from the hatch, which then began to close.

"Clear the area, clear the area," the pilot broadcast. *"All hands secure for takeoff. Preliminary countdown in sixty seconds."*

As one, Mik and Ibrahim moved forward to help the newcomers with their luggage. The bigger of the two adults turned toward them, and Mik saw a large man's face. *"Hey, Ben. Long time no see, man. I'm guessing this is your little prodigy?"*

"It's nice to see you too, Kyle," the Professor replied, taking up two of the cases. *"Yes, this is Mik. Introductions can wait until we're clear."*

The shorter figure was trying to deal with four different cases at once, so Mik grabbed two of them. The suited girl—Mik recalled that the Connaughts' child was a daughter—looked up with surprise evident on her features through the faceplate, then her eyes widened almost comically. Her lips moved, though the radio didn't activate, so she'd probably forgotten to switch it on. Absently, Mik read the words as, *'holy shit, you're really not wearing a suit'.*

There wasn't much to be said about that, even if Mik could've answered, so she smiled and shrugged, then hefted the cases. Immediately, she wondered if they were packed with bricks; the weight training Professor Ibrahim required of her notwithstanding, they were still a strain to move. Lifting the other two cases with relative ease, the suited girl followed her behind the blast shield.

Ibrahim was the last to join them, eyeballing the landing pad for any luggage before he made the call on the radio. *"Clear for takeoff. I say again, clear for takeoff."*

"I copy clear for takeoff," the pilot responded. *"Ignition in ten."*

Mik couldn't hear the countdown, but she ran through one in her own mind anyway. At the end, she was only about half a second off before the deep rumble impinged on her ears and vibrated against the soles of her feet. On the other side of the blast shield, the shuttle lifted off the pad, the main rocket engine glowing brightly. Quickly gaining speed, it ascended out of sight, arcing over toward the east along the axis of Valles Marineris.

Hefting the cases he'd picked up, Professor Ibrahim led the way back toward the Research Complex. Mik tottered in his wake alongside the shorter girl, feeling as though her arms were being pulled from their sockets but unwilling to complain. Fortunately, it was a relatively short walk, and mostly downhill; Ibrahim chose to go in through the vehicle airlock rather than one of the personnel ones, as five people plus all the attendant luggage would've made for a tight fit.

As soon as the large door juddered into place, Mik let the cases down onto the floor and straightened up, shaking out her arms. She was almost convinced that they were now at least ten centimetres longer than they had been before.

"Oh, sorry," said the girl, having now apparently remembered she had a radio. *"I should've taken those myself. That's my book collection."*

Mik had seen pictures of books before, and she even owned a copy of *Treasure Island* that someone in the facility had given her to read years ago, but she'd never thought anyone would carry *collections* around with them, especially when digital copies were so much easier to access. She gave the two cases a dirty look. Books were *heavy*.

Air hissed into the lock and the suits appeared to deflate, then the chime sounded. *'Vehicle Lock One cycled. Air pressure nominal.'* As the inner door rumbled open, Ibrahim unsealed his faceplate and pushed the hood of the suit back. "At last," he said with satisfaction. "Welcome to the Valles Marineris Research Complex."

The big man, Kyle, did the same and put his hands on his hips, looking around at the vehicle airlock. "Looks like a nice setup you've got here, man. What sorts of construction vehicles do you have for me to play with?"

"Nothing substantial as yet, but they should be coming in soon," Ibrahim promised. "I want Mik as competent as you can get her before the presentation."

Kyle dusted his hands off, apparently satisfied with the situation. "That'll be easy. I've got sim chips we can use to get started with while we're waiting on them to arrive."

The girl unlatched her faceplate and pushed her hood back, then turned to Mik. "Hi, sorry I forgot to turn my radio on out there, and sorry for staring, but when Dad told me about you, I didn't really *believe*, you know?" She put out her hand. "Dani Connaught. Pleased to meet you."

Mik held her own hand out, the dusty-black fingers slender against Dani's broader—even gloved, that was apparent—hand. Dani's grip was strong but not overpowering. "Mik Wallace. Nice to meet you too." On impulse, she added, "I'll be happy to show you around, if you want."

It was the right thing to say. Dani's eyes lit up. "Can we, Dad?"

Kyle looked to his wife, who had also pulled her hood back. She nodded, and he turned back to Dani with a grin. "Sure thing, kiddo. Just remember that you still need a suit to go outside, even if Mik doesn't."

"Woo!" Dani grabbed Mik's hand again. "So, what are we gonna see first?"

At this sudden burst of enthusiasm, the last of Mik's nerves melted away. She'd been terrified at the idea of being rejected for how she looked, but Dani was showing no sign of that. Heading through the inner door into the base proper, she pointed at the suit rack. "De-suit there and we can get started. How about the Observatory?"

"Ooh, sounds like fun. I like stargazing, but there's no place for it in Burroughs." Dani began unzipping the suit to reveal … t-shirt and jeans.

It was a stunning revelation to Mik. *She's just like me.*

A line from one of Professor Ibrahim's favourite movies popped into her head. *I think this is the beginning of a beautiful friendship.*

Chapter 3: Rock-Hopper

There were still fines in the air, but the haze was settling. The dust storm had only been a small one, over and done in about five hours, which was probably why the satellites hadn't been able to get a proper fix on it.

Wearing a toolbelt, Mik led the way up the walking track to the roof of the Complex, which had been partially built into the side of a monolith in the middle of Valles Marineris. Dani followed behind—suited up, of course—and watched as she carefully eyeballed each one of the forest of antennae and dishes that had colonised the roof.

"So, what are we doing now?" Dani asked, aiming a micro-cam at Mik. Apparently, she'd left a bunch of friends back in Burroughs, and she'd gotten permission from Professor Ibrahim to follow Mik around (except in any of the labs where classified research was ongoing) and record what she was doing. That, and she seemed to think it was amazingly interesting. *"Making sure the wind didn't push anything around?"*

Mik put the pony bottle mask over her mouth, inhaled half a breath, then activated the radio. "The fines are hell on exposed electronics, and dust storms have been known to build up static charges. So, I'm checking on worn components and covers and, yeah, making sure the dishes are still aligned correctly. It used to take me about twice as long to get this done before Professor Ibrahim started letting me come out without a suit on the regular."

Crouching, she took a meter from the belt and held it to the base of an antenna; a moment later, it showed a reassuring green light. One at a time, moving quickly but surely, she checked on each of the dishes and antennae. She frowned as the readout from one dish came up blinking yellow. Hanging the meter back on the belt, she took a wrench and tapped one of the struts a few times. The second time around, the meter glowed a solid green.

When one antenna came up a solid red, she popped the cover off the data-gathering module and examined it, then pulled a chip and replaced it with one from the holder on her hip. With a flourish, she replaced the cover and rechecked the antenna. It showed up as green.

"That one socket burns out its chip nearly every time we get a dust storm," she confided to Dani as she finished checking the last installation. "It's not any different from the rest of them, but it's just fragile. Nobody knows why."

Dani was silent as she panned the cam over the equipment Mik had just checked over, then back to Mik herself. *"You're really good at this,"* she said quietly. *"I mean, you're my age, and you know how to do all this important stuff. I've barely learned how to do anything. Dad's about to teach you how to work construction equipment. The most I've ever done like that was to sit on his lap and 'help' him steer."*

Mik put a hand on her shoulder. "But I've spent my whole life right here, with all these genius-level intellects. I couldn't help but learn. I bet you've had a lot more interesting life than me. Been more places, met a whole *lot* more people."

*"What, you've **never** been anywhere?"* Dani turned to look at her with surprise. *"Not up Olympus Mons? Not to Earth? Nowhere?"*

"I've never left this facility," Mik assured her. "The farthest I've gone is a few kilometres up and down Marineris on a rock-hopper." She paused, her eyes widening. "Wait, you've been to *Earth?*"

*"Well, **yeah.**"* Dani put her hand flat on her own chest. *"I was **born** there. Same as Mom and Dad. But I thought you'd been there too. I saw your photo frame."*

"No, that was just a birthday present." Mik's mind was whirling. Dani had just become a good fifty percent cooler than before. "What was it like? Where are you from? Where did you go?"

"Well, Dad helped construct the Chicago-Evanston arcology. By the time that was done, I was about seven. We travelled around the States a little, though we kept away from the quarantine zones. I guess Mom and Dad wanted me to see and remember stuff about Earth before we went to Mars. I remember taking a boat ride through New Orleans, and getting up to watch the sunrise. And walking ankle-deep in snow, on the last day before we took off." Dani's voice softened, as though she could still feel the crunch of it underfoot. *"We've been most everywhere on Mars, but mostly Burroughs. Until now. Dad says he's never going back."*

Mik had seen pictures of snow, but she had trouble imagining walking through it. It looked cold, which it had to be, seeing as it was basically fluffy water ice, but the rooftop she was standing on was a lot colder than the freezing point of water. Would she even notice how cold it was, or would it be basically the same as everything else? "It sounds weird to be on a planet where there's frozen water and liquid water at the same time," she said without thinking it through. "And clouds, so that makes it water vapour too. I mean, does it *feel* weird?"

"No weirder than it must feel to be able to walk around outside and do maintenance on satellite dishes and stuff while people like me gotta wear EVA suits," Dani noted. *"What's a rock-hopper, anyway?"*

"What?" Mik had been distracted by Dani's mention of Burroughs. "Oh, it's a rocket powered vertol. We use them for getting around Marineris."

"A vertol?" From the tone of Dani's voice, the subject had gotten her immediate interest. *"Would we be able to go for a ride in one? They sound like fun. Mom's a rocketry engineer and she works with stuff like that while I'm stuck in ordinary boring school."*

The tone of her voice was so dejected at the end that Mik had to put the breathing mask on just so she could laugh. "I can *take* you for a ride on one. I'm fully rated to fly them; all I have to do is ask Professor Ibrahim if it's okay." She started toward the walking-track that led down off the roof. "Pretty sure he'll say yes. Your dad was still setting up the training sims for the construction vehicles, last I checked."

"Oh, this is gonna be so cool." Dani's voice bubbled over with enthusiasm. *"My friends are gonna be **super** jel that I'm getting to do this stuff with you."*

Mik grinned and checked the gauge on her pony bottle. The needle had only moved down a few increments in the time she'd been on the roof, and most of that was because she had to talk. Even when it ran out, she still had her internal store. "Before we do anything, check your air," she said. "If it's more than half down, we'll go in and get you a fresh tank."

There was a pause. *"I read it from the top, yeah?"*

"That's right. If it's still outside the yellow, we're fine."

"About a centimetre to go before it hits the yellow. How's that sound?"

"Perfect." She'd overestimated Dani's air consumption. Being a teenager meant her companion used less oh-two than the adults Mik was accustomed to getting around with. "Give me a second." Switching channels, she called out on the one Professor Ibrahim used. "Professor, are you busy?"

The reply came back in a moment. *"Not overly, dear girl. What is the matter? Is one of the dishes giving problems?"*

"No, the dishes are fine," she assured him. "Number Three needed a whack again, like normal. And I replaced the same chip in Sixteen. Burnt out again. But I wanted to ask you if it was okay to take Dani for a ride on a rock-hopper. Just up and down the Valles a bit."

He paused for a moment, and she heard vague mumbling. She was almost certain she knew what that meant; he was asking Mr Connaught, or Kyle as the man had asked her to address him. His wife Diamantina was nice. She'd chatted with Mik while they were waiting for Dani to suit up again, and she seemed like an interesting person.

"I don't see any reason why not." Professor Ibrahim paused for a moment. *"Just remember, she is a guest. If she loses her lunch, you get to scrub the suit out."*

Mik smirked. "You know I wouldn't make her do anything like that.

Thanks, Professor." Nobody she'd piloted the rock-hoppers for had ever actually thrown up in their suits, though some had been a little shaky when they got off. It wasn't her fault that her vestibular system gave her an enhanced grasp on her placement and movement in three dimensions. Also, she never suffered from motion-sickness.

She still hadn't heard of anyone else looping a rock-hopper either, or even trying to. Not that she'd done it more than the once; Ibrahim had grounded her for *months* after that little escapade. She made a mental note not to mention it to Dani, just in case her new best friend wanted her to do it again.

Flicking the radio channel back, she grinned at Dani. "Okay, then. Come on, let's go."

"Woo hoo!" Dani punched a fist in the air as they headed over to where the rock-hoppers were parked.

An extremely basic, rugged design, rock-hoppers didn't need to be kept inside. They had a solid circular frame with two seats bolted on, bare-bones controls, a set of fuel tanks and nine rocket engines: a large one pointing straight down under the seats, and eight smaller ones around the perimeter of the circle to provide attitude control. Bolted-on ladders on two of the struts allowed Mik to climb up on one side, and Dani on the other.

"Okay, safety briefing." Mik pointed at the high-backed seats as they strapped themselves in. "While you're on a rock-hopper, the five-point restraints stay on at all times. No exceptions. If the computer detects an engine or fuel tank failure, it'll kick the seats free. The seats are padded, and weighted so they'll come down back-first. It'll be a hell of a bang, but everyone who's done it has survived. And there's a governor that won't let it go above one hundred metres altitude. Per safety regs, we're not permitted to exceed that. Got it?"

Dani nodded earnestly. *"Okay. Anything else?"*

"Nope." Mik snorted. "As the saying goes, keep your arms and legs inside the ride at all times." She flicked the first switch, waking the flight computer up. It ran a quick self-check, then queried the 'hopper's fuel and engine status. Given its high thrust to weight ratio, a rock-hopper didn't need big tanks. These were seventy-five percent full; this information came up on the rudimentary control panel.

When she flicked the second switch, the eight attitude-control rockets lit off; the thumb-wheel on the control stick increased the thrust to where she needed it to be. Gently, almost absent-mindedly, the rock-hopper wafted up off the rocky ground. She nudged the controls forward, sending it drifting away from the main building, dust and fines swirling up around them.

Once they were well clear, she flicked the third switch. This ignited the main rocket motor. A gentle nudge on the thumb-wheel raised the rock-hopper straight up out of ground effect; she eased it off at eighty metres, as smoothly as she knew how. Controlling the craft with just finger and thumb on one of the control sticks, feeling every aspect of the vibrations of the craft, she turned to look at Dani. "So, you ready?"

"For what?" Dani was staring around wide-eyed as she took in the sheer majesty of Valles Marineris. Mik had seen it more times than she could count, but even with that she was still impressed by the scale of the landform.

"The need." Mik grinned at Dani's confused expression. "Do you feel the need?" Casually, she strummed the thumb-wheel on the control column she was holding, causing the attitude rockets to rumble briefly.

"The need?" Dani looked at her dubiously. *"I don't understand …"*

"The need …" Mik drew it out. "For *speed.*" Taking hold of the control sticks, she tilted the 'hopper over and slammed the throttle wide open. At best acceleration, it could pull two Martian gees, or seven point four metres per second squared. Mik knew how to cheat a little by trading altitude for speed, so that by the time she levelled it out, they were already going faster than most ground vehicles.

As they barrelled over the floor of Valles Marineris, sixty metres up, Dani whooped and grabbed at the rail on either side of her seat. Mik grinned; wind resistance was barely noticeable even at this speed, so keeping up the acceleration was no problem at all. However, they were leaving the research complex behind, so she pulled a long, wide turn that ended up with them going back the other direction at a speed that would be frankly unsafe on the ground.

Three-billion-year-old rock formations passed them by as she concentrated on flying the rock-hopper ever closer to the six-kilometre-high valley wall. Dani had recovered enough to aim the micro-cam back the way they'd gone and then where they were going to, and she didn't notice the way Mik veered away from the cliff and then toward it … at least, at first. Then, it was impossible *not* to notice it.

"Mik, what are you doing?" As if Mik might not have seen it, she pointed at the towering rock-face now looming closer with every second. *"You're gonna hit the cliff!"*

Mik could've replied with a smartass comment, but right then she was concentrating fully on what she was doing. Using the attitude rockets, she angled the rock-hopper and flew into one of the tributary ravines that fed into the Valles itself. It was maybe a couple of kilometres wide at the top, but it came down in a vee-shape that had deposited a fan of debris onto the floor of Marineris.

Up the narrow channel they flew, Mik keeping the speed down and ensuring they had adequate clearance on both sides. Sedimentary layers never before seen by humans flashed by on either side as they ascended along the tributary. Under her, the rock-hopper thrummed steadily, the rockets powering them onward.

At last, they popped up and over the wind-eroded rim of the channel; Mik circled the rock-hopper around and flew back toward Marineris, then landed about two hundred metres from the edge. With the feet firmly on the ground, she killed the engines and looked around with interest. "Huh," she said. "First time I've ever been up here. Nice."

Slowly, Dani turned to look at her. *"What? You mean you've never done that before?"*

"Nope." Mik unstrapped from the rock-hopper and climbed down to the ground. On one side was a huge plain, dotted here and there with craters large and small. On the other, the straight edge that denoted the largest canyon complex in the Solar System. "Never bothered, until now. I've seen the photomaps, so I knew what the terrain looked like. Though I still want to free-climb that cliff someday, just so I can say I did."

"That huge cliff? The one we bypassed by flying up the channel? That cliff?" Dani shook her head. *"You're nuts."*

"I'm nuts?" Mik snorted. *"You're* the one who was born on a planet with stupidly high gravity. I'd need a mobility frame just to visit." She pointed toward the rim, then started that way. It looked like the edge of the world. "Let's go look. Show your friends back in Burroughs what they're missing out on."

"Okay, sure." Dani made sure her micro-cam got a good panorama of the plain behind them, then moved to catch up with Mik. *"I have to say, growing up on Earth gave me a good head-start with the gravity on Mars. I was the best athlete in my class in Burroughs for about five years in a row."* She sighed. *"I'd like to go back someday, even if it was just to visit."*

"What, Burroughs or Earth?" Mik kept an eye out for micro-fissures, both for herself and Dani. The last thing she wanted was for either one of them to put their foot in one and damage an ankle. Professor Ibrahim didn't discourage behaviour like this, but neither did he encourage it. His attitude, as far as she could see, was that she was allowed to push boundaries so long as she was sensible about it.

"Both, I guess." Dani seemed to be thinking about the question. *"Earth has got so many cool things and so much history, but Burroughs is where all my friends are."*

"So why did you and your parents leave Burroughs in a hurry anyway?" asked Mik. "All Professor Ibrahim would say is that it had to do with politics. Did your dad try to run for mayor or something?"

Dani shook her head. *"No. I was born with a genetic tendency to a rare form of lymphoma, so they made sure I got gene therapy before we left Earth to be certain it would never crop up. That went into my medical file, so when we went to Mars, it came with. It didn't matter at first, because we were going all over the place, but then we settled in Burroughs and I got sick with a local bug, so Mom took me to a doctor."* She shuddered. *"More like a witch-doctor, if you ask me."*

"Why, what happened?" Mik had watched enough movies to understand the reference, even if she lacked the context.

"There's a political movement called Pure Strain going on there right now. It's all about ensuring the 'purity' of the human genome by not 'polluting' it with genetic alteration or modification." Mik could virtually hear the quotes settling in around Dani's words. *"The doctor was a believer in this, and he nearly refused to treat me once he read the notes on my file. My parents had a screaming match with him over it. They actually had to threaten legal action before he finally agreed to check me over and prescribe some antibiotics. Mom stood there the whole time, giving him the evil eye until he finished."*

Mik felt a spark of anger, directed toward an agenda she barely understood. How could anyone turn away a kid who needed help?

They reached the very rim, or at least the part of it that was safe to stand on. Over the next twenty metres or so, it gradually curved over until it reached a near-sheer drop. Mik went over to where a boulder was half-buried in the dirt, and sat down on it. The view was, in a word, spectacular. "Wow, damn. So, was that it, or was there more to it?"

Sitting down beside her, Dani panned the micro-cam over the stunning vista before them. Far below, a metallic reflection from the westering sun showed where the research complex was. From this distance, Mik thought it looked like a scale model. *Is that all I've been living so far? A scale model of a real life?*

Dani took a while to answer. "No," she said at last. *"That was just the first symptom. It's been getting worse. There's a consortium called Cyberon or something that wants to corner the market on Mars-capable workers, and Dad says they're backing the Pure Strain idiots. They've been muscling in on the labour market, making it harder and harder for independents to get work. It's either fall into line or don't work at all. And somehow, someone got hold of my medical records, so Dad got blackballed from doing any construction work in and around the Hellas area. And that's why we came here."*

"Wait, Mars-capable workers?" Mik blinked a couple of times. Up until that point, it had been a weird story of bigotry, but that part hit home. "Like me? They want to make Mars-capable people, but they're in bed with the idiots who are against genetic therapy? How does that even work?"

"*I have no idea.*" Dani sighed again. "*I get it that we had to leave because of the politics, but I hated leaving my friends behind. Now I've got to start all over again.*"

"Hey, if it helps, I'm your friend." Mik put her arm around Dani's shoulders and pulled her close. "And I'm about the last person to look down on you for having genetic therapy."

Dani snorted. "*Yeah, you'll look down on me for other reasons. Like being about ten centimetres shorter than you.*" She laid her head on Mik's shoulder. "*But thanks. I appreciate it.*"

"You're welcome."

Together, they sat and watched as the sun slowly set along the length of Valles Marineris.

Chapter 4: Political Considerations

"We watched you on the rock-hopper today," Diamantina Connaught remarked at the evening meal that night. "You're very good. Is it easy to learn how to fly one?"

Mik blinked, unprepared for being singled out. "Ah … yeah, well, for me it was." She shrugged uncomfortably, not wanting to sound as though she were boasting. "It's basically translations in a three-dimensional phase space. Pick your vector and apply your thrust." A grin appeared on her face as the joke occurred to her. "I'd say it's not rocket science, but …"

Kyle Connaught chuckled. "But it's applying geometry and physics with rockets, so it more less *is*." He gave Mik a grin and a nod. "You're sharp, kid. I think we're gonna work well together."

"I was also going to say, Mik has that sort of aptitude built into her genome," Professor Ibrahim noted. "However, she has definitely applied herself to learning how to fly them better than anyone else at the complex, so she hasn't been coasting on her talents."

"Yes. Her lab work has been excellent as well." Kathy, at the other end of the table, bestowed an approving gaze upon their young mentee. "We're all very proud of her."

"I can see why." Kyle tilted his head questioningly. "One of the other guys I was talking to said that Mik once *looped* one of those things. Is that true? Is that even *possible*?"

Mik facepalmed as Ibrahim laughed out loud. She was just glad she couldn't blush. "Yes, I did it," she admitted. "*Once*. I wanted to see if I could, and I pulled it off, but the laser altimeter cut the rockets off when I was halfway over. I had to make it the rest of the way on inertia alone. I've never prayed so hard for the laws of physics to keep working as I did right then."

"And then I grounded her from flying them for two months, for scaring me out of twenty *years* of my life," Ibrahim grumbled. "She was so close to the ground when the rockets cut in again, the landing set off the eject function and she ended up fifty metres away. *And* it bent two struts on the rock-hopper."

"Which *I* had to repair," Mik chimed in. "If I'd known about the laser altimeter, I would've disabled the governor before I even started the loop, and I would've started a heck of a lot farther up."

"And *I* would have shown you how, if I'd known you were going to do it." The Professor lowered his brows in a mock scowl toward Mik.

"Yes," Kathy agreed. "Of course, that might encourage you to disable it for frivolous purposes, so it's good that you don't actually know how. Isn't it?" Her serious tone was belied by the grin lurking on her lips.

"Yes, Kathy," Mik replied, pretending meekness.

Across the table, Dani mouthed the words, *'you know how, don't you?'*. Mik smirked and winked.

Apparently oblivious to the byplay, Diamantina frowned. "What's the maximum acceleration derived from the rocket engine you use on the rock-hopper, and what sort of fuel do you use in it? You don't seem to be worried about excess usage."

Professor Ibrahim nodded and smiled. "Very good questions, madam. To answer the last one first, we refine and manufacture our own rocket fuel from the perchlorates abundantly available in the soil. It's something we'd have to filter out anyway, if we're ever going to grow anything in the ground. For your other question, the engines top out at about seven and a half metres per second squared with a two-adult load on the rock-hopper. Among other things, the Research Complex does geological surveys of the local sector of Valles Marineris, so they're useful in getting around and collecting samples."

"So, there's nothing stopping them from actually going higher except this laser altimeter cutting the rockets off?" Kyle frowned. "How high can you go, and why the arbitrary ceiling?"

"One hundred metres, and it's because anything higher than that is liable to result in severe pilot injury, or even death, if the bailout system triggers." Professor Ibrahim shrugged. "But yes, if the governor were to be disabled, there is nothing stopping you from theoretically reaching orbit. Except, of course, there is also no particular *reason* to do it when there are perfectly good shuttles available that have comfortable pressurised-air compartments."

Kathy cleared her throat. "Also, if you don't use up your fuel or your suit air going up, you certainly will on the way down. All that will need to be done after the fact is fill in the crater."

"Not necessarily," Diamantina said thoughtfully. "Honey, remember the hassles we had resupplying the Stickney depot? One of these rock-hoppers, beefed up a little, would've made our lives *so* much easier."

Kyle rolled his eyes. "*Do I*," he groaned. He looked at the rest of the table. "You're all aware of Stickney, right?"

"I'm going to go out on a limb here and presume you're talking about the crater on Phobos," Kathy said. "Unless there's another Stickney I'm not aware of?"

Mik didn't think there was. She tried to keep current with all the latest information regarding the Mars-Phobos-Deimos system, and she was fairly certain nothing had been double-named.

"No, you're on the money there," Kyle said. "While we were moving Robinson into areosynch over Pavonis, I decided that we needed a construction shack with resupply options in case someone looked like deorbiting because of a lack of fuel. So, we built one on Phobos. It ended up being a full-on emergency shelter, complete with spare oh-two, fuel stores and an emergency beacon that would light up receivers on half of Mars. The problem was, Phobos goes like a bat out of hell, so you had to be careful about matching velocities. However, the upside of that was that if you missed the connection, you only had to wait a few hours for it to come around again."

The preparations for the space elevator were something Mik had heard about, but she hadn't followed it closely. Now that she knew Kyle and Diamantina had been involved in it, she was somewhat more interested. She did know that a carbon-rich asteroid had been moved into stationary orbit (*areo*synchronous, as opposed to *geo*synchronous) over Pavonis Mons, a prominent mountain that sat right on the equator of Mars, and had been renamed Robinson (after some science fiction author, apparently). As she understood things, there were machines up there right now, gradually mining the asteroid and extruding carbon-nanotube cables both down toward Mars and outward into space. Eventually, in years to come, the downward cable would touch down on Pavonis, and the space elevator would be established.

Phobos was the nearer of Mars' two moons. Only six thousand kilometres above the surface of the planet, it had an orbital period of less than seven and a half hours. It was not uncommon to see the tiny moon pass overhead twice in one day.

Diamantina took up the tale. "It got so more people were dropping in to use it as a regular supply station than an emergency resource. We were spending more time resupplying it than bringing in supplies straight to the crewed satellites. Kyle ended up installing an air refresher, so people wouldn't just steal or use up the damn oxygen tanks." She looked at her husband. "Whatever happened to that place, anyway? Did we ever end up decommissioning it?"

"Search me." Kyle shrugged. "Wasn't by the time we were transferred out, and then we were put straight on to the Olympus spaceport and transit lines, remember? Haven't been back to check. Place might've been gutted, or left alone. Or maybe one of those damned meteorites punched a hole right through it."

"I know, right?" Kathy shook her head. "By the time Mars is fully terraformed and settled, they'll be coming across little caches and bunkers full of supplies everywhere, where someone set up an emergency stash then forgot about it."

Kyle frowned. "I don't know that it ever will be fully terraformed."

There was silence at the table for a moment, then Professor Ibrahim looked at Kyle. "You are going to have to explain that extraordinary statement, I think," he said carefully. "Terraforming this great planet is what Mik and her genetic descendants were intended for. Not to settle it, but to ensure that it can be settled by the likes of you and I."

"Yeah, well, some people have other ideas." Kyle glanced at Dani and Mik meaningfully. "This doesn't leave the room, okay, kids?"

Mik nodded. "Okay." She was well aware of what 'classified' meant; much of her own genome was still in the classified stage, back in Professor Ibrahim's lab.

"Sure thing, Dad." Dani sounded a little concerned. "What's up? Is more of that Pure Strain stuff?"

"In a word, yes." Kyle's jaw set. "Have you told Mik about the incident with the doctor? Okay, good. So, you know about Pure Strain then. They're basically a wholly owned subsidiary of the Cyberon Consortium by now. And with that sort of money behind them, and the carefully orchestrated public sentiment in the Hellas region, they'll be in legitimate control of the Hellas Legislature before too much longer. Which will give them a voice in how the ongoing terraforming efforts are maintained. Or *if* they're maintained."

"Wait, wait." Mik couldn't figure out what he was saying. Not the *how*—it was easy to see how one strong voting bloc choosing to abandon or even sabotage terraforming efforts could screw up the whole deal—but the *why*. "If they're supporters of Pure Strain, then they *can't* be modified like me. If they're ever going to leave the settlements and colonise Mars, they need to be able to breathe the air and survive the temperatures. How are they going to do that without terraforming the planet first?"

"Cyberon." Diamantina stated the name bluntly. "They're working on a prototype human cybernetics program to give people the ability to deal with the environment *now*, rather than wait a decade or three while Mik and her colleagues do all the hard work."

"That's stupid." Dani shook her head. "Implanting cybernetics has to be at least as invasive as gene therapy. Why doesn't Pure Strain have a problem with that?"

"And what do they have against genetic modification, anyway?" asked Mik. "It's not like *they're* being forced to get any."

Professor Ibrahim sighed. "There will always arise a certain type of person who, even though he is supported by the products of science on all sides, cannot understand it and in his ignorance decides that it is evil. Then he convinces others to join him in his crusade."

"What?" Dani stared at him. "We live on *Mars!*" Unspoken was the fact that it was science above all that was keeping every single one of them alive.

"Notice that I am not disputing your assertion one iota, dear child," Ibrahim pointed out. "Stupidity can usually be safely ignored, but it becomes dangerous when it is married to power. There are people, followers of Pure Strain, who consider all modification of the *'true human form'* —whatever that actually *means*—to be sacrilegious in the extreme, to the point that it warrants criminal violence."

"And while the Pure Strain leadership pretends to disavow them," Kyle noted, "they don't do much to stop them, either."

Kathy frowned. "And meanwhile, they're aiming to push invasive cybernetic enhancements on ordinary people to allow them to spread out and colonise."

"Exactly." Kyle's voice took on a particularly sarcastic tone. "Why wait for the air to be breathable when you can sell people the ability to breathe it?"

Mik still couldn't figure out the logic. "Shouldn't cybernetics also be a modification of the *'true form'*?"

"Yes, but money has a distressing habit of trumping principle," Ibrahim said heavily. "We are not paying Pure Strain anything, and the Consortium is: therefore, cybernetic enhancement is 'acceptable', whereas genetic modification is beyond the pale."

"But Mik wouldn't count as 'modified', right?" Dani looked from Professor Ibrahim to her parents and back again. "She's a whole new genome, not a modification of an existing one."

Solemnly, Ibrahim shook his head. "I fear, dear girl, that the distinction would be lost on them."

"*Lost* on them?" Kathy snorted. "Mik would be Target Number One in their eyes. They'll have a vested interest in seeing cybernetic modification win out over genetic enhancement, and Mik is the biggest threat facing them when it comes to that."

"Okay, ignoring the fact that they hate me, I'm still not sure how they're going to make it work." Mik shook her head. "Mars is hard on any kind of exposed cybernetics. The fines mess electronics up pretty good. Are they going to have some kind of warranty with an automatic replacement policy? Because that's the only way I can see it being fair on the colonists."

"Hardly." Professor Ibrahim snorted. "If I know Cyberon, and I fancy that I do, they'll be *leasing* the implants. It will start off at a very low price, but any replacements or upgrades will come with a hefty premium. Worse yet, it's all too likely that they'll maintain a permanent tracking and monitoring system on each piece of installed cybernetics, all the way up to the option of a kill-switch."

Dani blinked. "They want to *own* the settlers, not just supply them," she said, just ahead of Mik's realisation of the same thing.

Mik's stomach twisted. *I thought it was about money, not control.* The concept of personal agency was something Professor Ibrahim had instilled into her at an early age.

"They'll be able to dictate any terms they want, with that sort of hold over them." Dani looked pensive. "I can see people setting up private repair businesses to get around that."

"Yes, so can I," agreed her mother. "Right up until Cyberon, with the eager assistance of Pure Strain, applies pressure to the Hellas Legislature to outlaw *'unsanctioned cybernetics piracy'* and start vectoring in their security corps on these shops. Or remotely shutting down the cybernetics of everyone who goes to one."

"That sounds terrifying." Mik shook her head. "Like one of those dystopian novels you made me read. *'Big Brother is watching you'.*"

"Is there any chance that Pure Strain can shut down the research facility here?" asked Dani.

Professor Ibrahim shook his head definitively. "We are well outside their reach. Our funding comes from the Tharsis Corporation, and they've put their eggs firmly in the basket of genetic modification. As soon as the presentation goes live, they will be broadcasting Mik's face from pole to pole. She's going to be the face of the new Mars."

"It'll still take a while for the Martian Walkers to fully deploy." Kyle gave Mik a serious look. "In order to recoup their investment, Tharsis is going to have to fast-grow them. It'll be up to you, as the only person on Mars who can truly understand what it's like to be them, to teach them how to *be* people and not just robots who happen to *look* like people."

"Hey, I thought I was just the proof of concept, not the finished product," Mik said half-jokingly. "And now you want me to be the babysitter and mother figure to a bunch of … what was that line out of that weird movie where the guy got put in cryostasis …"

"Mini-me," Kathy said. "Well, you won't be doing it alone, you know. You'll have all of us helping you. And being the proof of concept is a worthy thing. You are literally the genesis of a new species."

"To a new era of life on Mars," Professor Ibrahim pronounced, raising his glass of reconstituted imitation fruit juice. "To Mik, the first Martian Walker."

When everyone had responded to that—even Dani, the traitor, grinning mischievously at her—Mik raised her own glass. "To all of you, and all the effort you've put into Project Martian Walker, and into making me feel more like a human being than a lab rat. If it wasn't for you, I wouldn't be here. So, thanks for that. I appreciate being alive."

"Hear, hear," Professor Ibrahim said heartily. "Every day, you repay us in some small way, proving once again that no matter your differences, you're as human as any one of us."

Mik gave him a mock glare. "Damn it, now I want to cry, though I know I can't, no matter how badly I want to. Because *someone* thought it would be a bright idea to engineer out my tear ducts." But her tone was more rueful than angry.

Kathy giggled. "She's got you there. Every year, she brings that up. And every year, you can't refute her."

"It was a logical thought process," Ibrahim protested. "We were sealing off the eye-sockets from external entry, and the tear ducts were a potential weak point. If I'd known that removing the ability to cry would be such a deal-breaker ..."

"You would've been married years ago," chorused Mik and Kathy, well aware of where this was going. Kyle and Diamantina laughed as well, in the manner of people who have also heard the joke.

It was clear that Dani hadn't, from the way she stared at the others around the table. "I guess this is one of those stories that are only funny to people who were there in the first place."

Mik smirked. "It's one of those things, yes. Every time the Professor finds out yet again that his extensive education did not prepare him for helping to raise a teenage girl on Mars, that's what he says."

"Oh, I get it now." Dani giggled. "I like it. That's funny."

The meal went on, slowly winding down to small talk among the adults. After a while, Mik excused herself and got up. Dani went with her.

They strolled through the dimly lit research complex, chatting aimlessly. Mik found herself thinking she hadn't enjoyed a meal so much in a long time. "I'm going to miss you," she said before she could think better of it.

Dani punched her lightly on the arm, her smile caught by a safety light. "Hey, I'm not going anywhere for a while. Dad's gonna be teaching you construction work, and Mom says she wants to tinker with the rock-hoppers to maybe get more efficiency out of them. Me, I'll keep up with my studies and hang out with you in between times."

"Yeah, I know." Mik sighed and rapped her knuckles against a doorframe. "After all this, I mean. Once the Martian Walker presentation goes forward and I'm a celebrity, and I'm helping to raise all the mini-me Martian Walkers. We won't have time to just chill and be you and me, not like we can right now."

"Yeah, well, there's an old saying that shit happens, and life goes on." Dani raised her eyebrows. "Just because we're teenagers doesn't mean it's not true for us." She clapped Mik on the shoulder. "Cheer up. Someday that'll be us in there, sitting at that table, talking about the important matters of the world and how to solve them."

"Yeah, true." Mik brightened. "Hey, wanna go outside and look at the stars?" At night, the research complex shut down almost all exterior lighting, which made the roof a prime viewing location, second only to the Observatory.

Dani smiled broadly. "*Now* you're talking."

They headed for Airlock Two, and Dani suited up. Using a hand-light, Mik led the way from the airlock up to the roof, where they sat with their legs dangling over the edge. Mik turned the light off, and they leaned back to look up at the sky.

The fines had all cleared away from the day's dust storm, and the sky was clear. Mars' thinner atmosphere meant that there was no twinkling effect, and they burned bright and clear in the vast over-arching gulf of the sky. Raising one hand, Dani pointed out constellations, naming them in a whisper. Mik did her best to keep up, but astronomy had never been her strong suit.

Still, she knew enough to be able to pick out the distant tiny dot of Deimos, and the irregular ellipse of Phobos. "Hey," she said, pointing. "That's Stickney." Even without binoculars, it was just barely possible to make out the smudge of shadow on one end of the fast-moving satellite.

"*Huh, yeah.*" Dani shook her head in the near-darkness. "*You know, that's the first time I ever heard them tell that story. You think we'll ever get up there to look for it ourselves?*"

Mik took a breath of air from the pony bottle so she could respond. "Cool idea, but I don't think it's ever gonna happen." As she moved the mask away from her mouth, ice crystals formed from her trace exhalation, gleaming coldly in the distant light of Phobos as they drifted to the rooftop.

"*Yeah, probably not. But it's nice to think about.*"

Another half-breath. "Yeah. It is."

Kicking her heels gently against the outside wall of the Valles Marineris Research Complex, Mik decided not to worry about the future. That had yet to come. Right now, there were stars to marvel at, and a friend to share them with.

She would deal with tomorrow when it came.

Chapter 5: Crisis Event

Over the next few days, Mik worked at familiarising herself with the various simulators that Kyle set up for his construction equipment. It was somewhat of a relief to find that even the catastrophic failure of an overworked gearbox wouldn't be nearly as dramatic—or fatal—as the impromptu deorbiting that might just result from screwing up a near-planet manoeuvre. However, given that most construction sites had people moving around on them, Kyle impressed on her that any mechanical mishap could lead to injury or death anyway.

A week later, after the machinery itself had been delivered and uncrated, it was time for her to get out there and translate simulator experience into real-world skills. Everything was set up and left out near a section of rough terrain that Kyle decided would be perfect for her to practice on. There was also an elevated gravity-fed hydrazine bowser for refuelling the machinery, plus a 'construction shack' in the form of a pressurised cabin (incorporating a small air refresher) that would allow Kyle to monitor her progress in comfort and safety.

Neither had Professor Ibrahim skimped on the machinery itself. Along with a classic tracked bulldozer, he'd acquired a front-end loader with an absurdly large bucket and a backhoe, and a heavy flatbed truck. More were due in later—a grader, a scraper, and an excavator, among others—but he deemed the initial equipment to be sufficient for the upcoming proof-of-concept demonstration for the Tharsis executives.

At Kyle's suggestion, she started off with the bulldozer. Per safety regulations, she wore a hardhat and high-vis gear, as well as her usual construction boots. The bulldozer controls and seat showed signs of having been adjusted for a large man in an EVA suit, which made it entirely unsuitable for her. Fiddling around a little, she adjusted matters so that she could see what she was doing and handle the controls with relative ease. Once she had that sorted out, she started the dozer up and began to familiarise herself with it, with Kyle offering guidance via radio from the construction shack.

He wasn't alone in there. Professor Ibrahim had firmly stated that he needed to observe Mik, at least for the first few days, and Dani had wanted to watch as well. Diamantina came along for a few hours then got back to her current hobby, which involved disassembling one of the surplus rock-hoppers and making it over into something that could achieve Mars orbit with ease. As Mik understood matters, it was more a situation of seeing if she could do it rather than making it for any particular purpose, but she was clearly enjoying herself.

Exposed to an entirely new learning curve, Mik applied herself to translating simulator experience to the real world, working to control the lumbering machines with her customary deft touch. They'd been designed with built-in oxygen supplies to plug into the pressure suits that the construction crews would have used; with a hose adaptor, she could take a breath every now and again, leaving the tanks mostly full by day's end. Even better, if she worked in a sleeveless shirt, her skin's pseudo-photosynthesis could augment her oxygen supply, to the point that the extra air would barely be needed.

But she took her pony bottle along anyway because, as Kyle put it, *'just in case'* was a complete sentence.

The training proceeded apace. Once Mik was secure in the basics, Kyle started her on more advanced techniques, swapping her from one machine to another to keep her mentally active, and so he could see how much she had retained when she got back to the first one. Dani had her own schooling to do, but Professor Ibrahim would drop her off to the worksite in the afternoon and she would ride back with Mik and her father. Overall, the work was both mentally and physically draining, but Mik had never been one to back down from a challenge.

About a month in, she felt she was getting pretty good at it. She was building new muscle in her arms from working the heavy controls, and she could tell by eye the best way to attack a new challenge. The area of rough ground she'd been working on had been bulldozed, scooped, trenched, built up, dug out, moved around and generally landscaped to within an inch of its existence. The demonstration for the Tharsis Corporation was not far away, and every member of the Research Complex was backing her to make a good impression, for both personal and professional reasons.

Which just made it all the more exciting when a shuttle came in for a landing at the pad one afternoon, just as Professor Ibrahim was dropping Dani off at the worksite. Working in the open as she was, Mik saw that the shuttle bore Tharsis insignia, but not much more than that.

"I thought the demonstration wasn't for another week?" she asked Ibrahim over the radio attached to her pony bottle.

"As did I," he replied, sounding puzzled. *"Perhaps they are moving it up. Or maybe a pre-demonstration inspection of the facility. A chance to meet you before the big day."*

"Oh, great," groused Mik. "I've been working all day, and I'm covered in dust and fines. I'm just glad I can't sweat. That would really make the first impression just perfect."

"No, no, it is good," he assured her. *"They will not want to see some perfectly dressed little doll. Showing them that you've actually been driving*

construction machinery is ideal. I will take Kyle and go and greet them. You and Dani can come along behind in the truck, once you've shut everything down."

"We can definitely do that," agreed Mik. "Want me to load some rubble on the back, just to prove we aren't playing patty-cake out here?"

"That is a nice touch, yes," Ibrahim agreed. *"It will prove to them that you can handle the work, over and above the Martian conditions."*

The two men emerged from the construction shack; Ibrahim tipped Mik a wave before heading over to where he'd landed the rock-hopper. Kyle detoured to where she sat on the idling bulldozer. *"It'll be fine,"* he assured her, giving her a thumb's up. *"This'll probably be just a few bigwigs wanting a sneak peek at their investment before the big event. Over and done, and back to work as normal tomorrow."*

"Sir, yes, sir," she replied with a smirk. Leaning back on the seat, she watched him head over and vault up onto the rock-hopper with an easy move that native-born Martians could never duplicate. Of course, it helped that the Connaughts were Earthborn and retained much of the heavy musculature gained from the stronger gravity field.

Once the rock-hopper had taken off and was heading down the Valles toward the Research Complex, she trundled the bulldozer over to the parking space she'd blocked out for it. Shutting it down, she jumped off and trotted over to where the loader was parked. It started easily enough—some of the lessons had involved maintaining the work vehicles under Martian conditions—and she rolled it toward a conveniently-piled stack of rocks. Edging the loader blade under the stack, she scooped a heap of them into the bucket.

The truck was parked nearby, and she took the loader over and dumped the rocks in the middle of the cargo bed. By now, this sort of thing was almost second nature to her, so she went and got a second load. Just as she was depositing them on top of the first lot, two all-wheel-drive vehicles came powering up the track from the Complex. As required by health and safety practices, she stopped the loader where it was and lowered the bucket to rest on top of the heap of rocks.

The AWDs were what the researchers from the Complex used when they wanted to move more than two people at a time, or bring back heavy rock samples. Four EVA-suited figures got out, then one waved and beckoned. Mik put the air mask over her face as she jumped down from the loader. "What's the matter, guys?" she asked over the radio. "Am I taking too long?"

There was no answer, but that wasn't unusual. Sometimes, people ended up on totally different frequencies and just plain forgot to switch back. But as she got closer, Mik recognised the suits in use. "Hey, Sven," she said, gesturing to the tallest of the newcomers and making the universally recognised hand-signs for '*switch to channel twenty-three, dumbass*'. "I thought you had an experiment you were married to, back in the lab. How come you're out here?"

Then they got a little closer, and she wondered why they had their faceplate polarisations turned all the way up. Behind them, the door to the 'construction shack' opened and Dani stepped out.

"Sven?" Mik frowned. "Kennedy? Hussein? Guys, come on, you're freaking me out a little here."

"*What's going on?*" asked Dani. "*These guys come to check on you or something?*"

"I don't know." Mik took half a step backward. Something about the ongoing radio silence—and the reflective silver polarisation on the faceplates—was setting off some deeply buried instincts. "They're acting a little weird." Sven crowded in on her at that moment, grabbing for her arm. "Hey!" she yelled, backing away again. "Cut that out!"

"*Mik, something's wrong,*" Dani said, her voice tight with tension.

"Why, what—" began Mik, then she saw where Dani was pointing. Back toward the Research Complex. The buildings themselves were out of sight, but then she spotted something that should never be visible on Mars.

A curl of smoke, climbing into the air.

Mik might not have had much in the way of experience in the ways of the world, and the Research Complex may have been situated in a valley, but there was always a satellite overhead, and the various dishes and receivers on the roof weren't there for decoration. Through them, she'd had access to all the online movies and books available through the Mars-wide information web. She'd marvelled at the (to her) exotic locations portrayed on the screen, but she'd also paid attention to the plots.

One particular genre that she'd watched quite a few of were detective movies. Her genetic heritage gave her above-average intelligence, so she'd enjoyed trying to solve the case before the detectives pulled all the clues together. It didn't always work—her lack of familiarity with some basic Earth concepts told against her in this regard—but it had been a fun hobby of hers for quite some time.

Now, despite the inclination to trust people wearing pressure suits she recognised, she came to a logical conclusion that she didn't like in the slightest. The people she'd thought were her friends were hiding their faces with polarisation and not replying to her radio signals. There was a fire at the Research Complex, or at least *something* was on fire.

That's not Sven. That's not any of the guys.

"What's going on here?" asked Dani.

"Dani, these aren't the people who should be wearing these suits." Mik ducked under a grabbing arm and backed off to avoid being encircled. These people were clearly unused to moving quickly over uneven terrain in unfamiliar EVA suits, whereas she was both unencumbered by a suit and entirely at home outdoors.

"Are they Tharsis security sent to bring you back to the Complex?"

"Doubt it." Mik retreated some more, alongside the truck. "They would've brought their own EVA suits. These guys wanted me to think they're from the Complex. But if they're not from Tharsis …"

Dani finished the thought. *"Shit, they're from Cyberon! They came here to grab you!"*

A ball of ice formed in Mik's stomach. "And make sure the Complex can't re-engineer me. What the hell have they done?"

"Mom … Dad … no. No, no, no." Dani sounded close to tears. Mik heard the whine of a hydrazine engine in the background. *"We've got to get back there."*

For a second, Mik thought Dani had taken one of the all-wheel-drive vehicles and headed back to the Research Complex on her own, leaving Mik to deal with the intruders. Then the AWD, with Dani at the wheel, came tearing around the truck, kicking up a cloud of fines behind it.

All four men were focused on her; their EVA suits severely limited their peripheral vision, and the thin atmosphere was insufficient to allow them to hear the high-pitched whine of the vehicle's engine. She gauged her moment, then jumped to the side. As Dani slowed down for her, Mik grabbed a convenient handhold and swung up onto the side of the all-wheel-drive. Dani kept going for about fifty metres then stopped, her shoulders shaking.

"Move over," Mik said. "I'll drive."

"I need to go and see what's going on." Dani sounded close to tears.

"Yeah, we need to do that." Mik had been trying to stay logical, but her brain insisted on injecting worry about Professor Ibrahim and Kathy and the others. "Let's make sure these jerks can't follow us, though."

Kicking up a rooster-tail of dust and fines, she pulled a fast one-eighty and gunned the engine. They blew past the four men and pulled up next to the other AWD; Mik jumped out, grabbed the ignition key (which was rarely if ever removed) then got back in with Dani.

A moderately strong wind (strong for Mars, that is) came down the Valles on occasion, and Professor Ibrahim hadn't wanted any more fines being blown down on the Complex than absolutely necessary. Accordingly, the worksite was about six kilometres from the Complex, and the road that connected them meandered between a few low hills.

Mik was normally careful and precise in her driving, but on this day she attacked each curve like a racing driver. She knew exactly how to get every bit of traction out of the large knobbly wheels in Martian gravity and she pushed her capabilities to the limit, the hydrazine engine howling like a banshee.

Passing through a small cut in the last hill, they emerged to a scene of utter horror. A bunch of suited figures stood before the frontage of the Valles Marineris Research Complex, with several more lying on the ground as though they'd been dragged out through the airlock and dropped there. The buildings themselves ... were alight. The large viewing windows were broken open, and flames blasted out through the gaps, giving vent to huge roiling plumes of smoke. More people were carrying cases up the rise toward where the shuttle pad was; in fact, Mik could see the shuttle resting there, behind the retaining walls.

Fire was normally impossible on Mars: in the open, anyway. Uncontrolled fire within the confines of an aired-up shelter was considered an emergency situation, and she'd been drilled in the various ways and means something like that could happen.

What she was seeing now was a runaway oxygen fire. Someone had opened up the emergency oh-two storage and flooded the Complex with pure oxygen, then struck a spark. While she'd only ever heard of it happening by accident, she had no doubt that this time was different.

Someone did this on purpose.

Her eyes searched both the moving and supine figures, and a sob escaped her. Professor Ibrahim's silhouette was unmistakeable, and she could not see him among those outside the facility. If he was inside, he was dead. That was as simple as it got.

She'd never hear him laugh again. Never get a proud nod when she got something right, or a stern lecture when she messed up. The grief clawed at her chest, raw and insistent, but she locked it away. *Later.*

Kyle Connaught was equally hard to miss, being brawny and broad-shouldered. Nobody she could see was moving like him, and nobody was being treated like a prisoner.

"Mom ... Dad ... no ..." She heard Dani's whimper from beside her, and she wanted to join in, but right then, she had a stronger urge.

The cases that were being transported had to contain all the classified work that the Complex had under development. Including, and this was important, everything that had gone into making *her.* Images sprang to mind of people who would commit murder to steal priceless industrial secrets actually creating and raising clones of her. Would those clones be treated as she had been, like a person?

She strongly doubted it.

"Hang on!" she shouted and turned the wheel. The all-wheel-drive responded nimbly, swerving off the road and attacking the slope like a hungry predator. She was halfway toward the group with the cases before one turned and saw her, and she angled her direction slightly to cut them off. What they thought they were seeing, she didn't quite know, but they froze for what seemed to be an eternity.

When one finally moved, it was to bolt for the safety of the retaining wall around the shuttle pad. He was clearly unused to running in an EVA suit while carrying a bulky case; within a few strides, he was off-balance and had to slow down. By the time he got his feet under himself, it was too late. Mik gauged the distance to a nicety and clipped him with one of the wheels. The impact jolted the AWD, but it sent him off his feet, sprawling on the ground and rolling over and over. The case flew off in a different direction.

Gritting her teeth, Mik spun the all-wheel-drive into a hard turn and arrowed toward the rest of the group. Designed with high clearance and off-road tolerances, the vehicle was clearly capable of going straight over the top of them, even if they left the path.

"What are you doing?" screamed Dani, hanging on for dear life. Mik didn't answer, being entirely preoccupied with driving.

The AWD came with large front-mounted floodlights for driving over rough terrain at night. Though it was broad daylight, Mik flicked these on as she bore down on the rest of the group. She was entirely willing to run them all down; this must have communicated itself to the interlopers, because they broke and ran. The cases themselves were not overly heavy—Martian gravity was nice like that—but they retained their mass and thus inertia, which made them awkward to run with. Accordingly, they discarded their burdens as they bolted.

Mik cast an eye on the main group as she skidded the all-wheel-drive to a halt. "Grab the cases!" she shouted. "Put them in the back!" The men were starting to move toward them, but they had some distance to cover.

Dani didn't argue; she scrambled to collect the scattered cases, hauling them back to the vehicle with frantic urgency, her movements quick and jerky with adrenaline. Mik already had the AWD moving as Dani vaulted into the passenger seat again. She gunned it back up the slope toward where the man she'd clipped was just starting to get to his feet.

He saw her coming and raised one hand defensively, but she smashed him again with the same wheel, sending him flying off his feet once more. Maintaining control, Mik pulled up next to the last case. Dani didn't need to be told this time, jumping out and tossing it in the back with the others.

"Okay, what do we do now?" Through her faceplate, Dani's expression was set as she got back into the all-wheel-drive, though tears were starting to make their way down her cheeks. *"Are Mom and Dad alive? Do you think we can save them?"*

Mik started the vehicle moving again. "I'm sorry," she said slowly. "That's an oh-two fire. It'll be hot enough in there to *melt* EVA suits. If these guys are willing to attack Tharsis property and destroy it like that, they'll be willing to commit murder to cover it up." She gunned the engine, heading back toward the worksite. "We can't bring them back. But we *can* make these assholes pay for what they've done."

"What about the ones that were lying down?" asked Dani desperately. *"What if they were—"*

"I'd say your dad fought back before they … did what they did," Mik said, wishing it wasn't true. "Those were their guys. The EVA suits weren't the same pattern as we use."

"So, they killed them."

Mik nodded, wishing she was able to cry. She'd never had to mourn anyone before, and it was totally messing up her emotions. Intellectually, she knew she had to keep it together until they were out of danger, but the other side of her wanted to scream and rage at the heavens. Somehow, she kept the AWD on track, driving between the low hills toward the worksite.

"Do you think they've got guns?"

The question brought her back onto even keel, at least temporarily. Guns could screw everything up. She wouldn't die from a pressure-suit puncture, but a bullet going through her would kill her just the same as anyone else. "I didn't *see* any," she said slowly. It kind of made sense. Guns weren't really a widespread thing on Mars, and knives would kill almost as easily. They'd also leave less in the way of incriminating evidence.

She just had time to be shocked at herself for being able to think like that before they rounded a curve to see the truck bearing down on them from the other direction. Adrenaline chased out everything else and she yanked the wheel to the side. As Dani yelped in surprise and grabbed for a handhold, the smaller vehicle swerved off the road. The truck lunged toward them, but Mik slammed her foot on the accelerator and sent the all-wheel-drive bounding up the slope, out of the way.

"Keep an eye on them!" she shouted. "Tell me where they're going!" The truck was too long to comfortably turn around on the relatively narrow road, even if the driver was used to the vehicle and the terrain. If it was her in the driver's seat, she would either keep going until she hit a wider point, or stop and try to reverse along the winding road.

Clinging to her handhold, Dani turned her upper torso so she could look back along the road. *"They're slowing down,"* she reported. *"I think they're going to turn around."* Her voice was brittle, as though she were hanging on by a thread. Mik knew how she felt.

"Good. That'll take time." She reached a decision for what she was going to do. "Do you feel up to driving?" In her time at the Complex, she'd gone through any number of emergency drills where all the adults were 'killed' or otherwise taken out of action, so she had to decide what to do herself. This meant that making life-changing choices wasn't totally out of her experience, but this was far outside what she'd ever trained for. Still, it was better than nothing.

"Yeah." Dani sounded on the edge of tears again, but she set her jaw and spoke with renewed resolve. *"If they get hold of us, we're both dead or worse. What's the plan?"*

Mik got the AWD back onto the road and turned it toward the work site. There was a possibility that the people who had set fire to the Complex were listening in on their radio chatter, so she took one hand off the wheel and tapped her ear, then held up five fingers, then four, then one. Channel 541 was clear off the bands that were used at the Complex, and Mik tended to use it when she wanted to have a private conversation with anyone.

The loader was still sitting in the middle of the work site, bucket poised in mid-air where it had been resting on top of the pile of rocks on the back of the truck. Mik pulled the all-wheel-drive to a halt next to it, and took the time to change channels. Jumping out of the vehicle, she reached into the back seat and heaved two of the cases out. "Get the rest," she grunted. "Bring them over to the bulldozer."

"Why? Are you going to bury them?" Dani grabbed two more cases and hustled in Mik's wake to where the bulldozer was parked.

Carefully, Mik laid her two cases down in a row behind the wide tracks of the bulldozer. "In a way. Drop those and get the last two."

Dani didn't argue, letting the cases fall to the dusty ground and running back toward the idling AWD. Mik slid them into position behind the first two. *"Uh … you know they'll just dig them up again, right?"*

"Won't do them any good. Put those behind the others." As Dani returned with the last two cases, moving somewhat faster than she herself would've been able to with that sort of burden, Mik climbed onto the dozer and fired it up. "Once you've done that, get back out of the way."

They were on borrowed time, and she knew it. But she had to do this right, for the memory of Professor Ibrahim, Kathy, and the others.

*Cyberon is **not** stealing our research.*

As soon as Dani was back out of the way, Mik started the dozer moving backward, the heavy treads crunching down on the cases like the metal frames were made of light plastic. She shut the bulldozer down once every case was under the track, then popped open the access panel and pulled out half a dozen components. Stuffing these into her pocket, she closed the panel again and jumped down off the dozer.

"What was that about?" asked Dani as Mik headed for the loader. *"Can't they just start it up and drive it forward again?"*

"Not without the parts I took. They're unique to the dozer. The only spares are back in the Complex. It won't start without them, and I bet they didn't bring any heavy-machinery engineers along." As she looked around, her eye fell on the bowser. "Get in the all-wheel-drive. We're going to need to move fast, but first there's something I've got to do."

Climbing up onto the loader, she kicked it over, the hydrazine engine whining to life. Then she raised the bucket and drove straight at the bowser.

"They're coming back!" warned Dani.

Mik risked a glance over her shoulder; sure enough, the men in the truck had figured out how to turn their unwieldy conveyance around and were just now driving back onto the worksite. "Okay, hang tight and get ready to follow my lead."

Throwing caution to the thin Martian wind, she ramped up the speed on the loader. All her practice with the heavy machine paid off as she gauged the moment just right, swinging the wheel as the corner of the bucket punched into the side of the bowser. Pressurised hydrazine fuel spurted out; she opened the throttle and swung the loader in a tight half-circle, ripping the hole even wider. *You don't get to use our fuel.*

The truck was coming on strong but swerved away as the bucket swung toward it. It came to a halt, and two men jumped out. Their faceplates, no longer polarised, showed angry expressions. Each of them was now carrying a heavy wrench, no doubt taken from the truck's toolbox. One headed for Dani and the other for Mik. With a shock of recognition, Mik realised she'd seen the one heading for her before. "Holy shit, I know this guy!"

"What? Hang on!" Dani gunned the engine, leaving her pursuer in her dust. *"What do you mean, you know him?"*

Mik started the loader moving, though she had to swerve to avoid the truck as its driver tried to come at her from the side. The guy on foot swung his wrench at her on the way past, but she ducked away; metal clanged against metal. "He was a security hire from Burroughs, last year. Wasn't here for long. That must be how Cyberon found out about me!"

"Sonovabitch." Now Dani sounded more pissed off than distressed. *"Can I run over him? Please?"*

It was tempting, but Mik had other plans. "No. Don't let them get too close. They might throw those wrenches. Let's go." Revving the loader all-out, she started on the road back toward the Complex. As the truck started to lumber in a large circle, she saw the men running toward it.

"Okay, so what are we doing now?" Dani was right behind her as she hit the road, the all-wheel-drive easily keeping up with the loader.

"Making sure these assholes don't get away with what they've done. Just stick close to me." She kept a lookout up ahead, concentrating on not swerving too wildly with the bucking, jolting loader. The scream of the hydrazine engine was vibrating through her hands as well as being actually audible through the air. She just had to hope that they hadn't gotten any more of the vehicles out before they set fire to the Complex.

"You know that truck's right behind us." Dani was starting to sound worried again.

"They'll have other problems in a moment." Mik hoped she sounded more confident than she felt. Her plan was tenuous as hell, but at least she had a plan. All that flight simulator time was hopefully going to pay off. "Try to keep up."

Up ahead, she saw the shuttle landing pad emerging from behind a hill. She spared a glance at the toolbox beside the seat, then grabbed the thing she needed. Slowing down as much as she dared, she turned the loader and headed off-road, avoiding the bigger boulders. The last thing she wanted was for Dani to get hung up trying to follow her.

"Where are we going? Are we going to hijack the shuttle?"

"Nice idea, but they'll have people on board." Glancing back, she saw the AWD gamely bouncing along behind her, Dani clinging to the wheel as she was jolted around in her seat. Behind the all-wheel-drive was the truck, but it wasn't built for this kind of off-road travel. Especially with a load of rocks on the cargo bed.

Over the small hill they went, then through a shallow gully that must have been a watercourse back when rain was still a thing on Mars. Then they were climbing the rise toward the shuttle pad itself. Gritting her teeth, Mik opened the throttle to full and lowered the bucket a touch.

"Mik, what are you doing? Mik!"

The retaining wall around the shuttle pad had wide gaps in it to allow service vehicles to reach anything on the pad itself. Mik guided the loader through one of these gaps, heading for the shuttle. The make was familiar from the endless simulator hours, and she was pretty sure she knew where the fuel tanks were. Leaving the loader aimed directly at the shuttle, she climbed onto the footplate and leaped outward.

Her landing was good, but she had far too much forward momentum to stop on a dime. Dropping into a tumble, she rolled over a couple of times before coming to her feet again. Somewhere off to the side, she felt rather than heard a solid *crunch*. Dani brought the all-wheel-drive to a sliding halt beside her as she looked around; the loader had swerved a little but not a great deal, and the sharp corner of the bucket was buried in the side of the shuttle. As they watched, fuel began to pour out.

"Can we go now?" Dani turned her upper body to look over her shoulder. *"I think you just pissed off a whole lot of people."*

"One second." Mik still had hold of the emergency flare she'd taken from the toolbox. Yanking the starter tab, she sparked the flare to life, then hurled it toward the growing pool of rocket fuel on the shuttle pad. While it was still in the air, she jumped into the AWD. "Go, go, go!"

Dirt sprayed out from beneath the wheels of the all-wheel-drive as Dani applied pedal to metal. Mik hung on as they shot out through the gap in the retaining wall. Despite the tenuous atmosphere, she knew exactly when the fuel caught; there was a tremendous low-pitched *whooom* and a flare of heat on her back.

Looking around, she took in the fireball that had bloomed from the stricken shuttle, scattering pieces far and wide. Amidst it all, the loader's tank of hydrazine went up as well, adding its small part to the whole.

Hanging on as the sturdy little vehicle bounced over the rocky slope, Mik watched the mushroom cloud climbing into the sky. *You burn my life down, I burn your life down. Assholes.*

"Okay, we can't drive out of here, so what do we do?" But Dani was already steering the AWD toward where they needed to go next.

"Rock-hopper," Mik agreed with what she hadn't said.

"The one Mom was working on?"

"Yeah." With the extra-sized fuel tank Diamantina Connaught had installed on it, it had far greater range than the standard model. Mik figured she could fly halfway around Mars on it.

"Where are we gonna go?"

That was actually a good question. If Cyberon was bold enough to attack a Tharsis resource in broad daylight like this, was anywhere on Mars safe? "How about that place your parents were talking about that one time? That depot?" Just on the off-chance somebody was actually listening in, she didn't want to spell it out for them.

Dani sighed. *"Yeah. Good idea."*

They jolted down off the rise and tore across the flat, scattering the invaders, who were currently running toward the burning shuttle. Fortunately, the rock-hopper 'parking lot' was a little way away from the Complex proper, so it hadn't been subjected to the same treatment.

The all-wheel-drive slid to a halt and they jumped out. It wasn't hard to figure out which rock-hopper Diamantina had been working on; it was bigger by half again than the rest of them. Mik clambered on board and began to decipher the new controls as she strapped herself in.

"Truck's coming," warned Dani. *"They're not going to the fire."*

"Damn it," muttered Mik. She flicked over the first and second switches, then nudged the thumb-wheel. Beneath them, the attitude rockets rumbled to life, lifting the reworked rock-hopper off the ground. She wriggled the control sticks, getting a feel for how it handled. "This is not how I should be learning—"

"Truck!" screamed Dani.

Mik reacted instinctively, throwing the third switch and opening the throttle. The main rocket engine blasted into life, driving them straight up into the air. An instant later, the truck blitzed past directly under them, ramming into another rock-hopper and reducing it to twisted scrap.

"Okay," Mik decided. "That's the tutorial over with. Time to go." Reaching under the minimal control panel, she flicked a hidden switch then glanced sideways at Dani. "Laser altimeter disabled. How's your orbital mechanics?"

"I've been keeping up my studies." Dani took a moment to think. *"Phobos will be overhead in forty-five minutes."*

"Okay, then." Mik gave the reconditioned 'hopper a bit more thrust. "Let's go see if Stickney's still there."

Dani reached across and clasped her shoulder. *"Let's do that."* There was a catch in her voice.

Turning, Mik looked into her best friend's faceplate and met her eyes. "I'm sorry about your parents."

Dani sniffled. *"I'm sorry about Professor Ibrahim and your friends."*

Mik took hold of Dani's hand and squeezed it. "I'm here. I'll always be here."

"Thanks. That means a lot."

Looking up into the sky, Mik opened the throttle some more. There seemed to be a lot more gradations on it than there had been before. She had it nowhere near full thrust, and the acceleration was gratifyingly strong. "Let's go to Phobos."

Dani squeezed her hand in return. *"With you all the way."*

Far below, smoke roiled upward from the Valles Marineris Research Complex and the burning shuttle. Above them, the stars waited.

Riding on a pillar of flame, they ascended into the Martian sky.

Chapter 6: Stickney

Mik had never been so grateful for the padding in the seats as she was right then. The rocket engines thundered below them, the vibrations transmitting freely through the frame as the modified rock-hopper accelerated upward.

As she watched the walls of Valles Marineris fall away on either side, she knew she'd never been this far up in her entire life. Just for a moment, she felt a twinge of agoraphobia—the Valles had always been there, subtly cradling and surrounding her with its towering rocky embrace—but she pushed it away. *Dani made it all the way here from Earth. I can ignore a little open space around me.*

Higher and higher they climbed, their speed mounting by the second. A two-Martian-gee acceleration wasn't unknown to her, but it was usually only momentary, such as when she was banking a rock-hopper into a hard turn. Or the time she'd nearly crashed one, looping it. There was a prickling around her eyes that made her wish yet again for the ability to shed tears, as she recalled Professor Ibrahim's exasperated words at the time.

Overhead, the sky was rapidly darkening to space-black as they pushed past the last of the tenuous atmosphere. She had no way to look downward, pressed into the seat cushioning as she was, but she could imagine the length of Valles Marineris spread out below, an immense scar stretching across the face of Mars.

Now, of course, it was the location of a crime scene, where the researchers of the Complex had been brutally murdered for the data they'd accumulated. Mainly data about *her*. With any luck, her actions would hold the Cyberon killers in place until some form of authority came to check.

Dani's voice sounded strange and remote in her ear. Personally, she didn't blame her friend. At least Dani was still holding it together. *"Cease thrust in five ... four ... three ... two ... one ... mark."*

Obediently, Mik ran the thumb-wheel down to zero, and the engines cut out. The upward pressure ceased immediately, leaving her with a floating sensation as though she was in free fall. Which, technically, she was. They were still hurtling upward at an impressive rate and would be for some time before they began to fall again, even if she didn't apply any more acceleration.

"Thrust at zero," she reported. "Do we have a vector for Phobos yet?"

"Not ... yet." There was a catch in Dani's voice. *"Can ... we just stay here awhile? I ... just want to not have to think for a bit."*

"Yeah, got it." Mik tried to sound strong and supportive, but there was a lump in her throat that wouldn't go away. It didn't matter that she physically couldn't cry and was in vacuum to boot. She wanted to cry anyway. A line from a story she'd once read crossed her mind: *the universe is a cold and malevolent thing, and it will laugh as it takes away everything you care about.*

Up until now, she hadn't believed it.

Now … she was absolutely a convert.

With a feather-light touch on the attitude thrusters, she nudged the rock-hopper gently, rolling it until they were facing 'down' toward Mars. In space, 'up' and 'down' were relative concepts, so she did her best to convince herself that she was looking *across* at the red-orange planet. In the middle of her view, of course, was Valles Marineris, seeming to split open the crust of Mars like an orange hacked at by a blunt knife.

It was a view she would've once sold her soul for, but right now it didn't help. About the only thing that gave her any measure of comfort was the fact that she'd well and truly blown up the bad guys' ride out of there. There would be no walking for help, and none of the vehicles held enough hydrazine to get them all to safety, or even most of them. If the Cyberon guys thought of it, they could load the AWD on the back of the truck (after removing the pile of rocks by hand) then drive the truck as far as it went, then go on with the all-wheel-drive after they ran out of fuel. This assumed, of course, that the truck didn't get into difficulties the moment it left the road.

Distantly, through the radio link, she heard Dani sniffling. Almost without her volition, she reached out and took the other girl's gloved hand, squeezing as hard as she could to be felt through the tough material. Dani's fingers closed on hers and they shared their silent grief, far above Mars.

"*Okay.*" Dani's voice was a little rougher than normal as she worked on the calculator built into the sleeve of her suit, but Mik wasn't about to point it out. "*Going to need a forty-five-degree tilt to the east and five minutes of two-emm-gee thrust, to begin with. I'll give you vector corrections as we get closer.*"

"Forty-five degrees tilt *that* way," murmured Mik, dancing the rock-hopper around with tiny bursts. Once she was certain she had it facing the correct direction and angle—her astrogation might be less than perfect, but when it came to orienting herself in a three-dimensional space, she had it *nailed*—she nodded. "Ready to fire on your mark."

Dani didn't hesitate. "*Go.*"

Mik rolled the thruster-wheel over with her thumb, feeling the acceleration as it built up behind her. Again, the rock-hopper leaped forward, going places its designer had surely not intended it for. On the other hand, unlike ninety percent of space-ships in general, it was light and agile enough to land directly on the surface of Phobos; a celestial body that Diamantina Connaught had once described as '*a collection of gravel orbiting in close formation*'.

To land there, however, they would first have to *almost* match its orbital speed and then let it catch up with them. Phobos orbited Mars at just six thousand kilometres of altitude, which meant that it whipped around its primary at a little over two kilometres per second. In astronomical terms, there were planets and moons that were a lot easier to pilot an intercept course with. Most had a gravity well that a ship could simply fall into. Phobos, not so much.

The minutes crawled by, and Dani gave Mik gradual course changes, occasionally heaving herself around in her straps to eyeball the approaching moon. Soon, they were so close that Mik didn't have to look hard to pick it out against the starscape. With movements so gentle she thought of them as *suggested* course corrections, she drifted the rock-hopper over until it was essentially hovering 'above' the enormous crater that was their goal. Stickney was only a little wider than Valles Marineris, but it took up a ludicrous amount of the surface of the tiny moon.

Suddenly, Dani pointed. *"There it is. There's the construction shack they talked about. And there's a landing pad there, too."*

Mik glanced that way and saw it: a blocky building next to a bare slab of raw concrete set into the rocky 'ground'. "Oh, good. They got any way of securing this thing on the pad? I don't trust the escape velocity here." She wasn't exaggerating; Phobos' mass was so low that even she would be able to throw a rock straight out of its gravity well with relative ease. Hell, Dani would probably be able to throw one all the way to *Earth*. A bad recoil on landing could knock them entirely clear of the tiny moon.

"I think I see chains or clamps or something. Get us down there, and I'll be able to secure the rock-hopper in place." Dani sounded surer of herself, now that she had something definitive to do.

"Just don't lose contact with the 'hopper," Mik reminded her. "I don't want to have to chase you all over Mars local space after you bounce yourself back out into the void."

"You got it." Dani went back to guiding Mik in for the landing.

The one real problem with the rock-hopper was that its design for use in a gravity well meant that the attitude jets couldn't be swivelled to point upward, because who needed upward-firing jets when gravity did the job just fine? This made manoeuvring the last few metres before touchdown downright painful, as she couldn't tilt the 'hopper to boost in the direction she wanted to go.

Fortunately, Phobos' minimal gravity took hold—*finally*—and almost infinitesimally drifted them downward over about thirty seconds or so, until they landed with a light jolt. Dani went over the side immediately, and Mik felt a metallic *clank* reverberating through the frame of the rock-hopper.

"All good?" she asked, hands still resting on the controls.

"Yeah, there's some basic shackles here." Mik heard panting, and the odd sound of EVA-suit soles against concrete; no doubt transmitted over Dani's radio. *"Should have it locked down in a minute."*

"Good to hear." Still, she didn't relax her vigilance, twisting her head to watch Dani where she could. "Let me know when I can shut the engines all the way down."

There was a second clank. *"That's two. Two to go."*

"Awesome." Mik hit the shut-down switch and unclipped her five-point harness, though she kept a careful hold on the control pedestal as she used it to pull herself upright. The microgravity didn't bother her, but she wondered if she should take her boots off to achieve proper ground contact with her feet. *Nah, I'll see how I go.*

Stepping off the rock-hopper, she let herself drift to the landing-pad next to one of the unsecured shackles. Hooking her boot under it, she crouched and took hold of it, then latched it onto one of the rock-hopper legs. Dani joined her at that moment, having secured the 'hopper at the fourth point.

"So, what now? We check out the shack?"

"That's the idea," Mik agreed. "Good work with the navigation and the shackles, by the way. I couldn't have done this without you."

"You could do it a lot faster with someone else like you," Dani said wryly, but her expression behind the EVA suit's faceplate was pleased all the same.

"Well, given that there *is* nobody else like me, I'm glad you're here." Mik pushed off from the rock-hopper, letting her boots skim over the rough concrete pad as she moved toward the blocky building that adjoined it.

"I'm glad I'm here too." Dani followed along behind Mik; not as gracefully, but she got there in the end.

They ended up at the heavy steel entrance hatch to the 'construction shack' together; Mik looked at the equally heavy spoked wheel set into it, and moved aside for Dani. "Yeah, this one's yours."

"Damn right it is." Dani took hold of the spokes and set her feet, then heaved. Mik heard a grunt over the radio link. *"Whoof. Damn, it's not easy for me, either."*

"C'mon," Mik urged her, half-jokingly. "Use those high-gee muscles you're so proud of."

"I've been on Mars for the last few years, in case you'd forgotten," snarked Dani. She threw her effort into it a second time. *"Jeez, it must be vacuum-welded or something."*

"You'd think they'd take precautions against that." Mik frowned, then took a closer look at the hatch. "What if you're trying to turn it the wrong way?"

*"There **is** only one way to turn it. Lefty-loosey, righty-tighty. I'm turning it left. Duh."* Dani strained against the metal bars, to no avail.

"Looks like not everyone thought that way." Reaching up, Mik tapped a faded arrow, curving from the left around to the right.

Dani stared at the arrow, then shifted her grip and applied pressure in the other direction. This time, when she heaved at the spokes, there was an almost infinitesimal shift. She tried again, and the spokes started to turn. The more they moved, the easier she seemed to find it.

When the wheel came to a stop, she heaved at it and opened what was clearly an airlock. They stepped inside and Mik helped Dani pull the hatch closed, then spin the wheel on the inside. Lights came up, reassuring Mik that the shack had power at least. "Lefty loosey, righty tighty," she murmured, just loudly enough for the radio to pick it up.

"Oh, shut up," retorted Dani, giving her a dirty look.

They finished sealing the outside door then applied their efforts to the inner hatch. As that wheel clunked against its stop in turn, vents opened and Mik felt the air pressure rising. It equalised at about thirty kilopascals, and Dani pushed the hatch open.

More lights came on inside the building itself as they stepped inside. Mik looked around as Dani pushed the inner hatch closed and spun the wheel to seal it. Oxygen tanks were stacked up on racks along one wall, storage cabinets held undisclosed contents on the other wall, and the air refresher took up a large section of the back wall. The air pressure was holding steady at thirty kPa.

Mik took a careful breath, then held the air mask to her face. "Oh-two partial pressure's not bad," she reported. "But it feels pretty cold to me, so you'd probably end up with flash-frozen lungs. It'll probably warm up soon enough."

"Well, I'm going to need to do something about my EVA suit." Dani gestured at herself. *"I'm getting notifications of air loss. It's not hard vacuum rated."*

"Shit!" Mik was stricken; she was the one who'd brought Dani up here. "How bad is it?"

"Could be worse, but could be a whole lot better, too." Dani moved across to the storage cabinets, then opened one. *"Score! Spare suits, from back in the day. And it looks like they were kept on trickle charge. If I can find one in my size, I'll be set."*

Mik felt a wash of relief, tempered by the direness of the situation. "How are you going to get from one to the other? I'm pretty sure you'll feel the cold."

"Pfft, I've walked barefoot in snow. If I hyperventilate first, I can hold my breath long enough to get out of the EVA suit and into the pressure suit." Dani was opening one cabinet after another, until she stopped and pulled a suit out. The helmet flopped forward, but it seemed to be in the right size. *"All I'll need then is full air tanks."*

"I can absolutely handle that part." Mik located a pair of air tanks on a rack and checked the gauges. Both read firmly in the green, so she attached them to the pressure suit. Then she unslung the pony bottle from around her neck and screwed a bayonet hose into it, fiddling with the controls until it started to refill.

When she turned around, Dani was partway out of the EVA suit, eyes tight shut. In front of her, the old-fashioned pressure suit was open, ready for donning. With careful precision, Dani climbed into the pressure suit and sealed it up, putting the helmet on last.

If Mik had been the type to hold her breath, she would've been doing so, right up until the helmet collar sealed and Dani gave her the all-OK signal then activated her radio.

"So, what's the plan?" Dani sounded happier now that she was wearing something more substantial than the EVA suit; Mik couldn't blame her.

"We spread the word," Mik said simply, glad that she didn't need the radio now that she was in pressure. "We can step off this rock and drop straight down to Tharsis in just a few hours. Tell everyone on Mars what's happened. Make Cyberon pay for everything they've done." It was clear, simple, and sharp in her mind.

"Oh. Somehow, I thought it would be a bit more dramatic."

Mik snorted. "I leave drama to the drama queens. If there's anything I've learned from growing up on Mars, it's that you make your plans as simple as possible, with fallbacks for anything that can go wrong." Grabbing another oxygen tank off the rack, she hefted it. "I'm gonna take this out to the rock-hopper and see if they haven't got fuel tanks here as well. You know, just in case."

"Because fallbacks. Gotcha."

"Got it in one. Never know when you might need that other half-tank of rocket fuel, or a spare oh-two tank." Holding the tank over her shoulder, she spun the wheel one-handed to unlock the inner airlock door then pulled it open.

Now that the doors had been opened, they were easy enough to operate, though Mik had to wait for the pumps to evacuate the airlock before she could open the outer door, and the sheer inertia of all that metal was still a pain to push around. After storing the tank on the rock-hopper, she then went to investigate a promising plate set into the base of the construction shack. The paint that had once coated the access plate was almost all worn away, but she could just barely make out the symbol for a refuelling station.

The clamps holding it shut were stubborn enough that she nearly went and got Dani to open it for her, but sheer bloody-mindedness got her through in the end. Once the plate lifted away, she saw coiled hoses, with fittings for several tanks.

Huh. They really did think of everything.

Hoisting one of the hoses out, she screwed it onto the outlet for the same type of fuel the rock-hoppers used, then attached the other end of the hose to the 'hopper's tank. The filler switch needed a little persuading before she finally got it to turn, but then the liquid fuel began to run through the hose.

Taking full advantage of the microgravity, she vaulted onto the rock-hopper and checked the readouts, smiling in satisfaction as the tank steadily refilled. Leaning back on the padded seat, she set about ticking off a list of action items in her mind.

Keep Dani alive: check.

Refuel rock-hopper: check.

Spread word about Cyberon: about to happen.

Something caught her gaze, and she frowned and cupped her hands around her eyes. Lights in the sky weren't exactly unusual once someone left atmosphere, but they generally followed predictable patterns of movement. These lights … they weren't moving much, but they weren't holding still in the sky either. And she couldn't be sure, but they seemed to be getting brighter.

Which meant closer.

Oh, shit.

She pawed at her chest for her pony bottle air mask before recalling that she'd left the bottle refilling, inside. More importantly, the attached radio was also inside, which meant she didn't have any way of communicating with Dani right at this second. And she *really needed* to get Dani's attention.

Launching herself off the rock-hopper, she leaped across the expanse of concrete that separated it from the main entry of the construction shack. Such was the minuscule gravity of Phobos that she made it all the way across in the one jump. Colliding with the spoked wheel, she hung onto it, set her feet, and heaved it around. Even knowing the correct way for it to turn, she still didn't have it easy.

Once the outer hatch was closed, she set the wheel spinning to secure it again, then turned to the inner hatch. Orbital construction workers, she decided, must have muscles out to *there,* just by way of opening these damn pressure hatches all the time.

After half an eternity, the pressure equalised, allowing her to shove the inner hatch open; in her haste, she almost fell through into the habitat. Dani, who had been getting used to the feel of her new suit by the look of it, turned toward her. *"Took you long eno—hey, are you okay?"*

"We gotta go!" shouted Mik, glad of the fact that the air itself would carry her words. "Like, right now! There's ships coming straight for Phobos!"

"What? What if they're rescue ships? Or, you know, tourists? Tourists who can rescue us?"

Grimly, Mik shook her head. "We can't afford to assume that they're friendly. Until we're face to face with Tharsis executives, nobody's on our side. Simple as that. We gotta go, right now."

She leaped across the room to where her pony bottle was still hanging off the hose, and detached it. Beside it, Dani had attached the one from the EVA suit. Yanking off the hard-hat and high-vis vest that she'd been wearing all this time, Mik discarded them; visibility absolutely was *not* her friend right now.

"Okay, but where?" Dani pointed at the floor. *"If we make a burn for Mars, they can probably crowd us to the point that we lose control and crash. They've got six thousand kilometres to play with. If we head outward, they can just keep harrying us until we run out of fuel, and I run out of air."*

"God damn it, I hate it when you're right like that." Mik slung her pony bottle around her neck. "So where should we go?"

Mik could actually tell when Dani took a deep breath. *"I have a plan. It's not a great plan; in fact, it's a shitty plan. You're going to hate it."*

"How do you know that?"

"Because I hate it."

"Oh."

Chapter 7: Desperation Move

Mik checked Dani's oxy-tank and found that it was in the green, so she disconnected it as well and tossed it gently in Dani's direction; two spares were always better than one. "Okay, so what's your plan?"

"We hide." Dani caught the tank with ease; in the near-infinitesimal gravity, it had barely made an arc through the air between them. *"I read this story once, where a guy hid out on a small moon and managed to evade a ship that was looking for him by always staying just over the horizon."*

"They'll land people," Mik said at once. She jumped back across the room toward the airlock hatch. "It wouldn't take a dozen men long to search the entire moon, spread out so they're all in eyeshot of each other. We'd be trapped and cornered."

*"No, no, see, **I** hide on Phobos."* Dani headed over to where her EVA suit lay discarded on the floor, the refreshed oxy-tank under her arm. *"You take the 'hopper up, get out a bit, and go dark. It's got the radar signature of a small rock. We strap this suit into the passenger seat, make 'em think it's me, so they don't look on Phobos."*

Mik frowned. She was certain she could play hide-and-seek with a bunch of Pure Strain bigots in surface-to-orbit tin cans until the sun went dark, but the plan felt awfully shallow. A twinge of uncertainty tugged at her gut. "What's the endgame? How do we win?"

"We activate the emergency beacon and outlast them," Dani shrugged. *"I keep coming back for oxygen top-ups and food. You just sit out there in the dark. Sooner or later **someone's** got to take notice and come up to ask questions. That's when we show ourselves."*

The plan wasn't entirely suicidal, Mik decided, just … desperate. Which matched it to the circumstances exactly. And Dani had been correct; she hated it.

"I don't like leaving you down here on your own," she said firmly. "Anything could happen. Suit failure, oxy-tank running out …"

"And you being with me won't help much if either of those things happen," Dani retorted. *"I've done pressure-suit safety drills."* She passed the EVA suit and oxy-tank over to Mik and laid hold of the airlock door handles. *"Once we're outside the shack, assume they're listening."*

Mik nodded. "Copy that." Her storage organ was replete with oxygen, so she could go for some time without needing even the pony bottle if she had to. Reaching over, she flicked up the cover on the button marked EMERGENCY BEACON and pressed it. A red light began to flash in the shelter.

The airlock door opened, and Mik lugged the oxy-tank and the spare suit inside. Dani closed the inner door, then set to work on the outer one. Due to either the comings and goings loosening the mechanism, or perhaps Dani's adrenaline levels, it opened in relatively short order.

When Mik stepped out, the ships were a lot closer. Just a few minutes away from landing or performing a fly-by, if she had to guess. As she watched, a retro-thrust illuminated one of the craft. "Shit," she said into the pony bottle microphone, "they're close!" That part, at least, was not feigned.

"What are we going to do?" Dani was playing her part in the deception perfectly. As Mik leaped lightly onto the rock-hopper, the Earth girl ducked under the skeletal craft and started unlatching the tie-downs.

"We're going to have to make a run for it." Mik braced her feet between her seat and the control column and pushed the empty EVA suit down into the passenger seat. "Here, let me get you strapped in." It was the work of a moment to secure it in place, then attach the oxy-tank and give it a burst. That inflated it just far enough to make it appear as though there was someone inside it. If someone had been watching with a scope from the beginning, the entire charade would've been pointless, but they were still far enough out that visual observation wasn't perfect—she hoped.

"Thanks," Dani ad-libbed. *"I suck at this microgravity stuff."*

The ships were coming closer with every second. "Okay, hang on. We're getting out of here." She yanked herself down into the seat, causing the entire 'hopper to bounce upward slightly. A vibration ran through it as she strapped herself in, and she glanced over to see that Dani had unfastened the refuelling hose from the rock-hopper. With a silent thumb's-up and a quick gesture that meant *'get the hell back'*, she thumbed over the wheel for the attitude rockets.

In Phobos' gravity, it didn't need much. The rock-hopper drifted up and away as the pale flames bathed the concrete pad. Out of the corner of her eye, Mik saw Dani scrambling away, skimming from rock to rock until she got around the far end of the construction shack. Only then did Mik ignite the main rocket and apply some throttle.

With a muted roar, only detectable through the vibration in the vehicle's chassis, the rock-hopper vaulted upward at over two Martian gravities. It was a strain on Mik's body, but she figured the end result would be worth it. She saw the effect on the two ships immediately, as they both did their best to adjust their courses toward her. This was what she and Dani were counting on; the interloper ships didn't have a fraction of the manoeuvrability she could muster with the lightweight rock-hopper, and she could lead them on a merry chase through Mars' orbital space for as long as the fuel held out. Which, given the outsized tank Diamantina Connaught had installed, would take some time.

Unwilling to give them a chance of spotting the fact that her passenger seat contained nothing but an inflated suit, she tilted the rock-hopper and gave the main rocket another burst that sent her zipping away at right-angles to their path of travel. Slowly, almost painfully, both craft began swinging around in pursuit, attitude rockets flaring. She grinned tightly, letting the 'hopper coast while she kept an eye out for anything else that might be encroaching on her current course.

Whoever had ordered these craft up to secure her, she decided, had made a significant tactical error. Two spacecraft could herd a third one away from a sensitive location if the third craft wasn't truly invested in getting close. Three could herd said craft with some efficiency, while four or more could englobe (as opposed to 'encircle') and capture. All of which, however, required them to be facing craft that shared their basic performance capabilities. The rock-hopper … didn't. As it was, her biggest problem was going to be boredom.

She waited until the ships had corrected their course and were beginning once more to accelerate in her direction. Tweaking her own attitude rockets, she set up her manoeuvre by hand and eye, then punched it. The vibration travelled through the chassis to her seat, giving her comforting feedback as she sank into the seat cushioning.

Her initial burst curved her away from the ships, then she angled over and swung back toward them. Inside the air mask of the pony bottle, she grinned again. As the distance between her rock-hopper and the two orbital craft lessened dramatically, she imagined the startled reactions of those on board. Another couple of bursts from the attitude rockets, in between more acceleration from the main engine, sent her weaving between the two and cutting close to the exhaust plume of the second one.

Time to go invisible. Stroking the controls, she turned the rock-hopper so that the main rocket (with its tell-tale thermal signature) faced away from the two orbiters, then cut all thrust. She concentrated, looking down at the dusty-black skin of her arms, and turned them all the way to a light-swallowing vantablack.

Silently, as close to ambient temperature as she could manage under the circumstances, she coasted away from the two orbiters. Her eyes searched the starfield, looking for moving lights and shapes blocking out stars; any sign at all that they'd tracked her through the manoeuvre and were still on her trail. There was none. If she'd been in pressure, she might have taken a breath just to heave a sigh of relief.

Okay, that was easier than I expected.

The thought raised red flags in her mind, and she redoubled her examination of the moving shapes and lights before her. Neither one was turning in her direction, and she was getting farther away from them by the second. Craning her neck around and examining her vector path also revealed there was nothing coming up toward her from that angle.

Slowly, she let herself relax. A glance down at Mars far below gave her a good idea of how far off Phobos' orbital path she was; some distance, but nothing she couldn't remedy once the Cyberon thugs gave up and went away. In the meantime, she could easily augment her oxygen needs with the pseudo-photosynthesis built into her skin.

"Mik? Mik, are you there?"

The voice on the earpiece shocked her. Dani should've been maintaining radio silence. Her friend wasn't stupid—far from it—which meant something had gone wrong. Worse, Dani was panting, which meant she was using air faster than she should be.

"I'm here," she said as quietly as she could and still activate the mic. "What's up?"

That was when the other voice cut in on the same channel. *"What's up, you slippery little abomination, is that we've caught your friend. And if you don't come down to Phobos right now and give yourself up, she's never going to make it off this rock alive."*

At the first sound of the harsh male voice, Mik flicked the switch on the outside of her breathing mask, setting the digital recorder to pick up both sides of the conversation. "I'm sorry, who is this again?" she asked. She didn't bother querying as to what had happened. That bit was clear: there'd been a *third* ship among the Cyberon crew, one that had seen through the deception and landed people on Phobos just in case. Or maybe they'd just gone to shut off the emergency beacon, and spotted Dani while they were there.

"Never you goddamn mind, freak." The guy had a one-track mind, alright. *"You listen to your little gene-tainted friend here and do what she says, or it's lights out for her, forever."*

Mik had enough oxygen in her system to go for quite some time, but she cracked the pony bottle for a single breath, trying to force her brain to work faster. "Okay, I'm listening. Dani, go ahead."

"Mik, they're wearing Cyberon pressure suits," Dani said rapidly. *"Go to Earth. Get away from them. So long as they don't have you, they can't risk killing me. You're the last witness. Go!"*

There was a sound that Mik couldn't decipher, followed by whimpers and half-sobs. She figured that Dani's captor had maybe gut-punched her through the pressure suit.

"Dani?" she demanded. "Dani? What've you done to her?"

"She's alive … for now." The harsh voice was back. *"Forget what she said. You come back here right now, or she dies."*

"Like hell." Mik's options had crystallised until the best of a truly bad series of options was all that remained. "I go to you, we're *both* dead. Just so you know, I'm recording this. I just recorded the voice of my friend Dani Connaught telling me that she's being held captive by employees of the Cyberon Consortium. You want that going viral? Because I can make that happen. And if Cyberon is pressured to produce Dani, and can't? You *don't* want to be in the crosshairs when that happens."

She waited for his response, but all she got was Dani's wheezing. On one of the exhales, she thought she heard the word, *"Go."*

Dani, I wish I could swoop in and rescue you. Once again, she wanted to cry and couldn't.

A movement in the starfield got her attention. While she'd been talking, the pursuing craft had not been idle; they'd clearly triangulated her radio signal, and they were closing fast.

She couldn't wait any longer. Rotating the rock-hopper until Mars lay behind her, she searched until she spotted the pale blue dot she'd peered at more than once through a telescope. While she wasn't the astrogator Dani was, she knew more or less what Earth was doing in relation to Mars. Specifically, it had just completed a transit of the sun.

Dani had shown her how the calculations went. If she aimed just right with the correct amount of offset, she could maybe intercept the Earth-Moon system without whipping past and impacting the giant solar orb beyond.

Well, this is gonna be interesting.

One of the Cyberon ships loomed in close. Too close.

"What do you think you're—"

Settling herself more firmly into the seat, she performed one last tiny correction, then pushed the throttle all the way to the stop. The rocket under her lit off with a concussion that shook her to her bones, then the rock-hopper began to accelerate. Diamantina Connaught had installed a reclining mechanism in the seats to better handle high G's; it activated now, leaning her backward.

The last coherent thought that passed through Mik's mind was how she and Dani had discussed the maximum acceleration of the upgraded rock-hopper on their trip to Phobos. According to Dani, it topped out at five gravities; that is, five *Earth* gravities, which came out to twelve and a half Martian gees.

Mik had never in her life gone past two and a half Martian gees.

At two Earth gees, her vision was a long narrow tunnel.

At three, as she was trying to throttle back, the strap around her neck slipped a little. The weight of the pony bottle on her left shoulder snapped the collarbone with a dry crack.

At four, she passed out.

Cyberon Consortium Headquarters, Burroughs City
Hellas Basin, Mars
Jarn Kolban, CEO of Cyberon

An encrypted radio com link buzzed. Kolban tapped the icon on his desk display. "Speak."

"Sir, there's been a slight … hitch."

"I don't employ you to report hitches. I employ you to solve them. What is this hitch, and how are you solving it?"

"The genetic freak got away, but we captured the Connaught kid. There … might be a recording, implicating Cyberon in all this, and that we've got the kid."

"Where is the recording?"

"With the freak."

"Where is the freak? How did it get away?"

"Uh … we think it's heading to Earth. It's riding some kind of stripped-down rocket that's faster than anything we've got."

"How in the hell … no, never mind. Get back here."

"And the kid?"

"Bring her. We'll keep her alive … for now. She may provide leverage in the future."

Kolban shut down the radio link and glared at the far wall, already calculating contingencies. Their flagship cybernetics program had run into repeated problems, mainly involving that damnable dust, and Tharsis had been on the verge of unveiling their genetic creation, so he'd taken matters into his own hands. But now he was thinking that having a monster like that under his control might be a good idea.

So, it's fled to Earth, has it?

He had assets on Earth. This might just merit activating them.

The tiny rock-hopper was far distant from the Mars-Phobos-Deimos system when the oversized fuel tank finally ran dry. Hanging limp in the straps was Mik Wallace, genetic refugee. Now it was coasting 'downhill' into the solar gravity well at a dramatically unsafe velocity, blitzing in toward Earth and possible salvation.

All it had to do at the other end … was stop safely.

Chapter 8: Orbital Rescue

Pete Janssen smiled as he pulled himself from the shuttle into the airlock of Oscar Romeo Five. It had been a fun week of furlough; getting back down into proper gravity was always exhilarating. Skiing down Mt. Kilimanjaro, exploring the flooded ruins of Los Angeles, and a helicopter tour past the perimeter of the Idaho Quarantine Zone had made up the touristy aspects of his downtime. The other four days he'd spent catching up with family and enjoying just one sunrise and sunset per day, with all the special effects a hundred-kilometre-thick blanket of air gave it.

But now he was back on duty; or would be, in another hour. He exited the airlock into Station Mainway as he heard the shuttle clamps disengaging from the exterior of the station. They had other personnel to drop off, so they'd be another day or more in orbit before they finally headed back into atmosphere. By that time, he'd be back into the routine like he'd never left it.

Slinging his duffel across his back, he kicked off from the bulkhead and sent himself gliding down Mainway, angled slightly to port so anyone coming the other direction wouldn't be on a collision course. From the hatchway leading into Engineering, he heard metallic clanging and a running commentary consisting mainly of swearwords, which made him grin. McPherson was on deck, it sounded like. The brawny engineer hailed from a city called Bendigo in Australia, but he'd bought into the 'Scottish engineer' trope so hard that by the time he'd been on OR-5 a week, his Australian accent had given way to his idea of a broad Scottish brogue.

The Commons were just up ahead, so Pete reached out and grabbed a longitudinal bar, squeezing it just hard enough to let the friction slow him almost to a stop. As he swung his legs in through the open hatchway, he reached out and let his fingers run over the metal plaque affixed next to it. The densest thing on the station, the plaque had been tooled from pure tungsten carbide to withstand wear and tear after the previous one had worn away altogether.

ORBITAL RESCUE, the plaque read, the words stamped across the equator of a globe with the continents shown in relief. Around the upper perimeter of the circle were the words, **YOU HAVE TO GO OUT.** Around the bottom was the rest of the quote: **YOU DON'T HAVE TO COME BACK.**

The words were not original; they had been the unofficial motto of the United States Coast Guard for many years. Every time a crew strapped in and launched, they knew there was a chance their names would end up being permanently marked in the rolls as being '*out on rescue*', but they did it anyway. Remarkably few Orbital Rescue officers treated it as just a job. Like Pete, they saw it as a calling.

Orbital Rescue featured two different types of craft. The first were the lightweight rescue single-ships designed to pull the crew out of a stricken ship that was too far gone to salvage; the second were the beefy heavyweights, designed to latch on and *lift* a ship back into orbit by sheer grunt power, or save the entire passenger complement of a larger vessel.

Predictably, these were called Lights and Heavies, and each had their proponents. Pete was a Light guy, himself; he enjoyed the delta-vee and manoeuvrability they could muster, especially when chasing some idiot pleasure-yachtsman who'd fouled up his re-entry vector.

"Hey, guys," he called out as he drifted into the Commons. "What's new?"

"Civil war on Mars, for one thing," Marj Weatherby replied, glancing over his way for politeness' sake before returning her gaze to the tablet floating in front of her. She was strapped into an exercise module, heavy springs forcing her to exert herself when she straightened her legs, one side then the other. "Started a couple days ago. Rival corporations going at each other. There's been casualties on both sides."

"What about their government?" he asked, hooking his leg through a convenient frame and opening his locker. "Shouldn't they step in?"

Boris Rankine, one-seventy centimetres and ninety kilos of brilliant Heavy pilot, shook his head and snorted. "Half the Mars government answers directly to Tharsis and the other half directly to Cyberon. They don't even pretend that it doesn't. One side enacts a law, the other side flat-out ignores them."

"So, what started it?" Pete unloaded his duffel into the locker, then started pulling out a fresh suit underlayer. It was identical to the one he was already wearing, but he hated having one on for more than six hours at a time. Sweat gathered in unpleasant places.

Marj rolled her eyes. "Tharsis claims Cyberon destroyed a research station, murdered all the researchers, and stole a high-value experiment. Cyberon says they went to investigate a distress call where one of Tharsis' researchers had gone nuts. When they got there, their ship was sabotaged and their men were left to run out of air. The UN is trying to get a clear picture of who's done what before they send in peacekeepers."

"... right. So, he-said-she-said." Pete knew the United Nations couldn't just unilaterally walk in and tell them both to settle down; that had been a major aspect of the Martian Settlement Agreement. All parties involved had to agree to outside mediation before it would happen. And if either side had anything to hide, all they had to do was say no. "Joy."

"Think it's bad now?" Boris raised a shaggy eyebrow. "Wait a week or so until the first refugee ships from Mars hit Earth system. They'll be lined up in the orbital lanes for re-entry all the way out to geosync and beyond. We're gonna be scrambling, every hour of the day."

"Great." Pete huffed in exasperation. "Welp, that's me for a shower. Which one's got the least green mould right now?" The green mould was harmless, but it thrived in the humid environment of a shower bag. No matter how hard the bags were scrubbed, or how long they were exposed to vacuum, missing just a single spore would allow it to grow back again.

"Four," Marj replied, continuing to work her leg muscles. Left, right, left, right.

Just about then, the all-hands alarm went off. Pete slammed his locker shut and abandoned the fresh underlayer to float there beside him while he grabbed the pressure suit on the rack next to the locker. It was SOP: when the all-hands went off, suit up *first* then ask questions.

Other people began to boil into the Commons about then, but Pete was concentrating on getting his own suit on. Each movement was quick and precise, practised over and over until it was second nature. He could do it—*had* done it—half asleep, dragged from his rack for a midnight drill. And then allowed to go back for half an hour of blessed sleep until the alarm had gone off again. And again.

By the time he'd completed the gruelling course, more than three-quarters of the aspiring recruits had washed out, or just plain quit. Pete had come close to doing just that more than once, but he'd hung on by the skin of his teeth. And at the end of it, when he got to pin on the coveted globe-and-spaceship badge, he'd decided it was all worth it, though it was possible they'd maybe gone a *little* over the top with the various emergencies.

A year later, he'd changed his opinion about that, too. There was no such thing as '*over the top*' when it came to emergencies in orbit. Murphy lived up there, and he wasn't shy about introducing himself at the worst possible moment.

Neither was the training a perfect shield against mishaps. There were two people Pete had known; one his training officer, the other a woman who'd graduated alongside him. Hollister and Abrams. Both had been as buttoned-down as they came. They'd gone out in two separate incidents, and they hadn't come back. Pure, unadulterated bad luck. Sometimes, you could do *everything exactly right,* and shit still happened.

But still they went out. They were Orbital Rescue; it was what they did.

He pulled his helmet down against the locking ring and twisted sharply left then right, both feeling and hearing the *click-click* as the lugs engaged. Air hissed and his ears twinged as the suit computer bumped up the pressure to check for leaks, then it reversed the cycle and brought the pressure down to standard operational; pure oh-two at three hundred millibars. All his HUD readouts were in the green.

He chinned the radio mic. "Janssen, suited." Already, other acknowledgements were coming in, voices tumbling over each other. Fortunately, they didn't have to keep a voice count; each radio had a distinct carrier band that registered on the central station computer. As he let up on the mic, he saw the red circle of 'transmitting' replaced by the blue circle of 'acknowledged', sent by the computer.

When the last of the stragglers had reported in, the radio channel opened. Commander Kenworth spoke, his voice dry and measured. *"All hands, all hands. We have a grazer coming in hot, sixteen hours out. Object is estimated to be one tonne in mass and has a metallic return. It lacks any kind of radar transponder, though we've been picking up a weak radio signal from it that we're still trying to decode. Vector is from the Mars subsystem, and incoming velocity is three five nine point four kilometres per second. I say again, incoming velocity is three hundred fifty-nine KPS. For those who haven't already done the math, this is just a hair under one point three million kilometres per hour. And yes, I know that's a magnitude higher than anything we've ever had to deal with before."*

In the pause that followed, Pete's mind exploded into speculation. A one-tonne grazer—shorthand for *'object aiming to graze Earth's orbit'*— hitting at three hundred and sixty kilometres per *second* … the damage would be comparable to a one-megatonne nuke. Nothing short of the Earth itself or the Moon would survive such an impact; no matter where it hit, it would absolutely leave a mark. If it struck in a populated area, the devastation would be catastrophic.

"Fortunately, we're projecting that it's going to go high; it's going to miss the Earth-Moon ecliptic by about ten thousand kilometres. We've already sent out word to clear a lane, so it can pass on by without hitting anything important. However, there's a distinct chance some poor soul has ridden this thing from Mars, given the recent unrest. If they expended all their fuel to get here and don't have any left over for braking purposes, then it's up to us to snag the fly ball before it hits the backstop."

Whoever was flying that thing, Pete decided, needed to have their pilot certification taken away and shredded before their eyes. It was the first rule of spaceflight: *'make sure you have enough fuel to slow down again'*.

Right alongside *'make sure you have enough air to get there and back'*. Food and water were lower priority; a person could survive far longer without those than they could with no breathable air.

On the other hand, he decided, maybe there was a good reason. A civil war could easily mean people were being killed for reasons he would personally see as unnecessary. With an unconscious pilot at the controls, a passenger may have panicked and jammed the throttle wide open without understanding what it really meant. In which case, they should count themselves lucky they hadn't been headed out-system at the time; there was remarkably little out there to help them come to a survivable halt.

As it was, all that was standing between the 'fly ball' and the aforementioned backstop—i.e., the sun—was Orbital Rescue. And even this wasn't a given.

"Wait a minute," someone asked. *"One tonne? How'd they get up to speed with something that size, and where would you put the life support?"*

Which was actually something Pete had been thinking about. One metric ton was a *ridiculously* tiny mass for something designed to actually carry passengers. But there were ways around it. "It could be a lifepod someone attached auxiliary engines and fuel tanks to, then jettisoned them once the fuel ran out."

"That's as good a theory as any. Now, how do we stop it?" Commander Kenworth cut right to the chase. *"Once it gets past us and into the solar clutter, we're going to lose it sooner rather than later."*

"I've got an idea," offered Pete. "Gonna need a Light with as many extra fuel tanks as we can attach to it. A couple of Heavies tow the Light *toward* where the grazer's coming from, then I boost back this way until I match velocities. That'll give me all the way to Venus orbit to find out what's going on with it, and the extra fuel will get us home again."

"Well, it can be done, laddie," McPherson adjudged. *"But ye won't be able to raise more'n two gees once I add all that extra mass. Won't be a Light anymore, that's for sure. Maybe a Mid."*

"Call it a cement truck, for all I care." Pete shook his head. "Can it be done before the grazer gets too close?"

"Aye, barely. I'll get to work the noo. By your leave, Commander?"

"Stand down all-hands," Commander Kenworth acknowledged. *"Janssen, your mission is approved. Get some rack time, you're going to need to be as sharp as possible. I'll need two volunteers for the Heavies to tow Janssen out to the launch zone once the Light is prepped. Everyone else, I'm going to need rotating shifts keeping the lane clear for the grazer to come on through. The last thing we want is some idiot blundering into its path and getting turned into confetti because they can't comprehend an emergency directive. Get to it."*

Pete sighed and started removing the pressure suit again. At least his first day back wasn't going to be *boring*.

Four Days Earlier

Mik awoke.

Every part of her hurt, but most of all her left shoulder sent stabbing pains into the rest of her body whenever she tried to move it. "Oww ..." she mumbled into the pony bottle mask. Slowly, she raised her head—her neck felt cramped and twisted, sending jabs of discomfort into her skull as she moved it—and looked around.

Starfield, everywhere except straight up. In that direction was the sun, bigger than she'd ever seen it. Tucked in alongside it was the tiny blue dot she figured to be Earth. Twisting in the straps to look down through the open frame made her fully aware that every internal organ she possessed felt *bruised*, and gave her a sharp reminder about her left shoulder. But Mars was no longer a huge looming presence; now, it was a tiny dot, barely larger than the one marking Earth's location.

She surveyed her surroundings again, seeking some indicator of the speed she had to be travelling at that moment. But there was none. The rock-hopper hung in space, apparently motionless. No science-fiction stars streaking by, no useful readout as seen in the best dramas. If she had woken up amnesiac (also seen in the best dramas), she could've been forgiven for believing she'd been dumped mid-system, stranded to drift forever between the planets.

Fortunately for her state of mind, she knew better. The fuel counter on the rock-hopper read a flat zero, which didn't surprise her; the last thing she recalled was feeling *far* too heavy, even as she strained to get her one good hand back to the controls. The rocket engine had run through the entire oversized fuel tank in one long burst, which meant she was headed for the general vicinity of Earth at a fair clip. Lacking the slightest idea of how long she'd spent at max acceleration (five Earth gees was a *lot*), she could only guess at just how fast that was.

Running it up to full power was perhaps a mistake, she reflected ruefully.

But if I hadn't, I might've been captured. And then Dani and I would've been dead.

The next thought hit home hard. *Dani still might be. I can threaten to expose them all I like, but the farther I get away from Mars, the less useful she is to them.*

Okay. One crisis at a time. It was an adage Professor Ibrahim had once taught her. The reminder of the kindly scientist made her bite her lip and wish for the umpteenth time that she could actually shed tears.

Mourn the dead later, she told herself sternly. *Get myself out of this now. Once I'm safe and I've told the authorities on Earth what Cyberon's done, I can try to get back there and arrange a rescue.*

Because she *would* be going back. She owed that much to Dani, and to the Professor, and the rest of her friends at the Valles Marineris Research Complex.

The first order of business was to improve her odds of survival. Her arms and face were currently absorbing sunlight, but she'd half-emptied the pony bottle while she was unconscious. If she was to recycle oxygen more efficiently, she needed more pseudo-photosynthesis. *More skin it is, then.*

Moving carefully, hissing between her teeth each time she jolted her left shoulder, she unstrapped herself from the rock-hopper and began to remove her shirt and jeans. Underneath, she wore a tank top and what Dani called 'bike shorts', though Mik had never seen a real bicycle in her life. As fresh sunlight hit her skin, she felt life flooding into her body and clearing her mind. The clothing, including the boots, she stowed in a cage under the seat. Then she strapped herself back in.

Activating the radio in the pony bottle mouthpiece, she took a breath of air from the bottle more to boost her morale than out of need. "Hello? Is anyone out there? This is Mik Wallace, calling for assistance. Hello?"

As her voice echoed outward into the uncaring cosmos and the rock-hopper hurtled through the void, she resigned herself to a long, lonely vigil.

Dani, I hope you're okay.

Hours passed. She called out again and again. Despite her best efforts, fatigue overcame her, and she slept.

Cyberon Consortium, Mars

"You can't keep me locked up here forever!" Dani glared at the smoothly dressed executive on the other side of the Perspex barrier. "Once the authorities find out you kidnapped me, you'll be in *so* much trouble!"

"The only authorities in a position to do anything about it are here on Mars, and they don't *care*," he corrected her with a supercilious smile. "The only ones who will care are on Earth, and they don't have the jurisdiction to do a single thing about it." He leaned closer. "But your freaky little friend ... *it* cares. However much it's capable of feeling human emotion."

"She's ten times as human as you'll ever be!" blazed Dani. "She'll come back, and she'll save me!"

"Oh, I'm counting on it to *try*." He chuckled darkly. "And then I'll have the Martian Walker genome. Tharsis can whine all they like, but possession is nine-tenths and all that."

Dani shook her head. "But … why? You hate her! Why do *you* want the genome?"

His lip curled. "I cannot abide freaks like that being allowed to pretend to be human, to be afforded rights *just like me* when they are nothing more than science experiments. But as weapons? *That* I can use them for. I'll show Tharsis the *true* capability of that genome, and every single one of *my* Martian Walkers will know its damn place."

Turning on his heel, he walked away. Dani curled up in the corner of her cell, trying not to cry. *Mik's smarter than him,* she told herself. *She'll come and get me, and he'll never see her coming.*

If she told herself this enough times, she figured she would begin to believe her own words. They would be hollow comfort, but it was better than no comfort at all.

Chapter 9: Preparations

"T*ugboat One calling Outfield One, come in. Wake up, Janssen, got a call coming in from the brass."*

Pete Janssen grunted with irritation. It was part of the job to regularly spend time enduring two-gee loads or more, but only a confirmed masochist would actually confess to *liking* it. He lifted his hand to toggle the radio switch on his (currently not in use) control column. "Outfield One here. Patch me through, Boris."

This was the part of the mission he'd been looking forward to the least. The Light he'd be flying had been stripped of every nonessential system, including the deep-space antenna that would've allowed Orbital Rescue to talk to him directly. Currently, two Heavies were towing it—and him—out to the turnover point like a piece of space debris. *I'm a pilot, dammit, not cargo.*

A Heavy could pull two and a half gees unencumbered, so it only took two of them to get all the way to two gees while towing the single modified Light. They were going to be burning at two gees on the slowdown, too. A lot of number-crunching had gone into calculating the ideal point they could bring the Light to a dead halt, cast off the tow, and still have enough delta-vee to make it home on the slow and steady route.

"Lieutenant, this is Commander Kenworth. We've managed to clean up the signal and get a usable image of the grazer with orbital telescopes. Sending both through to you now, over."

A moment later, two files dropped into the computer's inbox. "Copy that, sir. Both files received, over."

Several seconds passed before Kenworth responded. Lightspeed lag was definitely a thing out here. *"I copy files received. Godspeed, Lieutenant. Kenworth, out."*

The comms dropped a second later, and Janssen frowned as he accessed the first file, which was the recording of the radio signal. It started playing and he listened intently.

"This is Mik Wallace. I am in distress. Please help. Mik Wallace calling Earth. Please help me. I need assistance. Is anyone out there? Please help."

"Jesus," he muttered. "It sounds like a kid." The extreme speed of the oncoming craft had the potential to cause a Doppler effect and raise the pitch of a person's voice, but not *that* much. If he had to guess, he'd put her at somewhere between fourteen and seventeen.

After listening to it again and trying to tune out the desperate pleading note—he had to stay focused and professional—he called up the other file. It looked like an amalgam of several images, which was precisely what it was. The craft ...! He spent the next few seconds swearing at it. A circular framework with two seats bolted onto the top, side by side. Not an escape capsule as he'd suggested, not even a pressurised cabin. Just a frame with seats. Underneath, he guessed, were the rocket engine and tanks.

And strapped into the seats were two people. Someone in a suit, and a dead girl.

Whoa, hold back there.

Why had he immediately assumed she was dead? It was a fundamental aspect of any rescue organisation anywhere to assume rescuees were alive until proven otherwise.

He examined the image again. It had been taken at the extreme edge of the capability of the various orbital telescopes and amalgamated into one view, which meant a lot of the details were down to computerised guesswork. Extremely *educated* guesswork, but guesswork all the same.

The suit was a smaller model. Despite the blurred sections here and there, he recognised it as a non-vacuum-rated EVA type widely used on the Martian surface. The faceplate was too dark to see inside. Still, it would be about the right size to hold a kid. This was almost certainly where the radio messages were coming from.

Unless they set it up to repeat a recording over and over, before they ran out of air. If that's the case, this is gonna suck.

On the other hand, the people back at Orbital Rescue would've let him know if the message was a looped recording. Which meant he was going to go with the assumption that there was someone to save, until proven otherwise.

So, about the other one.

He was pretty sure she was a girl, from the general shape and the clothing. Tank top and bike shorts were not exactly OSHA-approved vacuum protective wear. The mohawk was a little odd, but he knew nothing about Martian fads, so that was a null data point.

She had a breathing mask on, but the best guess of the computers had outlined a pony bottle attached to it. Good for five minutes of air, or ten if the person was an expert at conserving their energy. Not an hour, not twelve hours, and definitely not the five or six days they'd guesstimated it had taken this thing to cross the distance from Mars. Even the air tank he could see fastened between the seats—also an older model— wouldn't have lasted a person that distance.

That wouldn't work for the kid in the suit either ... unless they had more, and they tossed them overboard when the tanks ran empty.

The seat cover was a light-coloured material, and her skin ... wasn't.

Vacuum exposure did weird things to human flesh, as did constant sunlight *in* vacuum. People didn't just pop like balloons when they hit zero pressure; that wasn't something they showed even in the stupidest space dramas these days. Most casualties of vacuum just swelled up a little, which she hadn't, but it didn't look as though she'd been heavily built to begin with. Or maybe she'd been exposed so long her body had outgassed everything volatile, her clothing had pulled the skin back into shape, and then the resultant vacuum mummy had burned black with exposure?

It was a theory, anyway. One he was going to be finding out the truth of, once he got next to the ridiculously inadequate craft and had a chat with its live passenger. Including *why* the girl had thought it was remotely survivable to travel that way.

The creepy thing was that the girl looked almost alive, limbs not set in odd or uncomfortable positions as dead people tended to do. The suit was the one with arms akimbo, but that probably meant the kid inside wasn't used to moving in zero gee. Or they were injured; that was always a grim possibility.

But no suit and no air meant no chance. If there was a survivor on that flimsy makeshift life-raft, it had to be the kid in the EVA suit, however they were maintaining pressure inside it. And while there was a chance of survival, Orbital Rescue was there to make a difference.

Hang tight. We're on the way.

He was going through the voice recording one more time when Boris got on the ship-to-ship comms again. *"Tugboat One to Outfield One. Beginning turnover. Hold onto your panties, Janssen."*

"Outfield One to Tugboat One, I copy turnover," he replied. "Don't screw this up, Boris."

"Tugboat One to Outfield One. I should be saying that to you. Out."

They'd given him four hours of rack time, of which he'd slept approximately two. That didn't matter; the closer it came to crunch time, the more alert and alive he felt. Three hours fifteen minutes of burning hard in the direction of the incoming grazer, followed by a turnover and three and a quarter more hours of deceleration. That would put him a little over two and a half million klicks away from Earth. Right where he wanted to be.

Once he cast off from Tugboat One and Tugboat Two, he'd light off his engines and start boosting hard back toward home, leaving his comrades far behind. Holding steady at two gees, or perhaps a little over, he'd have a four-and-a-half-hour run back to the Earth-Moon system while he pushed the tiny rescue ship to the highest velocity any of them had ever achieved.

If all went well, he'd pass back through about twenty minutes behind Mik Wallace. At that point, he'd have nearly ninety percent of her speed already under his belt. It would take him another forty minutes just to match her speed, and a tad bit more than that to overhaul her and get alongside. His vacuum suit was stocked up with caff tabs, and by the end of this he suspected he was going to need them.

The next three-and-a-quarter hours were just as painfully boring as the first three. The turnover had been achieved with minimal fuss—Kenworth had picked the best Heavy pilots for this mission—and Marj was running Sunward in her own Heavy in case he needed assistance after he slowed down. But all he could do was sit there and endure, with nothing to *do*.

When six and a half hours finally ticked over, he could've cheered, but he didn't. Celebration came at the end of a mission, not at any point during it. Tugboats One and Two ceased thrust, and all three ships hung motionless in the void. The cables connecting them curved slightly as they drifted a little closer to each other.

"Tugboat One to Outfield One, casting off now." There was a series of *clack-clack* noises from the outer hull as the tow-cables released from their attachment points. The cables writhed oddly as they were reeled in toward their respective ships. *"Good luck. Kick ass. Bring that kid home safe, over."*

There was a time for banter and smartass comments, but this wasn't it. Boris' voice was sincere, and Pete heard what wasn't said—*and come home safe yourself*—as easily as the rest of it.

He keyed his mic. "You know it. Outfield One, out."

There was nothing more to be said. Tugboats One and Two—their current designations would last until they got back to Oscar Romeo Five, but their part in this was done—turned and moved away on a course that would take them far away from the projected trajectory of Mik Wallace's craft. This had been calculated to a fare-thee-well, using up-to-date information about every possible gravitational influence within the Earth-Moon system. In the end, this came down to two objects: the Earth and the Moon.

The sheer speed of the oncoming craft would be helpful in this regard. At that velocity, the combined gravity of both celestial bodies wouldn't register so much as a speed-bump as it passed them by. Even though it was going to technically pass within Earth's Hill Sphere—the zone within which objects would normally enter orbit—it would exit again within seconds.

But the fact that it *was* going to enter Earth's orbital space, however briefly, made this a job for Orbital Rescue.

He checked over his instruments one last time, making sure everything was in the green and that he had a straight board. McPherson had outdone himself this time, and Pete made a mental note to have a bottle of genuine Scottish whiskey shipped up. The crusty engineer may never have set foot in his ancestral lands, but he did like his booze.

The timer ticked over to zero, and he hit the switch to ignite the rockets. One after another they kicked in, smoothly accelerating the rescue craft forward and shoving him back into the gee-couch as the familiar weight settled over him again. He'd already endured six and a half hours of this, and another eight or so awaited him, but that was fine. Now *he* was in charge of his own destiny. That made all the difference.

Checking to make sure his small antenna was angled rearward, he keyed his mic. "Orbital Rescue calling Mik Wallace. Orbital Rescue calling Mik Wallace. Come in, Mik Wallace …"

Mik came out of a fitful doze with a tinny voice in her ear, but when she tried to concentrate on it, it was gone. *Did I imagine it?* She thought the sun looked bigger, but that was what she thought each time she saw it. *How long have I been out here?* There was no way of telling for sure, without a clock readout. Seven days, maybe eight?

She'd never gone so long without actual food before. The pseudo-photosynthesis afforded by her unique dermis was designed to allow her to go without food for quite some time, and her body systems recycled water with a very low percentage of loss. But 'quite some time' was not 'forever', and no system was totally self-contained. She suspected she was drifting in and out of consciousness, even though the extra sunlight was ensuring she didn't have to breathe. That part, at least, was working as planned.

"… *calling Mik Wallace. Come in, Mik Wallace. This is Orbital Rescue. Can you hear me?"*

The voice in her ear, emerging from a cloud of static, startled her. It was scratchy and faint, but definitely understandable. She sat upright in the seat, ignoring the stab of pain from her injured shoulder.

"This is Mik Wallace," she replied, then took a breath from the pony bottle to give her more air to speak. "Come in, Orbital Rescue, I read you one by three. Mik Wallace calling Orbital Rescue, how copy?"

Rescue protocols had been drilled into Mik from the very beginning. Radio signals were rated on volume and clarity; 'loud and clear'. The clarity was better than the volume, but at least she could hear him.

"This is Orbital Rescue. I copy you one by two, Mik Wallace." She fancied the voice was a shade stronger this time. *"State current situation. How many souls on board, and do you have any braking capability, over?"*

"Mik Wallace to Orbital Rescue. Current situation is zero fuel, repeat zero fuel. No manoeuvring capability at all. One soul on board. I say again, one soul. Do you copy?"

Something that may have been a sigh travelled down the line. *"I copy, one soul and zero fuel. What was your plan for stopping, over?"*

She took another breath from the pony bottle, more for morale than anything else. "I'd planned on keeping some fuel in reserve, but I passed out due to acceleration. How fast am I going, over?"

The answer froze her blood. *"In the region of three hundred sixty klicks per second. That's three six zero Kilo Papa Sierra. I may have to ticket you for speeding in a built-up area, over."*

Involuntarily, she let out something between a sob and a chuckle. "I think you'd have to catch me first to do that, over."

"That's the plan. So, talk to me, kiddo. How old are you, anyway? Over."

"Sixteen," she said automatically, as hope surged within her.

Communication had been established. *Someone knows I'm here. They're going to help me.*

The next stage, of course, would be to save Dani from Cyberon. It wasn't going to be easy or quick, but she had faith in herself.

They think they're something?

I am Mik Wallace, Martian Walker.

*They ain't seen **nothing** yet.*

Chapter 10: Unexpected Complications

Pete was nearly an hour into the burn, pulling seventy klicks per second, when he caught the edges of radio chatter from far ahead. He had to sift through the static put out by the sun, but what he could hear was disturbing.

"… escue *Golf Niner Niner Whiskey* to unidentified ship, this is a restricted through-passage area. Vacate the area immediately, over."

"… I say again, vacate the area immediately, over."

"… er Whiskey to Oscar Romeo Five, we have an unidentified vessel encroaching on the grazer's through-passage line. Failing to respond to hails, no transponder return, over."

"… meo Five to Golf Niner Niner Whiskey, you are authorised to close with that ship **immediately** and remove it from the area of operations, do you copy? Over."

"… er Whiskey copies authorisation to remove unknown ship by force. Moving to comply. Golf Niner Niner Whiskey, out."

The radio was scratchy at best, but he could still hear the outrage in the pilot's voice. Orbital Rescue was in the job of keeping people alive, and the last thing they needed was some idiot blundering into the middle of a delicate operation like this one. One rogue ship ignoring priority routing could easily kill civilians and OR pilots alike.

In this particular case, the interlopers either didn't have a working radio, weren't on the correct frequencies, or were choosing not to answer the calls. Though keeping their transponder off wouldn't help them much if G-99-W got close enough to put a searchlight on the hull and read off their registration details that way. And once the Heavy got its clamps onto their hull and dragged them the hell out of the way, they wouldn't be going *anywhere* except where Orbital Rescue said they were going.

He hadn't spoken much with Mik after that first conversation, wanting to conserve her radio battery (and tanked air) as much as possible. Now, he wasn't sure if she'd heard that exchange. If she asked, he decided, he'd tell her what was going on, but otherwise he wouldn't worry her.

The minutes crawled by, his engines thundered, and his velocity steadily increased. A pair of the aux tanks went empty at the same time—this was deliberate—and used the last gasp of their fuel vapours to kick themselves away from the rescue ship in diametrically opposing directions. Each bore a radio transponder, so they'd be trackable if anyone wanted to retrieve them.

"Golf Niner Niner Whiskey to Oscar Romeo Five. We have a situation. I say again, we have a situation …"

Pete sat up in his seat, adrenaline pushing away the fatigue. A 'situation' was what Orbital Rescue called something that had gone seriously wrong. He fiddled with the radio, trying to narrow down the signal. Golf 9-9 Whiskey was still talking.

"… as I got close, the unidentified ship bolted. I still have them on radar, but they've dumped a load of gravel into the through-passage region. They did something to make it spread in all directions. There's minimal chance the region will be clear by the time the grazer comes through, over."

"Golf Niner Niner Whiskey, I copy the presence of gravel in the grazer's through-passage region. Is there any way you can speed the dispersal of the gravel, over?"

Chills ran up and down Pete's spine as he visualised the situation. For whatever reason, *someone* didn't want Mik telling her story. Passing through the Earth-Moon system at over three hundred kilometres per second, hitting even one tiny fragment of rock would be like an impact with an ordinary meteorite bigger than his fist. A whole cloud of them … she and her crazy craft would both be chopped into fragments in an instant, EVA suit or no. And dead girls told no tales.

"Oscar Romeo Five, I can try to push through the cloud and make a hole, but I can't guarantee to get everything, over."

"Golf Niner Niner Whiskey, I copy that. You are authorised to clear a path, over. Break, break. Oscar Romeo Five to Outfield One, how copy, over?"

Pete toggled the radio switch. "Outfield One copies four by four. Am aware of situation, over."

There was a long pause, one that he knew he couldn't simply attribute to lightspeed lag. *"Outfield One, have you been in communication with the grazer? Specifically, what is their manoeuvring capability, over?"* There was a world of subtext in that question.

"Oscar Romeo Five, that is affirmative. I have spoken with the grazer. One soul on board, zero manoeuvre capability. I say again, Zulu Echo Romeo Oscar, over."

Again the pause. *"Outfield One, I copy zero manoeuvrability. What is your fuel situation, over?"*

His mind racing in four different directions at once, Pete scanned his readouts. He was reasonably certain he knew what was behind the question, but it wasn't something he could be ordered to do. "Oscar Romeo Five, I'm ahead of the curve for fuel, and I'm down on mass since I dumped my first two tanks. If I redline it, I can get up to three gees. There's a good chance I can match velocities before we hit the gravel cloud, over."

There would be no chance of avoiding the hazard once he did get close, of course. And while the modified Light was far more robust than the ridiculous framework Mik Wallace had ridden in from Mars, hitting any gravel at all would be like subjecting a ground-effect car to a sustained burst of machine-gun fire. They'd both die, unless he dumped his fuel and rode it in tail-first. Even then, the odds were poor.

When Commander Kenworth came on the line, he knew he'd been correct. *"Outfield One, you've been at two gees for over seven hours now. Can you handle three, over?"*

This was the make-or-break question. His was the judgement call, to go ahead or abort the mission. Whatever he chose, they would support his decision one hundred percent.

But of course, there was only one choice he could make, and still live with himself. He took a deep breath, his muscles already aching. "I can handle it as long as it takes. Outfield One, out." Next, he switched to the rear-aimed dish. "Orbital Rescue calling Mik Wallace. Come in, Mik."

It only took a couple of seconds for her to reply; her voice was a lot clearer now. *"Mik Wallace responding. What's up, over?"*

"I'm going to need to match with you *before* we pass Earth, not after. Here's the situation …"

"I copy all that. Do you think it'll work, over?"

The Orbital Rescue pilot—she didn't even know his name yet—sounded calm and unflappable in her earpiece. *"We're going to have to make it work. Orbital Rescue, out."*

The radio went silent, and Mik settled back to wait. It was a sobering revelation that Cyberon could reach out this far and try to murder her before she could inform the authorities about what they had done, what they were doing right now. If she hit the gravel cloud and died, they'd only need a tiny sample of her DNA to grow more clones of her, to be raised the way *they* saw fit. At the same time, they'd have no more reason to keep Dani alive, so she would die too.

Not gonna happen.

Her stomach rumbled, but gently. The lack of food was becoming more of a thing, though with the way the ever-strengthening sunlight was providing her with both energy and oh-two recycling, it would take her a very long time to die of starvation or thirst. She just hoped the matter would be resolved before she got to that point.

Peering ahead, she tried to pick out the thruster-flare of the rescue ship ahead of her, but he had to be tens of thousands of kilometres away, if not more. She could only guess at which of the points of light ahead was her salvation, or if she could even see it against the glare of the sun.

Moving carefully in her seat, she took an eyeball inventory of what she had on hand. *Spare refuelling hose, check. The oxy-tank I threw on board at the Stickney depot, check. One empty EVA suit, size small, partially inflated, check. Toolkit, check. Outer clothing and boots, check. Breathing mask and pony bottle, check.*

There wasn't much else she could do. It chafed at her that she had to wait for someone *else* to come save *her*, but right now she was riding a roller-coaster without brakes (she'd seen one in a movie once) and there was no safe way off the ride. And even if they braved the obstacle and survived, there would still be the problem of stopping afterward.

Frowning, she considered the situation from all angles. An idea occurred to her, and she spoke into her radio. "Mik Wallace to Orbital Rescue. I have a question, over."

His reply, when it came, was severely strained, and she belatedly realised he'd gone to the full three gees. Internally, she shuddered; going to five gees by accident had nearly killed her. He was doing this *deliberately.* Also, he was still able to function under that load, whereas she would've been crushed into the acceleration couch, incapable of everything including speech. *"Orb-ital Res-cue rec-eiving. Shoot. Over."*

She took a breath from the pony bottle to give herself the air to speak. "What kind of fuel does your ship use, over?"

If Pete had thought two G's was bad, three was horrific. Moving *anything* was a chore, and his muscles ached just lying back against the gel padding. He figured his internal organs would be bruised for a week or more; but if he pulled this off, it would be worth it.

Also, Mik's little brainwave had provided the last piece to the puzzle titled *'how to get us both home safe and alive'.* Marj's Heavy running Sunward wouldn't have nearly enough delta-vee to match speeds with them without draining its tanks dry; and sending out *another* ship to rescue the first one held the potential of a cascade of catastrophe. Losing one ship on a mission was something that happened, but losing three or four would make *nobody* look good.

Fortunately, the ad hoc plan was *working.* Although Mik still had a lot of velocity on him, the hard burn would allow him to match with her around the time she caught up with him. More importantly, this would happen *before* they entered the Earth-Moon system proper, and give them a short amount of prep time before they encountered the deadly trap that had been set for Mik. Golf 9-9 Whiskey might have managed to clear most of the gravel out of their path, but 'most' was not 'all'.

He'd been sent a least-time rendezvous flight plan by Oscar Romeo Five, which meant all he had to do was check on the regular that the flight computer wasn't varying from it. He was fine with sitting there and doing nothing. Trying to fly the Light by hand to a specific point in space and time while *also* dealing with the rigours of three times his normal weight would've been asking for trouble.

When I'm done here, I'm going to locate the asshole who saw fit to dump all that gravel in our way and punch him in the face. Repeatedly.

Ahead of him, the gravel cloud spread inexorably outward in a steadily expanding sphere. Behind him, Mik Wallace hurtled ever closer to the near-certain doom posed by the gravel.

It was his job to make sure they never met.

Mik had never been so glad to hear a hail over the radio. *"Orb-ital Res-cue call-ing Mik Wal-lace, I read you as com-ing up on my six. Still haven't matched velo-cities yet, but I should be with you in about fif-teen mike. How copy, over?"*

His voice sounded strained, as he fought to get his words out past a three-gee — in Martian terms, nearly *eight* gravities! — load on his system.

She searched the starfield ahead, and finally spotted the thruster flare from the rescue ship. "Orbital, this is Mik. I read you five by five," she said, wanting to sigh with relief but not having the excess air to do it with. "I have eyes on you now, over."

"Ex-cellent. We've got four-zero mike before we hit the grav-el cloud. I say again, ren-dez-vous in fif-teen mike, over."

"I copy all that, Orbital. And thanks for showing up. I was starting to get a bit lonely out here, over."

He chuckled painfully at that. *"All part of the ser-vice, over."*

By the time he'd finished speaking, she'd whipped past him, but she fancied their velocities were close to matching even then.

She tried to keep watch for him, down through the framework of the rock-hopper, and finally caught a glimpse of his ship sliding *backward* toward her, decelerating as hard as he'd been pushing to catch up with her. He was a damn good pilot; she'd admit that for free. While she was adept at making the rock-hopper do what she wanted by hand and eye, the ship he was piloting was a lot bigger and heavier than a 'hopper, and its reactions would need to be anticipated.

On what she estimated as the final tick of the last minute, he slid into place alongside her; a single burst from the thrusters eliminated the relative motion, and they hung in space next to each other as if they were standing still. From the side of the ship, a jointed arm unfolded, the clamp on the end reaching out with the same delicate touch that had been used on the ship's controls and latching onto part of the rock-hopper frame.

However, Mik wasn't sitting by as an idle spectator. Releasing herself from the five-point restraints, she reached down with her one working arm and removed the spare refuelling hose from its clips. It turned out that taking off her boots had been a good move, because this let her hold onto the framework of the 'hopper with her toes while leaning over the side and attaching the hose to the filler neck of the tank. Not that it was easy, but she managed. Because she had to.

When the small airlock opened and the pressure-suited figure emerged, she waved with the end of the hose and mimed tossing it to him so he could get the fuel transfer started. Orbital Rescue didn't use precisely the same type of rocket fuel the 'hoppers did, but it was close enough that she wasn't worried. What she didn't expect was a sudden start, and the closest thing to a double-take she'd ever seen in anyone wearing a pressure suit.

"What the hell?" he demanded. *"**You're** Mik Wallace? Why aren't you wearing the suit? How are you even alive?"*

Well, that answered the question (that she hadn't actually asked) as to whether people on Earth had ever heard of the Martian Walker project. It was also weird in another way; the last time she'd faced disbelief of this type was when she first met Dani. She was *used* to people knowing who she was and what she could do.

"Long story," she said. "Fill you in later. Right now, how about we get this done?"

"Right. Yeah. Copy that." He sounded irritated with himself, as if ashamed of his outburst. *"Let's do this."*

When she tossed him the end of the fuelling hose, he caught it on the first try. Dragging a tether behind him—*yeah, that might be a good idea for me too, hey?*—he hauled himself around his ship until he found a place to latch it on.

In the piloting sims she'd played, zero-gee fuel transfers usually involved an inert gas—usually nitrogen—being pumped into the tank to force the fuel down the hose into the empty one. She couldn't see if he was doing exactly that, but the fuel gauge on the 'hopper was going up, so she wasn't exactly about to question his methods.

The twenty minutes they'd had in hand seemed to run down way too fast, but finally the guy straightened up from the connection on his end. *"Flow meter says zero. What've you got?"*

Mik leaned over to look at the rudimentary control panel. "Says full on this end. What's our time?"

"Ah ... five mike. We'll drain the fuel back through then disconnect, then I'll move over—"

Five minutes was cutting it way too fine. She shook her head. "No.

No time. We're too close. You tell your ship to let the 'hopper go and get over here. I'll disconnect from my end."

Just for a moment, she thought he was going to argue, but then he nodded. *"Copy that."* She didn't see him do anything else, but the clamp came loose and the mechanical arm retracted.

At the same time, she leaned over the side once more and worked the hose connector free. It came loose, spraying globules of rocket fuel randomly in its path. One got on her arm, and she wiped it on her tank top; nothing penetrated her skin that she didn't want in her body, but the stuff still stank. Hopefully it would evaporate by the time she got back into pressure.

By the time she pulled herself up to the seats again, the Orbital Rescue guy was there, staring at the decoy EVA suit and back at her. She could tell he still had questions, but they didn't have time for that right now. Working quickly and efficiently, she disconnected the tank she'd used to inflate the decoy and sent the suit drifting away from the 'hopper with a shove. Then she put the tank down next to the other one and pulled herself into her seat. "Strap in," she advised him. "Time?"

He did as he was told, having to let out the straps to their limit before they'd fit around him. His pressure suit was more substantial than a Martian EVA suit, mainly because it was designed to be used in hard vacuum. *"Three-zero sierra."* Thirty seconds.

Even down to one working arm, she had her straps done up before he did, but he was only a few seconds behind her. Was that a twinkling cloud of death she could see ahead of them, or just her imagination? She wasn't waiting around to find out.

Grabbing the control column, she hit the attitude thrusters, tilting the rock-hopper 'backwards' and scooting them toward the nose of the guy's ship. As soon as they were clear, she danced the 'hopper sideways to duck behind the bulk of metal, then spun the other way and flicked a quick burst to cut their lateral motion.

"Damn." His tone was deeply respectful. *"You can fly."*

From the person who'd neatly placed his multi-ton craft directly alongside hers with twenty-five minutes to spare, she figured she'd take that as a serious compliment. "So can you," she said. "I've got a genetic advantage, though. I was literally designed this way."

"I am definitely gonna want to hear more about that. Is that the same genetic mod that lets you not need a pressure suit? How did you make it from Mars to here without—"

Sparks suddenly erupted out of the ship ahead of them; off to the side, the still-drifting EVA suit … exploded. Just shreds were left. "Shit!" she blurted. "It's the gravel!"

"Sonova ..." he muttered over the channel, and pointed. Plumes were spraying out from the sides of the ship; Mik thought she could identify air, as well as what might have been fuel.

"I'm giving us some separation." She turned the 'hopper so the rocket bell-muzzle pointed the way they were going, then gave the main engine a brief burst. Letting them recede to about half a klick, she spun them end-for-end and let out another burst to maintain that distance.

"We should be nearly through by now," he assured her. *"With the spread of the gravel cloud, the ship won't be hit by more than a dozen fragments—"*

The ship exploded.

His voice faded away as they watched the fireball spread and then die, choked by the limitless vacuum all around them. All that proceeded onward was a blackened, twisted shell of a hulk, rolling aimlessly. Pieces broke off it, slowly separating and going their different directions.

"Yeah," she agreed. "But it only needed one to hit it in the right spot."

"True. In history classes, they called it the 'golden BB'. Right place, wrong time. Like ... you ever watch the classics, like Star Wars?"

She chuckled out loud. "Oh, heck yeah. I love that movie. Totally unrealistic on so many levels, but yes. I do see what you mean."

It was his turn to laugh. *"Unrealistic, right. Says the girl who went from Mars to Earth orbit in one week, without a pressure suit. Just saying."*

She rolled her eyes; not that he could see it with the protective membranes in place, but it was the thought that counted. "Uh-huh. Right. Sure. Me? I'm the product of applied science. X-Wings were built to look like fighter planes in space, and we both know it."

"Oh, not arguing." He looked around. *"Okay, we're past the farthest projection on the size of the gravel cloud. Now that you've got a full tank of fuel, how about we slow this puppy down some?"*

"Thought you'd never ask." Grinning, she rolled the 'hopper around until the main rocket was pointing vaguely Sunward. Thumbing the control wheel carefully, she increased thrust to the point that her shoulder began to pain her and kept it there.

Merely being back in control of the rock-hopper gave her a huge confidence boost. She didn't know how long the Earthman could go on a pair of oxy-tanks but there were spares on the 'hopper, so she felt certain help would catch up with them before it was too late for him.

"So, about my speeding ticket?" she asked with a smirk.

"Nah, don't worry about it," he replied, the chuckle audible in his voice. *"I left my ticket book in the ship, anyway."*

Her laughter trailed off into the void as they continued the deceleration burn.

Mars
Cyberon Consortium, CEO's Office
Jarn Kolban

"Just *what* were you thinking?" Kolban was a big man, and he used this to his advantage as he towered over his protégé.

"It's a danger to us." The younger man, smart enough to know that he *was* smart, but not wise enough to know what he didn't know, answered confidently. "They won't be able to connect the ship to Mars, and it wouldn't have been able to give them details about our operations here on Mars. Killing it is the best move."

"It's not that you tried to kill it. It's that you tried and *failed*." Kolban rubbed a hand over his eyes. "If it'd simply been rescued, we could've spun *everything* it said. The calibre of lawyers that we retain? By the time they were done, we would've been able to demand its extradition for multiple cases of murder one. But now … people will *listen*. Not to us, but to *it*."

"We can still salvage this—"

"Yes. We can." Kolban raised a hand and snapped his fingers once. "Security."

"Sir?" Two body-armoured men approached.

"This man's clearances and right to work in Cyberon have been revoked. He is to be let go." Kolban drew a deep breath, thinking. It was a pity to discard such a keen mind, but the boy had shown he couldn't be trusted not to overstep the mark. "Permanently."

More to the point, the boy couldn't be *trusted*. Not if he lacked the incentive to stay loyal.

"Sir?" asked one of the goons as they took the young man by his arms.

"Make it look like a depressurisation accident. Condolences to his next of kin, et cetera, et cetera."

"Sir."

The security men hustled his ex-protégé away, the young man's sudden yell of panic cut off by an elbow to the solar plexus. It was a waste of talent, but unreliable tools were best disposed of. Putting the whole grubby affair from his mind, Kolban frowned as he looked out the triple-paned window at the desolate Martian landscape beyond.

I need that specimen.

And what Jarn Kolban wanted, he always got.

Chapter 11: Recovery

Pete settled back in his seat and re-checked his straps. Facing back along the path they'd travelled—as was necessary, now they were pulling a deceleration burn—he could see Earth gradually creeping away from them. Beside him, Mik maintained a steady hand on the throttle. The rocket engine beneath them thundered endlessly, the sound transmitted as a vibration through the framework of the ridiculously tiny craft.

He'd probably been in odder situations, he decided, but he had no idea when or where.

"How's your radio battery and air?" he asked. He could see the pony bottle she was wearing, but he still had trouble believing that had sustained her over a week of travel. Hell, the two air tanks stashed between the seats wouldn't have kept him going for a day between them.

"I don't need air right now," she assured him. *"Even on Mars, I only need to breathe every now and again. This close to the sun, I can photosynthesise all I need. Radio batteries are probably getting low, though."*

"Okay, we'll conserve comms then." He didn't *want* to—there were so many questions he desperately wanted to ask—but the last thing they needed was for her not to be able to communicate in an emergency situation.

He figured they were running on about three-quarters of a gee deceleration, which was twice what Mik would've been used to on Mars. If his math on how much acceleration she'd used to get up to that speed was correct, they could maintain that for thirteen hours, maybe a smidge less due to his excess mass. This wouldn't bring them to a *complete* halt, unfortunately; over and above what he brought to the party, Mik would've been getting a slight speed boost from the sun's gravity since she started her downhill run from Mars. Not a huge amount, but it would certainly be more than zero.

Thirteen hours would be a damn long time, but it wasn't the end of the world. He had his air tanks, and there were the other two, of an older make but the attachment fittings looked compatible. Of course, that required them to be full.

"Quick question. Are those tanks fresh, or empty?" It was a question he didn't want to ask, but *absolutely* needed to know.

"One's full, and the other one's nearly so," she told him. *"Topped them off just before we left the Phobos construction shack. Used that one to inflate the EVA suit."*

And there were more questions again. When she finally got around to telling the whole tale, this was gonna be a doozy, he could tell. But the news was good, so he let himself relax again. The lower his heart rate, the less oh-two he would use. And after the hard three-gee burn he'd been pulling just before they'd rendezvoused, point-seven-five was a walk in the park. He could barely even feel it.

Time passed. The rocket engine continued its burn.

It had been a long, long day, and they still weren't out of it, but there was nothing he could do right now, so he slept.

Pete blinked his way awake, aware that something had changed. This triggered an immediate feeling of apprehension; in space, 'change' almost always meant 'bad'. Then he realised that the main rocket had been shut off and Mik was using the smaller ones to turn the craft, the starfield rotating around them.

The sun slid into view, and he began to wonder just how good his suit insulation was. It was rated for normal space operations, but by now they had to be millions of kilometres closer to the sun than any normal Orbital Rescue operation went.

"What's going on?" he asked as he pulled down the visor to augment his faceplate polarisation. "What are you doing?"

Her reply was patchy, which only proved she'd been telling the truth about her radio batteries being on their last legs. *"Rock...per bloc...un. Need ...enish photo...is."*

He puzzled over that while she turned the craft so they were directly facing the sun, still hurtling along on their course. A look at his suit chrono indicated that a little over two hours had passed; if he was right, they'd bled off between ten and twenty percent of that insane speed.

Okay. Rock something. Blocking the sun? She needs ... ahh. No sunlight, no photosynthesis, no oxygen, and this thing's been facing away from the sun for more than an hour. She needs to top up.

He watched with intense curiosity as she sat there, her good arm angled outward to catch more light, her eyes closed with a faint smile on her face. Her toes twitched occasionally, showing she was still alive. The weirdest part was how utterly dead-black her skin was; against her seat, it looked darker than actual space. He wondered how he could even tell this story in years to come, without people calling him a liar.

No shit, there I was, riding an open-frame lifeboat inside Earth's orbit, piloted by a skinny teenage girl who didn't need a pressure suit, and could get her oh-two straight from sunlight.

Yeah, that would get drinks poured over his head for sure.

Fifteen minutes later, she opened her eyes and gave him a grin and a thumb's up. Then she took hold of the controls and danced the craft back around to where she could recommence the burn. The renewed vibration of the rocket engine reassured Pete that they might actually get out of this alive.

More time passed. Pete dozed off again. He woke up once when his suit alarm sounded, notifying him that one of his air tanks was low. It was remarkably easy to communicate this to Mik, even without using radios, and with her assistance they changed it out for a fresh one. With both tanks safely in the green again, he was able to relax.

They raced on, across the endless expanse of space.

"Outfield Two calling Outfield One, do you copy? Hey, Pete, are you there?"

Pete's head came up as he registered the incoming call. This was Marj's Heavy, the one that had been pulling a hard burn Sunward just in case he needed assistance after snagging the grazer. They hadn't had all the information at the time, of course—specifically, the fact that whoever or whatever Mik was running from was willing to *kill* her to ensure her silence—but that was what contingency plans were *for.*

"Outfield One to Outfield Two, I read you five by five, over." He turned his head, searching the starscape. "Do you have eyes on, Marj?"

Her chuckle came back to him. *"I've got the teensiest, cutest little radar return I ever saw with a great big rocket plume coming off it, so I'm guessing that's you. I knew you favoured Lights, Pete, but isn't that a little light even for you?"*

"Oh, hardy har har," he retorted, abandoning any pretence of being pissed at her. "Drinks are on me when we get back into pressure."

"You can definitely buy me one," she agreed. *"But the others are gonna be getting you **wasted** for that little stunt you pulled going through Earth orbit. Word is, everyone from Kenworth on down started swearing when your ship blew. Is it true there's someone alive on that little bit of nothing?"*

"Surely is," he confirmed. "Her radio's down, though. Did you need her to cut the thrust or keep it going?"

"Keep it going," she advised. *"I'm still ahead of you, but only just. We've got a chunk of delta-vee to overcome yet. The more fuel I can save now, the more we'll have for later."*

"Copy that," he agreed. Reaching across, he tapped Mik on the shoulder.

She looked over at him curiously, making the gesture that meant 'do you need air?'.

Raising his sun visor and briefly turning on the in-helmet lights so she could see his face—these were never used in normal operation, but it was a good way of seeing if someone was okay after an incident—he shook his head. Then he made a gesture with both hands, as of two ships docking. Finally, he tapped the side of his helmet, right where the radio antenna was woven into the outer fabric. *I talked to them.*

The smile that spread across her face was amazing. She looked like she wanted to hug him but was constrained by both her injured arm and the safety belts. Narrowing her eyes—by now, he was almost used to the featureless white orbs she had in place of normal optics—she began quartering the starfield 'above' them. The Earth was still in view, though smaller than even the full moon from the planet's surface.

He got her attention and pointed 'down', indicating that the rescue ship was Sunward of them. She figured it out immediately; her thumb moved on the control stick, increasing the rocket thrust.

"Outfield Two to Outfield One, nicely done, over." Marj sounded pleased. *"That'll make things easier all 'round."*

"Yeah, just don't take too long matching speeds," Pete said, observing the way Mik was biting her lip. "Pretty sure she was injured getting away from Mars. This level of deceleration is painful for her."

"Copy that. Outfield Two beginning hard burn. Out."

It wasn't easy to lean over and look down through the frame—twisting and turning had always been a problem with pressure suits in general—but Pete wrestled himself into a position to get a look. After a few minutes of squinting and swearing to himself, he figured he had the thruster plume picked out from the background glare. It was coming in fast, but not too fast. Marj was a damn good pilot, which was why she was on this mission at all.

Another few minutes passed, then the Heavy slid backward into view with about half a klick separation, its drive still going hard. Mik turned her head, watching it intently, and clicked up the acceleration by a few notches. The moment they matched velocities, she cut the thrust, a move echoed by Marj in the Heavy.

With both drives inert, they hung motionless with respect to one another, as if sitting still in the void. Again, it was an illusion. They were both still hammering Sunward at perhaps one-eighty klicks per second. This was half the speed Mik had been doing when she passed through Earth local space, but it was still far too fast for comfort.

After half a second to ensure that Marj had indeed shut down her drives, Mik spun the little craft on its axis and sent it over toward the massive Heavy rescue ship. She tipped it the other way to apply retro-thrust and came to a halt barely five metres from Outfield Two.

"Well, damn," Marj commented from the cockpit. Pete could barely see her through the glare coming off the heavy polycarbonate. *"That's some neat flying. But who the hell is that in the pilot seat? It almost looks like they're not even wearing a suit."* As she spoke, a gripper-arm unfolded from alongside the Heavy and reached out to delicately take hold of the small craft.

Pete felt a fatigue-born giggle welling up inside him. "Trust me, you're gonna need to be sitting down for this one."

He and Mik held on while the gripper manoeuvred them into the open hold, then auto-adjusting magnetic clamps grabbed the craft's feet and locked them hard to the deck-plates. The gripper-arm withdrew, and the outer hatch closed. Lights, previously dim, brightened to show the size of the hold; big enough to take on a hundred or more people in an emergency.

He undid the five-point restraints and kicked off across toward the airlock leading into the control cabin. When he looked behind, Mik was following along. The airlock fitted both of them in; Mik was skinny, even for a teenager.

When it finished cycling and the inner door opened, Marj met them with one foot hooked into a grip-hold and first-aid case in hand. As was protocol in such instances, she was wearing her suit but with her faceplate open. "Okay," she said, looking from one to the other. "This one, I've *got* to hear."

Mik coughed a couple of times, then nodded. "Sure. I'll tell you everything. But it's a long story. Also, do you have anything to eat or drink? I'm *starving.*"

Marj grinned as she left the case floating in front of them and headed back to the pilot's console. "I stocked up, just in case. Take your pick. But I have to say, this is the first time I've ever rescued someone who *wasn't* wearing a suit, and they lived to tell the tale."

"Like I said, it's a long story." Mik pulled herself over to a free seat and strapped herself in.

Pete followed on with the first-aid case. "Just give me a chance to immobilise that arm, and we can get going."

"Copy that." Marj keyed the radio. "Outfield Two calling Oscar Romeo. Outfield Two calling Oscar Romeo. Outfield One and the grazer have both been secured. Returning to base, over."

Long moments passed while Pete finished strapping Mik's arm in place, then the reply came back. *"Oscar Romeo to Outfield Two, that's a big well-done from the boss. Come on back, over."*

"Copy that, Oscar Romeo. On my way. Out." Marj gestured Pete toward the rations. Once he and Mik had food in hand and they were both secured in place, she manipulated the controls and spun the Heavy end for end like a ballerina. "Everyone good to go?"

"Definitely." Pete tore his ration pack open and took a long drink out of a capsule of orange juice concentrate. "Take it away."

"You got it." Marj kicked in the main drives; rather more powerful than the little craft Pete had been riding for the last few hours, or even one of his beloved Lights, they rumbled throatily to life. As the acceleration slowly built, she looked over at Mik. "Okay, hon, we got nothing but time now. So, what's the story?"

Mik tore open her ration-pack one-handed and popped a freeze-dried reconstituted meatball into her mouth. "Well," she began rather indistinctly, "have either of you heard of Project Martian Walker?"

Pete glanced at Marj, who shrugged. They both looked back at Mik, and Pete shook his head. "I'm guessing that's you?"

"Yeah, I'm the prototype." Mik gestured at herself. "Genetically engineered to survive and work in micro-pressure and microgravity, and to photosynthesise oxygen from sunlight …"

As the Heavy forged its way on a long parabola back toward Earth orbit and safety, she told her tale; Pete and Marj listened with total fascination.

Chapter 12: Laying Plans

Mik blinked her way back to wakefulness and looked around. After telling her story, she'd taken the opportunity to get some actual sleep. Between that, the rations she'd essentially inhaled, and the water-packs she'd emptied, she was feeling much better. Pete had gone and collected her belongings from the rock-hopper into a mesh bag which he was holding on to for the moment, at least until she could get her collarbone seen to.

Some advice Kathy had given her an eternity ago came back to her, about dressing to the occasion. If she was going to see Pete and Marj's boss, she had to make sure she made the right impression. Dressed in tank top and bike shorts, she looked *tiny* next to the two Earth natives. She needed to add bulk to her profile, so they'd respect her enough that she had a chance of making her own decisions. Without that, they might well decide to override her needs and wants, and leave Dani to the not-so-tender mercies of Cyberon.

That's not going to happen. I'll ride the rock-hopper solo back to Mars first.

"Give me a hand to put some of this back on?" she asked Marj. She respected Pete immensely for putting *everything* on the line for her, but she'd found that guys got really embarrassed about stuff like that.

"Sure thing, hon. We've got a few minutes before I need to actually do anything. Pete, relieve me?"

"Yeah, I can do that." Pete unbuckled and pulled himself into the seat after Marj vacated it. "So, what's this big red button with 'Do Not Push' on it do, again?"

"Ha ha, funny man." Marj pushed off to glide over to where Mik waited. "What do you want to put on?"

"Jeans, boots, maybe the shirt?" Mik wasn't sure about the last one, but every little bit helped.

"Okay, gotcha." Marj took the mesh bag from where Pete had left it, and examined the contents. "No socks?"

"Nope." Mik shook her head. "I don't sweat. They redesigned my heat-exchange systems to not need it. Besides, skin pores don't go well with hard vacuum."

"Damn, sign me up." Marj expertly helped Mik shimmy into the jeans and fastened them shut, then handed her the boots to put on. "I'd *love* to not have that stank all in my underlayer when I take the suit off."

Mik carefully didn't shrug as she pulled the boots on, one at a time. Without being asked, Marj tied the laces. "Well, there are tradeoffs. I need certain additives to my diet, or I start feeling weird after a while.

Don't worry; they made me memorise the list, just in case. Should we try the shirt?"

"So you don't look like a little lost orphan in front of Commander Kenworth?" Marj considered it, then nodded. "I can guide your arm through and put the strapping back on, after. Your pony bottle can go on recharge and refill. The *'refugee from a war zone'* look won't hurt at all, I don't think."

"Okay, that works, I guess." Technically, Mik decided, she was indeed a refugee from a war zone, for a specific definition of the term. "Thanks."

"No problem, hon." Marj shook her head as she helped Mik remove the pony bottle, then started on the strapping. "I'm still getting over how you made it all the way from Mars on that … what did you call it again?"

"Rock-hopper," Mik said. "Dani showed me how to get close to Earth. I maxed out the throttle when I had no other choice."

"And broke your collarbone, just saying," Pete interjected from the pilot seat.

"Miscalculation on my part, not Dani's." Mik winced as Marj helped ease her arm in through the shirt. "I'm pretty sure it was the pony bottle that actually did the damage."

"Yeah, well, don't tell any of the idiots on board Oscar Romeo Five, or they'll want to try it too," Marj advised. From the grin she was wearing, Mik didn't think she was serious.

"I'll be happy to show you how to use the rock-hopper," Mik offered. "But I'm not about to pull that stunt again. Like, not *ever*."

"I can understand that. Okay, done." Marj leaned back for a look at her. "Yeah, you look all kinds of badass now. That strapped arm really sells it."

"Alien princess from Mars, here to beg assistance to free her home planet from the forces of evil." Pete grinned across at Mik. "What? You could totally be that."

She wrinkled her nose at him. "First, I'm not an alien. Second, I'm not a princess. Third … okay, maybe the rest fits."

Pete climbed out of the pilot's seat as Marj drifted over to it. "The term 'alien' can literally mean someone from the next nation over. And as the sole possessor of your genome, you're the highest-ranking member of your species. Being a queen implies that you need someone to rule over, but a princess doesn't exist to rule. She just *is*."

"And Pete Janssen wins the prize for number one bullshit artist today," Marj declared. "Okay, kids. Strap in. We're doing a decel burn in a few minutes, and I don't want anyone bouncing around the cabin."

"Yes, mother," Pete deadpanned as he pulled himself into the seat.

Mik grinned as she ensured her restraints were pulled in tight. This was the sort of banter she enjoyed. The decel burn, she knew, she probably *wouldn't* enjoy. "Secure," she reported, then turned to Pete. "Okay, *'princess of Mars'* I'll accept. But don't expect me to put on a jewelled bikini anytime soon."

As Pete mimed a shot to the heart, Marj laughed out loud.

Marj brought the Heavy back in to dock at the Orbital Rescue station with exquisite grace. The massive craft settled into the clamps as smoothly to Mik as though she were pulling on a glove. Mik had practised this sort of manoeuvre in simulations enough times to know exactly how hard it was. While she thought she'd be able to pull it off if she absolutely had to (say, if every other qualified pilot was incapacitated) she really, truly didn't want to be put in that position.

"Clamps locked, engines powering down," Marj reported. "Okay, we have a green board. You may unbuckle your seatbelts and move around the cabin, and thank you for flying Outfield Spaceways. Feel free to tip your hostess on your way out the airlock."

Mik unsnapped her safety belts, enjoying the freedom of microgravity once more. "Thanks for coming to get me, both of you," she said sincerely. "That was some amazing flying, back there."

Pete shrugged. "Amazing flying is what we do. Insane stunts like yours? They're what make life interesting."

"Yeah," added Marj. "Especially when some asshole's actively trying to murder the people we're trying to rescue. 'Interesting' is *one* way to describe it." She nodded toward the airlock. "You go ahead and get her to the Commander. He'll be wanting to debrief her soonest."

"On our way. C'mon, princess." Pete made for the airlock.

Mik followed along, looking around with interest at the corridors of Oscar Romeo Five as they glided through. She'd never been in a space station before; in fact, Marj's Heavy was the first spaceship she'd ever seen from the inside. Grip-holds designed for gloved hands and booted feet abounded, giving her plenty of options to move along quickly, even with one arm out of action.

As they passed by open compartments, curious faces gazed out at them. She could only guess at what they thought of her, because Pete wasn't stopping to chat. Nobody showed hostility in the brief glimpses she got, but that didn't mean anything.

Earth was where a lot of those idiots got their bigoted ideas from the first place; she knew that from the history lessons Professor Ibrahim had made her sit through. She decided to not trust anyone unless Pete or Marj vouched for them first.

They stopped at a hatchway with **CMDR KENWORTH** emblazoned on it, and Pete slapped a touch-panel. "Janssen reporting, sir, with Mik Wallace."

A moment later, the hatchway slid aside, and Pete entered. The office space within made full use of all six bulkheads, Mik could see as she followed him; there were screens, keyboards, storage lockers and other paraphernalia from one end of the compartment to the other. An older man with a neatly trimmed greyish beard, wearing a pressure suit underlayer with rank insignia printed onto the shoulders, was turning to face them.

"Ah, so you're our grazer," he said, not bothering to reorient himself to match Mik's alignment. She didn't care; part of the prep work on her brain for the eventual Void Walker genotype had ensured she never got disoriented in a three-dimensional space. "You've caused quite the stir, young lady."

"Yes, sir," she agreed; he was the boss of this space station, so the honorific seemed a good idea. "None of it was my idea."

"I'm fully aware of that, Ms Wallace." A wintry smile crossed his lips. "I've had the opportunity to review the verbal report you made to Lieutenants Janssen and Weatherby, and I've been double-checking what facts I could with my own sources."

"And what have you found, sir?" This was it, she sensed. This was where she found out what kind of a man Commander Kenworth was. *Will he help me, or is he going to stand in my way?*

"Exactly what I expected." His expression became warmer. "Nothing you've said to Janssen or Weatherby has proven to be false, while several of the statements by Cyberon were patently untrue, once I dug down past the rhetoric. I'm fully aware of the political stance within Burroughs these days, and how Cyberon has allied itself with the Pure Strain movement. I personally have no doubt of any significant detail of your story."

Pete frowned. "I'm hearing a 'but', sir."

"Your hearing is as acute as ever, Lieutenant," Kenworth acknowledged. "There is a considerable problem to overcome in this situation. In order for *anyone* to officially act on this, I would have to kick it up the chain of command. There, I suspect, it would be spread around to whoever was interested. The likelihood of someone with a direct interest in Cyberon hearing about it would approach one hundred percent."

Mik swallowed. "That … wouldn't be good."

"A succinct analysis, Ms Wallace." Kenworth laced his fingers together in front of him. "I foresee two possibilities stemming from that.

First, the powers that be in control of Mars simply deny anything untoward is happening and refuse permission for such an expedition to be sent. As Ms Connaught lacks any relatives with strong political ties, I suspect the will to push forward would rapidly dwindle. It would also become abundantly clear to those holding your friend that you are unlikely to ever come within their grasp, so her usefulness to them would just as rapidly diminish to zero."

"And if they let us go ahead," Pete filled in, "it would come to much the same result, only they would invite inspection of every one of their public facilities. Meanwhile, *if she's lucky,* Ms Connaught is being held offsite. In the end, same result."

"No." Mik shook her head. "We can't let that happen. Dani is depending on me." A deep and abiding pain clamped down over her heart.

Commander Kenworth's gaze softened. "I happen to agree. We are a rescue organisation. Saving people is what we *do,* Ms Wallace. And right now, nobody else is coming for Danielle Connaught, so it's up to us to get her out."

Mik blinked. "What? I mean … you mean that, sir?"

"I do." Commander Kenworth turned his gaze to Pete. "Lieutenant Janssen; as of this moment, you're on the sick list, due to the excessive G's you pulled during that frankly impressive rescue mission. Ms Wallace, you aren't even on our roster, but we're going to have to arrange some kind of minor masquerade to convince those who know you're here that you're *still* here. We're probably going to need a few more volunteers, but most importantly, we'll need all the information we can get about Cyberon's operations on Mars. Once we have that, we can determine where she's most likely being held and make our plans accordingly. And then …"

"We're going to go save her?" asked Mik hopefully.

Kenworth nodded. "You're going to go save her."

Pete frowned. "Won't that get you in trouble with the chain of command, sir?"

The glint of battle had come to Commander Kenworth's eye.

"It'll be worth it, Lieutenant."

Chapter 13: Return to Mars

Cyberon HQ, Burroughs, Hellas Basin, Mars
CEO's Office

"Sir, we have an update on the situation with the specimen."

That got Kolban's attention. He held up his hand to forestall his conversation with the Pure Strain rep and turned toward the screen showing his assistant's face. "This had better be something we can work with."

"Yes, sir, I believe so." The young man sounded upbeat, which was a good sign.

For the last three weeks, following his protégé's untimely demise in an 'airlock accident', people had been tiptoeing around him as if they were worried about being next. Which was stupid. All people needed to do to avoid that sort of thing was to actually *get him what he wanted.* Was that so hard?

"Well?" Kolban made a *go-on* gesture.

"Orbital Rescue retrieved the specimen and brought it back to their satellite Oscar Romeo Five. However, at some point, it must have blabbed about being genetically engineered, because they promptly placed it and the two pilots who retrieved it into quarantine."

He nodded. "Understandable. Stupid, but understandable. Well, that's reasonably good news as far as it goes. We know exactly where it will be for the next few weeks." Plans began to churn over in his mind: if he could replace one or more incoming crewmembers with his own men ...

"Sir, there's more."

"Really?" Kolban's attention, which had drifted away from his assistant, snapped back into place. "Well, don't just stand there. Fill me in."

"It broke out of quarantine and tried to steal a ship. The reports are incomplete, but it seems people got hurt, and it's being kept under lockdown while they are preferring charges against it. All being kept hush-hush, of course, but they can't maintain secrecy on this sort of thing forever."

"Well, now." His smile broadened. "That *is* good news. Do you have any idea of what it would take to convince them to simply deport the specimen right back into our arms?"

"Not yet, sir, but I'm making enquiries."

"Excellent. Keep me posted."

"Yes, sir."

The screen went blank, and Kolban looked over at his visitor. "You heard?"

"Yes." The man's answering smile was downright vicious. "Things like that need to be put in their place. I understand you have the other abomination? The gene-tainted child?"

"We do. She is currently being kept alive and healthy."

Distaste twisted the Pure Strain fanatic's features. "Why? Destroy her uncleanness and dispose of the body in some remote location. Mars is a big place."

Personally, Kolban thought the man was making too much of a fuss over one teenage girl, but he would never say that out loud. "She may come in handy as leverage, once we have the specimen in hand. Once that usefulness is over, of course ..." He made a throwaway gesture.

"Of course."

"I'm glad we agree. So, as we were saying ..."

Around the Same Time
In Mars Orbit
Mik

Mars loomed large in the forward viewport of the repurposed Heavy. Valles Marineris had just slipped over the horizon to the left of the image, while Hellas Basin dominated the lower right. Mik glowered at the inoffensive crater and by association the city that was dug into its rim wall, then pointed. "That's where the facility we're going to is, right? Somewhere near Burroughs?"

Marj nodded. "Got it in one, hon. So, was it called 'Burroughs' because it's partly underground, or because of the author?"

"Not sure." Mik shrugged carefully. "Could be one or the other, could be both."

Pete, in the copilot chair, noticed the movement. "How's the collarbone going, princess?"

By now, Mik knew damn well that asking him not to call her that merely encouraged him, so she ignored it. "There's little bit of a twinge every now and again, but I've got full use back." She demonstrated by moving her arm in every direction it could travel.

"That's good," Marj said warmly. "I'm still impressed that it healed so fast, given that you spent most of your time in zero G, and your bones are so fragile compared to ours anyway."

"Thank Professor Ibrahim and the others at the Research Complex." Mik tried not to let her voice catch in her throat. Many times over the past three weeks, she had wished she could shed tears. Her grief was no less intense without them, but the same biomods that ensured her capability to survive for a week in hard vacuum turned crying into a dry affair, leaving her unable to get rid of stress hormones quickly or easily. "Martian Walkers are supposed to be the precursors to Void Walkers, working in microgravity and micro-pressure for eight to ten hours a day. But whether we're on the surface of Mars or somewhere out in space, there's every chance we'd be suffering broken bones or getting hurt in other ways, so they made sure we didn't lose calcium in low G. And with the right additives in our diet, injuries like that heal faster than the human norm."

"I'm both impressed and a bit jealous." Pete shook his head. "Calcium loss is one of the reasons we've got to rotate downside regularly. I had a buddy, champion aeroball player in Luna Three, who was on track to hit the big time. He zigged when he should've zagged in a practice game and busted his thighbone. Never quite healed properly, and he lost his chance for the major leagues."

Mik frowned. "That can't be right. You're from Earth. Couldn't you get gene therapy, like Dani did for her cancer problem, and deal with that sort of thing before it ever happens?"

"Oh, that sort of thing isn't free, hon, or even cheap." Marj's tone was warm and understanding. "Plus, gene therapy for cancer potential has been around for decades. All it really does is suppress a gene we don't want expressing itself. What you're talking about is adding new options. While that's totally a thing, it's also very definitely an elective process, and almost prohibitively expensive."

"Oh." Mik was beginning to get the distinct impression that corporations on Earth weren't all that different from those on Mars. Profit was the bottom line: first, last, and always.

"Changing the topic." Pete gestured at the planet before them. "Is there really no single orbital authority down there at the moment? Because that sounds more than a little dangerous to me."

"That's how it is," Marj assured him. "I've looked into it all the way from Earth to here. After the Marineris raid, the whole situation devolved into a cold civil war, if that's a thing. The elements of the Martian government—such as it was—that were in Tharsis before this happened are in direct opposition to the parts that were in Burroughs, and vice versa. Each has declared the other invalid, and demanded that they *'dissolve their unlawful assemblies'* and cease issuing directives forthwith."

Pete shrugged. "If that's the case, why don't they draw a line on the map and each take half of Mars? It's what they've essentially done already, right?"

Mik knew the answer to that one. "Because Burroughs, with Cyberon behind them, wants *all* of Mars, so they aren't going to suggest it, and wouldn't honour an agreement like that even if they signed it. And the Tharsis Corporation knows it, so they're not giving an inch. They're the ones who've been trying to call in the United Nations, but every time they issue a request for intervention, the Burroughs section of the government countermands it."

"And in the meantime, everyone with half a brain who doesn't actually have a pressing reason to hang around is upping stakes and leaving," Marj said grimly. "Oh, and the best bit? Rumour has it that anyone who orbits too low over Burroughs is targeted by Cyberon ships for boarding and searching, on suspicion of espionage. There's no *proof* that they've forcibly deorbited anyone for noncompliance, but I wouldn't put it past them."

"Me neither." Mik unbuckled from her seat restraints and drifted toward the main console. "And on that note, I'm thinking we should make our final prep. Can I have another look at the sat map?"

"Sure thing." Along with her other talents, Marj had a knack for ferreting out information from the sprawling hive of information that the twenty-first century Internet had evolved and mutated into. "The place is owned by Cyberon through a bunch of shells and cut-outs intended to make sure the average member of the public never realises it. But despite its original intention of selling goods in 'rivalry' to Cyberon, it hasn't done business in weeks. No goods going in or out. But I've been keeping tabs on it, and there's staff on site, every day. A regular turnover. And it's well outside Burroughs proper."

She tapped buttons on the console, bringing a satellite image up on the screen. There was a small complex of buildings, with a shuttle pad and sealed tunnels leading from one structure to another. Zooming in showed an enclosed all-wheel-drive in the process of either entering or leaving a vehicular airlock in the largest building.

"Guards." Pete reiterated the point that they'd already agreed on. "A place like that could be monitored remotely for any problems if it was properly shut down. But keeping a human prisoner on site? You'd need human guards." He rubbed his chin. "I'm just wondering, if we *know* where she is, why don't we contact Tharsis for assistance?"

"Because for all that they're the 'good guys' in this," Mik said flatly, "the term is relative. They had me created for a profitable reason, and if I walked into their headquarters and asked for help, their *first* priority would be to whisk me away and run a million tests on me to figure out the effects of my trip. Dani's welfare would be *way* down their list of wants and needs, and by the time I got them to listen to me and maybe do something about it, the inevitable moles would've reported back to Cyberon that I was there. And then they either contact me under the table and use her as a hostage ... or they give up on me and murder her outright. I prefer our way."

"That, and Orbital Rescue doesn't outsource." Marj's tone was final. "This is our job, and we're going to do it right."

Mik paused, emotions welling up inside her. "I … seriously, I have no idea how I'm going to repay you, all of you, for doing this. You're going so far above and beyond …"

Pete got out of his seat and pulled his way over to her. "Don't sweat it, princess." One arm went around her shoulders in a side-hug. "When the next generation of your genome is ready to roll, send some of them our way. If I'm still around then, I'd be honoured to train them in orbital rescue."

"Seriously?" Marj sputtered with hilarity. "Did you honestly just ask for her *firstborn child* as payment for our help?"

Pete facepalmed, while Mik joined Marj in helpless laughter.

Pete

Mars rolled majestically beneath them as the Heavy gradually lost orbital altitude. Pete and Mik sat strapped into the rock-hopper with a teenager-sized pressure suit partially inflated and strapped into the third seat, installed by McPherson. Attached to the larger ship via a large grasper-arm, they were effectively part of it for the time being.

"*Okay, coming up on release point.*" Marj's voice crackled in Pete's earpiece. "*Final checks: go/no-go. Mik?*"

Beside him, Mik did a fast visual and tactile check of all her gear, as well as the rock-hopper's readouts. Watching her, Pete felt frankly inadequate. It wasn't just that she could sit outside the ship in near-total vacuum with nothing but a pony bottle and mask, wearing ordinary clothing, though that was unfair enough. However, she could also turn her head and see *everything* that was going on without anything impeding her peripheral vision. This was her element; she was the natural-looking one here, not him in his bulky pressure suit.

"*Mik here. I say go. Pete?*"

He'd already checked his suit readouts a dozen times. Pressure was holding steady, his oh-two was high in the green, and everything that was supposed to be attached to the outside was still there. He chinned his radio transmitter. "Pete here. I say go."

"*I concur with go. Green light, guys. Kick ass and take names.*" There was a faint vibration transmitted through his suit as the grasper released the rock-hopper; craning his neck around, he saw it retracting into the hull of the Heavy.

"*Copy that.*" Mik took hold of the controls—she'd tutored Pete and Marj in how to fly the flimsy little craft, but he didn't think he'd ever reach her level of instinctive understanding of how it was going to react—then tilted the rock-hopper sideways and eased them out to a hundred metres or so of separation. Then she spun the whole thing so that Mars was effectively over their heads. "*Last chance to back out.*"

That sounded ominous. Pete was aware of the plan, but all of a sudden, Mars was starting to look really big and really close. They couldn't just land the Heavy outside the facility; groundside radar would pick it up with ease. The rock-hopper, on the other side, could pass for a meteor until it got under the horizon for all the emitters that were tracking it. McPherson had even installed a sensor for telling them when that happened.

He took a deep breath. *Here goes nothing.* "Let's do this."

"*You got it.*" Up until now, she'd only been using the smaller thrusters, but now she ignited the main rocket. Not at full power—the last time she'd done that, she'd broken her collarbone and passed out— but definitely at more than one Martian G.

"Jeezus Chriiiiiiist." The exclamation was torn out of him by the feeling that he was falling straight toward Mars, along with the absolute *knowledge* that there was literally nothing between him and the ground except for his suit. It was great for holding air, but its shock-absorbing qualities were sadly lacking, especially for an orbital insertion like this. Grabbing for the minimal armrests on either side of the seat, he hung on for dear life; even though he was wearing the suit, he knew his knuckles had to be white.

When the main thruster cut out, he sagged in relief, though he was fully aware that they were still hurtling downward at a horrific velocity, aided and abetted by the gravity of the planet below. Mik nudged the attitude thrusters so they were now sitting at an angle, as though sliding down an endless slope toward Mars.

This didn't actually help.

Nor was he comforted by the fact that Mik was leaning forward slightly, her bared teeth visible through the transparent plastic mask. She was enjoying this. All that stood between them and a fiery death in a brand-new crater was her skill with something that wasn't supposed to travel more than a hundred metres off the ground, much less into space, and she was *enjoying* it.

She's certifiably nuts. And so am I, for going along with it.

Mik

The closer they got to Mars, the more she felt a sense of recognition, of familiarity. She *knew* the planet, how it looked, how the atmosphere felt on her skin. It wasn't a sense of homecoming; the only place she'd ever known as home was now destroyed and gone, along with everyone she'd ever cared for while growing up. Mars itself might become home to her, and it might not. *I'll have to see how things go.*

The radar sensor had been showing several lights steadily but now, as wisps of atmosphere made the frame of the rock-hopper judder and shake, they were starting to flicker. She flexed her fingers on the controls, ready to apply retro-thrust if she started feeling too much re-entry heat. Beside her, she could tell Pete wasn't having a good time of it, even without the air friction. She figured he was used to having a whole lot more separation between himself and any nearby planets.

The last radar light blinked off, and she grinned. *Showtime.*

Cutting in the thrusters, she began to angle their downward plunge toward level flight. They'd need to slow down some, but not a huge amount. By the time they got down to what she'd decided to call NOM—nap of Mars—altitude, they'd still be doing multiples of the speed of sound, whether measured on Earth or Mars. There probably wasn't anyone else on the planet who could pull this off.

Which was why they'd never see her coming.

Chapter 14: Insertion

The wind stirred Mik's mohawk and made her t-shirt flap noticeably as the rock-hopper raced across the floor of Hesperia Planum. Technically a plain (thus the name), Hesperia had a few craters here and there, but they were skimming across the surface just high enough for her to avoid both those and the wrinkle ridges as they came up over the horizon.

Dani had once told her how, more than a century after humans went into space, a tiny but vocal minority still hadn't believed in Earth's curvature. *Weird.* Mik had never been down to the surface of Earth, but if it was anything like Mars, the curvature was just *there.*

Having wind strong enough to notice was a new experience. At the elevation that had been designated as the 'datum' on Mars (equivalent to sea level on Earth), the pressure was about one percent of that turgid soup people laughingly called an 'atmosphere' on Earth. The only time anyone on Mars normally felt anything more than a gentle shove from it was during a dust storm, and nobody with any kind of sense was outside during that time.

But now they were belting along at several thousand kilometres per hour, and she could actually feel it. If her eyes had been exposed to the outside atmosphere (ignoring the laundry list of problems she would also be suffering because of that) they probably would've been watering. She could tell Pete still wasn't enjoying the ride, mainly from the way his gloves were gripping the armrests, but they both knew he'd been going much faster when he intercepted her rock-hopper back in near-Earth space. *The wuss.*

It was all relative, she figured. Velocity was just a number, unless there was a chance of hitting something. When that happened, everyone learned why (in the immortal quote she'd learned from Marj) *'Isaac Newton is the deadliest sonovabitch in space'.*

Tyrrhenus Mons loomed up over the horizon, the single biggest obstacle in their passage so far. Her areology lessons had told her that Tyrrhenus was one of the oldest volcanoes on Mars, and that it (and the landscape around it) had been gradually collapsing in on itself over the last few million years. It was very interesting, and under different circumstances she might well have spent several days climbing all over the massif. But they weren't there to have intimate relations with arachnids (that one was from the ever-crusty McPherson, while going over the rock-hopper with a fine-tooth comb); Dani needed rescuing, and that was what they were going to do.

Tweaking the controls, she eased the rock-hopper up into a gentle bank that allowed them to avoid the peak; the gullied flank flashed by beneath them. She grinned, reasonably sure she could feel the frame of the rock-hopper creaking under the strain of Pete's grip on the armrests. But she wasn't doing this just to tweak Pete's sensibilities. The speed was required to get them in close to the Cyberon facility before anyone noticed them, aided and abetted by the nap-of-Mars flying.

It was totally beyond the point that she'd always had a thing for going fast on rock-hoppers. They were light and agile, and she literally had the solar system's best-designed vestibular system in her head. It was a match made in whatever Heaven people decided to believe in.

Once clear of Tyrrhenus, it was time to start their decel burn. They were currently doing about five thousand kilometres per hour, down from the seven thousand they'd had under their belts when the rock-hopper first got down to ground level. She didn't want to subject her freshly healed collarbone to much more than two Martian G's if she could help it. Also, the smaller they could keep their thruster flare, the better.

Having Dani on hand, rather than being the person they were there to rescue, would've been useful; she'd always been better at the math side of things than Mik was. But Mik figured she could seat-of-the-pants it until they hit a more manageable over-ground speed. Giving Pete the hand signal to let him know she was about to do it—they were keeping radio comms to an absolute minimum, for obvious reasons—Mik waited for his nod, then flipped the rock-hopper up on an angle and thumbed the control for the main thruster.

Up until now, she'd been using the attitude thrusters to keep them from ploughing into the Martian regolith. At the angle it was now on, she couldn't use them all at once. Some of the retro-thrust had to go downward to stay level; the rest went toward slowing them the hell down.

She felt it at once, of course; rock-hopper seats didn't have the most luxurious padding, and she'd only been experiencing intermittent acceleration and deceleration since she left Mars. To have twice the gravity she'd grown up under smack her on the ass and compress her spine like that was a rude awakening.

But it wasn't going to be for long; one-eighty seconds, max. That was *nothing* compared to the *hours* at three Earth G's that Pete had willingly subjected himself to, just so he could intercept Mik before she encountered the deadly cloud of gravel in Earth orbit. There were many things she was willing to complain about, but that wasn't going to be one of them.

The seconds crawled by as the main thruster roared, reducing their forward speed. Not as fast as it *could*, of course, but Mik didn't need any more broken bones. One was two too many.

Close enough to the right moment, a rille opened up in front of them and she dropped the rock-hopper down into it while continuing to apply deceleration. The sound of the main thruster was a lot more audible in the confined area, though nowhere near as loud it would be in breathable pressure. Fines kicked up in a massive cloud from the floor and walls of the narrow ravine as they slowed to a halt.

As the forward motion dropped to zero, Mik rotated the rock-hopper to level keel, until they were hovering a few metres above the rocky floor. She rolled the thrust back, dropping them smoothly to the ground. Just as the landing struts kissed the floor of the rille, she killed power altogether, then turned to grin at Pete. Around them, the fines slowly settled to the ground again.

"Piece of cake," she said, secure in the knowledge that the rocky terrain would block anyone nearby from picking up the signal. "Now, that's what *I* call a re-entry."

Pete forced himself to let go of the armrests. He was honestly surprised the metal wasn't bent out of shape from the force with which he'd been gripping it. "Jjjeeeeesus Chriiiist," he managed. "You do that sort of thing *all the time?*"

"Well, not the re-entry part, and not usually as fast as that, but yeah." She didn't seem overly fazed. *"It was how we got around if we wanted to go somewhere the all-wheel-drives couldn't reach."*

"I … see." He didn't yell at her, mainly because he'd *seen* how good she was with the rock-hopper in free-fall, where it wasn't even supposed to be. Under Martian conditions, it was in its element, and so was she.

More to the point, she *had* threaded the eye of the needle with a craft that made his preferred Lights look bulkier than a Heavy, going by eye and genetic talent. Taking a few deep breaths, he sipped from his suit water dispenser to dispel the dry taste in his mouth. That had definitely been the fastest he'd ever gotten from orbit to planetary surface, he had to admit.

Damned if she didn't make it look easy.

Though it would've only worked on Mars. Trying that stunt on Earth would've resulted in immediate arrest by the authorities of whatever nation they'd overflown on the way down, and that would be the *preferred* result.

The other result probably involved a fiery death in a medium-sized crater.

"So, you good to go?" She unfastened her five-point straps, then dug under her seat to get her coat. It had seemed odd to him for her to want the garment at all, until he saw the camo pattern she'd had the guys print on the outer side. In contrast to the mottled grey of urban camouflage, this was shades of dusty red; if she stood with her back to him and flipped up the hood that came with it, she'd be damn near invisible against the side of the rille.

"Yeah, I'm good. How far to the complex?" He undid his own belts, then deflated and collected Dani's pressure suit, along with its oh-two tanks. No matter how dashing and daring they were, the rescue would come to a screeching halt if she couldn't actually leave the complex.

"Half a klick, maybe more. How well can you cover ground in a suit?"

"I did the standard surface pressure-suit training on Earth and the Moon before I went on to Oscar Romeo Five, so I know *how*." Pete grimaced, leaving the rest unsaid.

"But you're not used to it," Mik finished diplomatically. *"Well, I'll take point and try to find an easy way for you to go. Hand signals only, once we're out of this ditch."*

"Copy." Pete was a professional, and very good at what he did. The trouble was, despite the fact that he was wearing a pressure suit designed to fit him perfectly, sneaking around on the surface of Mars was not part of that category. He hated feeling like an amateur, and hated even more that the success or failure of the mission rested (mainly) on the shoulders of a skinny teenage girl. A teenage girl whose genetic modifications made her *ideal* for the mission, and who was tall for her age, but still ... *a teenage girl.*

He watched as Mik went up the side of the rille without needing to use her hands, totally in tune with her environment. Were it not for the Martian sky overhead and her dead-black skin tone, she could've been a kid messing around back on Earth. Reaching the edge, she peered around then ducked out of sight. A moment later, her arm came back into view and she beckoned him upward.

It took him considerably more effort than it had taken her to get up the side of the narrow ravine, even under Martian gravity. Between the suit he was carrying (the spare tanks were slung across his back) and the awkwardness of his own pressure suit, he had to work for every metre. By the time he got to the top, he could feel his underlayer wicking away the sweat, and he was breathing hard.

Mik was just within sight, between two standing monoliths that would've each out-massed a Heavy. She waved for him to come on, then vanished. With a sigh, he started in that direction, feeling every inch the clumsy Earth cousin come to visit.

She met him at the gap when he arrived there, and looked at him with concern. *You okay?* she asked with basic hand signals.

He nodded in confirmation and added a thumb-and-forefinger circle. It wasn't a total lie; he still had physical reserves he hadn't tapped, but he also hadn't expected things to be this strenuous on the surface of a planet with just thirty-nine percent of Earth's gravity. She looked critically at him, then nodded in return.

Away she dashed again, showing off more of the irrepressible energy that she'd demonstrated on OR-5. Mars, he figured, was just about big enough for her to get along in; nothing smaller was.

He plodded after her, trusting the path she'd picked. She was as good as her word, ensuring that he didn't have to deal with much in the way of difficult terrain. While he was certain he could leap higher than she could if he had to, she was definitely the better pick when it came to having someone scout out the path.

They came to a halt next to a large angular boulder; via hand signals and a little drawing in the fines at her feet, Mik conveyed that the complex was only about ten metres away. He wouldn't have known it was there until she told him, but he accepted her word on the matter. The big problem, as she pointed out, was the security camera on the airlock on that side.

They'd talked it over on the Heavy coming to Mars, and figured out a number of scenarios, along with the potential responses for those scenarios. This had been one of the situations they'd gamed out and decided on the optimum response for.

Holding up his hand, he spread all his fingers. *Five?* he asked silently.

Three, she corrected, holding up that many fingers, showing how many minutes she figured she needed to get into position.

He copied her gesture, then formed a fist. She bumped it with hers, then nodded and ducked away between the rocks.

Unslinging the spare oh-two tanks, he put Dani's suit on the ground and attached the tanks to it, then manually opened the valve on one to reinflate the suit. Within a few seconds, it looked reasonably humanlike, so he shut the valve off again. All he had to do after that was wait until Mik's three minutes were up.

Then it would be showtime.

Cyberon Consortium Headquarters, Burroughs, Mars
CEO's Office

Jarn Kolban's new assistant spoke urgently without sounding over-the-top. *"Sir, we've just learned some troubling information."*

He nodded to acknowledge the statement. "Is it about the specimen?" If it wasn't, then he'd probably downgrade the 'troubling' rating.

"Yes, sir. I nudged a few of our assets in the Earth-Moon system, and they demanded to interview the specimen and ensure that it was healthy and being well cared for. Orbital Rescue held out for a suspiciously long time, then the commander on site requested a warrant. I had to pull a few more strings before sufficient legal pressure could be applied, but eventually the commander's superiors were obliged to order him to produce the specimen. That was when he revealed that it had left the station some time previously. The specific details were only made privy to a few people, and I'm still working on getting access to them, but I think there's only one viable conclusion."

Kolban sat up, eyes widening. "It's coming to Mars. It intends to rescue its human friend."

"Or it may already be here, sir. The commander was irritatingly vague about its exact departure time. There is a significant window."

He resisted the urge to put his fist through the screen as the familiar rage flared up. *God damn it. Why can't things just go smoothly for once?* "Put out word to all our subsidiaries to keep an eye out for a human-presenting girl of that height and body type, wearing skin-tone makeup. Did they say how many people went with it, or how it intended to get to Mars?"

"No, sir, on both counts. I'm still pursuing those details."

"Understood. Was there anything else?"

"No, sir."

"Very well. Keep me posted." Kolban ended the call and spun his ten-thousand-Martian-dollar executive chair so that he could glower out through the thick UV-opaque glass at the city of Burroughs and the raw, savage landscape beyond.

Where are you, you little genetic money machine?

Chapter 15: Infiltration

The clock was ticking as Mik moved quickly but carefully around the building. Finally, she reached the point she was aiming at: an area of blank wall, with no entry points and thus no security cameras. She'd known where it was, having scoured the overhead imagery to the very limit of its resolution capability. More to the point, she knew what was on top of the building.

Here was where the mindsets of the Cyberon employees who had built and were staffing the structure would inevitably fail them. They required at least twenty kPa of atmosphere around them at all times (and that was just the oxygen), otherwise various nasty things would start happening to their bodies, starting with depressurisation and ending in death. And while EVA suits were a good stopgap, and much handier than full pressure suits would be, they were still relatively bulky and clumsy.

As such, anyone (apart from Mik) attempting to gain surreptitious entry to any airlocked structure on Mars would have to go in via ground level or use stairs to access the roof. The thick gloves and heavy boots built into such suits had a minimal chance of allowing a suited person to climb even a conveniently placed rope; the concept of free-climbing straight up the side of such a building, out of the sight of cameras, simply wouldn't occur to them.

When she reached the base of the wall, Mik took a moment to pull off her boots, hanging them from her belt by the laces. Thinking ahead, she picked up a rock and put it in her pocket. Then she reached up, hooked her fingers into a couple of convenient crevices, and started to climb.

The concrete, as with most large structures on Mars, had been poured in a rough and ready manner. Outward appearance held far less importance than the ability to consistently hold air pressure. So external flaws such as crevices and shallow cracks (unfortunately common with some of the temperature shifts) were overlooked as being superfluous to the security and safety of the buildings.

Mik aimed to prove them all wrong.

It wasn't so long ago, she mused as she steadily made her way up the vertical surface, that she'd told both Professor Ibrahim and Dani how she wanted to free-climb the wall of Valles Marineris, near the complex where she'd grown up. She'd probably never do that now, but this was an acceptable substitute, especially if it got Dani safely away from the clutches of Cyberon. Making that a permanent situation still wasn't a guarantee, given how they'd almost managed to kill Mik with a spread of gravel inside Lunar orbit. If that was any indication of the reach of the rogue Martian consortium, it was frighteningly long.

But one crisis at a time, as the Professor had often said.

Her internal clock wasn't perfect, but she was pretty sure that by the time she reached the top, the three minutes she'd allowed Pete were up. This meant his part of the distraction was due to start, and the window of opportunity was going to start closing soon. Pulling herself up to the top of the roof, she paused to survey the expanse.

Signal dishes, check. Airlock for roof access, check. Total lack of guards on top of the roof, check.

Okay, let's do this thing.

Still barefoot, she darted across to the nearest signal dish and examined the box built into the base of it. One of her jobs back in the Research Complex had been to check on the various dishes on the roof, especially after a dust storm came through. That hands-on experience, plus the formal tutelage from half a dozen brilliant minds, had left her with a thorough understanding of how such dishes worked … and how to best simulate an equipment malfunction.

With this in mind, she popped the cover off the control box, examined the fuses and breakers she found there, then grinned and pulled one out. That particular brand of fuse was finicky as hell, and always needed to be firmly seated or it would play hob with the signal. Removing it altogether would be a dead giveaway that someone was up there on the roof, but Mars itself had a ready solution.

Fines, the micrometre-scale Martian 'dust', got *everywhere*. Proofing Mik's body against them had been one of the tougher challenges of the Martian Walker program, or so Kathy had once told her. It was one of the things that would've propelled the Tharsis Corporation, and Mik herself, into the forefront of the terraforming initiative.

Wiping some fines off the sole of her boot onto her fingertip, Mik transferred them onto the fuse then replaced it in its socket. She knew from personal experience that the resultant signal would be jittery at best, and would cut out altogether at worst. Just the sort of thing that would require someone to come up and check it out.

Leaving the box partly open as though left unlatched by a careless tech, she scrambled up on top of the roof exit airlock and set about putting her boots back on. The airlock would be electronically secured from the inside, of course, but the thing about boredom was that it made people lazy. She'd seen it herself a dozen times; if someone was just ducking out for something, they'd leave the outer door open, because why bother closing it when it was just going to be opening again in a minute or so?

Thirty seconds after she finished lacing up the second boot, the airlock rumbled open. Someone in an EVA suit stepped out, carrying a toolkit. Predictably, he headed straight for the dish she'd sabotaged.

EVA suits were utterly shit for peripheral vision, so Mik didn't waste any time. Grabbing the upper edge of the airlock, she swung down and in, then slapped the button to close the outer door and cycle the lock. Her sinusoidal channels registered the rise in air pressure, and soon enough her sphincters relaxed, as did her abdominal muscle bands.

Stepping out of the airlock, she took the rock from her pocket and wedged it into the channel to block the inner door from closing all the way. The safety interlocks would kick in at that point, preventing the outer door from opening. It was an old trick, dating from the first days of the Martian colonies, but it was still an effective one.

While she didn't have anything in particular against the guy who'd gone to repair the dish, he *was* one of the assholes holding Dani captive, so keeping him out of the way was a good idea. By now, Pete would've knocked on the front door, so the timer really was ticking. Reaching up to her ear, she activated the mastoid earpiece, so they could talk if necessary.

Step One: infiltrate the base. Done that.
Step Two: find Dani.
Okay, so where are you?

Pete

The last few seconds of the timer in Pete's suit chrono ticked down, and he took a deep breath. *Okay, showtime.* He was fully aware this was not part of his job description—*I'm Orbital Rescue, not SpecOps, dammit!*—but this was where the rescue operation was, so he was just gonna have to man up and do the job anyway.

Holding the inflated suit meant for Danielle Connaught in a way that made it look like there was someone inside and he was helping them along, he headed for the airlock Mik had already spotted. When he knew he was within range of the video pickup, he waved his free arm and activated his radio on the universal Guard channel. "Hey, help, can you see me? Need help here! Crashed our transport and the kid's hurt!"

Nobody had answered by the time he got up to the airlock, so he hit the oversized entry button. It depressed but the airlock didn't open, as he'd predicted. He didn't even try to figure out the coded keypad, instead slapping his palm on the exterior alarm panel. That would sound a loud buzzer inside the building, indicating that someone was locked out and needed to get in.

"Hey!" he called out over the radio again. "Help! I need help out here! I got a hurt kid! We need medical attention and we need air! Help!"

Four things were working in his favour here. The first was that this secret facility was trying hard to pretend not to be a secret facility. Second, the pressure suit meant for Danielle and the mention of a 'hurt kid' would throw them off the track. Third, the people inside *would* want to know who had been wandering around in their back yard, and why. And as for the fourth, it was simple. He'd been born on Earth and had spent an extended period of time down on the surface a lot more recently than any Cyberon employee he was likely to encounter.

The light over the airlock door turned green, then the door itself rumbled open to reveal an EVA-suited figure. *"Come on in,"* said a masculine voice over the same channel. *"Bring the—"*

He got no further than that, because Pete had dropped the suit and launched himself into the airlock. Orbital Rescue pilots had to be fit and good at hand-to-hand combat, both in and out of pressure suits. They weren't combat troops, but it wasn't unknown for potential rescuees to act thoroughly unreasonable in the face of extreme stress, up to and including physically assaulting the people trying to rescue them.

When it came to subduing people in a hurry, Pete knew the value of depriving them of their own breath, so he led with a sucker punch to the solar plexus. Letting out a pain-filled gasp, the Cyberon goon doubled over, allowing Pete to smack the close-door button with his elbow. In the interval before the airlock finished cycling to full pressure, he shoved his involuntary dance partner against the side of the small compartment and gave him another couple of gut punches to keep him honest.

When the inner door opened, he pulled out the half-metre-long metal bar he'd stashed in his leg pouch, and came out swinging. There were two men waiting for him, neither one in an EVA suit. Both were wearing uniforms with Cyberon patches, which only confirmed what he and Mik had already known.

His initial swing took the one on the right in the left shoulder, and Pete felt the snap of a bone transmitted through the bar. The guy screamed and fell away, leaving Pete clear to turn his attention to the third guy. That one started backing away; he'd clearly been prepped to grab and subdue a man and a child at three to two odds, and this was not turning out that way.

Suit-clad, even if he wasn't outside anymore, Pete knew damn well that he was slower than anyone wearing normal clothing. His peripheral vision was also limited, which meant that he had to finish this fight *fast*. His one big advantage was his strength, incidentally allowing him to also move more quickly than expected in the pressure suit.

The guy he was heading for pointed something at him; for a moment Pete thought they'd miscalculated badly, and he was about to be shot. Fortunately, he heard the faint warble of a wireless taser instead and felt the vague tingle of a charge passing across the outside of his suit. But just because the guy had tried something that wasn't going to work didn't mean Pete could relax. Lunging across the intervening distance, he grabbed the guy by the front of his shirt, spun him around, and slammed him against the wall.

Only because he was facing in the right direction did he see the one in the EVA suit coming out of the airlock. Still hunched over a bit from the gut punches, he was clearly recovering by the second. Worse, Pete could see his mouth moving inside his faceplate, indicating that he was on the radio to *someone.*

They were far too close to Burroughs to want to play hide-and-seek with Cyberon security, so he had to shut this down *now.* Dragging his stunned captive back across the room, he swapped the bar to his left hand and rammed it hard into the EVA guy's solar plexus. The guy bent over, and Pete's knee drove into his faceplate. While the faceplate didn't shatter or even crack (they were built tough), it was a solid impact all the same; the guy stumbled sideways and fell over.

Pete turned to check on the one whose collarbone he'd broken, and found him just climbing to his feet. He didn't trust the guy to not cause trouble, so he towed his captive in that direction and kicked the injured one's legs out from under him again. Unsealing his faceplate, he flipped it up. "Danielle Connaught!" he shouted. "Where is she?"

"Wh-what?" asked the injured one. "Who?"

"The Earth girl!" Pete was starting to lose patience. "If someone doesn't give me a straight answer, I'm gonna be tossing one of you in the airlock and cycling it, just to see if that wakes the other one up!" He wasn't sure if he'd actually be able to do it, and he hoped fervently that they wouldn't make him find out.

"Oh, *that* Earth girl," the guy who'd tried to taser him said in tones of groggy enlightenment. "Yeah, she's in room ten-thirty-eight."

Pete flipped his faceplate closed again and keyed his radio. "Papa Juliet calling Mike Whiskey," he said tersely. "I'm in. Guy here says she's in room one-zero-three-eight, do you copy?"

Cyberon Consortium Headquarters, Burroughs
CEO's Office

"What do you mean, you're under attack? Is it the specimen? Is it *there?*"

Adrenaline flushing through his system, Jarn Kolban stood up from his desk. At the same time, he slapped the privacy button, so that the door to his office shut and locked. While there were none under his employ who would dare gainsay his right to do anything he wanted in the interests of furthering Cyberon's market share, it was still a good idea to ensure that nobody heard any details of things they weren't cleared to hear.

The voice he was listening to was pained and labouring, but still audible. *"No, sir, I haven't seen it. Just an Earthman, on foot, in the chaotic terrain. Said he had a hurt kid, then he gut-punched me. Hits like an ore-loader."*

"A hurt child?" He zeroed in on that, to the exclusion of all else. "Did you see the child?"

"No, just a—" There was a burst of static, then silence.

"Say again your last!" he snapped. "Just what? What did you see?"

But the signal had cut out. He was talking to dead air.

Slowly, thinking furiously, Kolban lowered himself back into his chair. It was the specimen. There was no other possible reason for that *specific* complex to be under attack by someone from Earth. The specimen had somehow suborned Orbital Rescue into aiding it in its misguided efforts. It was the only scenario that made any kind of sense.

Fingers moving swiftly, he called up the radar imagery over that area for the previous two hours. No unexplained ships had landed anywhere near the facility in that time; everything that had touched down in the vicinity was accounted for and squawking the appropriate transponder codes. For a moment, he glanced at the trace of a meteorite that had come down on Hesperia Planum, well to the north-east of Hellas Basin. Then he shook his head; the thing had massed no more than a thousand kilograms, far too light for any kind of assault lander.

The only viable explanation was that the specimen and its Earth patsies had come in via ordinary channels and his precautions had missed them altogether. Once it was captured, he'd have to see about backtracking its movements and arranging a suitable punishment for those who'd been asleep at the switch when it came through. But for now, he had to make sure it could not get what it wanted.

Kolban didn't have anywhere near total control of the facility, given that it was outwardly supposed to be owned by interests opposed to those of Cyberon. But he'd arranged the security precautions around the Connaught girl himself, and those he could access and activate. Calling up the appropriate screen, he checked the camera views around the purpose-built cell—originally intended for the specimen itself—then entered a specific command.

                                    Alan M. Atkinson

While the cell itself was airtight, the corridors around it were now a trap. The moment anyone who wasn't authorised to be there showed up on camera, vents would kick open and the atmosphere around the cell would be reduced to that of the outside pressure. If the Earthman had taken off his EVA suit to get to her (and Earthmen *always* got out of their suits as soon as they could), he would die in the near-vacuum of Mars-normal atmosphere. On the other hand, the specimen would survive, but it would be forced to stand helplessly outside the cell in the knowledge that there was no way of getting the Earth girl out without dooming her.

With that taken care of, he sent off pre-prepared messages to his security people. They were to flood the facility and take all intruders prisoner. None but the specimen needed to be captured alive, and even it could die if necessary. Once it (or its body) had been secured in Cyberon's deepest laboratories, the superfluous captives could be disposed of in ways that would obscure their origins and actual cause of death.

Jarn Kolban smiled coldly, flexing his fingers against each other in anticipation of victory. Who said good things didn't come to those who waited?

Chapter 16: Rescue

Mik's mastoid earpiece crackled to life. *"Papa Juliet calling Mike Whiskey. I'm in. Guy here says she's in room one-zero-three-eight, do you copy?"*

"I copy one zero three eight," she replied quietly. She looked up at the room numbers and noted that she was at least on the correct floor. "On way now, over."

It was a good thing that even evil corporate secret facilities had their safety procedures. As she jogged along the corridor in what she thought was the right direction, she spotted an evacuation map of the facility, complete with room numbers. Studying the plan for a moment, she traced out a path, memorised it, then took off running.

Although people fresh from Earth often complained how hard it was to run properly on Mars due to lack of traction, Mik had no such issues indoors. The floors weren't the best for cornering on, but she saw no issue in running halfway up the wall to kick off in the direction she wanted to go. Her enhanced vestibular systems aided considerably in keeping her balance, no matter where her feet were placed at the time.

Now that she knew where she was going, she reached the corridor that she needed in less than a minute. But then she encountered something that wasn't a barrier as such, but certainly caused her to think twice about what was going on.

At first glance, there was little to worry about. What she'd found was an airlock of a make and model ubiquitous to half the buildings on Mars. Given that the outside atmosphere of Mars could only be survived by *one* person currently on the surface of the planet, the presence of an airlock would normally have been easy to explain away as an essential safety precaution.

What gave Mik pause was the fact that the airlock was *inside* the building, and in fact was between her and the person she was here to rescue. This made her ask herself a very specific question:

Which side of this airlock is expected to be depressurised, and why?

There was only one logical answer, and it did nothing for her peace of mind. If she had this figured out, the person behind Dani's abduction had set up the circumstances of her imprisonment with lethal intent. This was a deliberate screw-you aimed at Mik; left where she was, Dani wouldn't die immediately, but any attempt to get her out would push the meter from zero to fatal in very little time indeed. And if the airlock was code-locked on the other side, it would also serve to trap Mik inside, allowing Cyberon to simply walk in and scoop her up at their leisure.

If I keep going, I'll be trapped, and she dies no matter what. Cyberon security's probably on the way, so Pete might not be able to get us both out in time. If we pull back, they might decide she's no use as bait and kill her anyway. Bad end, do not want.

Okay, so I've seen the trap. How do I turn it around?

Dani

The cell was cold, the floor hard to sleep on, and the ration bars they'd been feeding her tasted like salted sawdust, but that wasn't the worst part. Dani had been uncomfortable before; some of the places her father had worked had lacked many civilised creature comforts. But she'd had friendly company and she'd been able to keep track of what was going on in the larger world.

Here, she had neither.

She wasn't sure if it was deliberate torture or just a total lack of care factor about her wellbeing, but the lighting outside the Perspex panel that fronted her cell never varied. Neither dim nor overbright, it was just constant. They'd taken her watch at the same time as they'd sequestered the rest of her belongings and shoved her into an anonymous coverall, so she had no way of keeping track of time, except by way of her biological rhythms and the delivery of the food and water rations (which in itself was worryingly irregular, like they kept forgetting that she needed to eat and drink).

Even the Suit, as she called him (she didn't have a name for him, but she had a *huge* number of highly unflattering descriptors for him) hadn't shown up in some time. At first, she'd been able to mark off the days in her mind by his visits, either gloating over how Mik was going to walk straight into his trap or attempting to interrogate her about Mik's habits and potential actions. She'd given him no joy either way, which in hindsight was possibly a mistake, as he hadn't visited in some time.

All she got these days was a guy walking past the cell every few hours and glancing in to make sure she hadn't miraculously dismantled the lock and spirited herself out of the building. They didn't talk to her, even when she called out and tried to open lines of communication. She knew they could hear her, but their faces just closed off and they walked on.

It had been many days, she was sure of that much. A month, maybe two? She couldn't be sure. Sometimes she dreamed she'd been rescued, or that the cell wall had opened up and she'd walked out; the emotional crashes when she woke and discovered the reality of the situation were devastating. Pretty soon, she figured, she'd be hallucinating even when she was awake, and it wouldn't matter anymore.

So, when she saw Mik herself step into view in front of the cell, wearing her usual t-shirt and jeans and heavy boots, along with a badass-looking long-coat, she didn't bother to react at first. Either it was someone else and her eyes were playing tricks on her, or she was asleep and dreaming the whole thing, or her mind had finally cracked. Didn't matter: Mik wasn't there.

She waited for the apparition of her friend to morph into one of the guards or to evaporate altogether, or maybe rip the door off its runners, but none of that happened. Instead, Mik examined the lock and frowned. Then she pulled out a notebook and pencil—pens had a really hard time working in vacuum, so Mik always went old-school when it came to passing notes—and scribbled something.

Dani had never been able to read a damn thing in a dream. The words and letters always came jumbled up, probably because reading was a logical thing, and dreams were by their nature illogical. So, she was fully prepared for whatever pure gibberish the note showed to be.

Instead, to her surprise, it was totally readable. NO AIR OUT HERE. PREP FOR DECOMPRESS, CLOSE EYES. WILL GET U OUT. DO U TRUST ME?

She read it through several times, trying to make sense of it. Mik was still standing there, waiting, though she'd glanced from side to side a couple of times. The writing on the notepad was holding steady, not changing to something else.

Is this real? Is this actually happening?

Tears sprang to her eyes as she first began to allow herself to consider the concept. She tried to keep herself under control; every other time she'd believed she was getting out, her expectations had been cruelly dashed. But she could read the note. She could *read* the *note.*

Climbing painfully to her feet—there was little chance for exercise in the cell, and the nutrient bars had left her with zero excess energy—she went over to the Perspex panel that served as a door. "Are you real?" she asked, putting her hand on the panel. "Are you really there?"

Mik nodded, then flipped a page and scribbled some more. IM REAL. IM GETTING U OUT OF THERE. DO U TRUST ME? Then she tore the page from the pad and dropped it.

Instead of fluttering lazily to the ground—under Martian gravity, it always took even longer than it did on Earth—it fell straight down, at the standard three point seven metres per second squared.

Okay, that's not something a hallucination would bring up. There's only Martian air pressure out there. She'd had dreams of walking unprotected on the surface of Mars. The human brain couldn't create the consequences of low air pressure out of whole cloth. That was a leap of logic that it couldn't make.

Dani took a deep breath and nodded. "I trust you," she said, aware that Mik was practised at reading lips. "I just don't know how long I can go without air." Attempting to hold one's breath in micro-pressure, she knew, was a recipe for ruptured lungs. "Should I hyperventilate?"

Instead of writing more notes, Mik made the hand gestures for *'no time'*, then pointed at her first note. Dani nodded, then stepped back. Closing her eyes, she opened her mouth, working her jaw to allow her ear canals to connect to her sinus cavities.

She heard it when the door began to open, the thin high screech of escaping air, deepening to a rumble as the air pressure dropped. Her ears popped, then popped again as she kept working her jaw. Air flowed out of her lungs, then an involuntary belch joined it.

Her skin prickled and her eyes were uncomfortable behind her tightly closed eyelids, but she didn't dare open them. Micro-pressure did nasty things to exposed eyeballs; they didn't pop (that was something even the stupidest of space dramas didn't do anymore), but the sheen of tears on the exterior surface had been known to freeze or evaporate, neither of which was good for the eye.

Pressure was building unpleasantly in her gut, and she did her best to relax her sphincters. Another burp was followed by a small *frrrt*, and she silently blessed the fact that the nutrient bars were designed for vacuum workers, who didn't want to share their pressure suits with abdominal gases.

And then a mouthpiece was pressed over her face, and air flowed into her lungs. Reaching up, she grabbed the pony bottle, amazed that she'd actually forgotten how Mik carried it everywhere. Once Dani had it, Mik let go and grabbed her arm, urging her forward.

Under the guidance of her friend, she stumbled out of the cell then turned left. They moved as fast as she was able, though she had to keep her eyes closed. How Mik had located her and then gotten into the Cyberon facility, and what the plan was to get her out, she wasn't sure, but she trusted her friend implicitly.

They went down the length of one corridor and then another one, much farther than she would've been able to go with her eyes closed and no air. Alone, she would've stumbled aimlessly until she died. Then they entered what she figured was an airlock, the supposition borne out when a door closed behind them and the air pressure started rising.

When she felt it was safe, she opened her eyes and handed the pony bottle back to Mik. "Th-thanks," she rasped, her voice rusty from disuse. "You came back. I didn't know if you would."

"It's been a month, let me tell you," Mik said lightly. "I had to go a hell of a long way for reinforcements, but here I am."

Something clanked at floor level, and Dani looked down to see that Mik had just knocked over a bucket. "Okay, what's a bucket doing in an airlock?"

"Holding the inner door open so nobody can lock it remotely behind me," Mik explained. The outer airlock door opened, and she stepped through. "C'mon, we've got places to be."

Dani followed along. Her joints still felt creaky and stiff, but she was *damned* if she was going to slow Mik down now. "Where'd you go for reinforcements? Tharsis? Wouldn't they just send stern memos to Cyberon or something?"

"Yeah, that's why I didn't go to them." As Mik and Dani turned a corner, Dani saw two of the guards on the ground, along with a third one in an EVA suit, and a *fourth* person in a vacuum-rated pressure suit standing over them with a metal bar in his hand. "Hey, we're ready to suit up and go."

The standing man flipped up his faceplate. "Good. The suit's just outside. I'll keep watching these clowns while you go get it."

"On it." Mik tipped Dani a wink, then ducked out through the airlock. A moment later, she was back, dragging in a pressure suit in Dani's size.

"I was *wondering* how you were going to get me out of here." Dani didn't waste time, starting to haul on the suit even as she addressed Mik. She didn't know the guy, but Mik trusted him, so she was totally willing to give him the benefit of the doubt.

"It was either this or terraform the whole planet so you could just walk out normally, and terraforming was taking too long." Mik eyed the guards unfavourably. "How badly were these assholes treating you?"

"They didn't hit me or anything," Dani said. "Just fed me and watched me. It was their boss who said all the nasty stuff about how you were gonna fall in his trap."

"Mmm." Mik looked like she didn't want to drop the matter, but the guy put his hand on her shoulder, and she subsided. "Okay, then. Ready?"

"Nearly." Dani locked her helmet in place, then triggered the oxygen flow. The telltales showed up green, so she nodded and gave the thumb-to-forefinger all-good gesture.

The guy with Mik flipped down his faceplate, and all three of them stepped into the airlock, which was big enough to fit them all with room to spare. *"We're going to have to move fast,"* the guy said over her radio. *"I have a feeling Cyberon security will be incoming with everything they've got."*

"Yeah, no crap." That was definitely Mik. *"Just by the way: Pete, meet Dani; Dani, meet Pete."*

"*Pleased to meet you,*" Pete added. "*Lieutenant Pete Janssen, Orbital Rescue, at your service.*"

Even while Dani was trying to figure out what an Orbital Rescue pilot was doing on the surface of Mars, the airlock opened and they hustled out. The surrounding terrain was the very opposite of flat, and Dani had no idea which way to go. And then Mik's eyes opened wide, and she turned her head, looking up into the sky.

"*Lander,*" she said. "*I can hear it coming in.*"

Dani had very little experience with matters like this, but she had an idea what was coming next anyway. "They'll be bringing in ground troops, won't they? Looking for us?"

"*Got it in one.*" Mik started off into the rocks. "*We have to get to the 'hopper before they catch up with us.*"

"*Copy that, princess.*" Pete hooked one arm under Dani's. "*Let's move.*"

Dani had thought the nightmare was over but as she discovered, it was just beginning. Even with Pete and Mik helping her up and over the obstacles in their way, she quickly ran out of energy. Fear-generated adrenaline was well and good, but it had its limits, and her arms and legs were soon powerless noodles.

"Leave me," she begged. "If they catch you, this'll all be for nothing."

"*And if we leave you, it'll also be for nothing,*" Mik told her grimly. "*I had to do it once. It's not happening a second time.*"

"*Take her.*" That was Pete. "*I'll go and draw them off. Even if they catch me, they can't—*"

Mik cut him off. "*If they can't use you to get us back, they'll kill you. You take her, you can carry her if necessary. If they've got guns, which I'm pretty sure they do, they're less likely to shoot at me than you. I'll meet you at the 'hopper.*"

Not giving Pete the option to argue, she let go Dani's arm and vanished into the chaotic terrain.

"*Wait—*" began Pete, but it was too late. "*Dammit! Okay fine, she's not giving us a choice. Let's get to the 'hopper.*"

As they moved off, Dani had to ask the question. "Why did you call her princess, earlier?"

"*Well, she'd just told us her story, and I made a joke ...*"

Mik

The security troopers were good at moving in EVA suits, and these ones definitely had guns. There were also a lot of them, which was going to make this tricky as hell. Still, Mik had a few advantages on her side, some of which they hopefully didn't know about.

She peered around a rocky outcrop at a bunch of them, who were conferring over some kind of digital map. If they wanted to use that thing to make any kind of straight path through this labyrinth of Martian terrain, they had to be dreaming. The trouble was, if they just pushed forward en masse, they could comb every last hiding place, no matter how tricky she was. Which was why she had to pull them away from the '*logical thinking*' mindset and into the '*chase me*' mindset.

Picking up a friable-looking rock, she stepped into view, then hurled her missile directly at the faceplate of one of the troopers facing her. It burst on impact, leaving a cloud of dust behind. Before they could bring their guns to bear, she ducked out of sight again, heading down a twisting, turning alleyway of rock. Her natural agility and balance made up for the uneven footing, allowing her to move much faster than the troopers behind her.

The call would be going out now, converging every security trooper in the area on that spot. This included any of them that might've been on course to discover the rille where she and Pete had hidden the rock-hopper. If they were chasing her, they weren't going after anyone else.

She paused after a minute or so of movement, listening hard with her hands on the rocks on either side. Sound didn't travel well in this atmosphere, though her ears were attuned to pick up what little there was. Vibrations through the ground were sometimes more useful, and she fancied she could feel the security troops coming her way, just as much as she could hear the scuffing and stumbling among the chaotically tumbled boulders.

The next time she nailed someone in the faceplate with a rock, one of the troopers shot at her. It didn't come close enough to worry her, though the whole experience of being shot at in general was a new and unpleasant one. She got her target though, dusting the man plus his comrades with the ever-present fines. The fewer of her pursuers who could see properly, the better.

And then Pete's voice crackled in her mastoid earpiece. *"We're at the 'hopper. Want a pickup?"*

"No, don't," she replied, talking quietly into the mouthpiece even though she knew the troopers couldn't hear her. "They'll shoot you out of the sky. Hold tight, I'm coming to you."

A dozen troopers swung around as she jumped out of concealment, almost within arm's reach. She was holding two large rocks that she'd selected carefully, each with the consistency of chalk. Both left her hands before her feet touched down; not aimed at the troopers, they instead hit the rocks on either side. A great cloud of fines billowed over all the troopers, but she wasn't waiting around for it to dissipate.

There was a nice straight pathway for her to retreat down, but she didn't take it. Instead, she ducked into the first niche she found that was barely large enough to take her, crouched down, then flipped up the hood of the long-coat so that it covered her head. Thus concealed, facing the rock and holding still, she hopefully looked like part of the landscape.

She both heard and felt the rush of booted feet behind her; yelling inside their helmets so loudly that she heard that too. Thirty seconds ticked by in her head, and there were no stragglers following along. Cautiously, she peered out from behind the hood. She was alone.

By now there would be enough troopers spread through the chaotic terrain for false sightings to be happening on the regular, and in fact she heard a few random shots here and there which bore out that idea. But that wasn't her problem, so she slipped unseen through the dragnet until she came to the rille. Jumping from foothold to foothold, she descended to where Pete and Dani were just getting settled on the rock-hopper.

"Oh, good," Pete said. *"You're here. I was starting to worry."*

"Can we go now?" asked Dani plaintively. *"I just want to get out of here."*

"We can," Mik confirmed, scrambling up onto the rock-hopper and strapping herself into the middle seat. She flicked the wake-up switch on the upgraded flight control computer (also supplied by McPherson), then activated the controls and lit off the attitude rockets. Slowly, then with more power as she fed fuel to the main rocket, the rock-hopper climbed into the air.

"Straight back up to the ship?" That was Pete.

Mik shook her head. "Not quite. They've almost certainly got ships up there that can shoot us down if they see us coming up out of their area of interest, so we're going to have to stay low for the moment until we get out from under their umbrella. Our best chance for doing that is to leave their turf altogether. And I know just the place."

Angling the rock-hopper westward, she applied more thrust. They shot away across the tumbled landscape.

Chapter 17: Working Things Out

In the minimal Martian atmosphere, the rock-hopper could maintain a considerable over-ground velocity without suffering significant drag, but they were a long way from safety. Fully aware that she was going to be pushing the 'hopper to the outer edge of its range, Mik kept a careful eye on the flight control computer, working to extend that range as far as possible. Her genemods assisted in this, allowing her to gauge the local kPa and the performance of the rock-hopper even more precisely than the sensors attached to the computer.

Travelling slower would increase fuel efficiency slightly, but balanced against that was the distance they had to travel and the available air in Pete's and Dani's pressure suits. The spare tanks they'd brought along would help, but their air still wouldn't last forever. Fortunately, it didn't have to; it just had to last long enough.

"So, uh, where are we going?" asked Pete after a few minutes. *"Because I don't know how much fuel we need to go for orbit, but it's got to be more than we used coming down, especially with a third person on board."*

Dani leaned forward and poised her hands over the flight control computer. When Mik gave her a nod of assent, she started typing in calculations, using the pre-loaded formulae. After a few moments, she sat back again. *"We've only got a narrow window if we want to try for orbit. Another ten minutes at this rate, and we'll be past the cutoff point."*

Mik shook her head. "We're not going to try. Still too close to Burroughs. If we broke radar shadow and made a run for it, they'd be vectoring ships on us like fines on exposed circuitry. We'd never be able to climb fast or far enough."

Pete proved he could read a screen with the best of them. *"And I don't care how good a hotshot pilot you are, we'll never make it all the way to Tharsis."* He turned to face Mik. *"So, spill. Where are we going?"*

"Marineris." The name tasted sour in her mouth, but she forced herself to keep talking. "I want to pay my respects, and pick up some stuff I left behind." And although she didn't mention it, in a pouch on her belt were several items she'd brought from Mars, and now she was returning them. In a manner of speaking.

"What stuff?" The catch in Dani's voice indicated that she was still suffering emotionally from being reminded of where her parents had died. Mik had also gone through it, but she'd started when she began planning the operation. She'd never be *okay* with knowing that Professor Ibrahim and the rest had all died because they'd been deemed surplus to requirements, but she could deal with it for the moment.

"Remember what I did after we blew the shuttle? Yeah, that stuff." Saying it like that, Mik felt like a character in a bad spy drama, but on the outside possibility that Cyberon had a satellite in low orbit focusing a high-gain dish on them, she figured cryptic was better than just saying it in the clear.

"*Oh.*" Dani remembered; from her nod, she understood what Mik intended.

"*Ah.*" Although he hadn't been there, Pete had been briefed on everything Mik and Dani had done from the moment Mik realised something was wrong to the point she overdid the acceleration toward Earth. His response, little more than an exhalation, indicated that he'd also figured it out.

They shot onward, over the unforgiving Martian terrain. Pete was bigger and bulkier than Dani, but he had long practice with conserving his oh-two intake, so they were closer in consumption rates than Mik would've immediately thought. This was good, because they only had one spare tank apiece.

The rock-hopper was travelling at what would've been a shade over twice the speed of sound on Earth, but the wind-rush was barely noticeable. Her only real worry was for dust storms; fortunately, the sun was bright and clear whenever she checked it, so that fear at least could take a back seat.

The rocket engine thundered endlessly, its noise a comforting background rumble, while the Martian landscape rolled by under them.

Cyberon Consortium Headquarters, Burroughs
CEO's Office

"Does anyone have anything?"

Jarn Kolban sat in his made-to-order chair and glowered out through the triple-paned window at Hellas Planitia. The floor of Hellas Basin, it was over two thousand kilometres across. This meant that for someone standing at one end of Hellas Basin, the crater rim at the far side would be out of sight over the horizon.

Usually, he liked to consider the view as proof that he exerted control over an area that could not be observed all at once, except from orbit. Now, it mocked him, since the specimen had broken its human 'friend' out of holding and vanished over that self-same horizon.

"*Uh …*" There was a long pause after that first noise. "*I think we might know where the specimen is going, sir.*" It was his personal assistant.

"Tell. Me." Kolban would hunt the specimen down, wherever it went. Never mind that the Board of Directors disapproved of his fixation on it. He had the veto power; more importantly, he had leverage over each and every one of them, stored on the computer built into his desk. They *would* do as he said, or he would ruin their careers forever.

The specimen would be his, and with it the keys to a brand-new Mars. If just one teenage specimen could pull off such a coup, a company of spec-ops trained Martian Walker soldiers could dominate the planet.

"Sir, uh, we just got a datadump from one of our ships in orbit. They picked up a fragmentary message from west of the facility. Only a few words, but one came through clearly. 'Marineris'."

He sat up, his eyes widening. "Marineris. Are you sure?" But even as he asked the question, he knew it was correct. That was where the specimen had been created. It was returning to the only place it knew. What it intended to do there, he had no idea. Perhaps attempt to nest in the burned-out ruins like a wild animal. But that didn't matter; what mattered was that he knew where it would be.

"That's what the datadump said, sir."

"Good." Kolban came to his feet and paced across his office. The smart-mic on his desk followed him with its sound dish, so that every word would come through crisply. "Launch a combat shuttle, with a dozen men. Give orders that anyone else accompanying the specimen is superfluous to requirements. If the specimen can be captured alive, do it, but it's not essential. A tissue sample is all I really need."

"Yes, sir. On it, sir."

"Good. Report back to me when the specimen is in hand."

"Yes, sir."

The end-connection beep sounded, but Kolban barely heard it. Pacing over to the window, he leaned against it and stared out at the raw Martian landscape. Triumph filled his soul, and he laughed harshly. "You think you've won, don't you? You think I can't get you. Well, you little abomination, even if you leave Mars, even if you go all the way back to Earth, I'll follow you and I'll have you dragged back here, to where you belong. Under. My. Control."

It had been a long month, but now everything was coming together.

*It will be mine. And when I've properly leveraged it, **Mars** will be mine.*

Two Hours Later

The EVA-suited figure was face-down and covered with a dusting of fines, but Mik caught a glimpse of it as the rock-hopper blitzed past, fifty metres up. So did Pete, from the way he craned his head around to stare back along their path. Dani's light snores indicated that the girl was asleep in her suit, for which Mik didn't blame her.

"Did you see that?" Pete gestured back toward the now-distant suit. *"That man was in trouble."*

Mik shook her head, her weariness more emotional than physical. "He's dead. Been that way for a month." Even if she hadn't known the exact reason for his death, anyone who lay still long enough for fines to collect on them had to be deceased.

Another suit whipped under them, then another. Pete stared at her. *"Were they from …?"*

"Marineris, yeah." The second word was more of a sigh. "These guys must've tried to drive out, then started walking when they ran out of fuel." The truck passed under them; from the looks of it, the front end was hung up on a slightly larger rock than normal. It had never been intended as an all-terrain vehicle, and there were no roads in this part of Mars. The pile of rocks on the cargo bed probably hadn't helped. She thought she'd seen a suit slumped over the wheel, but it might have been her imagination.

"Jeez. Why didn't they just, you know, call for help?" They passed by an all-wheel-drive, upside down in a small rille. Someone hadn't been watching where they were driving.

Mik took a quick breath from the pony bottle. "Because they burned the complex, where our radio setup was, and I blew up their shuttle, where *their* radio setup was. The vehicles didn't have radios, just larger antennae for the suits to plug into. We didn't need a great amount of range. Someone would have to be pointing a dish straight at them to pick up any Mayday calls."

He was silent for a few moments. *"I suspect some were rescued, from the details in the accusations they made against you. But from the looks of this, most weren't."*

Mik had already come to the same conclusion. "Yeah."

She didn't wish on anyone the fate of dying alone out on the Martian surface, watching the needle on their air gauge reaching the bottom of the red and then choking on nothing thereafter. During her time at the Marineris facility, there'd been enough accidents and close calls that she felt real empathy toward those who suffered such tribulations. On the other hand, she couldn't help feeling that those who had killed Professor Ibrahim and his fellow researchers might just *deserve* such a prolonged and agonising death.

Had she crossed a line she couldn't uncross? She didn't know if it was even her call to make.

She'd deliberately blown up the shuttle, cutting them off from their only real form of transport out of there. At the time, she'd known exactly what she was doing, and not cared. Now, a month older and wiser, without the immediacy of the moment to spur her along, she was beginning to wonder if she should've paused and reconsidered her actions.

Pete was a good man, someone whose opinion she valued quite highly. Over and above that, he'd literally made a career of saving lives. If there was anyone she could depend on to be unbiased in the matter, it was him.

"Pete?" The ground was rising under them, and she adjusted their altitude upward a little. It wouldn't last; the long since dried-up outflow of Marineris had turned to the north before all the water evaporated or sank into the ground, so they had a short stretch of highlands to cross before they entered the canyon proper.

"Yeah?" He turned his whole upper body to look at her. *"What's on your mind?"*

"When I blew the shuttle, I killed these guys, didn't I?" No asking for absolution, no excuses. Just the facts, and a question.

"You did. Are you asking if you were justified? Taking revenge when you could've just left?"

"It wasn't just revenge." The shuttle could have easily followed them into orbit. It was what shuttles were *for.* "But mainly, yeah."

He was slow in answering. *"I don't know if I would've done exactly the same. I'm from the United States, like Dani. Sure, we've got a pop-culture tradition of lone heroes going against the grain, but we've also got laws aplenty. What happened here wouldn't happen there. Or if it did, there'd be a regulatory body that would come down on Cyberon with both feet. Here, you're very much in the same place as those pop-culture heroes, where not fighting back means capture or death, and there's nobody both willing and able to uphold what laws you've got."*

The highlands dropped away again, forming a steep downslope. As Mik adjusted her altitude downward again, she spotted the wreckage of the second all-wheel-drive, half-buried under rocky detritus.

Must've hotwired it after I took the key. Much good it did them.

It looked as though the driver had tried to take it up the slope and triggered an avalanche. Mars had thirty-nine percent of Earth's gravity, but that didn't mean the landscape was any more forgiving: cliffs were higher, and rockslides went farther.

Pete fell silent then, perhaps mulling over what he was going to say next. Mik watched the nearest canyon wall start to rise above them; the farthest one was out of sight over the horizon. Still, she knew they'd reached the Valles itself, indicating that there was only a short way to go. This was good: the fuel readout was already perilously low, and getting lower by the second.

"Which means …?" she prompted.

His sigh was audible over the radio link. *"Which means that you're in the position of an Old West lawman, possibly apocryphal, who once said, **'There's more men needing shooting than horses needing stealing.'** In a place with no law, you are the law. Cyberon started this by killing your people. If you could stop them, you were right to. And it's not like those men who died out there were innocent in all this."*

"No, true, it's not. They all either participated, or stood back and let their buddies do the dirty work." Of this, she was certain. Cyberon had enough money, and Pure Strain had enough fanatics, that there'd been no *'reluctantly going along with it'* types at Marineris on that day. "Just one question. What if they don't stop, just keep chasing me and Dani?"

Pete nodded to acknowledge her words. *"In a perfect world, I'd say to remove yourself from the situation and let the law handle it. It's not a perfect world, so I'm just going to say, protect yourself any way you can. I've seen you in action. If they want to play stupid games, I've got no sympathy for them when they win stupid prizes."*

"Wow." At some point, Dani had woken up, and now she spoke. *"That's pretty blunt, coming from a guy whose job is literally to save idiots from the consequences of their own actions."* There was a teasing note to her voice, though Mik suspected at least part of it was an attempt to distract herself from thinking about her recent ordeal.

Pete snorted. *"The Coast Guard down on Earth still goes armed, because not everyone they meet is a good guy. Right here and now, you two are my sole responsibility. Other than that? Not my planet, not my jurisdiction."*

Which fitted perfectly with Mik's experience of the man. During her time on OR-5, Commander Kenworth had exuded 'protective uncle' vibes, bending regulations as needed to arrange Mik's return to Mars with Pete and Marj. Pete, on the other hand, had stepped right into the 'older brother' role, showing her around the station and setting aside a place for her to call her own while she was there.

"Well, let's hope it doesn't come to that." Mik nodded in lieu of pointing ahead. "ETA thirty seconds. Brace yourself." The warning was more for Dani than Pete; seeing the place where their respective families had been brutally murdered (the Marineris research team, especially Professor Ibrahim and Kathy, had been just as much Mik's family as any more traditional arrangements) would be an unavoidable emotional jolt.

Dani bit her lip and nodded jerkily. *"Okay, I think I'm ready."*

Already starting to decelerate, they lofted over a low rise. The remains of the Marineris facility came into view before them. Dani audibly gasped over the radio link, and Mik found herself blinking in astonishment.

Because there was a massive crawler there with Tharsis markings, and the site was swarming with people.

Okay, yeah, I didn't expect this.

Chapter 18: Marineris

Dani's voice came over the radio. *"Those are the good guys … right?"* She had evidently seen the markings on top of the crawler, but it seemed she still wasn't ready to take everything at face value.

Mik privately approved of that thought process. "Technically yes, but don't trust them."

By the time she'd said it, they'd swept clear over the top of the gutted ruin of the Marineris complex—people below looking up and pointing—and were bearing down on the ad hoc construction training area. In fact, due to her distraction, they were going to overshoot. She began a harder deceleration and swung the rock-hopper around in a huge circle that terminated back at the construction area. As the 'hopper settled onto the dusty ground next to a large dirt berm, the rocket motors started to stutter and miss, so she shut them down.

She'd known it was going to be tight, but not *that* tight.

It was eerie, returning to a place she'd been only a month ago. So much had happened in the interim that it felt like years. Still, there were the crisp, clear wheel-tracks of the AWDs, the loader, and the truck; all absent now. The dozer was still there, which didn't surprise her in the slightest. If they'd managed to move it, *that* would've astonished her.

"Dani, do you remember if there were spare oh-two tanks in the shack?" As she asked the question, she unbuckled her belt and climbed down off the rock-hopper.

"I think there were. I'll go check." Given a purpose, Dani roused herself and jumped down as well. While she hadn't had the intensive training that Mik had gotten in using the construction equipment, she'd enjoyed making herself useful in small ways, and had become familiar with the equipment stored in the shack.

Pete followed Mik as she headed for the dozer. *"Wait, what did you mean when you said not to trust them? Aren't they your parent company?"*

"They are, and that's the problem." Mik swung herself up into the open cab of the bulldozer. Designed for EVA-suited operators, it had worked just fine for her, once she'd adjusted the seat and controls for her smaller frame. "Remember, Marineris engineered my genome more or less from scratch, so the paperwork says that I'm their property. On Mars, I have no legal rights unless someone chooses to give me some."

"And they're not going to do that?" He seemed to be wrestling with the idea, even though Mik had discussed the broader topic with him a few times. *"Why wouldn't they? I mean, conscript syndrome is a thing. They'd be a lot better off having you work with them willingly."*

"You'd think that, but no." She settled into the driver's seat, then leaned forward and popped open the same inspection panel she'd accessed when she was last in this position. Unzipping the pouch on her belt, she took out the electronic components that she'd been carrying all this time. Each one slotted back into place with nary a problem, and she closed the panel with equal ease. "See, these execs don't want to gamble on their genetic constructs choosing to work with them. They want a sure thing. So the way their lobbyists have shaped Martian laws, I'm not a person so much as a biological robot. Emotions and the need for personal agency? Superfluous to efficient functionality."

Professor Ibrahim had thought differently. He and the rest of the staff at the Marineris complex had treated her as their child or younger sibling, and raised her accordingly. She'd had her own space, access to entertainment and leisure time, and the chance to express herself however she liked. While it hadn't been a normal life, it had been *her* life, and she'd been enjoying herself.

There was one other thing that Ibrahim had alluded to a couple of times; she didn't know precisely what it was, but she intended to check it out the instance she got the chance to do so. In the meantime, however, she had something else to collect. Pressing the start button, she grinned as the dozer rumbled to life.

The airlock into the construction shack opened, and Dani came out with a pair of oxygen tanks. *"Found them!"*

"Nicely done." Mik gestured to Pete. "Help him with his and change yours out, then see if you can locate the shaker siphon." She knew the Cyberon guys hadn't taken it, because the bulldozer's fuel gauge was still showing mostly full.

Not even bothering to ask questions, Dani came over and assisted Pete with changing his lowest-pressure tank out for a fresh one, then accepted his help with doing the same for hers. Taking both used oxy-tanks with her, she headed back toward the construction shack.

Checking her mirrors, Mik looked over her shoulder before pulling the lever to raise the blade. She could've just gone, given that Pete was in plain view, but the habits of safety that Dani's father had drummed into her were pervasive. Also, she wasn't about to disparage Kyle's memory like that.

With the blade raised, the dozer trundled backward with zero hassles, then she turned it and drove it up onto the berm alongside the rock-hopper. Another press of the start button shut it down, and she climbed off the machine and headed back to where Pete was waiting. When she got there, he was eyeing the wreckage that had been crunched into the ground under the dozer's tracks.

"And that's it?" he asked. *"All the research material?"*

"Everything that wasn't nailed down, and a few things that were." Mik went to one knee alongside the line of the dozer track. "All the backup drives. Probably a few genetic samples." The latter would be well and truly ruined, having been crushed then exposed to the raw Martian soil for a month, but the former were a lot more robust. She began to sort through the bits and pieces, finding it considerably easier than he would have. "I'm subject number three one one three six eight. They can have the rest. I don't care."

As she spoke, she located a storage drive with that number emblazoned on it. She took a moment to examine it; while scratched and scuffed here and there, it wasn't even cracked. *Good.* Those things were built to take serious punishment; if they were breached in any way, it was game over, but actually damaging them took a lot of effort. The drive went into her pocket, and she kept looking.

"Found it!" Dani emerged from the shack, bearing the shaker siphon. Looking around, she evidently spotted the dozer up on the berm. *"Right. We're refuelling the 'hopper, then?"*

"Got it in one." Mik grinned; Dani was pretty fast on the uptake. "We're gonna have company really soon, so it'll be good to have the option of leaving in a hurry." She didn't necessarily think it was going to come to that, but *'better to have and not need'* was an attitude she'd learned from Professor Ibrahim.

"On it." Dani headed toward the bulldozer at a fast trot.

"Need a hand?" Pete crouched down awkwardly next to Mik as she went back to sorting through the wreckage of the crushed crates.

Mik gauged his ability to work through the bits and pieces as fast as she was, then shook her head as she heard the whine of approaching engines. "No, I'm just about done here. If you could run interference with the Tharsis guys for me, that would be great."

Pete

"I can do that." Straightening up again, Pete turned toward the road leading to the main complex. "They're not going to just come in shooting, are they?"

"I sincerely doubt it." She sounded sure of herself. *"I'm their proof of concept, and one of two living witnesses to what Cyberon has been doing."*

"Well, that's good." He took several steps away from her, toward the rising dust that he could see over the road. Up until now, he'd been going anonymous, but now he reached into a pouch and slapped his Orbital Rescue insignia onto the pressure suit. It probably wouldn't impress them for long, but even a few minutes might be useful. Also, it would help distance him in their minds from their Cyberon rivals.

The two all-wheel-drives came skidding around the nearest low hill, wheels barely holding traction in the low gravity despite the chunky, knobbly tyres. They were painted in the same colours as the crawler and the men riding in them wore sleek EVA suits, possibly incorporating body armour. Most ominous, they carried pistols and SMGs, no doubt adapted for Martian conditions.

Raising his hands in the most obvious 'we come in peace' gesture he could perform, Pete walked forward slowly. "Hey," he said, knowing they probably couldn't hear him but could see his face. "Good to see you. Can you hear me? Lieutenant Pete Janssen, Orbital Rescue."

When he was halfway through saying it, the dead air in his earpiece turned into the static of a carrier wave. *"Orbital Rescue? Where the hell did you come in from?"* The voice was sharp and commanding. One of the men who got out of the AWDs was wearing black and red patches on his shoulders, and the others deferred to him; Pete decided that he had to be the one doing the talking.

"Burroughs, actually." He kept his hands up, noticing how a couple of the men put their hands on their guns when he mentioned the name. "The girl back there at the rock-hopper, her name's Danielle Connaught. She was abducted by them, and we just got her out."

"Still doesn't explain what you're doing here." The man in the decorated EVA suit stopped in front of him. *"And for God's sake, put your hands down. We're Tharsis security, not Cyberon gun-thugs."*

"Thanks." Pete did as he was told. Nobody was aiming a weapon at him yet, so that was a bonus. "When Mik Wallace came through our orbital space asking for help, I volunteered for the duty. Came back here to rescue her friend. Soon as we're refuelled, we'll be out of your hair."

"Slow down a bit there. Nobody's going anywhere until we've got answers to our questions." The ranking guy didn't reach for his pistol, but the air of tension over the whole group redoubled. Pete mentally crossed out the 'until we've got answers' section of his statement. This guy wasn't about to let anyone go anywhere at all, end of story.

"You want answers?" That was Mik's voice. She strolled up alongside him, as nonchalantly as anyone could while walking around unprotected on the Martian surface. *"Cyberon landed a shuttle painted like one of yours. They murdered everyone in the complex and torched the place. Dani and I were right here when they came to get us. We fought back, I wrecked their shuttle, then we got the hell out of here on that rock-hopper. They grabbed Dani after we stopped off at the Stickney depot on Phobos. Then I went to Earth and asked for help."* She tilted her head toward Pete. *"I got it. End of story."*

The security guy didn't actually salute her, but he certainly reacted with a little more deference than he'd shown Pete. *"You're actually **the** Mik Wallace? The Martian Walker?"*

If she'd had eyebrows, she would've raised one right then. As it was, the skin over her right eye wrinkled slightly. *"You see anyone else outside without a suit right now?"*

"They say Cyberon's working on cybernetic enhancements to do the same thing." He wasn't arguing with her, so much as politely raising an opposing viewpoint.

She made a rude noise inside the air mask. *"When one of them can work outside for a complete sol without any problems, then I'll believe it. We both know fines can screw up circuitry faster than solar flares can."* A 'sol', Pete had learned, was a Martian day, 40 minutes longer than a regular Earth day.

"Okay, yeah, point. So, we're going to need you to come back to Tharsis Central with us, so we can debrief you on everything that happened." His tone of voice indicated that it was very much a done deal. *"Your friends are free to return to Earth."*

She shook her head. *"Like you said, slow down there a bit. Before I go anywhere, I'm going to need to see everything you pulled out of the complex. There's stuff in there that I want."*

Pete wasn't sure where she was going with this. If Dani got the rock-hopper going and he delayed the security guys until Mik got on, then they *might* get out of there without anyone shooting at them, but he really didn't want to bet on their restraint. Tharsis had poured billions of dollars—both Martian and Earth currency—into developing Mik's genome, and would not be willing to just let her go.

Right now, they were playing nice, hoping to keep her on side. The moment she started really pushing back, that was likely to change. Pete had a sinking feeling that he and Dani would transition from 'bystanders' to 'inconveniences' at some point, and he hoped to avoid that point until he could engineer an out for all three of them.

Fortunately, the security chief was still talking to her. *"Right now, Tharsis' well-being hinges on us taking back as much as we can find. We're salvaging what we can, but all the research is gone, including the backup drives. Cyberon's got all that. They've got a month on us. Everything the big brains were working on here."*

Mik shook her head, her tight smile visible through the translucent air mask. *"They've got jack shit. Dani and I grabbed the stuff they stole, and I parked the dozer on top of it. You should be able to salvage most of the backup drives."* She hooked her thumb back at the bits and pieces crushed into the dozer track.

"Jesus. Okay." A peremptory gesture sent two men forward to start digging through the detritus. *"That's a hell of a lot better than nothing. Good thinking."*

"They killed my friends." Mik stated the fact as plain as day. *"I was **not** going to let them win."*

It was also a subtle warning, Pete realised a second later. Pete and Dani were Mik's friends. If the security guys aggressed against them, the evidence of just how personally she would take it lay for all to see, on the long grim trail of death leading eastward toward Burroughs.

"Found some drives, sir!" One of the men at the dozer track waved his arm in the air. *"They're intact!"*

"Well, halle-goddamn-lujah. Keep looking. There'll be a bonus for every man here for each one you find. Ms Wallace, you just saved Tharsis a metric ton of grief." Inside the armoured EVA suit, Pete saw the guy's shoulders relax.

"That's good to hear. I—" Mik raised her head and peered eastward, shading her eyes. *"Wait, you hear that? There's a shuttle incoming."*

Pete was familiar with how good Mik's hearing was, even in the thin Martian atmosphere, so he looked in that direction as well. Predictably, he neither saw nor heard anything. "Is it from Tharsis?"

"I wasn't advised of one. And that's the wrong direction, anyway." The security chief turned his head. *"Sure you're not just hearing things?"*

"Absolutely. The hundred-hertz band carries forever. My stereocilia are tuned for it." Mik's light-hearted tone dropped away. *"If that's not one of yours, you need to tell everyone to take cover, right now."*

"Copy that." The security chief went silent then, though Pete could see his mouth moving through the tinted faceplate of his EVA suit.

Different channel, right. Pete turned to Mik. "Did you mean me too—" But she was already gone, sprinting toward the rock-hopper as only someone unencumbered by a suit could.

"Dani!" Her tone was urgent. *"Unhook now-now-now! Hostiles incoming! Drive the dozer off the berm and get under it!"*

Dani

"Got it!" Dani flipped the stop-flow catch on the shaker siphon and pulled it out of the rock-hopper's tank, then secured the cap. "You're good to go!" As Mik scrambled onto the 'hopper, she started clambering up the side of the berm, taking the siphon with her.

By the time Dani got up next to the dozer, Mik was already strapped in and kicking over the rocket motors. She ducked away, shielding her faceplate with her arm as the rock-hopper lifted off. Hot exhaust gases washed over her for a moment, then dissipated.

She wanted to watch and see what happened, but Mik had told her what she needed to do, and her friend was absolutely the expert in this situation. So she held the siphon hose high and opened the stop-flow to let the rest of the fuel drain back in, then yanked the siphon out, secured the dozer tank fuel cap, and dropped into the driver's seat.

While she'd never taken formal training, Dani knew which control did what. Stabbing the start button, she yanked on the lever to raise the blade, then jammed the two drive levers forward. The dozer rumbled forward and down off the berm; once it was on level ground, she dropped the blade and shut the whole thing down.

A distant explosion reached her ears, and she looked up to see the newcomer shuttle in the sky and a new plume of smoke rising from near the location of the wrecked facility. *Please be okay, Mik. You're all I've got right now.*

Diving off the dozer, she darted around the rear and wriggled underneath. There wasn't a whole lot of room, but she made it work anyway. It wasn't as though she had many other options.

"*Room for one more?*" Pete's voice sounded in her ears as he came crawling under the dozer.

"*Sure.*" She moved aside a little, trying to sound more confident than she felt. "You can take the sofa, I've got the armchair."

He chuckled at her weak attempt at humour as he moved up alongside her, his air tanks clinking gently against the underside of the dozer. "*Nice. Love what you've done with the place. A little bit cramped, though.*"

Right on cue, there was a **BOOOM** as something blew up nearby. Shrapnel pattered off the side of the dozer, sounding like hail on an old-fashioned tin roof. Dani hunched her shoulders inside the pressure suit. "I'm good with cramped. Cramped works for me."

"*Totally agree. Cramped is amazing right now. Thinking about moving in here for good.*"

Dani took a deep breath. No more explosions sounded, but that meant nothing. She cast around for something to distract her. "Um, Mik said her stereocilia were tuned to a hundred hertz. What does that even mean?"

His tone, when he answered, sounded bemused. "*Stereocilia are the tiny hairs in the ear that pick up sound vibrations. A hundred hertz is really low-frequency sound, the type you also feel in your chest. No idea how you tune hair, but I'll take her word for it.*"

"Me too." Talking was helping her keep calm, so she asked the next question that popped into her head. "So, tell me about Orbital Rescue. What's it like?"

"Well, *have you ever sat on your front porch on a moonless night, and the whole sky is full of stars?*" Now he sounded introspective.

"Yeah, I have. It's nice." She was reminded briefly of the nights where she and Mik had sat on top of the Marineris facility, looking up at the constellations and sharing dreams of the future.

"*Orbital Rescue's like that, but all the time. Just step out of the airlock, and you've got the whole universe surrounding you. I remember one time …*"

Chapter 19: Finishing Move

As soon as Dani was clear of the immediate blast area, Mik took off straight up, boosting as hard as she was comfortable with. She couldn't hear the incoming shuttle anymore, of course, but as she gained altitude, she picked out the black dot in the sky. Pulling the mask down, she let it dangle around her neck. There was nobody she needed to talk to, right now.

The shuttle was coming in a lot faster than the rock-hopper was moving right now, but long hours on simulator programs had taught her that speed plus mass equalled a huge turning circle. If she could get inside its minimum arc, she could dance around it all day, and it would never get a bead on her. Mik didn't yet know exactly *how* she was going to bring that bad boy down, but she figured once she got close enough, she'd be able to work something out.

Just about that point, she saw two smaller dots separate from the shuttle and accelerate away from it, toward her. Acting on instinct, she pitched the rock-hopper way over and went for the ground, using the first small hill as visual cover. One of the missiles shot over the hill—way over her head—and kept on going down the Valles, target lost and unable to reacquire. The rumble of a nearby explosion clued her in on the fate of the second one.

When she showed her face around the side of the hill, ready to duck back if another missile was to come her way, she saw the funeral pyre of the crawler. Smoke boiled upward as the stored oh-two and other oxidants fed the flames. Above it, the shuttle hovered on vertol thrusters, nose angled down slightly.

Mik took a moment to figure out what the shuttle was doing. As she watched, one of the Tharsis Security guys broke cover to fire his gun up at the shuttle. It was a pretty badass move but it also got him killed, if the dust and dirt that kicked up around him were any indication; he jerked briefly, fell, and lay still.

Then the shuttle started moving in Mik's direction.

Uh oh.

A twitch of the controls skated the rock-hopper back into cover. As soon as she was out of direct visual contact, she lit off the attitude rockets and sent the 'hopper zooming laterally behind the hill, only slowing when she reached the other side. There was a gully, fossilised evidence of ancient water, that ran alongside the road; she slid the tiny flying vehicle down into that and scooted along about five feet below the level of the road.

The shuttle loomed overhead, having gone straight over the top of the hill. It was moving more slowly now than it had on approach, probably because it was below the level of the nearest cliff and its handling was somewhat less than nimble. Mik's head jerked up as a missile erupted from one of the shuttle's launch tubes; about one second later, the construction shack detonated in a massive fireball. Sitting innocently nearby, the bulldozer seemed unharmed by the shrapnel. Voices filtered in through her earpiece.

"I'm good with cramped. Cramped works for me."

"Totally agree. Cramped is amazing right now. Thinking about moving in here for good."

Okay, so Dani and Pete were still fine, but that wouldn't last if the assholes in the shuttle decided to blast the dozer for target practice. *Time to go loud.*

Tuning out the rest of the conversation, Mik flicked her eyes from one point to another, working out her plan of action. Then, before she could talk herself out of it, she hit the throttle and blasted up out of the gully. This time, she wasn't sticking to low-and-slow; the main rocket motor boosted her up to just above the shuttle's altitude, before she banked around and flew directly across in front of the main cockpit viewport. If that didn't get their attention, she figured the finger she gave them on the way through should do the job.

Even as the massive craft began to turn ponderously—she'd deliberately baited it in the wrong direction, so it had to make a full two-seventy-degree turn before it could line up on her—she was accelerating harder, using every trick she knew to trade altitude for speed. Her destination was the nearest cliff face, several kilometres distant, and she was betting her life that she could reach it before the shuttle turned all the way around and acquired her again.

Reaching down, she flicked the catch that locked the reclining mechanism of the seat. It was good for prolonged high-G manoeuvres, but not right now. Temporary discomfort, she could live with.

The gamble she was taking wasn't as huge as it might have otherwise seemed; the Cyberon contingent could only have shown up so coincidentally if they were in direct pursuit of her unique genome. If they wanted her so badly, they wouldn't risk hitting her with something that obliterated her body altogether. In short, they would be trying hard to capture her at least partially intact. On the downside, 'alive' seemed to be very much an optional extra, especially after all the trouble she'd given them so far.

A growing thunder behind her indicated that the shuttle had finally completed its turn and was coming after her.

In the meantime, she'd been working to squeeze out every last ounce of performance she could from the overpowered rock-hopper, without actually passing out from the acceleration (as had happened the *last* time Cyberon had been chasing her). The six-kilometre-high cliff in front of her was a lot less forgiving than the same volume of hard vacuum, for one thing. And for another, she wasn't pointed anywhere *near* Earth.

Boosting at three Martian gees, which came to just over one Earth gee, she did her best to ignore the strain on her body. *How do Earth people live with this all their lives? Geez.* At the same time, she kept an eye on her over-ground speed, which was scrolling upward all the time.

Something *pinged* off the frame of the rock-hopper, and she realised that the subtle pulsing in the roar from behind her wasn't a flutter in their rocket engine, but actual gunfire. Even though this wasn't the first time she'd been shot at, it was just as unwelcome. Tilting the rock-hopper forward, she dove for the ground clutter.

This was where (she hoped) all the effort that had gone into designing her genome and training her on the rock-hopper would bear fruit. Due to her unique capabilities, she'd been *the* best rock-hopper pilot at the Valles Marineris Research Complex, and the rock-hopper was the most agile flying vehicle on Mars. The stick-jockey in the shuttle behind her had neither of those advantages, though he did have guns and missiles.

To be fair, those *were* pretty good advantages in their own right.

Flying nap-of-Mars was something she'd done recently; that very day, in fact. This time, however, she was trying to avoid being shot up by a trigger-happy asshole working for a power-hungry sociopath. She wasn't going as fast, but now she needed to go a lot lower.

Streaking along mere metres above the dusty, rocky terrain, she knew her rocket-wash was kicking up a huge rooster-tail of dust and fines, hopefully obscuring her from the guy flying the shuttle. Still, she stuck to the lowest elevations she could, weaving between the terrain features and using them as cover. Firing blind was absolutely a thing, as were heat-seeking missiles.

She heard the deep rumble as the shuttle pilot opened his throttle a little, pushing to overtake her, or at least not fall back so far. Then she heard another sound, too prolonged to be a gunshot, and weaved behind a small bluff out of pure instinct. The missile hit the far side of the bluff, detonating with stunning force.

Rubble, along with dust and smoke, filled the air, and the shockwave gave the rock-hopper a solid jolt. Fortunately, the Martian atmosphere was thin enough that it didn't give her a concussion or turn her lungs inside out; she'd read that both of those were possible on Earth. Living inside an atmosphere that thick sounded *weird.* And totally unsafe.

She'd dodged the missile, but she was still going to cop the crap anyway. Tons of rubble had been blasted into the sky, and what went up had to come down, even on Mars. She didn't really feel like dealing with her own personal meteor shower, so it was time to change the rules of the game.

Flipping the rock-hopper around to bring the rocket motor facing forward, she gritted her teeth as she pulled it up into a hard loop. Her thumb pushed the throttle wheel forward, increasing the thrust to fifteen meters per second squared; a hair over four Martian gees, or one and a half Earth gravities. She could feel herself being pressed down and back into her seat, her spine compressing with a palpable creak.

Blackness edged her vision, and she had a flashback to when she'd lit off the rockets to go to Earth. But this time, she hung onto the controls for dear life. There was never a good time to lose control, and this was worse than most.

Two pieces of rubble shot past her, while a third bounced off the rock-hopper's frame with a massive CLANG. The 'hopper tried to swing out of alignment, but she corrected automatically for the impact as she shot up out of the cloud, with the shuttle still coming on strong. Two seconds after that, she reached the top of her loop and eased off on the throttle, her vision clearing again as if by magic.

The Immelmann turn had been developed by a pilot in a war that ended centuries before Mik's genome was created in the Marineris facility, but it still had its uses. More to the point, she knew how to perform one, allowing her to roll the 'hopper upright and swoop down on the shuttle from above and to the side. *How does it feel now, asshole?*

The shuttle pilot reacted with commendable speed, banking the craft and accelerating in an attempt to shake her off. Unfortunately for them, she had a lot more manoeuvrability and power-to-weight ratio to play with. And while the rock-hopper lacked guns or bombs, she still had an offensive capability … but most of all, she had a plan.

While she'd managed to bait the shuttle into chasing her, it hadn't been pointed directly at the upcoming canyon wall. At least, not until her swooping attack had startled the pilot into turning away from her, and *toward* the rock-face.

Now, as the shuttle groaned its way into the turn, Mik brought the rock-hopper forward to a point just over its main cockpit viewport. Her main thruster bell-muzzle came down to within half a metre of the viewport, then she lit off the rocket engine with a one-second burst that compressed her spine again and bounced her upward by seven and a half metres. Banking over as she dropped down again, she surveyed her handiwork with satisfaction.

The shuttle viewport was now solid black from side to side; while even the thousand-degree heat of the rock-hopper's main rocket engine firing at full intensity wouldn't have affected the silica glass, every viewport on Mars bore a polymer coating designed to repel fines, and that had melted and burned just fine. *Whoops.*

Blinded as they were, they would only have basic instrumentation to work off, and there was no convenient auto-landing system in the Valles. (Or rather, the only nearby landing pad with an auto-landing system still had the wreckage of their previous shuttle on it.)

They're going to try to get the hell out of here.

Normally, this would have been fine. Mik would've been okay to let them go. But this was the second time that Cyberon had come to her home and killed people, and that was not a precedent she could be comfortable with.

If I don't do this now, they'll just keep trying.

So, just as the main engines lit off and the nose of the shuttle began to tilt upward, she landed right above the viewport … and ran down her own engines to minimum. Even with its open-frame construction, the rock-hopper still massed a solid tonne; accordingly, the shuttle's nose fell away again. They'd already committed to the main-engine burn, so the shuttle was accelerating forward and down—toward the canyon wall—by the time they registered the disastrous change in pitch.

She felt the shuttle's forward vertol thrusters increase power to lift the nose, but they lacked the wherewithal to offset the effect of the extra weight, Martian gravity or no Martian gravity. Perched on the rock-hopper, Mik watched the cliff looming closer. She waited until the point of no return, then ran the engines up and lifted off the shuttle, angling away from the vertical mass of rock.

The shuttle's nose came up hard then, but its forward momentum was too great. Under the impetus of its main engines, it smashed belly-first into the Valles wall, half a kilometre below the rim. Metal crumpled and the engines died, then it tumbled toward the floor of Valles Marineris, far below. The impact was impressive, as was the resultant explosion. Fire and smoke trailed upward from the twisted wreckage.

As Mik watched, large sections of rock fractured and separated from the cliff face where the shuttle had struck. The shards and chunks of rock landed on and around the still-blazing remains of the shuttle, half-burying it and sending sparks and detritus in all directions.

Mik slowly turned the rock-hopper back toward the Marineris facility. Bringing up the mask to cover her mouth, she took a breath of oxygen. "Okay, guys. You can come out now."

Later
The Ruins of the Valles Marineris Research Complex
Pete

It was amusing to observe the respect with which the Tharsis security people treated Mik. Before, they'd been polite, but now their deference was almost exaggerated. A third of them were dead, killed in the initial attack or during their attempts to fight back; the remainder owed their lives to her, and they knew it.

"This is what we salvaged from the area shown in the layout as Professor Ibrahim's personal quarters." The security chief gestured to a section of the tarp that had been laid down. *"And those, I believe, are from yours."*

Mik knelt down next to her belongings. There was a paperweight, the upper part covered in charring which she wiped off with her thumb to reveal a cityscape in miniature; New York, as far as Pete could tell. Next, she took up an electronic frame that looked like it would have displayed stored photos. It was irreparably warped, but she popped off the rear cover and retrieved its memory card, which she slipped into her pocket.

Standing up again, speaking to nobody, she went over to Professor Ibrahim's small pile. The most prominent item was a safe that had evidently been pried out of the wall it was mounted in. From what Pete could see, it was solidly constructed, designed to protect its contents above all else.

Again, she brushed the charring away from its face, then she paused for a moment with her hand resting on the metal, as though communing with its former owner. Her features were still, but Pete could feel the grief radiating from her.

"If you want, we can drill the lock out," the security chief offered awkwardly. *"If there's a drill around here, that is."*

Mik lifted the air mask briefly to her face. *"Don't bother. I got it. He shared his combination with me years ago."* Carefully, she began to turn the safe dial, first one way and then the other. It rotated smoothly, despite the abuse it had taken.

Nobody spoke; everyone was watching Mik at the safe. Pete keyed his radio to the alternate channel he'd arranged with Dani. "How's it going with the refuelling?"

"Nearly done." The day's events notwithstanding, she sounded remarkably upbeat. *"How's Mik holding up?"*

"As well as can be expected, I guess." Pete grimaced. "She's opening Professor Ibrahim's safe right now."

"Oh. Okay. When you get a chance, tell her I've done that other thing, too."

He frowned. "When are you going to tell me what that is?"

"When it's time. Did they find any of my stuff?"

"There was a case of books from the guest quarters. When I checked, they were a little scorched, but mostly intact. They yours?"

The teasing note gave way to happiness. *"Oh, wow, yes, thank you! That means so much to me. Mom and Dad gave me most of those books."*

"Good. We'll grab those too." He watched Mik turn the dial one last time, then work the handle. "Huh, she got it open."

"Cool. Let me know how it goes."

"Will do." He switched back over to the common channel, just as Mik turned the lever and opened the safe. There was a puff of vapour around the edges of the door as it unsealed, and he blinked. *Damn, that thing was even airtight.*

She reached into the safe and pulled out a wad of documents. Lips moving soundlessly, she scanned each one in turn, handing them up to the security chief. And then she came to a sealed envelope; as she turned it one way and the other, Pete saw the words *'For Mik'* written on the front.

"What's that?" asked the security chief.

She handed him the remainder of the papers but kept the envelope, then attached the air mask to her face. *"He always said he had something in his safe for me, in the event of his passing or for when I turned eighteen. Never said what it was. This must be it."*

Pete took a couple of steps closer as Mik opened the envelope. Within was a set of papers, which she carefully unfolded. She started reading the first one, then audibly gasped and began again. *"No."* Her voice was a whisper, on the ragged edge of hearing. *"I can't believe it."*

"What?" Pete came closer. "What is it?"

Blindly, she held them out to him, then turned away with her arms wrapped around herself, hunched over. He looked over the papers, frowning.

… sound mind and body … I, Benjamin Murgatroyd Ibrahim, hereby adopt Mik Wallace as my legitimate child … full beneficiary of my will … per the Martian Settlement Agreement … dual Earth-Mars citizenship …

He stopped reading, and scanned all the way to the bottom. A messy signature was scrawled there, along with those for the witness and lawyer. As far as he could tell with his limited legal understanding, it was fully signed and sealed.

How well it would hold up against a legal challenge, he had no idea. But it sure as hell *looked* real.

"What is it?" The security chief asked the question again.

Pete took a deep breath and gestured toward Mik. "Her ticket home."

He'd been planning to assist her in leaving anyway; she clearly had no desire to stay on the same planet as Cyberon (or Tharsis, for that matter). At best, she was a useful asset. At worst, a target.

The trouble was, until the document was invoked, she legally belonged to Tharsis; they could raise a massive legal stink and try to have her returned to Mars if she left the planet. It wouldn't even be kidnapping if they dragged her away by force, merely repossession of property. But that one document changed everything.

Benjamin Ibrahim's hole card had been sheer brilliance. Adopting her—he was actually one of her gene donors, which gave him the legal standing to do so—meant that, by definition, she shared his dual citizenship. Of course, while this technically made her a Martian citizen, Pete didn't trust Tharsis *or* Cyberon not to push their respective legislatures to overturn that particular aspect.

However, neither legislature had any hold over Earth's legal system. And since the adoption papers *also* decreed her a citizen of that planet, both corporations could whistle in the wind as far as legal extradition went.

Mik Wallace was going home.

Mik

"You okay?" Dani put her arm around Mik's shoulders and squeezed.

"I'll be fine." Not for the first time, or even the tenth, Mik wished she could cry. No sniffles, no nothing. While there were many aspects about her odd physiology that were pretty damn cool, that one truly sucked from time to time. "I just can't believe he did that for me."

"He was your dad. You were his kid. I could see that from day one." Dani hugged her again. *"He just made it legal."*

Mik leaned into the embrace. "Yeah. He did." She turned her head. "Pete, ready to go?"

"Sure." Pete vaulted up onto the rock-hopper and waved to the Tharsis security guys. Most of them were clustered around the dozer, and its large supplementary oh-two tank. *"I'll be calling this in as soon as we get to orbit. Reckon their air'll last until help gets here?"*

"It should. Tharsis is a lot closer than Hellas." Mik waited until Pete was strapped in, then kicked over the rocket motors. "Just by the way, Dani? If we look like not having enough fuel, I'm tossing your books overboard first." She gave her friend a gentle elbow-nudge to show she wasn't serious.

"What about that dead weight?" Dani pointed at Pete, an answering grin clearly visible on her face.

He turned to look at her and raised his eyebrows in an older-brother-is-not-impressed kind of way. *"Yeah, good luck getting onto the Orbital Rescue ship without me."*

"… okay, fair point."

Mik chuckled, then switched her radio to the channel used by the Tharsis security guys. "Before I go, can you pass on a message to your bosses for me?"

"Yes, ma'am, we can." The security chief spoke respectfully. *"What's the message?"*

"Tell them that I've retrieved all the backup drives for the Martian Walker project. If they want to keep it going, they need to come and negotiate with *me* about who has control over my genome. Nobody else. Got that?"

He nodded. *"Understood, ma'am. And, uh … good luck."*

"Thanks. You, too." She rolled the thumb-wheel over.

The rock-hopper lifted off into the Martian sky.

Chapter 20: Endgame

"Oh, good. You're back. I was about to call out for a search party." Marj's warm voice was welcome in Pete's ears. *"I see you found her. Is this a bug-out-now situation, or can we take our time?"*

"Oh, I figure we can take our time—"

"Can we have the engines warmed up?" interrupted Mik. *"You know, just in case? Cyberon might not be so pleased that I'm getting away, and I don't trust them not to try to intercept us. Or Tharsis, for that matter."*

"You got it hon." The hatch in the side of the Heavy opened, wide enough for Mik to fly the rock-hopper all the way in. *"And you'd be Danielle Connaught. Hey there, I'm Marj."*

"Hi." Dani sounded weary. *"It's good to be here."*

Mik edged the rock-hopper sideways, but put it down close enough to the edge of the hatch that it protruded out of the ship. The magnetic clamps automatically adjusted position and locked onto the feet of the small craft. *"Okay, everyone off. Dani, grab your books."*

"Uh, hon, you might want to move your little buggy," Marj warned. *"Otherwise, it's likely to get bent when I close the hatch."*

"Sure," Mik replied casually, almost absently. *"Do me a favour and unclamp it once Dani's off, please?"*

Kicking off from the rock-hopper and floating toward the nearest handhold, Pete looked from Mik to Dani and back again. He didn't have a huge amount of experience with teenagers, but Mik was definitely up to something. There was no way in *hell* she'd flub a landing that badly.

Moving carefully, Dani took hold of her case of books, then kicked off from the rock-hopper. Pete watched her to be sure she'd catch a good hand-hold, then switched his gaze back to Mik.

"Unclamping now. Do your thing, hon."

The clamps unsnapped and lifted clear, then Mik acted. In one smooth sequence, she released her five-point harness, pressed a button on the flight control computer, and bailed out herself. Half a second later, the attitude rockets ignited, jetting the rock-hopper straight *out* of the hold and clear of the ship. *"Whoops."*

"What the hell?" demanded Marj. *"What's going on here? Why did that thing just launch?"*

"I think the flight control computer's acting up." Dani's tone indicated that butter wouldn't melt in her mouth, even the synthetic stuff.

Flight computer, my ass. I knew they were up to something. Pete had a sudden flashback to the radio conversation with Dani, about the 'thing' she'd done. Things were becoming a lot clearer now.

"Yeah," agreed Mik. *"So, uh, I was thinking we might want to leave. Like, right now."*

Outside the open hatch, the rock-hopper rotated on several axes at once, as though seeking something. With one last burst from the attitude rockets, it firmed up on a particular alignment, then the main engine fired. Pete watched it recede into the distance until it vanished from his sight a few seconds later.

"… gotcha." The hatch began to close again. *"All hands, secure for boost, two-four-zero seconds. Wallace and Connaught, control room, now. I'm gonna want some answers. Even if it's just so we can all get our stories straight."*

"Yes, ma'am."

"Yes, ma'am."

Pete followed the two girls through into the control room, letting them use the airlock first. Once they were all secured in acceleration seats, Marj applied thrust and the Heavy surged forward reassuringly.

"Okay," she said, turning in her chair with her faceplate open. "What in the howling blue blazes was all that about? Where did you send it?"

Pete cleared his throat. "Before we get into this, I need to make a radio call. After that …" He gave Mik and Dani a stern look, shared between the two of them. "I'm going to want to know too."

Mik and Dani shared a quick glance, then Mik nodded. "Yeah, that's totally fair."

Cyberon Headquarters, Burroughs
CEO's Office

All was quiet in the office. The encrypted radio, tuned to a specific frequency, emitted only static. Even the latest hourly status call had failed to come through.

All Kolban had was a single garbled call three hours ago, something about *'blinded'* and *'falling'*, then … nothing. The most effective assault shuttle in the Cyberon arsenal, crewed by the most ruthless men and women that he'd recruited from Pure Strain, attacking from surprise … it should have been a quick in-and-out. The presence of Tharsis security had been an unwelcome surprise, but he'd planned for contingencies like that.

And yet, the shuttle was not answering.

The specimen was not yet in his hands.

He *needed* the damn thing in one of his labs. Strapped to a table, dissected, every last secret extracted from its tissues, then improved and cloned off to form his private army. It was his destiny, his *right* as a man of vision.

And he would not let that destiny go to waste. No matter where the creature fled to.

Abruptly, Jarn Kolban stood up and strode from his office. His earpiece would inform him if the radio received a signal. In the meantime, he needed refreshments. He would return to his vigil afterward.

For the past few hours, the rock-hopper had been skating across the top of Mars' atmosphere. If anyone had been paying attention, they would've registered that it was drawing a straight line toward Hellas Basin. But it was a tiny metal object in a huge orbital volume; and right then, the political tensions on Mars meant that nobody was looking *up*.

As it passed over the western rim of Hellas Basin, it turned slightly and oriented itself downward. Its final coordinates locked in, it fired off its main rocket, accelerating rapidly down into the atmosphere. There was nobody on board, no hand on the controls.

No way to stop it.

With the rocket engine blasting at full strength, the only thing preventing it from reaching its full acceleration capability was the tenuous atmosphere, and even then, the gravity gave it a boost there. It streaked down toward the surface, its speed mounting rapidly. The only time it had gone faster than this was when it had been bound for Earth.

This journey would be considerably shorter.

Losing altitude all the time, it crossed over Hellas Basin. It began to heat up as it went, more from the atmosphere compressing before it than from actual air friction. For the last five hundred kilometres, it left a glowing trail in the sky.

Four minutes forty-five seconds after it began its final run, it struck its target. The window of the CEO's office in the Cyberon building was triple-paned and reinforced to withstand stresses exceeding the most strenuous of projected dust storms; it stood about as much chance as a sheet of tissue paper against a heavy calibre bullet. The rock-hopper struck it left of dead centre, tore through the office in an instant, and hit the building proper like a bomb.

A *large* bomb.

Nearly a hundred gigajoules of energy were released in the instant of impact. The shockwave spread in all directions, shattering walls and windows, and hurling people from their feet. Parts of the building collapsed or were otherwise exposed to the outside atmosphere. Other parts held; emergency doors slammed shut, retaining pressure.

Sirens howled. Chaos reigned.

A Hospital Bed, Burroughs, Mars
Jarn Kolban, Cyberon CEO

Kolban's first thought upon waking was, *pain. Why do I hurt so much?*

"Oh, good. You're awake." The voice was familiar, but not in a good way. He prised his eyelids open, and found himself looking at the head of the Board of Directors. "That will make this easier."

"What?" Kolban's throat was scratchy, his voice a thin rasp, but nobody offered him water. "What happened?" His last memory was of being struck by a ballistic door.

"The building was impacted by an object travelling at re-entry speeds. Your office was specifically targeted. The person you have been seeking to acquire left Mars orbit only a few hours before the strike. There is no way of proving that they are responsible, but you have used our resources to attack them twice. We will not allow this to happen a third time."

He was still trying to gather his wits, but it wasn't easy. There was a connection he wasn't making. "The next time, I won't fail."

"You are not listening. Half the Board of Directors were killed when the building was struck. The rest of us held an emergency meeting and expelled you from the CEO position and the company as a whole, under the grounds that you are officially a danger to Cyberon."

The cold, dry delivery made the whole revelation all the worse. "No. I have the veto to any decision you come to."

"Not this one. You're out. We are officially pivoting away from your dangerous pursuits, and away from Pure Strain as a whole." A folded document was dropped onto his chest, even the minor impact sending shards of pain through his sternum. "This is your official notification."

Panic began to belatedly flare through his body. "You can't do this!"

"We already did." The Director moved to the door, then glanced back. "Don't worry about coming in to clear out your desk. It's not there anymore. Everything in your office was vaporised." Then he was gone, the door clicking shut behind him.

Kolban blinked, slowly digesting the situation.

They can't do this! It was a silent scream of denial. *I'll reveal everything I've got on them!* Every member of the Board of Directors had things they didn't want coming out. He had leverage on everyone, all stored on his personal computer, built into his desk …

… in his office.

Oh.

A Little Earlier
Mik

There was silence in the control cabin after Mik and Dani finished explaining what they'd arranged. Dani was downcast, the emotional reaction finally catching up with her. Mik was trying to look defiant, but she wasn't sure how either one of the adults was taking it, and goddamn it, she wanted their approval.

"Well, Marj." Pete let out a gusty breath and slapped his thighs. "Someone's about to find out the truth of your favourite saying."

Marj nodded, though her smile was a little forced. "Isaac Newton's definitely the deadliest sonovabitch in space."

Pete looked over at Dani. "And you programmed this? How accurate did you make it?"

Dani bit her lip. "The Cyberon building's the most prominent one in that part of Burroughs. I knew the address. Told it to go in through the biggest window."

"It was my idea." Mik kept her voice low and steady. "If you want to yell at anyone, yell at me. They already kidnapped her once, and they were willing to torture her to get to me. You didn't see the cell they were keeping her in. And they'd totally do the same to any of you. They weren't going to stop."

"They killed my parents, and everyone else who was working with Mik." Dani hugged Mik's arm to her. "Laws don't matter to them. They sent *two* shuttles into Tharsis territory, specifically to murder people and abduct Mik. You think you know what they're like, but you don't. I've been screamed at by their boss, spit flying in my face and everything. He came *that* close to just opening the cell and letting me choke to death, more than once." She held up her free hand, fingers only a few millimetres apart. "And they would've stood there and let him."

Pete glanced at Marj, and she looked back. Finally, Pete grimaced. "Okay, yeah. I get it. If they aren't willing to abide by the rules, then they can't exactly complain when people break the rules to target them."

"You know they're gonna try." Marj raised her eyebrows. "People like that always do."

"Screw 'em." Pete nodded to Mik. "Hey, princess, what are your thoughts about taking Orbital Rescue training? Pretty sure we can skip the pressure suit drills. And I've never seen anyone who's a better hand with a light singleship."

Mik raised her head, interested. "I could do that, but what about Dani? If she's down on Earth, they might sneak in and grab her again."

Marj ran a thumbnail over her bottom lip. "Not everyone in Orbital Rescue flies a ship. If she wants to do the training, she could be a dispatcher or other support staff."

"And *nobody* messes with Orbital Rescue personnel." Pete's tone was definite. "If they grab either one of you, it won't be just a single semi-authorised mission to get you back. We've got more ships than Cyberon and Tharsis put together, and we *will* roll on into Mars orbit and put the beatdown on whoever took you. We take care of our own."

Dani took a deep breath and nodded. "Okay. Yeah, that sounds good."

Marj grinned. "Welcome aboard."

"So, Mik." Pete's voice was thoughtful. "I was thinking, if you wanted to collaborate with McPherson, he could put together something like a rock-hopper, only with gimballing so it can go in any direction. Without the need for pressure or life support, we could make it seriously lightweight. Put a regular-sized drive on it, and you could pull major acceleration."

"Not too much, thanks." Mik gestured at her collarbone, recalling the weeks it had taken to mend properly. "I'm not built for it like you are."

Marj tilted her hand from side to side. "Still, not a bad idea. You'd be *amazing* for exterior examination and repair."

Mik privately conceded that she had a point. "Okay, I'll think about it. But first, I've got to actually get into Orbital Rescue, yeah?"

Marj and Pete glanced at each other, and Marj laughed. "Oh, hon. That'll be the *easy* part."

The End (For Now)

Bug Eyes

Chapter 1: The Human is Out of Place

When the human entered the tavern, it didn't take Vrikk more than a few wingbeats to decide that he'd blundered into the wrong establishment. Since her unit's arrival in the village, the tavern had been unofficially designated as military territory, and while she understood humans could have soldiers—of a sort—this was probably not one of them. The trick now would be ensuring that he also figured this out and left before one of the drones took offense to his presence.

Drones weren't bad, in their own way. Heavily built and suspicious of outsiders, they were clustered up at their own end of the bar-room, conversing among themselves via antenna-touch. Vrikk had never had a conversation with one that didn't involve her giving it orders, but from what she knew of them, they weren't exactly deep thinkers. They didn't tend to dwell on abstract concepts such as philosophy and beauty and impending mortality, which surprised her not in the least. Bred to be workers and soldiers, they carried out that function perfectly, without ever questioning why.

But they did tend to be territorial, and it showed. Drones never squabbled between themselves; any pecking order disputes were resolved via antenna-touch or (at worst) an agreed-upon contest. However, if Vrikk or one of her fellow sub-queens thought to go and sit at their end of the bar, they would *look* at her, awaiting orders, until she got the message and retreated to officer country.

Staring was about the most aggressive thing a drone could do to an importunate superior, but they could do it very effectively. Vrikk had been on the receiving end of it a few times, and had no wish to repeat the experience. It didn't help that while higher castes had eyes that reflected a variety of hues, drone eyes were uniformly black, making them somewhat intimidating.

Vrikk hadn't met many humans before, but she was reasonably sure she could pick out one of their soldiers. This one lacked the tightly defined endoskeletal musculature, and was almost as wide in the abdomen as a queen heavy with eggs ready to be laid. Furthermore, he (she was aware that aliens could be female, but they didn't fulfil the same roles that she was used to, so she defined them all as 'he' until given more information) wore an odd contraption over his single-lens eyes, the glass catching the light occasionally. It looked far too fragile to wear into combat.

Oblivious to the hostile stare of the drones, the human moved over to the bar and used a few basic phrases in Trade, plus a translator module for Frizz undertones and overtones, to order a drink. *Zarzz* was a potent brew, consisting of a fermented honey base, that had apparently become a huge hit with human visitors. Vrikk enjoyed a sip of it every now and again, but anything more than a single proboscis-draft was likely to leave her feeling like her antennae had just exploded. From the size of the vessel the human was negotiating for, he either didn't know how strong it was, or thought he could take it.

As the human stepped away from the bar with his oversized mug in hand, one of the more belligerent drones blocked his way. "Human," the drone said in passable Trade. "That drink is not for you."

All conversation had ceased with the confrontation, so Vrikk heard the human's words clearly. "Excuse me for any misunderstanding. This drink is mine. I paid for it." He took a mouthful to prove his ownership.

The drone reached out with an upper manipulator capable of crushing stone and closed it around the human's mug. Showing a certain amount of intelligence, the human did not try to keep hold of it, but instead let go as soon as the drone began to pull on it. "Not for you," the drone repeated.

"You can have that one," the human said. "I'll just get another." To Vrikk's mounting astonishment, he turned back to the bar and ordered an identical drink while the drone just stood there, staring. It seemed the stare of a drone had little effect on a human; once he had his second mug in hand, he seemed surprised (if Vrikk was reading the body language correctly) to find the drone still there when he went to move away from the bar.

"That drink is for Frizz, not for human," the drone said once more. "Human is not Frizz."

"Oh," replied the human brightly, clearly misunderstanding the drone's belligerent attitude. "Humans love this stuff. It's like old-fashioned Earth mead, only not as strong. Here, let me show you."

Putting the mug to his mouth (those mobile lips were just *weird*), he began to drink. And drink. And drink. Along with the rest of the patrons in the bar, Vrikk stared as he almost literally inhaled mouthful after mouthful of *Zarzz*.

The mug tilted farther and farther back, and still he showed no signs of being affected by the potent brew. Finally, with a triumphant flourish, he smacked the empty mug down on the bar. "See?"

Oh, Hive. If drones couldn't establish dominance via orders, they would do it by contests of physical prowess. Whether the human knew it or not, he'd just challenged the drone and laid down the rules of the contest. Would the drone understand that an impossible standard had just—

The drone wrapped its mandibles around its mug and inserted its proboscis into the sweet-smelling drink. It began to drain the mug, siphoning it out via its proboscis (the *natural* way of drinking something like that, Vrikk silently maintained), keeping the human well within its field of vision at all times.

It was a large and healthy specimen of its kind, and it stayed on its feet until the mug was empty. Then, just as its fellows were raising a group hum of congratulations for its fortitude, it swayed and fell over, raising dust from the floor with an almighty crash. The mug clattered to the floor beside it.

The human stood looking down at it. "Oh. Wow. Uh, is he okay?"

Impulsively, Vrikk stood up from her table and beckoned to the human. "It will be fine, once it sleeps off the excess drink. Come and sit with us." She evidently didn't know as much about humans as she'd previously assumed, if they could imbibe enough *Zarzz* to send herself and half a dozen Frizz like her into a drunken stupor without showing it. As a sub-queen of her own Hive, it was her job to learn as much about the world—and potential allies or enemies—as possible.

"Uh, thanks." The human came over and slid into a free chair. "Have I done something wrong?"

"Not wrong, no." Jarskk, a slightly senior sub-queen, spoke up. "Drones do not like anyone intruding on what they see as theirs. Why are you here?"

The human did something very strange with its eyes. Behind the glass lenses, thin fleshy coverings flicked down over them once, twice. "I'm a ..." He spoke a word Vrikk did not know.

"That does not translate," Jarskk said. "What is a ... [*too-wrist*]?"

"Um." The human turned his head, as if seeking an escape route, though he did not appear fearful. His insanely mobile eyes—*single lenses*, Vrikk reminded herself, *so he has to look at everything to see anything*—darted from point to point around the room, though they did not seem to fixate on the exit. Finally, although it didn't seem he'd found what he was looking for, his attention returned to Jarskk. "I have paid to travel here so that I can experience your culture and your drink. Your ancient Hive cities are exquisitely beautiful."

"They are," agreed Jarskk. "But what is it to you? You are human. You have your own cities, your own beautiful things." She twitched an antenna toward the bar. "Your own drink, from your own world."

"How did you drink so much?" Vrikk asked. "There was *alcohol* in that!"

The human only had one pair of manipulator limbs, and now he made a motion with their upper joints which abruptly reminded Vrikk that he possessed an endoskeleton as opposed to a carapace, as was right and proper. Joints normally did not move that way. "Not much," he said with a certain amount of authority. "One of the major pastimes on Earth over the past ten thousand years or so has been figuring how to make alcohol out of just about anything, and then competing to see how drunk we can get on it."

"Ah." Jarskk stared at the human, then twitched her antennae in a way that conveyed *'aliens are crazy'*. "Back to the first question. Why do you come here to see cities and beauty?"

"Because it's a *different* beauty to what we have," the human explained earnestly. "I've been taking lots of photos, see?" Pulling a flat electronic device from his pocket, he activated it and displayed beautifully sharp images on its screen. "People are going to love these, back home." He paused, then went on in a more subdued tone. "And besides, if the civil war you people are having rolls this way, it might not be here in another week. And I'd hate to see stuff like that just vanish, without someone making a record of it."

"What is that image?" demanded Prakk, a younger sub-queen. She tapped at the screen with a manipulator. "How did you get it so close?"

Vrikk leaned in to see what she was referring to. It was the Tower of Harmony, in the middle of the ancient Hive city of Varoskk. Just the upper cupola was visible in the picture, but it was so clear and sharp that it could only have been taken by someone in a flying vehicle. The nearest tall buildings were too far away.

Jarskk closed her upper manipulator over the human's shoulder. "Why are you *really* here?" she demanded. "Are you spying with your human devices for the Hive Breaker?"

"No, no, absolutely not," the human said, holding his soft pink hands up in a defensive posture. "I'm just here to take photos and drink *Zarzz*, I swear."

"Then how did you acquire the image so clearly?" asked Vrikk. "I have seen devices like yours, and they do not allow such a close focus."

"Oh, I've got a [scope]," the human explained. He paused, apparently realising that the looks he was getting indicated confusion. "Uh, it's got a series of lenses that magnify an image, so I can look through it and see something far away?" Reaching up, he tapped the frame of the lenses he was wearing. "Like these, only a lot better."

Vrikk and Jarskk briefly touched antennae. Pictures flicked into Vrikk's mind, of scientists standing around a screen displaying an image of the moon. She sent an impression of agreement back.

"Ah," said Jarskk. "Like an electronic distance-magnifier."

"Yeah, but what I've got isn't electronic," the human said. He held up his device. "This is the only electronics in the whole thing. Frizz don't use scopes? At all?"

"Not ones that focus light into a single point," Vrikk explained, gesturing to her compound eyes. "If we need to see far away and we do not have an electronic magnifier, we have several drones touch antennae, and then the best artist of them draws an amalgamation of what they all see."

"Ah. That kind of sucks, I guess." The human's head came up. "But the antennae-touch thing is pretty cool. You can read each other's minds and talk silently. And your *Zarzz* is amazing. A lot better than the stuff I've tried back on Earth."

"They have *Zarzz* where you come from?" Prakk was curious now, instead of hostile. "How is that so?"

The human spread his hands. "Someone came here and tried some, then talked to some Frizz about selling it to us, I guess. But it looks like they're only sending the second-rate stuff to Earth. Because what you've got here is a whole lot better."

"What is your name, human?" Vrikk asked. "I cannot think of you as 'the human' all night. I am Vrikk, and that is Prakk." She did not introduce Jarskk, for her superior had not given permission for that to happen.

"Oh, right." The human nodded in what seemed to be a friendly fashion. "My name's Francis Hopewell, but everyone calls me Frank. It's good to meet you all."

"It is also good to meet you, Frankk," Jarskk replied, speaking his name in the way that sounded familiar to them all. "I am Jarskk. What are your plans for tomorrow morning?"

"I hadn't actually decided," he said. "So, um, how easy is it to climb that hill behind this village?" Self-deprecatingly, he slapped his thorax with his open hand. "As you can see, I'm not exactly athletic anymore. If I ever was. I was just thinking, there might be some nice views from the top."

"There are several angles of view from the summit," Vrikk confirmed. "I have climbed it. It is not a difficult ascent."

Tilting his head as he looked at her, he formed his overly mobile lips into a strange expression. "I think I'll try it, but I strongly suspect that you would've found it a lot easier than I will."

Prakk had been paging through the images on his device, which he'd left lying on the table. She pointed at one. "How do you make the image so steady with this *scope* of yours, if it is not electronic?"

"Well, first, you wait until the wind dies down," he said; if Vrikk were not mistaken, his tone was one of humour. "Even the tiniest vibration makes it very blurry. Then you set the timer for five seconds or more—"

A subtle vibration impinged on Vrikk's antennae. Her head came up, as did that of every other Frizz in the bar.

"Drone strike!" shouted Jarskk. "Take cover!"

Within a wingbeat, Vrikk was diving under the table with the other sub-queens. At the far end of the bar, a commotion made it clear that the drones were doing the same. Only Frankk was left sitting in his chair, clearly ignorant of what was going on. *Can he not **hear** them?* The massed wingbeats, as they came closer, were impossible to miss with the dullest of antennae.

*Oh, Hive. He doesn't **have** antennae.*

Reaching out from under the table, Vrikk seized his arm with her upper manipulator. "Get *down* here, pupa-brain!" she snapped.

The direct command, and the sudden drag, jolted him into action. Almost falling from his chair, he wriggled under the table, his bulk suddenly making the limited space even more cramped. "What do you mean, drone—?"

At that moment, the windows blew in.

Chapter 2: The Human is Educated

Frank Hopewell woke up, and immediately regretted it. He felt like *shit*.

Where he didn't feel a dull throbbing ache—mainly centred on his right hand, but also radiating from his feet—he was suffering from cramps of varying intensity, mostly in his legs. There was also an empty grumbling in his stomach, a familiar morning pressure in his bladder, and a taste like something with *leprosy* had died in his mouth after a prolonged illness.

All this was made much worse by the *terrible* state of his mattress; he didn't know how the Frizz did beds, but he was reasonably certain this one was stuffed with rocks. His ribs and hipbone spoke up at this point, wanting to claim compensation for pain and anguish. He told them to wait their turn.

"Ghuh," he groaned, levering his eyelids open. They hurt, too.

There was far too much light in his room, temporarily dazzling him. Ignoring more sundry aches and pains as they were awoken by his movement, he brought up his left hand to shade his eyes so he could figure out exactly who to complain to about his terrible living accommodations.

Which raised another point, once his vision cleared. Where *were* his accommodations?

Instead of the snug little guest-house room he'd paid to sleep overnight in, he was lying on grassy, rocky ground, under a tree. Also, he belatedly discovered, on a tree root. Morning sunlight—at least, he hoped it was morning, because otherwise he'd been asleep for *far* too long—slanted downward between a whole lot more trees. Buzzing chirps filled the air, and what he figured had to be bird-sized bugs flitted from branch to branch.

Oh, yeah. The Frizz have that bug ecosystem, don't they? But this doesn't explain why I'm—

All of a sudden, he was looking into the face of a Frizz drone. Like the rest of them, it had dull red eyes, though even as he yelped and recoiled, he registered that it was smaller and not as mean-looking as the ones he'd seen just before ... just before *what?*

His involuntary reaction drew a similar one from the drone. Jerking back away from him, it held up all four arms in a weird posture. "Isz me!" it buzzed. "Szorry for szcare! I am good kid!"

"Ah," he heard from off to the side. Now, *this* was a familiar voice. "He is awake."

Turning his head in that direction—his neck creaked and crackled like someone had lubricated his neck vertebrae with crushed glass—he saw one of the Frizz sub-queens approaching. Without his glasses, he couldn't see the finer details of her markings, but he was pretty sure she was the one he'd been talking to in the bar just before … well, whatever happened, happened.

"Uh, hi," he began, then cleared his throat to get the horrific taste out of it. "Sorry. Excuse me." Turning his head aside, he spat a couple of times, then wiped his mouth. Carefully, using his left hand only—someone or something seemed to have encased his right hand in a dull lumpy brown substance, and it still ached—he sat up properly and turned to face her.

"Are you well enough to travel, Frankk?" she asked, using that same weird stutter on the end that she'd done the previous night. "Does your hand pain you?"

He frowned, looking down at it. Now that he was thinking about it, a sudden twinge shot up his arm and he winced reflexively. "A bit, but I can handle it. What happened to it? What happened to me? Where *are* we?"

Oh, god. It was that Zarzz, wasn't it? I had to show off, didn't I? I thought it was impossible to get drunk on that stuff.

"You do not remember?" The Frizz—Vrikk, that was her name—looked down at him with her azure-gold tinted eyes. All Frizz compound eyes reflected light slightly differently, which also made it easier to tell them apart. The further up the hierarchy, the closer to ultraviolet—which they could see, and he couldn't—their eyes got. It was apparently a genetic thing.

He frowned. "Uh … I was sitting with you guys, and telling you about how your *Zarzz* is better than the stuff we buy, and then someone yelled something about drones, and you yanked me out of my chair, and then it got really loud, and that's all I remember."

"You are suffering from memory loss." Vrikk sounded concerned, or as concerned as any Frizz could sound to a human ear. "Is this common with you, or your species?"

"It's not unknown, especially in the aftermath of stressful situations," Frank explained. "Just give me the highlights, and I can probably figure out the rest from there."

"Very well, then." Vrikk settled into a seated position entirely unlike Frank's, mainly due to her anatomical differences. "Hive Breaker forces must have discovered that we had a garrison in that village, because they sent air-capable drones carrying high-explosive and incendiary devices, and armed with plasma pulse rifles. After dropping their munitions, they circled overhead, shooting down at us. We armed ourselves and fired back. When half of them had been downed, the rest flew away. We had no air-capable drones, so we could not pursue."

Frank blinked. "Well, that explains what happened to the village, but what about the rest of it? Why does my hand hurt, and why is there a baby drone acting like my best friend?"

"Ah." Vrikk tilted her head and moved her antennae in a way he couldn't decipher. "Humans are designated non-combatants, so I assigned Prakk to watch over you. She says you ran off almost immediately after we got out of the bar, babbling something about getting your 'stuff'. She caught up with you as you left your lodgings, carrying several items. Then you diverted to another building, where the immature drone had been trapped under debris and was calling for help. Prakk says you were attempting to lift a piece of wall as heavy as you are when it slipped and trapped your hand, fracturing part of your endoskeleton. She freed you, and incidentally freed the drone at the same time. However, your efforts to free it caused it to temporarily imprint on you."

Frank turned to look at the drone, which was watching him steadily. "I am good kid!" it said proudly.

That didn't sound like something a Frizz would say. For them, the words 'good kid' were just sounds. Frank turned back to Vrikk. "And the rest of it …?"

Patiently, she continued the explanation. "Your hand was paining you, until you explained that the 'bones' need to be 'set'. A drone did this for you. It seemed quite painful. Then another, which was specialised in hive-building, encased it in hive material to immobilise it, again at your direction."

He was suddenly glad he couldn't remember that bit. The mass surrounding his hand seemed to be working well as a cast, and he wasn't in agony, so hopefully they'd set it okay. "Well, thanks for that bit. It would probably be swollen up bigger than my head by now if you hadn't done that."

Vrikk gave a very human-like nod. "So you said at the time. We gathered what troops we had — several drones, and our commanding sub-queen, Kaskk, were killed in the bombing — and left as soon as we could. Unfortunately, our scout drones were dead, so we made very little progress until you revealed that your eyes can adapt well to darkness. Jarskk had you at the front, guiding the way, but you were not able to travel far or fast without suffering distress. We were forced to halt on two occasions while you voided your digestive system, quite violently."

And that explained the cramps, the sore feet, the nasty taste in his mouth … well, almost everything, really. "I'm pretty sure I told you I wasn't fit," he said, for want of a better explanation.

"Your ability to drink large amounts of *Zarzz* made us think otherwise," she noted. "On the way, you fell several times, and dropped your belongings. Your drone retrieved them for you and carried them along, which is when you named it." Her antennae made an odd motion. "Drones are rarely given names of their own, and never at that age. That was most irresponsible of you."

Frank looked at the young drone again. On cue, it brightened up again and said, "I am good kid!"

*Good kid … **oh.*** "Let me guess. I said something like, '*you're a good kid*' when he picked up my stuff?"

"Yes. You are remembering?"

"No." He chuckled, then winced as his *everything* complained about the sudden muscular contraction. "I'm thinking the translator doesn't quite understand it when I run those words together. I was just calling him an excellent child for doing that. It wasn't a name."

"It is now," she said, a reproving tone in her voice. "Drones are very impressionable, especially at that age. It has fixated on your command-scent. You have given it a name, and reinforced that name several times. It will now only answer to that name, and follow your directives above all others, until its next moulting."

"Command scent?" He was confused. "I haven't got a command scent." He vaguely recalled from the educational package that Frizz society was heavily pheromone-based, but that humans could barely smell these pheromones, and were never affected by them.

"You exude several very distinctive odours, especially when agitated," Vrikk said. "Your drone—*Good-Kid*—has fixated on these odours. As far as it is concerned, this is its command-scent."

"Until he moults next?" he asked, recalling what she'd said. "When's that likely to be?"

"At this stage in its growth cycle, several months." She gave him as direct a stare as he could've expected from a species with compound eyes. "Until then, you are effectively its commanding sub-queen."

Well, shit. He looked again at the drone, at Good-Kid. "I, uh … sorry." Even as he said it, he wasn't sure if he was apologising to the kid or to Vrikk.

"At this stage, apologies will do little. Be more aware of the consequences of your actions, next time." She turned to look at the drone. "Unless you would prefer that we disposed of it for you?" It was more a suggestion than a question.

He blanched. "No! You can't just … *kill* him."

"It is a drone." Her words were matter-of-fact. "There are always more drones."

"We're not killing him." Frank painfully got onto his knees, then struggled to rise to his feet, his joints cracking and popping with the sudden strain. Even using the tree as a support, it was difficult with only one hand, until he suddenly found himself lifted up from behind. Once he was steady on his feet, he looked back to see the young drone standing there.

"I am good kid!" declared the drone. If his features had been capable of a smile, Frank bet he would've been grinning all over his face.

"Yeah, you are." Frank patted Good Kid on the shoulder. "Thanks, you were a real help. You brought my stuff along?"

"Yesz!" Good Kid pointed at a small pile of zipper cases neatly stacked against the tree. "Isz your sztuff! Good Kid bring!" He held out something else. "Good Kid szave thisz!"

Wonderingly, Frank accepted his glasses from the young drone and inspected them. The frame was only slightly twisted, and the lenses were both intact. From what Vrikk had described of the night, he was astonished that they'd survived at all. "Thanks," he said, carefully putting them on. All of a sudden, his surroundings became crystal clear again. Poor eyesight sucked balls. "You're a real good kid."

"I am Good Kid!"

That could get a little tiresome. "You, uh, you don't have to say that you are Good Kid every time I tell you that you're Good Kid, okay? If someone asks you who you are, you can tell them, but that's it."

Good Kid twitched his antennae. "Yesz! I will do that!"

"Okay, cool." He turned to Vrikk, who had risen to her feet in the interim. "Is it just me, or is he really enthusiastic about being my personal servant?"

"You are paying it attention," she explained. "Most drones are given orders, then ignored until it is time to give them more orders. It is still learning, and so it is eager to know what you want to tell it."

"Right." He grimaced. "I don't want to just ignore him. I mean, he grabbed my stuff without even being told. Saved my glasses, too. I think he's smarter than you guys think he is."

"Drones can be intelligent if they are encouraged to use their minds," she said. "For most of them, intelligence is not required, so they do not receive this encouragement. It is unfair to them if we awaken their curiosity and then assign them to a task where it is never needed."

That made sense, in a dark and horrifying way. "But what if they *want* to be smart?"

"Frankk." The tone of her voice drew his attention to her. "You must listen carefully. I understand your query, but only because I have met humans before. Your species has an insane amount of self-determination capability, compared to Frizz. We are bound about by genetic imperatives, which force us to excel in some ways and limit us considerably in others. *We are not the same as you.* Do you comprehend?"

Reluctantly, he nodded. "Yeah, but I don't have to like it."

"I am not asking you to approve, merely to understand." Vrikk gestured outward, toward the forest around them and beyond. "Those beautiful places you created your images from, they only existed, and continue to exist, because those same genetic imperatives have preserved our culture from the very earliest days of the original Hive. None go hungry, none are left in poverty or ignorance. Every member of Frizz society has their place, and they fit into it neatly. Of discontent, there is none."

Curious, he tilted his head slightly. "So, what's with this civil war, if everyone's happy in this best of all possible worlds? How's that work?"

"You do not know?" She looked at him for a moment. "Of course you do not. Why would you? Walk with me, and I will tell you."

"Okay, sure." He stretched, feeling his back crackle and crunch. "Is there going to be breakfast involved? My belly-button's currently wearing a hole in my backbone."

"Is your endoskeleton always so noisy?" she asked. "And I do not understand the latter statement at all."

"Only when I wake up. I was just saying that I'm hungry."

"We have rations." She started toward where the rest of the Frizz were grouped, away from them.

Frank turned to Good Kid. "Wait here and watch my stuff, will you?"

"I will do that!" agreed Good Kid.

"Thanks." Frank started after Vrikk. "So, about your civil war? Why didn't your genetic imperatives make it impossible?"

"They *should* have made it impossible," she replied. "The Hive Breaker is a genetic anomaly. A drone that is able to issue commands to itself, and to other drones. It does not respond to pheromone control, but it can force other drones to take on the role of sub-queen and birth eggs. The hatchlings are also under its control."

Frank considered that. "Whoops. How'd *that* happen?"

"Unknown, because the Hive in which it was birthed has been destroyed. But the conjecture is that an outside party deliberately induced the genetic anomaly to cause problems within Frizz society."

"Well, that's gotta suck."

"Indeed."

Chapter 3: The Human is No Longer Neutral

With Vrikk at his side, Frank approached the group of Frizz. They seemed to be engaged in intense discussion, though half of it was taking place via their pseudo-telepathic antennae-touches. Jarskk, who seemed older than Vrikk, looked around as Frank got close. He was still only vaguely conversant with their body language, but at least she didn't look hostile.

"You are awake, Frankk," the Frizz sub-queen noted. "Are you capable of moving quickly, if the need arises?"

"Gonna have to, aren't I?" Frank wasn't looking forward to it, but 'shit happens' was a long-standing saying for a reason. "So, what's happening? Are you going to be linking up with the rest of your forces, doing the guerrilla thing, or aren't I allowed to know?"

"I do not know that word, but we are out of contact with our forces." Jarskk gestured to the drones, which were standing in an odd formation, facing away from Frank and her, antennae touching. "We had a contact-drone, but it was mortally injured during the bombing attack last night. Until we have two more form a contact, we will not be able to communicate with our senior sub-queens."

Frank blinked. "I'm missing something. What's a contact-drone?" He was aware that drones could be guided into various specialisations by way of pheromones secreted by a sub-queen, but he'd never heard of that particular designation before.

Vrikk twitched her antennae. "By your leave, Jarskk?"

"Yes. Explain to him," Jarskk agreed. She turned away to the group of drones.

With a sinking feeling in his stomach—it looked like he wasn't going to be getting back to civilisation any time soon, and he was way past the age to be running around in the boonies for fun—Frank looked at Vrikk. "What am I missing?"

"Normally, any two Frizz can communicate by touching antennae," Vrikk began. "You are aware of this, yes?"

"Yeah, that part I got," he agreed, then he began to figure it out. "Contact drones … don't have to be touching antennae?"

"That is correct." She sounded mildly surprised that he'd gotten it so fast. "We take a pair of drones and put them through the process together. From then on, what one knows, the other does also."

He grimaced. "And let me guess. You can't just make another drone into a contact drone, because it won't be able to link up to the other one. Each pair has to start fresh?"

"Correct," she said. "We will need to either create a drone pair here and send one back to our forces—in which case, we may as well all go—or they will need to create one and drop it off with us. But in order to do that …" She trailed off.

"But in order to do that, they need to know you're just out of contact and not dead. Also, where you are." He nodded. "That's a problem, sure."

"Yes, it is." She tilted her antennae. "That word you used. What does it mean? I get an image of a large hairy primate, very strong. This does not make sense to me."

"Oh, 'guerrilla'?" He chuckled, pleased to be able to clear something up. "My language—English—borrows words from many other human languages, some of which sound very similar to pre-existing ones, but which are too useful to discard."

"I do not understand," Vrikk said. "What do you mean by 'other' human languages? Why do you need more than one human language?"

"What, you don't?" Frank thought about it for a moment. "Well, of course you don't. You've always been a monoculture. Every time you guys touch antennae, you reinforce the language on both sides."

"And you do not possess antennae." Those appendages on Vrikk's head flared, as though aware of the attention.

Frank nodded. "Yup. As you said, humans aren't like Frizz. The farther we spread across our homeworld, the more our languages shifted. It's gotten to the point where two educated adults who live a day's walk apart might be entirely unable to get their points across to each other without resorting to sign language and drawing pictures."

"That sounds complicated and ridiculous," Vrikk declared. "This is the benefit of having a Hive structure. All Frizz can communicate with each other fully at all times. But what does that word mean, if not a large hairy primate?"

Frank nodded. "I was getting to that. It basically means being sneaky when it comes to warfare. Attack and disengage. Sabotage behind enemy lines. Pinprick attacks to wear them down."

Vrikk's antennae twitched into a different configuration. "All that in one word? I am impressed. But yes, that is what it appears we will need to do, at least until we can contact our other forces."

"Wait." Frank went to delve into his pocket with his right hand, but all he managed to do was bump the ad hoc cast up against his pants. "I might be able to help you out with that. Can you, uh, can you get my phone out of my pocket?"

"No."

Frank blinked. "What?" It had been a reasonable request … hadn't it?

Vrikk's azure-gold eyes seemed to be staring at him, asking him to understand. "I am a sub-queen of the Frizz. I do not fetch things for anyone other than a senior sub-queen, or for the Hive Queen herself. To be seen doing so would lower my standing among the drones and other sub-queens. This is not a matter of pride. This is a matter of fact. I can order one of the drones to do it, once they have completed their current task."

"Don't bother." He turned and looked over at where Good Kid was guarding his stuff. Raising his left hand, he beckoned. "Hey! Good Kid! C'mere! Bring everything!" If they had to move out in a hurry, he didn't want to have to abandon his gear.

In another moment, he saw the immature drone collecting the equipment up; the secondary arms sported by all Frizz, halfway down the torso, were certainly useful for that. Moving at a steady trot, the drone—Frank couldn't help thinking of him as 'he', even though he knew drones were genderless and sexless—came up to him and stopped. "Good Kid isz here!"

"Yeah, you are." Frank gave the top of Good Kid's braincase a fond rub. "Okay, I need you to fetch my phone out of my pocket." He gestured with his cast.

"Good Kid can do that!" Wearing an expression on his mandibles that Frank was almost sure was beaming pride, the kid eased one of his secondary arms into Frank's pocket and brought the phone out, held carefully between his thick 'fingers'.

"Thanks, kid. You done good. You can put the gear down if you want." Frank took the phone and awkwardly turned it on with his left hand. Entering the wake-up code was a little difficult, but he managed it on his third try.

"You are aware that giving a drone a choice in its actions is likely to foster an independent state of mind." Vrikk's tone seemed to be more cautionary than accusatory. "This might well interfere with future interpretation of orders, especially when the drone is not in possession of all the facts."

"So, I'll give him all the facts." Manipulating the phone's interface one-handed was harder than it looked, but he managed to tap the icon he wanted. "Ah-ha!"

"Sometimes that is not possible." Vrikk tilted her head. "What does that exclamation mean?"

Frank grinned. "It means that we're under the path of a comms satellite that's due to be above the horizon in half an hour. It'll be in range for two hours, so I'll be able to call the embassy, and they can contact your high command."

Jarskk re-entered the conversation. "I do not believe that is permissible. The human presence on our world, which includes the human diplomatic embassy, is officially neutral. They would not be permitted to pass on information useful to our armed forces, and our armed forces would not be permitted to accept it."

"What?" Frank wanted to face-palm, but he had no desire to either break the phone or give himself a concussion. "Can't your guys bend the rules just once?"

"Not under the eyes of the Hive Queen herself," Jarskk stated. "The ongoing integrity of our culture does not work in the same way that your human chaos does."

This was irritating and bizarre. "Okay, just to check. If I found out something useful to the war effort and tried to tell you, you'd listen, right?"

Jarskk's expression was unreadable, even for a Frizz. "Are you stating that you are ceasing neutrality in this matter, and allying yourself with us? You, as an individual?"

"Yeah, me as an individual." Frank nodded. "Those other jerks tried to kill me. You saved me. I am definitely on your side, here."

"Your petition for ally status has been noted. Vrikk?"

"He could have led us severely astray last night, but he did not," Vrikk said. "On the other manipulator, he has expressed doubts as to the structure of our society, especially as far as drones are concerned. I withhold judgement."

"Vrikk, your position has been noted. Prakk?"

The younger sub-queen looked Frank over. "I have not spent enough time with the human to make an appropriate judgement. I withhold."

Jarskk turned to Frank. "We can not accept you as a full ally until more evidence is presented. However, your divestment of neutral status has been noted, and we will be permitted to accept militarily useful data from you, should you present it."

It took Frank a few seconds to decipher this in his own head, then he nodded. "Okay, then. Glad we got that sorted out. If I find any, I'll let you know. Anything else involved in me not being neutral anymore?"

"Yes." Jarskk's posture was relaxed again, or as relaxed as Frizz ever got. "As you are no longer classed as a noncombatant, our obligation to deliver you safely to human authorities has been obviated. You have entered this conflict under your own recognisance, and all decisions you take from now on are your concern, not ours."

"Oh." Well, that was a thing. "I'll, uh, I'll try not to hold you back. But does this mean, if I get through to the embassy, we can do the information trade thing?"

"No. They are still neutral." Jarskk's tone was unbending. "While you are now permitted to convey such information to our forces, they are not."

Frank mulled that over. He'd met a few interesting characters during his stay on-world, some of whom he'd gotten along quite well with. "What if I could contact another human, not connected to the embassy?"

"That would have to be dealt with on a case-by-case basis." Jarskk turned abruptly back toward the bunch of drones and touched antennae with them.

Reminding himself that Frizz didn't do the '*if you'll excuse me now*' thing, Frank turned to Vrikk. "Um, so, what *is* going on with these drones? Are you trying to make a connection with your other contact drone anyway?"

"No." Vrikk took several steps to one side, drawing Frank with her. She gestured with one of her upper arms, toward the valley several kilometres below. There appeared to be activity going on down there, but his eyesight wasn't good enough to get any kind of real detail. "We are attempting to study the enemy camp below, but we lack the number of drones necessary for effective imagery at this range."

"Enemy camp?" Frank shaded his eyes, staring at the valley floor. "That's an enemy camp?"

"Yes, it is." Prakk appeared at his shoulder. "What do your human eyes tell you?"

"That it's a really long way away, and I can see movement, but that's about it," Frank said honestly. "But you're serious about letting me give you military data? How far away's that camp, anyway?"

"Approximately one and a half thousand wingspans," Prakk said, after a moment of silence.

"And a wingspan is …?" Frank knew that drones could be made flight-capable—that was what had bombed the village the previous night—but not how big their wings got.

Prakk looked at him. "Stretch your arms out to the sides." As he complied, she appeared to measure him with a glance. "Perhaps half again as far as that."

Frank did the math in his head. If a wingspan was about nine feet, then that made the distance to the camp in the region of thirteen to fourteen thousand feet; maybe two and a half miles. He smiled.

"I think I can help you out, there."

Chapter 4: The Human is Useful

*"V*rikk, *what is Frankk doing?"* asked Jarskk, via antennae-touch.

Vrikk hesitated for a long moment, hoping to gain more information so that she could answer properly, then conceded defeat. *"I am not certain. I believe he is attempting to view the camp more clearly. What I do not know is how he intends to do this."*

"The images he said he had gained via 'scope' were very clear," Jarskk reminded her. *"Perhaps he is doing this again?"*

At that moment in time, Vrikk did not care if Frankk turned himself invisible and went down to spy on the camp in person, but she did not convey that to Jarskk. *"At least he is willing to assist."*

"This is true. I still have trouble understanding how one human can act against the neutrality of other humans, but I will not question this."

"I believe it has to do with how they lack antennae and diverge into different cultures, even across the surface of the same planet. Their lack of Hive requires each of them to become a Hive unto themselves."

Jarskk looked at Vrikk, her antennae set in a surprised posture. *"That is a different and intriguing notion. This will be discussed, once we are back in contact with our forces."*

As they watched, the human continued to set up a strange apparatus, with the willing assistance of the drone that he had accidentally named. Oddly enough, rather than the almost mechanical cooperation that most drones afforded to sub-queens, the bizarrely named 'Good Kid' seemed to be virtually anticipating its alien commander's orders.

Whether this was due to the way Frankk was treating it, or an anomaly within the drone's own mind, Vrikk had no idea.

Frank

"Okay, that's the tripod sorted." Frank leaned down as best he could to make sure all three feet were solidly planted on the gentle slope. Good Kid had done a great job with extending the legs and locking the catches in place; after the first couple, he hadn't even needed instruction. "Next up is the universal swivel head. Good Kid, can you grab that bag for me, please?"

"I can do that!" Good Kid picked up the bag Frank had pointed at and handed it over.

"Thanks." Cradling it between the ad hoc cast and his stomach, Frank unzipped it and took out the universal head. Turning it over, he showed the bottom plate to Good Kid. "See that screw-hole there?"

Good Kid nodded enthusiastically. It wasn't a gesture many other Frizz used, so Frank figured the immature drone had picked it up from him. "Yesz. I can szee the szcrew hole."

"Excellent. Can you screw it onto the bolt on top of the tripod? Firm, but not too tight." Frank indicated the bolt with a tilt of his head.

Good Kid looked at the screw-hole, then the bolt, and nodded again. "I can do that!" Carefully, he took the universal head from Frank, then paused and swapped hands. With his upper hands—which Frank had already noted were stronger and less dextrous—he took hold of the tripod itself, then used his lower appendages to lift the universal head above the tripod and began to thread it onto the bolt.

"What is the use of that device, Frankk?" asked Vrikk. Apparently, asking questions was something she was allowed to do.

"Well, the scope's going to need to be steady," he explained as he re-zipped the case and put it back with the others. "Otherwise, we're not going to see a damn thing. But we also need to be able to move it around, so we can look at what we want to see. The tripod makes it steady, and the universal head there will allow me to change alignments. And, more importantly, it'll let me go back to something I've seen before. How's it going there, Good Kid?"

"I have finished szcrewing on the universzal szwivel head!" the drone replied proudly. "Firm, but not too tight."

"You're doing great, Good Kid." Frank indicated the last case. "If you can get the scope out and bring it to me, I'll show you how to attach it."

"I can do that!"

Vrikk had barely any of the tells of a human, but Frank could almost *feel* the intensity of her curiosity as Good Kid unzipped the scope case and lifted out the venerable instrument. It was nowhere near as old as the science of building telescopes, but he was certain it was considerably older than he was. Good Kid carefully brought it over, and Frank took hold of it in his good hand.

"See this?" he asked, turning it over to show Good Kid the attachment plate. "This clips onto the top of the universal head." Following his instructions, Good Kid was able to get it done; finally, the scope was in place.

"I have done well?" asked Good Kid.

"You've done marvellously, Good Kid," Frank said sincerely. "Now we take off the rear cap, slide the front cover all the way out so the bad guys don't spot any reflection from the objective lens, then open it up." With his free hand, he put the rear cap in his pocket and hung his glasses on his shirt, then leaned in to peer through the scope. "Huh. Like I thought, way out of alignment and focus."

"How do you see anything?" asked Vrikk. "That is a tiny aperture. And I thought you needed those frames and lenses to see correctly."

"The pupil of my eye is *also* a tiny aperture," he reminded her. "And the scope takes the place of my glasses. Now ... let's see ..." Losing himself in the moment, he turned the knobs on the universal head, swivelling the scope and angling it downward. When he figured it was lined up about right, he teased the focusing knob until the image was as sharp as it was going to get. A fraction of a turn of an alignment knob ... and he was looking at a camp full of Frizz.

Vrikk wasn't sure what was going on. The human was using his one good hand (which showed the inefficiency of human body structure; were he a Frizz, he would still have three working manipulators) to adjust the controls on the 'universal head' while making random sounds under his breath. His drone, lacking other orders, was tidying the cases the 'scope' had come in.

"Whoaa ..." said Frankk softly, stepping back from the 'scope'. "Good Kid, look in the scope case. Gonna need my phone bracket."

"What is it?" asked Vrikk. "Can you not see anything?" She was unable to determine how he could, even with his odd single-pupil eyes.

He turned to her and made the human gesture known as 'grinning', which meant showing his omnivore teeth in a non-threat display. She had seen this before, so she didn't step back. "Oh, I can see *everything*. The trouble is, I don't know what I'm looking at. So, I'm gonna have to show you."

"Everything?" Vrikk looked at the distant camp, barely a blur down on the valley floor. "Is this a human exaggeration for effect?"

"While we've been known to do that on occasion," he admitted, "that's not the case right now." Turning away from her, he accepted a small piece of shaped plastic from the drone. "Excellent. Now, can you slot my phone into the bracket so the camera looks out through this hole?"

The drone studied the bracket and phone for a moment, then nodded. "Szlot the phone into bracket szo the camera can szee through thisz hole. I can do that."

"Great. Let me know when you're done." Frankk turned back to Vrikk. "Sorry about that. We should be ready to roll in a minute. You might want to let the other sub-queens know."

"Let them know what?" Vrikk felt as though she was being left behind by the conversation. "What is that supposed to achieve?"

"Phone isz szlot into bracket," Good Kid reported. "Isz thisz correct?"

Frankk *again* turned away from Vrikk, to pay attention to the drone. "Yeah, that's perfect. Probably better than I could do with two hands. Okay, see this, how turning this *this* way opens that clamp, but turning it the other way closes it?"

Vrikk reminded herself that Frankk was a human and a professed ally to the Frizz. *He does not know the level of disrespect he has perpetrated.* Leaving them to their activity, she went over to Jarskk.

"Well?" asked Jarskk. "Is that 'scope' of use? It looks a little small. Is it a weapon?"

Vrikk's antennae twitched. "He did not say that it was a weapon. He merely said that he could see 'everything' and that I needed to get your attention."

The look Jarskk gave her was long and thoughtful. "Then I will come. You appear angry. Why are you angry?"

It felt good to vent the justified upset that she felt. "The drone is far lower ranking than I am, but the human spent more time paying attention to what it was doing than what I was saying. Humans have no sense of the way things should be!"

"It is as you said earlier," Jarskk replied. "Humans form Hives of one, or perhaps two. Frankk does not see us as part of his Hive, but does see the drone as such."

"Oh." Vrikk felt the anger drain away. "I am not used to dealing with non-Hive."

"None of us are used to it, but humans are our trade allies." Jarskk touched antennae with her, giving her an encouraging emotional boost. "Let us go and see what he meant by 'everything'."

When they returned, the human's 'phone' was attached to the end of the 'scope' via the bracket. Frankk had replaced his glasses-frame device over his eyes and was watching the screen of the phone as he moved the knobs very carefully.

"Well, Frankk," announced Jarskk. "Vrikk says you have something for us. Is this the case?"

"I'm pretty sure I do." Frankk stepped back from the scope. "Feast your eyes, ladies."

The idiom sounded bizarre at best, but Vrikk ignored it. Humans were like that. She of course deferred to Jarskk as the superior sub-queen moved in to examine the screen, but there was room for her as well.

"Hive …" breathed Jarskk, and Vrikk silently agreed with her. Where the camp was a distant blur, what they could see on the phone screen was so detailed that many of the Frizz in the image were individually recognisable.

"So, figure your high command could use this?" asked Frankk.

Jarskk leaned in until her compound eyes were half a metre from the small screen. "How many images can you capture from this?"

"I can take all the pictures you like." Frankk performed one of those endoskeletal shrugs. "If you want, I can get footage."

"Footage, yes." Jarskk's head twitched minutely; Vrikk knew she was trying to use different angles with her compound eyes to bring the screen into better focus. "And I will need images of each prominent Frizz there. If I am not mistaken, I recognise some of them."

"Sure, I can absolutely get all that," said Frankk. "I'm pretty certain we can even get a good layout of the camp. But what are we gonna do with all this? You're still out of touch with your high command."

Jarskk was still studying the screen. "You mentioned a potential contact, not a member of the human diplomatic team."

"Yeah, I can try to get in touch. There's just one thing, though …" He trailed off, as though reluctant to complete his statement.

Once more, Vrikk was struck by the contrast; when dealing with other Frizz, what needed to be said was stated out loud. Humans seemed to work by a whole different set of rules. *How do they ever get anything done?* "What is this thing you speak of?" she asked.

"The guy I was talking about … he's not necessarily totally legal in his dealings. And he's gonna want some kind of [*quid pro quo*] for helping out. Because he *will* be asking what's in it for him."

"He will not choose to assist you simply because you are both human?" asked Vrikk, deciding not to ask what the words meant. She was learning that many supposedly simple human phrases had layer after layer of meaning cloaking them.

Frankk swivelled his head back and forth on his neck in the human negation gesture, as though shaking off flying pests. "He won't care about that part at all. But if you can maybe offer him some sort of exclusive trade agreement, he'll more than likely agree to pass information on."

Jarskk spoke up. "Frankk, I need your scope to look downward. There is something happening."

"Okay, gimme a second," said Frankk. Peering at the screen, he reached up with his good hand and moved a knob slightly. The view scrolled downward, and then both Vrikk and Frankk saw what Jarskk was referring to.

"Those are *humans*," Vrikk said, trying not to sound as though she were accusing Frankk of being in league with them. *Humans have their own individual Hives,* she reminded herself. "What are humans doing in a Hive Breaker camp? Have they allied with our enemies, as you have with us?"

Frankk pulled at his flexible lower lip as he stared at the unmistakeable form of several humans among the Frizz. "Those two idiots there look like they have, yeah," he said, pointing at the screen. "But the others … they aren't happy about being there. Not even a little bit." He brushed his finger across the screen, and Vrikk heard a *click*. "I'm pretty sure our diplomatic corps will be really interested in hearing about *this*."

"Once we get into contact, yes," agreed Jarskk. "But what happens then? We cannot simply direct an attack to destroy the camp, or the unwilling humans may be harmed."

"Yeah, true." Frankk looked thoughtful. "Quick question. In your culture, do you have the concept of the [*prison break*]?"

Vrikk and Jarskk touched antennae for a moment, searching for the phrase, then separated. "No," admitted Jarskk. "What is that?"

Frankk smiled.

Chapter 5: The Human Has a Pack Bond

"No." Jarskk's tone was uncompromising, to the point that Vrikk would have had the greatest difficulty in even *considering* not doing what she said, and Prakk would have no chance at all. Yet Frankk stood firm against it, disregarding tone, stance and command pheromones … everything.

"Why not?" he argued, as though asking why the sun did not stand still in the sky for them. An entirely unreasonable question, yet he *did not see it that way.* "We need to get more information, and we need to get those innocents out of there."

"That is not in question, Frankk." Jarskk spoke evenly. "But if you go down there, they will discover your plans and all will be lost."

Frankk's mobile features contorted oddly. The tufts of hair above his single-pupil eyes lowered while the flexible skin of his face creased in ways that chitin never could, ways Vrikk had trouble looking at. He also spread his manipulators, apparently forgetting that one of them was injured. "I'm sorry. Do you think I'm just going to tell them everything up front?"

"No." Jarskk's antennae assumed a satisfied posture, now they'd reached the point that she could explain his error to him. "But they will of course ask where you came from. You will then tell them about us."

"Uh … no." Frankk shook his head again in a negatory gesture. "I'm gonna spin 'em a line. Sure, I'll tell them I'm a tourist, but I'm pretty sure I can come up with a story that doesn't involve a ragtag band of plucky loyalists fighting back against the revolutionaries. Even though popular culture where I come from does tend to favour the Rebellion over the Empire."

Most of the terms he used were understandable, though Vrikk suspected there existed deeper connotations than were visible at first antennae-touch. However, she spared only a fraction of a wingbeat for that thought, because something else had pushed to the front. Jarskk, it seemed, had seen it as well.

"What do you mean, *'come up with a story'*? What story can you tell, other than what is so?"

Frankk, once more, did not appear to comprehend her deeper meaning. "Hey, give me *some* credit. I'll tell 'em I was climbing one of those godawful steep mountain paths and fell and lost all my supplies, and I've been wandering around tired and hungry ever since." At that moment, his internal organs literally uttered an audible noise. "Well, *that* part I won't have to fake, anyway."

"I … fail to comprehend." Jarskk's antennae assumed the posture of *'needing more information'*. "How is it that you can speak of events that did not happen?"

If Frankk had been a Frizz, both his antennae would have stood up straight at that moment, so clear was his moment of realisation. "Wait. You guys can't *lie*?"

Vrikk at least knew the word, though the concept was fuzzy to her. So, fortunately, did Jarskk. "Misrepresenting what is so rarely happens among Frizz. If we are speaking with a lower caste, no explanation is required. Commands are simply followed. To a higher caste, we do not misrepresent, from duty and from pheromones. And, of course, any unpalatable facts that we attempt to conceal will be revealed at the first antennae-touch. So, we do not. But the way you asked that question seems to indicate that … you *can*?"

"Well, yeah." Frankk made a noise that may have indicated amusement. "I can lie my ass off all day long. There's nothing stopping me except social convention. But I thought you knew that. Otherwise, why'd you debate over allowing me to act as your ally?"

Jarskk flicked her antennae. "Just because you are opposed to the Hive Breaker's forces to the point that you will act against them, does not mean that you agree with every aspect of regular Frizz society. After all, we and they are a different species to you, and you may find yourself in opposition to some of our regular practices as well."

"Huh. I guess that makes a weird kind of twisted sense. And you're right: I don't necessarily like everything about your society. But as of right now, the Hive Breaker's people are the only ones who've attacked me. So, I'm totally willing to lie on your behalf and work with you."

"But will other humans not detect your lies and force you to recant them?" Jarskk indicated her antennae. "I understand that you do not possess these, but … how else would you keep order in your society?"

Vrikk's own antennae straightened in surprise. *How could I not have seen that?* She had gotten so used to associating with Frankk as a fellow sapient that she had forgotten the one basic fact differentiating them. Humans did *not* possess antennae, which meant they could not simply pass information from one to another via that means!

Again, Frankk made the noise that indicated amusement. "Oh, man. Order? We don't have *order*. Human society is barely controlled chaos at the best of times. We spend the first eighteen years of our lives learning how to act in civilised society, and even then way too many of us ignore all that and just … do whatever. You've got your social hierarchy; if we get caught breaking a law, we're punished by way of financial penalties, or actual imprisonment away from society."

Vrikk knew what money was. It was used to a certain degree among the lower castes, to pass on social credits in return for goods and services, but at her level she rarely if ever needed to handle tokens. From the way Frankk was speaking, humans *hoarded* the tokens instead of simply passing them on. Not for the first time, she reminded herself that humans were alien in more ways than mere outward appearance. "And that works?" she asked before she could stop herself.

"Eh … well …" Frankk shrugged again. It seemed to be a favoured gesture of his. "It's not *perfect*, and in fact there are many abuses of the system, but it's a lot better than some of the previous systems we've had."

"You did not answer my question." Jarskk spoke sharply. "Can other humans not detect your … lies? And use force to compel you to speak of what is so?"

"Whoa, steady back there." Frankk spoke in a reproving tone. Vrikk got the impression that had he been a Frizz, his antennae would have been bristling. It was an exceedingly odd mental image. "I'm choosing to work with you because I think it's the best thing to do. This does *not* give you the right to talk to me like that. I'm not one of your sub-queens, and I'm for damn sure not a drone. But to answer your question, maybe. Some humans can tell when others are lying, from observation, but it's very much a case-by-case situation. And if I tell them what they want to hear, they're a lot less likely to question my story."

Had Vrikk's mandibular construction possessed a lower jaw, it would have dropped at that moment, as she had seen in images of humans who were shocked and surprised. As it was, her antennae flattened back against her head and she crouched slightly, as did Prakk. Neither of them wished to draw the attention of their senior sub-queen at that moment.

Jarskk's antennae twitched to an angry posture, then to one of reluctant acceptance. "I … believe I understand what you are saying. Do you think they are likely to see through your misrepresentations?"

"That, I don't know," Frankk admitted. With her new awareness of humanity's ability to lie without consequence, Vrikk now understood that he could have stated his certainty of passing muster and they would have known no different. "But it's our best bet. If you're going to paste that camp down there, I need to get the poor bastards who *don't* want to be there out of the way. And the best chance to get that done is me going down there."

Jarskk twitched her antennae in agreement. "That is true. But will they not ask you where you received the cast on your arm, if you have not seen any Frizz since you were injured?"

Frankk's lips pulled aside to show his individual bony teeth, quite different from the grinding plates of a Frizz. From what Vrikk understood, his expression was that of strong distaste rather than the happiness that a similar expression could convey. "God damn it. That's right." He lifted his head to look at Jarskk. "Would it be possible for your guys take it off again, remove any trace of it? I'll have to rig a sling for the arm."

"You are willing to jeopardise the ready healing of the limb?" Jarskk sounded no less shocked than Vrikk felt. "Your manipulator may never work properly again, if it is badly treated."

"I'll survive. But what I'm worried about is Good Kid."

Prakk and Vrikk each turned to look at the juvenile drone. It stood alongside Frankk's tripod and scope, watching them with a very *aware* set to its antennae.

"What about it?" Jarskk's tone was dismissive.

Frankk took a step closer to her. "You don't touch him. You don't hurt him. I know your culture sees drones as expendable, but his life and wellbeing are *my* price for going down there and helping sort out *your* shit. Is that understood?"

Vrikk found herself struggling with yet another alien concept. Frankk was not Frizz, certainly, but how could he be so concerned with the life of a simple *drone*? Of a species not remotely similar to his, at that?

"… agreed," Jarskk said eventually. It could not have been easy for her. To see a drone taking orders from a non-Frizz and acting in such a non-drone fashion was hard enough for Vrikk, and she was not the senior sub-queen here. "It will not be harmed."

Frankk went to speak, then paused thoughtfully. "You know, it's just occurred to me that you can lie to me as easily as I can lie to you, and you don't have any superiors here to answer to. But you can't lie over antennae-touch, can you?"

"No," Jarskk said tightly. "But you lack antennae, so I would not be able to confirm my words to you in that fashion."

"Hm, true." Frankk gestured to Good Kid. "Tell *him* via antennae-touch, then. He can confirm to me what you said."

Vrikk had heard it said that humans were good at thinking sideways, but she had not understood what it meant until now. Good Kid was *not* under the command of any of the sub-queens present, and was in fact subservient to Frankk. Should Jarskk attempt to lie to the drone, it would know, and it would inform the human.

If Jarskk's antennae had been any more tense, they would have been throwing off sparks. "You would have me report to a *drone* in the same way I would do with a superior sub-queen?"

"No." Frankk was not conceding an inch. "While he's my subordinate, he's not a drone. He's an independent person. And you talking to him is the only way I can be certain that you won't 'accidentally' murder him the moment I'm out of sight."

"And if I do not speak with the drone?"

"That call I was going to make, passing on all that information for your armed forces? I don't make it." Frankk ostentatiously tapped an icon on his 'phone'. "Looks like the comms satellite is above the horizon now. In two hours, it'll be down again. I can't guarantee how long it will take to send the data. But if you want to hold out on me, that's totally your choice."

"Frankk." Vrikk stepped forward, attempting to reason with the human. "I told you that there are things we cannot do, due to caste. Treating a drone as equal or near-equal is one of those things."

"Can't do, or don't want to do?" Frankk's lips were pressed tightly together at the end of the question. Vrikk imagined mandibles grinding together.

"Jarskk is the highest-caste Frizz here. It is literally below her to act as though your drone deserves her active attention." Vrikk knew her words may serve to anger Frankk more, but could not imagine a way of telling him in a different fashion.

But instead of escalating the conflict, Frankk creased the skin above his eyes once more. "Okay. How about you? Can *you* speak to him via antennae-touch? You're the second highest Frizz here, and he's the second highest in the Frank organisation. Or is that *still* too much of an imposition?"

Vrikk's antennae rubbed together in agitation, but she made a gesture of assent. "It is not. If I am passing on information, not receiving direction, it can be done."

"Good." Frankk looked at Jarskk. "If you can tell Vrikk specifically that you're not going to harm Good Kid or give orders for him to be harmed, then Prakk does the same, then Vrikk tells Good Kid exactly what both of you said, and adds her own assurances, that should work."

"You humans are strange beings. Violent to your own kind, yet you go far to protect those you barely know of another species." Jarskk touched antennae to Vrikk and passed along the message.

"It's a thing we do," agreed Frankk, while waiting for Prakk to do the same. "Once upon a time, thousands of years ago, a member of a savage predator species spent too long following humans around and eating scraps that were thrown to it. Now the original species is almost extinct, but the off-shoot from that species is almost as numerous as humanity itself."

Vrikk tensed her mandibles as she leaned over to touch antennae with the drone named 'Good Kid'. *Jarskk told me that she would not harm you or order you harmed. Prakk told me that she would not harm you or order you harmed. I will not harm you or order you harmed.*

As soon as the information transfer was complete, she stepped back, breaking the link. Despite the necessity of it, she still felt as though her antennae had been somehow soiled in the process. She determined to spend extra time on her next grooming session.

"Okay, Good Kid, what did they tell you?" Frankk asked.

"Szub-Queen Vrikk szaid that Szub-Queen Jarszkk and Szub-Queen Prakk both szaid they would not harm me or order me harmed," recited Good Kid proudly. "Szhe alszo szaid szhe would not do it."

"Great," Frankk said. "So, this guy is all about the profit motive. I was thinking you could maybe offer him the following deal ..."

Chapter 6: The Human Negotiates

Jimmy Argus, owner and sole operator of the grandly titled 'Argus Shipping Enterprises', paused in his collating of goods to go on board the one dilapidated freighter that he had to his name. The civil war didn't seem to be dying down any time soon, and he didn't want to be caught on the ground when or if it rolled through the capital. The trouble was, he had more in his warehouse than he could legally fit on the *Argus One*; if he took just the stuff he knew would pass scrutiny with the outgoing inspectors, it wouldn't all fit on board. And if he took the bits and pieces that would *not* make it through an inspection, it wouldn't all fit into his scan-shielded hidey-holds.

Life had been much easier, he decided, before the Frizz decided to have a civil war. How they'd even managed to *have* one was beyond him, but the universe seemed intent on screwing him over no matter what he did to get ahead. Whatever he left behind, he just *knew* would be gone when he got back, either stolen by whoever broke into his warehouse or discovered and confiscated by the authorities.

He honestly didn't want to know what the Frizz did to punish people who absconded with bits and pieces of their precious heritage. Just looking at the dull red eyes of their soldier drones as they passed by was creepy enough. Would they just deport him, or would he end up in some distant Hive, paralysed and being eaten alive by their young?

His phone chimed, interrupting his less than pleasant reverie. Taking it out, he stared at the number and the name. He didn't know anyone called Frank. But then, answering calls from strangers was an occupational hazard of the job. "Argus Shipping, Jimmy Argus speaking. You crate it, we'll ship it. How can I help you today?"

"Jimmy, how are you? It's Frank Hopewell here. We met a week ago in the bar. I'm the guy with glasses who was asking about where to go to get good photos. I just need a moment of your time."

Jimmy frowned. The name still escaped him, but he vaguely recalled a guy on the pudgy side with glasses, who'd been rabbiting on in detail about capturing the beauty of Frizz architecture. He'd also bought Jimmy several drinks and listened to a bunch of his stories, which had endeared him to the smuggler enough that they'd swapped contact details.

However, this was not a good time for old home week. "Yeah, it's good to hear from you, Frank, but unless you're already off-planet, I'd advise you to get there. I'm busy sorting out my affairs as well. So, if you don't mind—"

"Jimmy." Frank's tone became a great deal more definite. *"How would you like to become a very rich man?"*

Well, of *course* Mrs Argus' little boy wanted to become very rich. Who didn't? But there would be a catch. There was always a catch. "What have you got? It's going to need to be under one hundred kilos, if I'm going to fit it into—"

"Jimmy." There was that tone again. *"This isn't a smuggling thing. This is legal. Zarzz, you know the stuff?"*

Everyone who had heard of the Frizz knew about *Zarzz*. It was a rite of passage for new visitors to try it out. Barely fermented, it was popular among some, but he didn't really like it. He preferred his booze to have a kick to it. Also, the stuff you could get on-planet was light-years better than what they let leave the gravity well.

"Yeah, I know the stuff. Who doesn't? And why?"

"How would you like the rights to ship the good-quality version back to Earth, with the chance of making it exclusive?"

Jimmy blinked. He knew it was already popular on Earth, and that was just the basic version. If proper *Zarzz* made it back home, it would be *the* big new thing. Even with a non-exclusive trade deal, he could make an absolute killing. "You have my undivided attention. How did you get your hands on this, why not hold onto it for yourself, and what do I have to do?"

"Long story, don't want it, and nothing illegal. I just need you to deliver a message. Can you do that for me?"

"Message? Who do you want me to deliver a message to, and what's the message?" He was harbouring severe doubts about the 'nothing illegal' aspect, but in his line of business, illegality was more of a detail than a deal-breaker.

He heard Frank take a deep breath. *"I'm going to send a datadump to your phone. A big one. I need you to go to the Frizz military headquarters in the capital, and ask for a Sub-Queen Preskk. Tell her that Sub-Queen Kaskk is dead, but you have a message from her subordinates. Pass the datadump on to her."*

"Holy Mary, mother of cargo." Jimmy pushed his fingers through his hair. "The Frizz are already on edge. If I just walk in, they're likely to shoot first and interrogate my smoking remains."

"No. They won't. Humans are neutral in this conflict, so at worst they'll escort you out. Oh, yeah, before you turn the datadump over to Preskk, you have to explain that you're relinquishing your neutral status and applying for ally status with the Frizz. That's the only way they're allowed to accept the information from us."

"And they'll give me the right to export *Zarzz*?"

Frank cleared his throat. *"Not right away. They don't know about this deal yet. But I have three sub-queens with me right now who are willing to sell you the excess from their home Hives on the cheap, to re-sell elsewhere. If this datadump is as valuable as they think it is, you might just get awarded the exclusive license from the Hive Queen herself as a reward for being a trusted ally."* He paused. *"Maybe."*

Well, at least he was being honest about it. "So, what's in it, anyway?"

There was a pause, then a chuckle. *"You're a smart guy. You've already figured out it's valuable to the loyalist side of the civil war. And the type of guy you are, you're wondering if you could get more from the other side."*

Jimmy had indeed been wondering exactly that, but he didn't have to admit it out loud. "What sort of a person do you think I am, anyway?"

"The sort of person who will grab whatever opportunity that comes past. I get that. But I want you to think about this." Frank's voice went serious again. *"This deal is already set up. Deliver that datadump, you are guaranteed three Hives' worth of Zarzz, with the potential for more. Screw us—me and the Frizz—and you're not guaranteed a damn thing from the Hive Breaker's people. They don't know you from whatever the Frizz version of Adam is. Also, revolutionaries are historically bad at remembering promises made in the heat of battle, once they become the new ruling class."*

Put that way, he could definitely see Frank's side of things. "Okay, right. What's the time window on this?"

"Sooner rather than later. So, it's a deal?"

Jimmy took a deep breath. Doing this would put him directly on the radar of the Frizz military command, in more ways than one. Until now, he would've been just one more human to them, but that was no longer the case. If the data was somehow bad, he *knew* they'd blame it on him. But if he did it right …

"Okay. It's a deal. Datadump me."

"Incoming now. Please don't let us down."

The call ended, then his phone beeped and flashed up a screen. *ACCEPT INCOMING FILES?*

He tapped **Y**, and the download began. When he saw the size of the datadump, his eyebrows rose. *Holy crap, Frank, what are you up to?*

He knew it would be a while, if ever, before he found out.

Frank wanted to hold the phone up in the air to improve reception, but he knew it wouldn't change a damn thing. There were two numbers ticking down on the screen; one showing the progress of the upload, and one showing the interval before the satellite went over the horizon. The satellite's countdown was steady and inexorable, while the upload jumped forward in irregular steps.

When the countdown dropped to less than a minute, he held it in the air anyway, staring fixedly at the screen. "Come on …" he mumbled, trying to recall what the very last part of the datadump had been, or if it would even have gone in sequence. "Come *on*."

Forty seconds to go. Three uploads.

Thirty seconds. Still three uploads.

Twenty seconds. Two uploads.

Ten seconds. Two uploads.

Five seconds. One upload.

Beep. **UPLOADS COMPLETE. SATELLITE OUT OF VIEW.**

He sagged, letting his good arm flop to his side, still holding the phone. "Arrgh. I am not cut out for this crap."

"What is wrong, Frankk?" Vrikk stared at him with her azure-gold eyes. "Did it fail?"

"No." He shook his head. "It went through, I think. I'm just not built for this kind of high-stress lifestyle. Slow and steady, and taking my time with a photoshoot, that's me."

"Are you saying you cannot go to the camp, Frankk? That will be stressful."

He shook his head again. "I can do it. I won't exactly *enjoy* it, for obvious reasons, but it's something that's gotta be done, and I'm the only human on site."

"You mean, you are the only one who can lie to them." Vrikk's gaze was as steady as only something with compound eyes could manage.

"Well, yeah. If I don't go down there and make up a good story, those humans who don't want to be there will be trapped when Preskk's forces come on down that valley and steamroller the whole camp into a greasy paste." Frank held out the phone to Good Kid, who accepted it. "I can't let that happen."

"If you do not get out in time yourself, you may be trapped as well." Frizz overtones and undertones weren't really equipped to show concern, but he thought he heard it in her voice anyway. "If you had not allied with us and passed on that information, your fellow humans would not be in danger, and you would not be needing to break them out now. Why did you do this?"

He wasn't sure about that himself, but he forced a chuckle. "They attacked me, and you saved me. It's as simple as that."

Vrikk stood alongside the group of drones, touching antennae with one. Their antennae were interlinked, so she could see the amalgam of what they could all see. Frankk was most of the way down the hill, making steady progress. He had fallen three times that she could see, but had gotten back to his feet each time. She could not see if his damaged appendage had become more injured than it already was from his falls; unlike with a Frizz, it was impossible to tell from external observation.

"He will be there soon." That was Jarskk, standing nearby.

"He will," Vrikk agreed. "Do you think his accomplice will indeed deliver the information to Sub-Queen Preskk?"

"I am in no way equipped to make that prediction," Jarskk chided her. "Humans are strange and incomprehensible. They live by no rules except those they choose to abide by. There is no inherent order to them. If one human gives a command to a lower ranking one, the other human is not compelled to obey."

"And worse," Prakk added, "their chaos is infectious." She turned to look at the anomalous drone, which was doing something with Frankk's 'scope'. "It acts more like a human than a Frizz, merely by spending time with him."

"It is no act." Vrikk ran her upper manipulators over her antennae. "Its mind is not like that of any other drone. It *thinks*. All the time. I saw this in its mind when I antennae-touched with it."

"Will this be a problem?"

"I don't know. It does what Frankk says, and he is allied to us, so … perhaps not?"

The drone with the name 'Good Kid' did not say a word as it attached the phone to the scope as Frank had shown it. It knew that sub-queens always talked in front of drones as though they were not there, because drones didn't normally think about what was being said, only about their orders. But the interactions between it and Frank had opened up new pathways in its brain.

Instead of giving it unequivocal orders, he had made suggestions and given it options. That, and the positive reinforcement he had given it, had pushed it to think for itself and make real decisions about its actions. Even in his interactions with the sub-queens, he had assigned it equal importance to them, which had caused a major upheaval in its evolving worldview.

Yes, I think. And I listen. I hear what you say when you speak about me. You know I am listening and thinking about your words, and yet you still speak where I can hear.

Despite the promise that had been extracted to neither harm it nor cause harm to come to it, Good Kid knew that if it spoke its thoughts out loud, that promise might be retracted. Most drones did not hold a very high value on self-preservation, mainly because sub-queens treated them as expendable. Frank, however, acted as though Good Kid had value beyond its immediate service, so it had picked up that attitude.

It did not hate the sub-queens for thinking in that way, because it did not know what hate was. This was just the way things were. Other drones were what they had been made to be. It was a fact of Frizz society; regimented, rigid, orderly.

Frank thought differently; and now, so did Good Kid. This was *also* just the way things were.

Its lower appendages finished fitting the phone in its proper place while its upper appendages held the scope steady. The phone was already activated, and it could see the image on the screen. Adjusting the swivel head as Frank had shown it, it panned the scope downward until it picked up the distant figure of Frank trudging toward the camp.

Getting down the hill had been both easier and harder than Frank had anticipated. Easier in that much less effort had been expended than going up and over the previous hills; harder in that he'd fallen three times, barely avoiding breaking his *other* hand on one of the falls, and so he was even more bruised, scratched and generally pissed off than before.

But now he was on the flat, which meant he had his next obstacle to overcome. The gates of the huge compound loomed ahead of him, along with the Frizz traitors guarding it. They held plasma pulse rifles, which he imagined could punch a smoking hole right through him if he made the wrong move.

"Human!" barked one of the guards, stepping forward. "What are you doing here?"

"I'm lost," he said, which was almost true. The fact remained that he personally had zero idea of where he was in relation to the city, despite having sent off the map coordinates to the location with the datadump. "I've been wandering around the hills for the last day or so. Fell down a gully and busted my hand and lost my stuff. I am *so* glad to see you guys. You wouldn't have some food or water I could scrounge, would you? I'd be glad to pay for it once I get back to civilisation."

The two guards touched antennae for a second, then one turned and loped back through the open gates. The other stayed where it was, its weapon not quite pointing at Frank. "A superior is coming."

"Awesome." Frank kept the mild expression on his face, not letting his real thoughts show.

'Superior' instead of 'sub-queen', huh? All hail the new boss, same as the old boss.

"We muszt move."

Vrikk turned to look at the anomalous drone, which was quickly and efficiently packing away the scope and tripod. "Why?" she asked. It had been hard enough to accept Frankk treating it as a near-equal, but there was no way she would take anything resembling an order from one.

"An enemy Frizz came to szpeak with Frank. He wasz allowed in, but the enemy hasz arranged for dronez to szearch his back-trail. They will be coming szoon." With the scope and tripod packed away, the drone began moving off toward a thick clump of trees.

"How do you know this?" Vrikk understood that the 'scope' allowed closer observation, but that level of understanding seemed more akin to what would be gained from a pair of contact-drones.

"Frank thought they might be szuszpicziousz. He szhowed me hand szignalsz he would usze if that happened. I szaw the szignal. They are coming." The drone was halfway to the trees by now.

Vrikk turned and looked at Prakk and Jarskk. "If their drones come here and see us, it would put us in danger. And Frankk, as well." They could flee; Frankk could not.

Jarskk twitched her antennae, evidently as uncomfortable with following the directive of a drone as Vrikk was. "We will seek cover."

"As you command." Vrikk hustled in the same direction the drone had gone.

By all the Hives combined, I will be relieved when this is done, and everything is back to normal.

Chapter 7: The Human Uses an Exploit

Frank's right hand was managing to both ache and throb at the same time, not improved in any way by the lack of a cast to protect the broken bones, nor by the fact that he'd fallen over several times on his way down the hill. The makeshift support he got from tucking his injured limb into the front of his shirt wasn't exactly perfect, but he had bigger things to worry about.

Most specifically, the pair of armed humans in front of him, both eyeing him suspiciously.

"What's *your* deal?" growled the one on the left. "Where'd you come from?"

"Back up that way." Frank half-turned so he could gesture at the hills behind with his good hand. "Name's Frank Hopewell. I'm a tourist. Photographer, mainly. I was looking for some nice vistas to get some shots for the folks back home when I slipped and fell. Knocked myself silly, busted my hand up, lost all my gear, and got myself totally turned around. I tell you what, I was never so glad as when I saw you guys. I didn't even know there was a Frizz town here. Where's the closest doctor?"

The two humans shared a glance, then bestowed another dubious look on him. He hoped suspicion was their default, not something he'd accidentally triggered through his words. If they were used to being suspicious, they'd probably decide eventually that he wasn't dangerous so long as he didn't do anything untoward.

"No doctor," grunted the one on the right. Frank decided to call him Mojo and his buddy Jojo, after a popular comedy duo that had been making the rounds when he left Earth. "Get over there with the others, and stay put until we tell you to do something else."

"Okay, sure, but this is really starting to hurt. Also, I lost all my food, too. Is there anything to eat?" Frank knew he was pushing his luck, but he had to play up the oblivious lost tourist angle as hard as he could.

"They got food. Git." Mojo pointed again at the small group of humans sequestered in their own enclosure in the middle of the camp.

Frank held up his good hand in surrender. "Okay, I'm going, I'm going."

As he headed in that direction, he saw a flight of winged drones lift off and range outward in the general direction of where he'd come from. He did his best not to stare after them, but he was hoping really, really hard that Good Kid had been on the ball, and that Jarskk and the others hadn't been stupidly stubborn.

"I might not be able to tell if they're going to launch drones to check out my back trail," he'd told the young Frizz. "You're going to have to watch the camp and use your own judgement. If it looks like they're planning to do that, pack up the scope and get under cover, and tell the others to hide too."

"Frizz szub-queensz will not take ordersz from a drone." Good Kid hadn't sounded resentful or angry; it was just the way things were.

Frank had sighed. "Right. Good point. Tell them that we arranged for me to make hand signals, so it sounds like it comes from me. Can you do that?"

Good Kid had nodded. "I can do that."

Well, no matter what had happened, he couldn't do anything about it now. His job was more immediate: find out what these people knew, and figure out how to get them out of here before the Frizz assault troops rolled in, shooting at everything that moved.

As he neared the dispirited group huddled under their makeshift shelter—it appeared to be a tattered tarpaulin propped up on several sticks—they looked around with dull curiosity. Any hopes he might have been harbouring that one of them was a special-ops soldier on vacation were swiftly dashed; there were two women and three men, all of whom were either too old or too unfit to suit the profile.

Looks like it's still up to me. Wonderful.

The older of the two women, a tired-looking brunette, stood up to meet him. "You should've stayed away." Her words were blunt and fatalistic rather than deliberately rude. "Who are you, and what are you doing here?"

He lowered his voice. "Name's Frank, and I'm here to get you out."

That got her attention. In fact, it got everyone's attention. They started asking questions, words tumbling over each other, until the woman waved them to silence. She glanced past Frank and he looked around as well; fortunately, it seemed their human guards hadn't picked up on the sudden noise.

"You're going to have to explain that one." The woman gestured to the ground. "Pull up some dirt. We need to talk, and I don't think you want to draw attention while you're doing it."

"Yeah, okay." Gingerly, Frank lowered himself to the ground. It was more of a controlled crash than a soft landing, and he suspected he would need assistance to get up again, but at least he was on the same level as everyone else now. "So, uh, what are all of you doing here? And what's with Mojo and Jojo over there?"

"Mojo and Jo— oh, you mean Hank and Pete?" She grimaced as she sat down beside him. "That was my mistake."

One of the men, maybe in his sixties with a grey beard, patted her awkwardly on the shoulder. "You couldn't have known, Bronwyn."

"But I should have at least *checked*, Cass." Her reply came so quickly that Frank figured this was not the first time the argument had been played through. She sighed and turned to Frank again. "We're all scientists, here to study the Frizz and their planet. I'm an anthropologist, Cass is a sociologist, Penny here's an archaeologist, Doug's a geologist, and Ben's a botanist. When we got here, I decided in my infinite wisdom that we needed a couple of strong backs to do the grunt work out in the wilderness. Those two were hanging around the spaceport with no visible means of support, so we hired them on." Her tone turned bitter. "I'm willing to bet that they've got a criminal record *somewhere*."

Penny, a petite blonde, spoke up. "And I'll match that bet with one that says if we'd dug up anything valuable, they would've stolen it and made tracks straight back to the spaceport."

Frank glanced over at the two humans. "Yeah, that wouldn't surprise me. So, what, you just happened to stumble on this camp?"

Doug shook his head. "We were looking over some ruins when a bunch of them showed up and took us prisoner. Hank and Pete basically started kowtowing and telling them that they'd love to join the glorious people's revolution, and got accepted straight into the ranks. *We* tried to tell them that we weren't part of this fight, but they pointed guns at us anyway."

"Hmm." A plan was forming in Frank's mind. It was basic as hell, but he thought he could make it work if the right conditions came together. "Okay, I've got a question. Did you hear the names of any of the higher-ups here in camp? Any at all?"

The five researchers looked at each other, then Ben put his hand up. "I'm pretty sure I heard one of them mention a Krozakk. Maybe a general? Not sure if I heard that part right. I thought Frizz high command were all queens and sub-queens and sub-sub-queens."

"Not with the Hive Breaker." Frank was damn certain he knew what he was talking about. Vrikk had been very emphatic on the topic. "He's overturned the whole natural order where it comes to the Frizz hierarchy. They don't owe allegiance to each other. They all owe allegiance to him, and to the ones he assigns authority to. Whatever word they used, your translator probably decided 'general' was the closest match."

Cass' shaggy grey eyebrows rose. "I hadn't heard anything about that."

"I hadn't either," Bronwyn agreed. "Who the hell are you, Frank Hopewell, and what was that about getting us out of this camp?"

                    Alan M. Atkinson

Frank drew a deep breath, then looked the motley group over as he let it out again. "Okay, so, last night I was in a little village, drinking and talking with some of the Frizz military. This bunch attacked, and we had to make a run for it. This morning, we were up in those hills where those drones went to investigate, and I managed to collect a whole bunch of actionable intel for the Frizz, and I've sent it off to someone I know who's going to pass it on to their high command." *I hope,* he added mentally.

Ben stared at him, eyes wide. "Jeez, are you some kind of spy? Because that totally sounds like something a spy would do."

Looked at from the outside, Frank could see how it might seem that way, but he dismissed the idea. "Just a tourist in the wrong place at the right time. The thing is, we need to get the hell out of this camp because once the loyalists decide the data is legitimate, they're gonna send in a whole bunch of drones with orders to kill everything in sight." He glanced around again at the two human guards. "How often do they take breaks? They *do* take breaks, yeah?"

Bronwyn nodded. "They do, yes, but they always put one of those drones on to relieve them. In case you didn't know, drones are very strong."

"Oh, I'm aware. Though they can't hold their *Zarzz*." He ignored the surprised glance shared between the anthropologist and the sociologist as he kept talking. "And there's one other thing I'm betting I know about them, and they don't know about us."

Doug hesitated. "Uh ... what's that, exactly?"

Frank grinned.

Sub-Queen Preskk was having a problematic enough day already without having to deal with an importunate human attempting entry into her headquarters. Unfortunately, humans were trade allies with the Frizz, and they were very specifically non-hostiles in the current conflict with the Hive Breaker, so she couldn't simply order the drones to dispose of it with lethal force. In addition, it seemed to know her name, which had gotten it past several drones and some of her subordinates before one with more initiative than the others had stopped it.

She found she was unable to concentrate on the reports before her, mainly due to her antennae tingling from the repeated shouts of her name, so she ceased trying. Placing a scent marker on the page so she would know where she had been, she rose from the desk and made her way through the outer office to where two drones had the human in what she understood to be a firm but non-damaging hold. "What is occurring here?"

The query was directed at her direct subordinate, Griskk, but the human answered. "Are you Sub-Queen Preskk? I've got a message for you. Military stuff. You're gonna want to see this."

Preskk did not respond to it, instead awaiting Griskk's reply. She would not be permitted to view any military-adjacent data originating from humans, due to their avowed neutrality. In addition, she had addressed Griskk, not the human. Even non-Frizz needed to learn their place in protocol.

Griskk stepped forward and touched antennae with her, reporting concisely and accurately the series of events that had led to this moment. After asking a few brief clarifying questions, Preskk broke contact and looked at the human. "You are Jim-my Ar-gus, human freighter pilot. You are on record for several irregularities in conforming to the regulations."

"Yeah, yeah, but that's not important." The human called Jimmy Argus drew a deep breath. "A buddy of mine called Frank Hopewell called me with a message from some Frizz, subordinates of a sub-queen called Kaskk, who's dead now. He sent me a huge datadump, and I'm supposed to give it to you. It's about the rebels."

Preskk had known Kaskk. To hear that she had been killed was quite a blow, and it would explain why her contingent was no longer in contact, but regulations were still regulations. "I cannot accept it. Humans are neutral in this conflict."

"Oh, right!" The human's singular-lens eyes opened their strange fleshy lids wide. "Sorry, I forgot. I'm supposed to apply for ally status, or something? Does that let you take this stuff from me?"

Preskk touched her antennae together for a moment to let the mental feedback centre her thoughts, then addressed the human. "Are you saying that you wish to relinquish neutral status as an individual, and apply for ally status, also as an individual?" *Can humans even do that?*

"Well, yeah." The human prodded itself in the upper thorax. "Just me, not everyone."

"I understand." That was not entirely true. There was much Preskk did not understand about the situation, but she did comprehend the meaning behind his words. "Very well. I will recognise you as being no longer neutral, and accept your ally status on a provisional basis."

"Provisional? What does that mean?" The human's eyes visibly switched from her to Griskk and then back to her. It was odd, knowing precisely where its attention was at any given moment.

"It means that we will examine the data and possibly act on it. If it is found to have been given to us with malicious intent, your status will be adjusted to 'hostile', and you will be dealt with accordingly."

This was all true, but it was also a useful way of testing if treachery was being attempted. Preskk was vaguely aware that humans did not always have to speak the exact truth, and so she was attempting to guard against being taken in by a ruse of the Hive Breaker's creation.

The human seemed to swallow involuntarily. "Okay, sure, but if it pans out, I'm super allied to you guys, right? Like, I get let off any fines and stuff that I might've forgotten to pay, yeah?"

Preskk strongly suspected that the human had not forgotten to pay anything, but was hoping to avoid such payment. The human addiction to amassing markers of exchange was just another bizarre thing about them. "I make no promises."

She accepted the device that the human offered, and took it back to her office. Being entirely familiar with human electronics, she was quickly able to delve into its storage and begin viewing the contents. *Now let us see what we have here …*

The first image made her antennae flare. By the fifth, she had called drones into her office and was sending them out with messages. Within a thousand wingbeats, her office and the surrounding part of the building was thrumming with as much activity as the average Hive, and analysts were scouring through the images and footage that she had copied to their devices.

The conclusion was irrefutable. A truly massive enemy encampment, thousands strong, had been located within strike range. She knew where it was, how many traitorous Frizz were located within, and even the names of some of them. Yes, there were human prisoners within the perimeter, but she also knew of the proposed extraction attempt.

Whether the latter succeeded or failed was immaterial to her. For the safety and security of all Frizz, the camp needed to be crushed beyond all recognition. Only after resistance had been dealt with would the soldiers come in on the ground, to take what prisoners they might.

She gave her orders. On this day, the battle would be taken to the traitors, and a threat to her world would be eliminated.

For the Hive.

Cass stared at Frank. "You're kidding me. They can't *lie*?"

"Well, no, it's more that very few Frizz have ever been in a situation where lying would do them any good." Frank shrugged. "They can't present a lie over antennae-touch, and they automatically do what a superior tells them, so where's the leeway?"

"No, no, I get it." Bronwyn's face lit up. "And because they can't or don't, they won't be expecting it out of us." She paused. "So … how do we use that, exactly?"

"Well, we can't, not while Mojo and Jojo are on guard." Frank surreptitiously checked on their guards again. "They're likely to ignore anything we say, on principle. But once we get a stock standard drone watching us …" He paused as he saw 'Mojo' gesturing over a drone. "Well, in the next few minutes, we're going to see how good my plan is."

Penny shivered, even though the day was quite warm. "I just hope you're as smart as you think you are, and drones are as dumb."

"They're actually pretty bright, if you give them the chance to be," Frank said absently, watching as the two human turncoats went out of sight into a larger structure. "Hopefully, these ones haven't been." He went to get up, and grunted as his legs refused to cooperate. "Can someone give me a hand up? It's been a day."

Between them, taking care with his damaged hand, Cass and Doug got Frank to his feet. He winced as pins and needles ran up and down his legs, then stumbled toward the drone that had been placed on guard, the others trailing behind.

It wasn't a rush (not that he would've been capable of one) but the drone spotted their movement long before any such attempt would have reached it anyway. "Stop. Orders say prisoners will remain inside enclosure." An aimed plasma pulse rifle merely underlined its words, but wasn't necessary. Frank knew it was entirely capable of ripping his arm off and beating him to death with the wet end.

Time to see how smart I really am.

"I have new orders," he said, speaking as crisply as he knew how. "Orders from General Krozakk. My fellow humans and I are allies to the Hive Breaker. We are to be escorted from this encampment by you, where we will gather information from other humans and return with the information for the general. Do you understand your orders?"

The time he'd spent talking to Frizz, and hearing them speak around him, let him pronounce the name exactly as a native speaker might. As he'd hoped it might, dropping the name gave the drone pause. "Prisoners are allies? Prisoners have orders from General Krozakk?"

"We are allies, and I have orders from General Krozakk," Frank confirmed, continuing to move forward. "You don't want to disobey a general, do you?"

"No," agreed the drone. "Orders will be carried out."

As much as Frank wanted to say something like *'that's good'* or *'excellent work, soldier'*, or even *'you'll get a medal for this'*, he refrained. Frizz didn't talk that way, and he didn't want to give the drone anything odd to think about. It was self-evidently not as smart as Good Kid, but he didn't want to push his luck.

As they proceeded down the laneway toward the exit gate, he felt an unbearable itch between his shoulder-blades. If Mojo and Jojo had been watching, they'd be running out and shouting any moment now, and any further escape attempts would be a hell of a lot harder. But there was no running, no shouting.

He wanted to look over his shoulder, but kept the impulse under control. *Just keep walking, like you own the place.*

The two drones on guard at the gate turned to face them, and brought up their weapons to bar the exit. Frank's gut clenched. "Stop," ordered one. "There is to be no exit without orders."

"Orders from General Krozakk," their guard drone replied with all the assurance of one who has received them personally. "Prisoner humans allied to Hive Breaker. Are to be escorted from encampment. Carrying out orders."

The moment stretched out, tension twanging in the air, then the gate drones stepped back. "Pass," they intoned in unison.

Frank felt a hysterical giggle rising in his throat, but he kept his teeth and lips clenched firmly together. Moving with their escort, they left the camp and headed for the treeline. Once the ground started sloping upward, Frank turned and faced their guard. "We're good from here. Escort is no longer required."

"Yes," Bronwyn seemed to get the gist. "It would be hard for us to gather information from other humans with a Frizz nearby. You're probably needed back at the encampment."

"Orders have been carried out?" asked the drone.

"Yes." Frank spoke firmly. "Orders have been carried out."

Without further ado, the drone turned and started back toward the camp walls. Frank nodded to the others. No words were needed; they headed into the trees and started up the long slope into the hills.

They were all tired and hungry, and his hand still needed medical attention. But he didn't give a damn.

They had escaped.

Chapter 8: The Human Tells Lies

Ben raised his head. "What's that noise?"

Penny paused, and looked along the valley. "I can hear it too. Some kind of buzzing."

"Hey." Doug pointed back at the camp. "They're getting all excited. Running around a lot."

Frank looked back as well. Suddenly, despite the distance they'd come, the camp looked far too close. "We need to move. Now."

"Why?" Bronwyn was leaning against a tree. "They're not paying attention to us anymore."

"Shit." Cass started up the slope. "Basic Frizz psychology. Drones are pathologically literal. If you tell them to kill everything in an area … well, we're in the area."

Oh, good. Someone gets it. "Damn right." Frank followed along, though his tired legs made every step harder as the slope steepened.

"But we're *humans*!" Bronwyn didn't seem to want to relinquish her tree; whether from fatigue or stubbornness, Frank couldn't tell. "We're not even part of this whole stupid thing!"

"Think the drones'll care?" Ben began scrambling uphill, tugging Penny with him. "Frank, did you tell them about getting us out?"

"Yeah." Frank was breathing hard by now, but he didn't dare slow down. "If I know Frizz, they'll assume we're out of the danger zone and flatten the place with extreme prejudice."

"And if we're not?" Doug stared up at the sky with dawning realisation. "They'll just … kill us?"

"Yes!" Frank shouted the word, echoed by Cass and Ben.

The sound of wings from above was a lot louder now. With one last frightened glance back at the camp, Bronwyn abandoned her tree and scrambled uphill after everyone else. Doug joined her, and they quickly passed Frank.

He struggled onward, panting heavily from the exertion. The earlier descent, compounded by his overall lack of blood sugar, had been bad enough. But now, tackling that same slope, his general lack of fitness had turned his legs into soggy noodles. Worse, the sharpening grade required two hands to climb, and one good hand wasn't going to cut it.

He barely heard the first explosions at the far end of the camp over the roaring in his ears. The rescuees were far upslope from him and climbing strongly; that part, at least, he'd gotten right. As for himself, every upward step drained more from him than he had left in the tank.

I'm not going to make it. I'm going to die here.

Footsteps sounded alongside him and a supporting arm lifted him up. There was too much sweat in his eyes for him to see who'd come back to help him, but he protested weakly anyway. There was no way any of the researchers could get him up the hill fast enough; merely trying was going to get them killed too.

"You need help! I am here to help you!"

There was no mistaking the bright, cheerful tone, or the strength that lifted him and moved him onward. Good Kid may not have been fully grown, but drones were immensely strong in their own right. From that moment onward, Frank's shoes barely touched the ground, his young helper using all three free arms to their best advantage. They powered up the hill at a blistering pace as the explosions came closer and closer.

Still, it seemed Good Kid might have left it too late; the ground was shuddering under their feet, and splinters were starting to fly through the air. The Frizz were taking no chances that some of the Hive Breaker's forces might have escaped into the treeline. Frank couldn't actually blame them, but he would rather not have been in the thick of it.

"Go!" His yell was a pitiful thing against the surrounding cacophony. "Leave me!" If he couldn't save himself, at least Good Kid could live.

"No!" It was the first time the young drone had ever directly opposed his wishes. "I will szave both!" With a powerful heave, Good Kid pulled Frank into cover behind a fallen tree, where they both fell flat in the leaf litter. Frank clamped his good hand over his head and squeezed his eyes shut as the concussions slammed into his ears from all directions.

Multiple impacts pounded the far side of the log he was pressed against, hard enough to move it a little. While he absolutely was *not* raising his head to look, he could hear smaller trees all around being demolished under the onslaught. Exhaling as hard as he could, he sucked his gut in and did his best to present the lowest possible profile, for both his benefit and Good Kid's.

After what felt like several centuries but was probably only ten or twenty seconds, the barrage moved onward. Cautiously, as the ringing in his ears began to clear, he risked a peek. At the same time, he took his first deep breath in forever. The air smelled like ash and burned dirt.

All around, the previously tree-covered slope had been devastated. As the dust and smoke wafted aside, he found he had a clear view down to the valley and all the way across it. Nothing remained of what had been there before.

Mere shattered stumps had replaced all the trees downslope of him, and a few upslope as well. Had he and Good Kid been caught in the open, they would've ended up as fertiliser, just as the trees themselves were basically mulch at that point. The camp had been reduced to rubble and craters, the traitorous Frizz either fled or dead.

"Damn." He coughed as the dust caught at his throat, and tried again. "Good Kid, thank you for that, but ..." *God, how the hell do I say this?* "I know you basically owed me one for helping you out, but that debt is done, once and for all. You understand? We're square. You don't have to serve me anymore." Not that he'd been overly comfortable with it before, but now he was putting his foot down. *We did away with the feudal system centuries ago, for crying out loud.*

Good Kid helped him to his feet. He had to admit, having someone around with that much strength packed into their frame was useful at times. Red compound eyes surveyed him; when Good Kid spoke, his voice was more solemn than before.

"Frank, I have think — been thinking. You have done more than szave life. You have given name to me. You have given *thought* to me. Am needing to do what you szay because isz way Frizz isz. But would help anyway. Isz human word for not-drone, not-queen? Juszt ... juszt wiszhing to help becausze other isz szpeczial to them? Dronesz do not have feel. I have feel. Good Kid hasz feel."

Frank took a deep breath, feeling the world shifting under his feet in a way that the bombs had not managed. *No wonder they want to kill him. This is even more dangerous to their society than the Hive Breaker.* "Friend. The word is 'friend'. And I want to be your friend, too." *Better than being your master.*

"Friend." Good Kid said the word slowly, as though tasting it. "'Friend' isz good word."

"Yeah, it is. But do me a favour? Don't use it around other Frizz." Frank wasn't sure exactly how much human body language Good Kid understood, but he lowered his glasses and gave the young drone a serious look all the same.

"Frank szhould not worry. Good Kid isz drone, not sztupid."

When they finally got to the top of the slope, the researchers were standing in a sombre group near the Frizz. All five of them had made it, he was pleased to see. There were two new Frizz with the group; a drone with a slender build and large wings, and another with elaborately segmented antennae. Jarskk was touching antennae with the latter, ignoring all outside stimuli.

Or maybe she just didn't care that Frank had survived. He gave that about a fifty-fifty chance of being true as well. While he'd been useful to their cause, he presented a metric ton of procedural problems to their highly regimented society, not least being his accidental imprinting of Good Kid.

Vrikk, on the other hand, turned as soon as she registered his approach. "Frankk. Are you injured? We assumed you had perished in the bombing." She left the Frizz and came over to him.

He noted without surprise that she chose not to acknowledge the survival of Good Kid, despite the fact that the young drone was right there as well. "Nothing that won't heal. Good Kid got me far enough up the hill that we could go to ground and wait it out. Little guy's a hero, is all I can say. Saved my life." *Go on, keep ignoring him. I dare you.* He knew he was deliberately jabbing at her preconceptions, but her callous attitude toward the young drone was annoying the crap out of him.

"When the bombs started to fall, it left us and went down the hill." There were probably subtleties in her posture and tone that he simply wasn't picking up (not to mention the pheromones), but he got the impression of someone narrowing their eyes suspiciously. "Did you leave it with orders to save you?"

He thought quickly. *If I say no, she might figure out the whole 'friends' thing. Frizz might have weird thought patterns, but they're no idiots.* "Yeah, I did. Kinda glad of it now."

Good Kid turned his head slightly. "Good Kid followsz ordersz!" The statement was both true and entirely deceptive; his self-preservation instincts were definitely firing on all cylinders.

"Ah." Vrikk nodded human-style. "It was wise of you to anticipate that possibility. Hive knows what would have happened if you had continued the folly of allowing it to make its own judgements."

Frank shrugged carefully. "Yeah, well. We'll never know now, will we?"

"That is what I said. Does your hand continue to pain you? I will have one of the drones encase it once more." Again, he had trouble reading the subtextual cues, but he got the impression she was simply checking off an action item rather than speaking from actual concern: *ensure alien ally receives available medical care, done.*

"Thanks, yeah. That'll be really good." Now that the adrenaline was starting to ebb from his system, his wrist was aching in earnest. Having a cast on it wouldn't fix all of that, but it would certainly help.

As the construction drone commenced re-casting his wrist from fingertips to elbow—they seemed to chew up plant matter then regurgitate it in a paste form that hardened in seconds—Frank found the researchers moving in his direction. He nodded to them as they came up to him, trying to ignore the near-awe in their expressions.

"I thought you were dead." Doug stared at him. "When you came walking up just now, I didn't know what to think."

"Nobody could've survived that," declared Cass. "I've seen carpet bombing, but that was horrific. You're saying that drone saved you?"

"His name's Good Kid. Long story." Frank winced as the cast began to warm up as part of the chemical reaction (or so he guessed) of setting into a solid block. "I'm just glad all of you got out alive."

Bronwyn smiled wanly. "I'm glad we *all* got out alive. You saved us. We should've helped you. I'm sorry for that."

"I would've slowed you all down." Frank looked down at the lumpy cast on his wrist. "We probably wouldn't have made it out of the blast zone at all. I guess I underestimated just how badly the Frizz wanted that camp wiped off the map." He looked around. "Where's my stuff?"

"It isz szafe!" declared Good Kid, either reverting to his enthusiastic-servant mindset or emulating it really well. "I will fetch it!" He trotted off without a backward look.

"The attack was a success," Vrikk observed, once more acting as though there was no such thing as an anomalous drone. "Our ground troops are meeting with no real opposition. Much information is being retrieved about the Hive Breaker's organisation, including the locations of other camps."

"Oh. Good." Frank smiled. "Given how they bombed the crap out of the place, I'd be surprised if anyone was able to fight back. Did any of the idiot humans survive?"

"I do not know. Will your government want them back?" *Is this going to get political*, she meant.

Frank pursed his lips. "That's something Jarskk going to have to hash out with our ambassador, but I strongly suspect that everyone will be happier if it all just … goes away." He made a throwaway gesture with his uninjured hand. "We don't need that kind of diplomatic tension, and neither do you. If it never happened, nobody needs to worry about it."

Vrikk addressed the researchers directly. "But each of you saw these humans. What will you say, if asked?"

"Humans?" asked Ben. "I didn't see any humans down there. Did you guys?"

"Not a single one," agreed Bronwyn. "What a silly idea."

"Renegade humans?" Cass shook his head. "Never happened."

As Penny and Doug nodded in agreement with the others, Frank turned to Vrikk. "See? There were no humans down there. Makes life a lot simpler."

"Human lies." Vrikk turned her head to face each of them in turn, despite the fact that her compound eyes could observe them all at once. It had to be something she'd learned for dealing with humans. "Is this how your society operates? All agreeing on the same lie, and proceeding as though it is the truth?"

Frank caught Cass' eye, and his lips twitched in amusement. Cass chuckled. "Pretty much, yeah. It's definitely as good a description as any."

"I see. Thank you for your insights. I will report them to Jarskk." Vrikk turned and went back to rejoin the group of Frizz.

"Little bit rude," complained Penny. "When we came up the hill, most of them looked at us once then ignored us. That one asked us if we were injured, then she ignored us too. What are they even doing?"

Frank took a deep breath. "Okay, if I'm right, that one there's a contact drone—"

"I have brought your sztuff!" Laden down with Frank's possessions, Good Kid stopped in front of him.

"Hang on a second." Frank nodded to him. "Thanks, Good Kid. You're a marvel."

"It isz all szafe!" The young drone presented each part of Frank's equipment in turn, unzipping the soft cases one at a time for his inspection. All of it was in good condition, which surprised Frank not at all. Finally, Good Kid unzipped a pouch and produced Frank's phone. "Good Kid took photosz!"

"I'll definitely be looking those over, when I get the chance." For now, he tucked the device into his pocket. "You can put the rest of it down, if you want. You've done really well."

It was only true, but Good Kid's back straightened anyway. Frank was pretty sure he was doing the equivalent of beaming in pride.

"Okay, *this* one isn't rude, I have to admit." Bronwyn looked Good Kid up and down. "He's not as big as the others, but … he does what you tell him to?"

"Yeah." Penny nodded. "How does that even work, anyway?"

Frank sighed. "Like I said, long story. Remember how I said the village was bombed? Well, Good Kid here was trapped under rubble …"

In an Undisclosed Location

"Is it true? They hit the staging camp?"

"Yeah. I got word from one of our guys just before the bombing started. No warning, no chance to get ready. Just total annihilation. And it gets worse."

"Oh, shit. Don't tell me …"

"Yeah. The big guy himself was inspecting the place. He's either dead or in their hands."

"Sonovabitch. Six months of prep, millions in developing the gene therapy, down the drain. How did it even happen?"

"Hell if I know. They've been rolling up his network like a mouldy carpet. If we're going to make this work, if we're going to destabilise them enough so we can move in and start making a real profit, we need to make another Hive Breaker."

"And how are we gonna do that, genius? You shot the last smuggler in the head. Tying up loose ends, you called it."

"I've got that covered. There's a guy I know. He'll smuggle anything for a profit, especially if he doesn't know what it is."

"Yeah? What's his name?"

"Argus. Jimmy Argus."

Chapter 9: The Human Goes Home

Frank had never met Sub-Queen Preskk before, but her role in all this was obvious. Her word was what would determine Good Kid's fate. So far, it wasn't promising.

The other human in the room, Raymond Carruthers, was from the ambassador's staff. Carruthers had cheerfully introduced himself as a 'troubleshooter', though Frank wasn't quite sure what the man considered to be trouble, and how literal the shooting aspect was likely to be. He'd raised an eyebrow at the fact that Frank's right arm was in a sling, but no comment was made.

"I have reviewed the facts of the case." Preskk's brisk and businesslike tone came across even through the translators he and Carruthers wore. "You, Frankk Hope-well, are here on a non-business visa, which will be elapsing soon."

"Ah …" Frank spoke into the silence that followed her statement. "I *was* going to be staying a few more months, but …"

Her voice sharpened, leaving no doubt as to her meaning. "It will be elapsing very soon."

"Sure, okay." Frank did not want to argue with her. "I'll be leaving very soon."

"Yes. As an ally to the Hive, you have done us a great service. However, due to your history of problematic interactions with our drones, you are no longer welcome on our planet." She was speaking almost conversationally once more, but he wasn't fooled.

"Would it help if I said that it wasn't deliberate?" It was worth a try.

"That has already been taken into account. It is why this is an interview and not an interrogation." Preskk's antennae twitched as Carruthers shifted slightly. "It is not your status I will be addressing here, but that of the drone currently known as 'Good-Kid'." She didn't have a lip to curl, but the meaning of it came across in her tone anyway.

Frank was not the fighting type; he preferred to relax and enjoy life, not jump into brawls. But he squared his shoulders as much as he could and leaned forward slightly. "You want to kill him, don't you?"

This was where human bureaucrats differed from their Frizz counterparts. Any desk-warmer back on Earth would have blustered and bluffed and weasel-worded their way into a conclusion that amounted to '*no, but yes*' while not admitting to a damn thing. Preskk simply said, "Disposing of it would solve many problems, yes."

Frank took a deep breath. "Well, killing him would be a huge problem for *me*, so can we maybe look for another solution?"

Preskk touched her antennae together for a moment, then seemed to focus on him. "We have already reimbursed you the entire cost of the trip here and back to Earth, as well as all the medical costs regarding your injured hand. Aerial drones have recorded multiple images of the most aesthetically pleasing locations of our cities, for your files. Your damaged and destroyed possessions have been replaced. You have the thanks of the Hive for your actions. Where are you lacking? I fail to see the problem."

"Excuse me one second, please." Carruthers cut in before Frank could respond. "Frank, is it that you've gotten used to having a drone follow you around and carry out your orders? Because to be perfectly honest, that's not a good look."

"It's not that. It's not that at all." Frank itched to be able to tell Carruthers exactly what was going on with Good Kid, but he still wasn't one hundred percent on whose side the staffer would come down on with that kind of revelation. "I just don't want him killed off for being an *inconvenience*. He saved my life, damn it! *And* he helped unravel the whole Hive Breaker thing, if you'd forgotten!" They hadn't, he was certain, but it never hurt to remind them.

"You are speaking of the incident this morning, in the office of Jimmy Argus." Preskk had one hell of a poker face, or whatever passed for one among the Frizz. She neither winced when mentioning it nor showed any reluctance about discussing it, even though Frank would've bet she'd rather arm-wrestle a soldier drone than go there.

"That's exactly the incident I'm speaking of." Frank raised his eyebrows. "Good Kid was the reason it turned out the way it did—"

"Excuse me," Carruthers interrupted. "I haven't been briefed about this. What happened this morning with Argus?"

Frank jumped straight in, because (among other pertinent details) he'd been there at the time. "So this morning, on the way to this meeting no less, Good Kid and I stopped in at Jimmy's office to thank him for coming through with the datadump, and to congratulate him on getting the *Zarzz* contract. But we weren't his only visitors ..."

Earlier That Morning
The Office of Jimmy Argus

Life was finally coming up roses for Mrs Argus' little boy. He'd hit the big time for sure, and it hadn't even required a shady deal concocted in the back room of a dive bar. One phone call, a datadump accepted, and a moderately nerve-wracking encounter with the Frizz ... and that was it.

Preskk had required him to stay until the data was shown to be genuine, then he was allowed to leave. By the time he got to the front door, the whole place was swarming like … well, he couldn't get away from the simile … a disturbed beehive. Only with a lot more plasma pulse rifles involved.

Nothing more had happened until late that afternoon—even the news services were coming up empty on what was transpiring—when three Frizz sub-queens visited his office with paperwork in hand. Right there in his office, they had signed contracts giving Argus Shipping exclusive access to the excess *Zarzz* produced by their home Hives, to sell when and where he chose. The legalities concluded, they walked out with their copies, sparing him not so much as a backward glance.

He lay awake most of the night, waiting for the good dream to end.

When he woke the next morning, having slept briefly and poorly, he returned to his office and began the arrangements for having his freighter converted for shipping *Zarzz* across the vast distance to Earth. The contracts were still in his files, something he felt the need to check on every half-hour or so. He was in the process of researching the ideal temperatures for long-term storage of the beverage when his office door opened and two men entered.

"Jimmy Argus?" That was the one on the left. "Of Argus Shipping?"

"Ah, yes, that's me. Can I help you gentlemen?" He didn't know them, but very few of his customers tended to call ahead with introductions. In fact, anonymity was something most of them prized.

"Yeah." The one on the right stepped forward. "Got a rush job for you. Pickup from the Coronado system, coming straight back here."

Jimmy's mouth opened to agree on automatic reflex, then he hesitated. The Coronado system was light-years in the opposite direction from Earth, which meant an unavoidable delay in his first shipment of *Zarzz* to its intended destination. Also, there was one other aspect of the situation.

"Before I say yes or no, gentlemen, I have to ask you: is this cargo legal?"

It was a question he'd never asked before in his life, but one of the contract clauses stipulated that if he was caught with contraband in his hold—entering *or* leaving Frizz space—the *Zarzz* deal would take a header into the nearest black hole. He was all for making some cash on the side, but there was no way he was going to queer *this* deal for the sake of a quick buck.

The two men shared a quick incredulous glance before advancing on him. "What the hell kind of question is that?" demanded the one on the left. "Of course it's goddamn legal."

Jimmy was starting to feel decidedly claustrophobic at that point. "Then, uh, then you won't mind if I have the Frizz inspect it in orbit before I land? It being legal and all?" *Go on, get the hint. Find some other operator. I'm off the market.*

He still had no idea who they were, but he knew exactly what their business was. They wanted to ship an illicit cargo into Frizz space, and they'd picked him as their catspaw to do it. Worse, they were clearly working on a tight time frame, which made them desperate, and desperate people were liable to do rash things.

The worst part of this was that the rash things almost always happened to other people, and Jimmy felt that their target lock was dead-centre on him.

Just as the one on the right got a good grip on his shirt-front and hauled him up out of his chair, the door behind them opened. Both of them turned and looked; Jimmy looked also, and his heart sank even further. Of all the potential saviours who could've walked through that door, a chubby, bespectacled amateur photographer was not high on his wish list. Especially not one with his arm in a sling.

"Hey, what's going on?" It seemed that despite having literally helped stop a civil war, Frank Hopewell's survival instincts were woefully underdeveloped. Far better to back the hell off and seek help than stand there and ask stupid questions. "Leave him alone!" That wasn't much better; the number of leg-breakers who would actually respond positively to that order was possibly in the negatives.

The one on the left went for Frank, while his buddy kept hold of Jimmy. "You sure picked the wrong office to walk into— what the— hey! Get off'a me!"

Jimmy had no idea what was going on, especially when the guy was hoisted into the air, protesting all the way. Before the one holding him could react, the other one was *thrown* bodily across the (admittedly small) office; Jimmy dropped behind his desk just in time. There was a complicated crash, and the two unwelcome visitors ended up on the floor next to him, cursing weakly.

"How the hell …?" Scrambling to his feet, he stared at Frank.

"I am Good Kid!" It was an immature Frizz drone, apparently quite proud of itself. "I will not let bad men hurt Frank!"

"And that's a fact," agreed Frank. "Jimmy, was this about something you did to them? Because we can get out of your hair if you want."

"Uh, no. No, it isn't. They wanted me to smuggle something in through Customs." Jimmy straightened his back, puffing himself out with virtue. "I don't do that, and I told 'em so." He figured adding the word 'anymore' would just complicate matters.

Frank gave him a mildly dubious look, then turned a somewhat more unfriendly gaze down at the two men. "I'd advise you two to stay down. Good Kid might not be up to pulling your arms clear out of their sockets, but I can attest to how much broken bones hurt. Jimmy, call the authorities. Let's find out exactly what's going on here."

As Jimmy pulled out his phone, he found he was starting to revise his opinion of Frank Hopewell. The man was definitely a survivor.

Frank

"… and it turned out that they'd been behind the whole Hive Breaker thing. Targeted genetic alterations to a single drone adjusted how it reacted to pheromones and also what it put out. Their first candidate got caught in the bombing so they needed another one, and for that they needed someone to smuggle in the genetic material." Frank gestured with his left hand. "Without Good Kid being there to kick their asses, there's a strong chance we would've been well on the way to Hive Breaker version two point oh."

Preskk appeared unmoved. "There were many factors involved in the uncovering of this conspiracy. The drone was hardly the most integral part of it."

"I don't know." Carruthers rubbed his thumbnail over his bottom lip thoughtfully. "Without Good Kid's assistance, Mr Hopewell would not have survived the bombing yesterday. Accordingly, he would not have visited Mr Argus this morning. The smuggling would almost certainly have gone ahead undetected, if not by Mr Argus then by someone else. Even when specifically loyal to Mr Hopewell, this drone has managed to act to the benefit of the Frizz."

"Your logic is sound," admitted Preskk. "Am I to assume you are taking the drone's side in this matter?"

"Well, I'm certainly not discounting the idea that the drone *has* a side. It is no automaton. It thinks. It acts on these thoughts. And I know that to you, such a thing in drones is anathema, but to us it is the very basis of affording rights to a living creature." Carruthers didn't raise his voice as he spoke; his tone stayed the same all the way through. *Very much like a Frizz,* Frank realised after the fact. *This guy negotiates for a living, and he is **good** at it.*

"Your point is understood and acknowledged." Preskk allowed Carruthers a nod. "To build on it, you are correct: we do not encourage independent thought in drones. The Hive Breaker was an extreme instance of such independence, and you can understand why we do not wish for that to recur ever, under any circumstance."

"But Good Kid *isn't* like the Hive Breaker!" Frank hoped he wasn't screwing up whatever point Carruthers was trying to make, but he had to defend his friend. "He's not trying to tear down your system or take over. Can't he just, you know, live his life?"

"I was going to make very much the same point." Carruthers caught Frank's eye and shook his head slightly: *let me do the talking*. "There is aggressive independence and passive independence. Good Kid is not intruding on your system of government, or even your way of life. In fact, I'm going to ask him that very question. Good Kid, answer me honestly; if you had the chance to take over Frizz society at the very top, what would you do?"

"I would not," Good Kid replied immediately. "I am not Hive Queen. Isz not for me to do. Frank would not like it."

"And if Frankk ordered you to do it?" Preskk leaned forward slightly.

"I …" Good Kid hesitated for half a second, and Frank's heart seemed to stop. "… would advisze him that I am not szuited for it, and that I am not Hive Queen."

"And if there were no Hive Queen?" pressed the Frizz sub-queen. "What would you do then?"

"When the Hive Queen returnsz to the greatnessz of the Hive, a mechaniszm exisztsz to anoint the higheszt ranking szub-queen to her poszition. I would explain thisz to Frank. It isz not my placze." Good Kid appeared to have regained his poise.

"You would *refuse* his order?" Preskk, on the other hand, seemed to have lost hers.

"Would you rather it didn't?" Carruthers also seemed to be drawn in by the unfolding narrative. "Madam Sub-Queen, it seems to me that you are determined to ensnare Good Kid in a logical trap, where no matter which option it chooses, it's the wrong option."

She was not to be deterred. "A drone that refuses orders is a dangerous drone. Drones do not 'advise' sub-queens about why they *should* not perform a task. They do as they are told."

"You have two drones here." Carruthers raised a finger and pointed. "Order that one to answer my next questions honestly, if you will."

Preskk froze. "My drones are not the issue."

A few seconds later, Frank caught up with what was going on. *Damn, this guy is good.* "Actually, I'm curious as to how it would answer, too." He didn't know if he was helping or making things worse, but he couldn't stand to see Good Kid treated like a loose cannon.

Carruthers was politely relentless. "If we cannot compare how your drones would act under the same circumstances, it is not a fair test for Good Kid."

"What questions will you ask it?" If Frizz could sweat, Preskk would have been wiping her brow by now.

Carruthers shook his head with an urbane smile. "We both know better than to prime it with the answers beforehand. Please give it the order, madam."

"And if I say no?" It was her last-ditch defence.

"Then I report to my superiors and yours that you are intent on arguing in bad faith, and this becomes a diplomatic incident. Good Kid is extremely photogenic. Believe me, you do not want this to go to the court of public opinion." The diplomat's expression never changed as he called her bluff.

As with the lack of sweat glands, Frizz had no teeth to grit, though Frank fancied he could hear her mandibles grinding together. "Drone, come here." She gestured for it to bend down so that she could touch antennae with it.

"Verbally, if you don't mind." Carruthers was on top of things. "We are all aware that Frizz do not make a practice of lying, but there will inevitably be those who say, *'but what if'*. So, let's keep everything above board, shall we?"

If Frank hadn't spent so much time with various Frizz over the previous day, he would've sworn Preskk was entirely fine with the situation. However, the tiny twitches of her antennae clued him in that she could see the trap closing in on her, just as she'd done her best to trap Good Kid. He couldn't help but feel sympathetic toward her, but that only went so far. Good Kid's welfare was at stake here, after all.

"Drone." The word may well have been dragged out of her by a hundred-megawatt power winch. "Answer that human's questions honestly." She pointed at Carruthers.

The diplomat nodded briefly, then turned to the drone. "If the position of Hive Queen were vacant, and Sub-Queen Preskk were to give you the order to do so, would you take the position of Hive Queen and rule the Hive in her place? If so, why? And if not, why not?"

There was a long pause, during which Preskk's antennae seemed about to twine together from the sheer tension. Frank stopped breathing altogether. Only Good Kid seemed at ease with the situation, probably because he knew exactly how the drone would answer.

"Yes." The drone's voice was blunt and uninflected. "It is the place of sub-queens to give orders, and the place of drones to carry them out."

"I have no more questions." Carruthers returned his attention to Preskk. "And there you have it. Good Kid, even under outside control, would not attempt to usurp control of your government, whereas your drone admits that it would, if given an order to do so. Who, exactly, is the danger here, again?"

"That was not a reasonable question." Preskk was rallying again, seeking the slightest crack in Carruthers' logic. "I would never give such an order. No sub-queen would. We are all loyal to the Hive Queen, unto death." She raised one of her thick upper-arm fingers in imitation of his earlier gesture. "The reports of Jarskk, Vrikk, and Prakk all indicate that humans are capable of lying with great ease and zero compunction. It may have learned the habit of deception from Frankk Hope-well."

Carruthers seemed to be briefly on the back foot with this, but Frank was able to step in. "You can't lie over antennae-touch. If Good Kid tells your drone the same thing as he told us, and your drone was ordered to report honestly, then we'd know the truth."

"I will be pleaszed to do that," added Good Kid.

Preskk hesitated. "I … am willing to accept that its statement is truthful." It was either that, Frank surmised, or have her own drone embarrass her for a second time. "However, what would you have me do? It is a wilful drone, under human control. Unscrupulous humans have already corrupted one drone in a way that threatened to shatter Frizz society. Far from our oversight, we cannot control what happens to it."

Frank figured it was time he stepped in again. "And if he stayed here, you'd be worried that he'd pass on his habit of *thinking* to other drones, and you just can't have that."

"Yes." Preskk didn't seem to pick up on his sarcasm. "Precisely."

"I may have part of a solution." Carruthers was leaning back in his chair, rubbing his lip with his thumbnail again. "Each and every drone that lands on the Hive world can be interrogated by a suitably selected sub-queen as to its intentions, via antennae-touch, rather than simply passed on through. I feel certain that you could easily come up with a series of questions that would uncover any duplicity."

"Not just drones." Frank spoke carefully. "Everyone. Every sub-queen. Make it so nobody's exempt."

Preskk's antennae stiffened. "Impossible. Nobody would assent to being questioned by a lower-rank sub-queen."

"They're gonna have to be." Frank looked from Preskk to Carruthers and back again. "This isn't about Good Kid anymore, or even about the Hive Breaker. They've just shown up the vulnerabilities in your system. Killing them doesn't remove the larger problem. Take the easy way out now, assume everything's fixed, and I *guarantee* you'll have ten times as many problems in a few years' time."

"Explain." The tension in Preskk's figure was such that Frank almost expected sparks to jump between her antennae.

In contrast, Carruthers nodded slowly. "I believe I grasp your point. Please continue."

Frank hadn't wanted to go there, but now he had no choice. "If Frizz eggs aren't already being smuggled off-planet, then they will be, sooner or later. They hatch as drones, but with the right pheromones or gene therapy, they can be made over into sub-queens with zero loyalty toward your Hive. You *need* to be able to know that whoever's making landfall is someone who belongs here, not a ringer." He shrugged with his good shoulder. "Fortunately, you've already got a head start there. Antenna-touch means there's no way to lie."

Carruthers raised a finger. "And you must be cautious of those who present with injured or missing antennae, no matter the reasoning behind it."

Preskk's antennae flared. "Have you *studied* how to undermine our society?" Her tone held equal amounts of anger and fear. Behind her, the two drones shifted slightly.

Frank didn't know how to answer that one without setting her off more, but fortunately Carruthers was on the ball. "No, but there are many humans who delight in overturning our own institutions, so we must devote much thought toward forestalling their efforts. As a result, we're exceptionally good at figuring out how to break things in theory, if only to prevent others from doing it in reality."

Preskk

The human diplomat's words made sense. Several passages from the reports made by the three sub-queens rose to the top of her memory: *'Human society is barely controlled chaos at the best of times,'* and *'Is this how your society operates? All agreeing on the same lie, and proceeding as though it is the truth?'*.

With that as perspective, the immediate problem presented by the anomalous drone receded somewhat in importance. "I ... see what you mean. Do you believe this is how the Hive Breaker came about?"

"I'm no expert, so I'm not even going to speculate on that." Raymond Carruthers (not an easy name to pronounce, but she did her best) touched his fingertips together. "The important part is that we all agree that it *can* happen again, and that it's better to prevent it by positive action, rather than raising unnecessary tensions by going after a drone who has no intention of causing problems, yes?"

She had to reluctantly admire the way in which he had assembled that statement. The incentive was all front-loaded, whereas the warning not to target the anomalous drone was almost an afterthought, where it could easily be missed. "That is the important part, yes." She pointed at the anomalous drone. "However, it must leave the planet with Frankk Hope-well, and never return to Frizz space." *That* part of her statement, she meant with every fibre of her being.

Frankk was already nodding as she finished speaking, as though he had expected her words. "That's totally fair. Good Kid, what do you think?"

Preskk was still recovering from the cognitive dissonance of *asking* a drone for its opinion when it replied. "Isz good idea. Do not wiszh to die. Am curiousz about what isz out there. Will go with you."

She suppressed a full-body shudder—drones *should not* be able to express those concepts, much less feel those emotions—and nodded sharply, once. "It is settled, then. The *Argus One* is lifting off tomorrow morning with its first cargo of *Zarzz* for Earth. You will be on it, and so will your drone."

And, Hive willing, I will never hear from either one of you ever again.

The Next Morning
In Orbit
Good Kid

Weightlessness was a whole new experience, as was the panorama visible through the main viewport. Good Kid had vaguely known that it lived on a planet, but it had had no way of knowing what that *meant*. And now it knew.

"So whaddaya think, kid?" That was Jimmy Argus, the pilot and master of the ship. "Homesick already? Or just spacesick?"

"Am learning much." Good Kid thought about that for a moment. "Will alwaysz remember where I wasz hatched, but it isz not home. Intereszting to look at from outszide, though."

"Oh, hey." Frank pulled himself in through a hatch, then kicked off gently across the compartment toward them. His damaged arm was strapped to his chest for the moment; he had explained to Good Kid that slings just didn't work right in microgravity. "Admiring the view?"

"Something like that." Jimmy nodded toward the acceleration seats. "Better get yourselves strapped in. We'll be getting underway in a minute, and you don't need any *more* broken bones."

"I will help you, Frank." It was easy to do so; between them, they had five working arms. Good Kid was mildly impressed by how well humans got along with just two, but losing the use of just one halved their capability. After Frank was secure, it found its own seat and fastened the straps, feeling proud of itself.

"So, Frankie." Jimmy spoke over his shoulder as he entered the last commands into his console. "What are you gonna do with Good Kid when you get back to Earth? I mean, indentured servitude is kinda out of fashion these days."

"Yeah, I know. I was more interested in just getting us out of there in one piece." Frank's face moved in ways that Good Kid's couldn't, indicating that he was thinking. "We were talking with Carruthers, and he suggested adoption as the simplest way to go about it. It's not like the Frizz want him back. What do you think, Good Kid? Adoption's the way to go?"

Adoption was a novel concept in Good Kid's experience, but once the idea had been explained to him, he had been entirely on board with it. "Yesz. I would like to be adopted."

"Excellent." Frank made a noise of amusement. "Can't wait to see the look on my sister's kids' faces when they meet their new cousin."

Jimmy shook his head. "And here I thought you groundsiders liked your peace and quiet. Everyone ready?"

"Ready," Frank said at once. Good Kid took one more look at the planet below, then echoed him.

"Good. Here we go." Jimmy pushed a lever forward and the *Argus One* began to accelerate, building up for the jump out of Frizz space …

… and into a whole new life.

The End

Hammer and Anvil

Part One: Unexpected Allies

The Xan'thuilli ship hit us in hyperspace, lurking in the mass-shadow of a star and then striking as we passed by. We tumbled, flailing. Our hyperspace engines stuttered and cut out, and I heard the alarms as one of them failed. From the sound of it, something was on fire.

With a horrific wrench that almost made me shed my vestigial tail, the *Promise Upheld* was suddenly back in realspace. The alarms were still wailing, but our battleshields went up so that when the Worms slid out of hyperspace and slammed another attack into us, it splashed harmlessly into the void. However, a second set of alarms soon joined the first.

"Field calibration has slipped!" warned the shield-tech, a Deep Dreaming amphibioid that was in the middle of its asexual cycle. Its name sounded like water gurgling down a drain, so we'd called it Burble. "We lost three-sixteenths in that hit alone!" Dreamers had eight fingers and eight toes, so when they went civilised, they jumped straight into tech with a base-sixteen number system. It wasn't the weirdest xeno-habit I've ever had to adapt to.

I worked the electronic warfare (known for some obscure reason as 'Weps') console, ensuring they didn't lock us up with their weapons, while the gun crews fired back and the rest of us did what we could to not get dead in the next few micro-cycles.

"How long to recalibrate?" snapped Captain Ja'kara. She was a warm-blooded reptilian like me, but she was a Pillan while I was a Fastrek. Still, species doesn't matter when you're fighting for your life. Crew is crew is crew, as Ja'kara told me once.

"Seven-sixteenths of a demi-cycle!" Burble replied at once. "Five-sixteenths if I slice the edges off."

The ship lurched, and I saw three close stars whirl by, then shots skipped off the edge of our shield. Everything shuddered. "Helm, take us into hyper again!" ordered Ja'kara. "Shields, get calibrating! Weps, blind the bastards!"

The good thing about crewing the *Promise Upheld* was that everyone trusted everyone else to do their job. Ja'kara didn't need to tell me *how* to blind the Worms; as soon as she started giving orders, I was already setting up the biggest hyperspace flare I could manage, to slow the Xan'thuilli ship down so we'd have a chance to calibrate our battleshields properly.

We curled around another incoming shot, returned fire (which they skipped aside for) and then dived straight back into hyperspace, my flare ejecting just in time. "Flare gone, ma'am. Figure they'll be sensor-blind for maybe half a demi-cycle."

"Nice one, Weps. Sensors, what do we have? How did they manage to blindside us?" Ja'kara somehow moved from behind me to looming over Pishka without appearing to cross the intervening space. On the small side, mammalian with a stripe of fur down his back and along the backs of his upper arms, Pishka was a Kromalan. Up until then, I would've accepted without a doubt that he was competent.

"Looking now, ma'am." Pishka's nimble fingers danced over the response-board in front of him. "Playback's got nothing on sensors until … ah. I see. I think I see." He hunched forward and began working the magic that all good sensor techs are capable of.

Some captains would've snapped at him and demanded answers. Ja'kara stood, still as an obelisk in the Plaza of the Lost Deities, until he sat back again. "Sneaky, ma'am. Too sneaky. They fluctuated their hyperspace engines to blend into the solar mass shadow. Now I know what I'm looking for, I can see it, but I didn't before."

"Very good, Sensors. Can you make sure it doesn't happen again?"

"Assuredly, ma'am." He was already working on it again. "I'll set it up in a datapacket to be sent out to other Fleet ships, once we get in hailing distance. We don't know if this one's just a smart one, or if it's a change in tactics."

"Knowing Worms, it's the latter. Make it happen. Shields, how are we doing?" She pivoted, moving toward where Burble was working at its own console.

"Just a few more micro-cycles," the Dreamer replied without pausing in what it was doing. "We took a bad hit, though. Some of the projectors are damaged."

"Do your best. Helm, what's around here that we can use for cover?"

Before the question could be answered, Pishka called out. "Xan'thuilli coming up fast!"

However they'd fooled him before, he was on the ball now. He sent the sharpened image out, and I saw the waveform clearly. There wasn't much I could do to confuse their aim in hyperspace, but I gave it everything I had. I even tried fluctuating the drive signature to make it look as though we had a bad hyperspace impeller.

"Drive overheating!" With a huge shudder, we dropped back into realspace. Again, there was a star nearby, but only one this time.

Oh, wait. We didn't *have* to pretend about that bit.

"Shields up!" called out Burble. "On and holding."

"Throwing out all the chaff I can," I added. "Don't think it's doing much." And it was true. The enemy ship was sliding past the waves of electronic fuzz like they didn't exist.

"Ma'am, we're in an occupied system." Pishka reported. "Planet three's in the water zone. I'm picking up modulated radio signals."

"Are they spacefaring?" Ja'kara pointed at the diagram of the system that was drawing itself on the main screen. "That gas giant with the ring system. Helm, get us there." I could see her strategy. It wouldn't be hard for the *Promise Upheld* to conceal itself among the ever-moving, ever-tumbling chunks of rock and ice.

"Sublight at the most, ma'am," Pishka said. "Satellites in orbit, but nothing on even the closest planets."

"Something's wrong." I focused my sensors, trying to burn through the Worms' own electronic warfare. "The Xan'thuilli should've come in firing by now."

"Excrement of the sun god," hissed Pishka, working his own console like a sapient possessed by a bio-organic computer virus. "They've also picked up the signals. They're going for the locals!"

It made a sickening kind of sense. Xan'thuilli weren't out for conquest. They just wanted to eat. And what they ate was the nervous systems of carbon-based life forms, slithering in through the skin and following the nerves all the way to the brain. Sometimes they kept the bodies as puppets to perform tasks that their squirmy little bodies couldn't manage, but most times they just discarded them and kept going.

The war between the Xan'thuilli and every carbon-based life form in the galaxy (my own included) had been going on since long before I was born. There was no quarter given, no prisoners taken. It was a war of extinction, though they tended to leave unintelligent creatures alone. Apparently, highly-developed brains just tasted better to them. Also, when they ate the brain, they got the ideas. Which was where they got the tech to build the ships they flew.

So, they'd been going after us for our tasty, tasty brainmeats, but when they sniffed out the signals of civilisation, they tossed the appetiser aside and went straight for the main course.

"Not if I can help it!" snapped Ja'kara. "Helm, get us there first!" She didn't order us to attack the Worm ship, because they were on a different course to us, and pulling an intercept would've been difficult in the extreme. But we knew where they were *going*, which made life easier. "Weps! You're good at signals analysis. Get me a language breakdown by the time we're over that planet. We need to be able to talk to them. Warn them about what's coming for them."

Yes, ma'am, of course, ma'am. Would you like me to run all the way there in my underclothes as well? But all I said was, "On it, ma'am." Fortunately, Pishka had already gathered a huge amount of data from his sensor sweep of the planet, and he shot all of it to me with a little hand-scrawled 'good luck' in the corner.

I resolved to buy him whatever brew he favoured most, the next time we hit port.

As we blazed through into the inner system, I set my most tenacious pattern-matching algorithms to digging into the secrets of whatever language the locals spoke. Or even if they spoke a verbal language. Stance, tone, overt or subtle body signalling, it all had its place.

On the first pass, I thought my software was glitching. There were matches and correlations, but some were hard, some soft, and some kept switching from one meaning to another. I paused and took a breath, trying to look past what I was seeing to the metadata beneath.

Then I had a hunch. *What if they've got more than one dialect?* I'd seen it before. Linguistic shift could turn *ano'oka* at one end of a continent to *nokka* at the other end. So, I told the software to treat it as a phase space of simultaneous problems, to bunch the correlating results, especially where populations would be separated by water or other geographic barriers.

It worked, but all too well. I stared at the result, trying to figure out if the software had gone mad or *I* had. By the time we slid into high orbit around the planet—Pishka calling out notifications about artificial satellites to be avoided—I had a rotating globe, with a series of colours denoting the local dialect spoken in that region. Which was all well and good, except for two things.

One, these weren't *dialects*, not the way I knew them. The linguistic shifts were *insane*. Populations barely a tenth of the way around the planet from one another were using entirely different words and tonal variations, not to mention rules of grammar, from each other. A native speaker of one would be *entirely unable* to understand the other.

And two … there were a *lot* of them. The software was hard put to give each local speech-pattern its own colour on the map, and that didn't even factor in the areas that didn't broadcast. Were there yet more down there that we hadn't sampled?

"Weps, do you have a lexicon for me?" Ja'kara was suddenly right behind me.

"Yes and no, ma'am," I said. "I'm still filling in the gaps, but … there's not just one common language down there. There's dozens of supra-dialects, all related, all distinct. *Hundreds.* The software's categorising them as fast as it identifies them, but there's so many."

"Space it. I'll work with what I've got. Transmit this to them. *'Danger danger danger. Alien invader. Big ship is enemy. Evacuate cities'.*"

One of the tactics of the Xan'thuilli was to swoop low over a city and drop a canister carrying several hundred thousand of their kind. The canister would burst on impact, sending the threadlike worms in all directions. When they located a sapient being, they latched on, burrowing their way up nerve trunks toward the brain. From what I understood, this was absolutely agonising, and if they got to the brain, that was it. Once they'd eaten about half the brain, they'd lay their eggs, eat a bit more of the nervous system then dig their way out of the body and go after their next target. They could depopulate a city in hours.

The worst bit was when the young hatched and finished eating the brain, then started piloting the body, looking for another meal. Seeing your loved ones lurching down the street, reaching for you ... well, it had driven more than one being to the point of despair. Some destroyed the stricken ones then ended their own lives, while others embraced the dead ones and became infected as well. It had never happened to my family or friends, and I had no idea how I would handle it if it did.

I put the message into the computer and told the software to encode it into as many supra-dialects as it could match the terms for, then broadcast it on those frequencies. Just as I was finishing, the *Promise Upheld* shuddered as enemy fire hit us.

"Shields are holding, but those damaged projectors need replacement soon!" called out Burble before Ja'kara could ask the question. "If they go, we lose one hand of our shield capability!"

One hand: in Dreamer jargon, that equated to four-sixteenths, or one-quarter. We all knew what that meant; every subsequent hit on that area would put additional strain on the remainder of our defences. It would become a cascade of component failures, pushing our shield system closer and closer toward total collapse.

In battle, ships could avoid this by linking up with 'shield buddies', each ship covering the other's weak point. But we were on a solo patrol, showing the standard as it were. We had nobody to buddy-shield with.

Or did we?

"Get down close to the planet!" I shouted. "We'll buddy-shield with the ground, and the atmosphere can funnel away shield overheating!" Shields gathered energy when shot at, and this had to be either radiated away or absorbed in heat-sinks, which were by definition limited in capacity. Fighting in atmosphere, the thicker the better, meant energy could be drawn away by conduction and convection.

"And we'll be between them and the ground if they try to drop anything," Ja'kara agreed. "Good thinking. Helm, make it happen."

We lurched and dived, Ja'kara latching onto the closest overhead handgrip to deal with the bobble in internal gravity. I busied myself with trying to spoof the Xan'thuilli ship's sensors and targeting arrays. And then I got an incoming signal, one that made me squint.

"Captain, the locals are hailing us," I said, scanning the message where it had been converted into Galactic Trade, the common language we used on the *Promise Upheld*. "They've got questions. Requests for information."

"Tell them no, we don't want to meet their leader. Or their sister," she shot over her shoulder as she leaned over Pishka's shoulder, eyeballing the diminutive sapient's display. "They just need to stay out of the way until we finish this."

I studied the message again. "No, they're asking for the specs on the Worm ship. Any weaknesses, that sort of thing. I think they want to help."

I didn't recall the Captain having any arboreal creatures in her ancestry, but the way she swung from hand-grip to hand-grip across the bridge to me certainly suggested it. She needed the assistance; we were bucketing through the lower atmosphere by then, and a sea-level pressure of seventy-six *fnarg* per square *krass* could make for some hefty wind gusts.

Her eyes slitted as she read the message from below. "Well, I'll be spaced," she muttered, then raised her voice. "Sensors! Package everything you've got on the Worm ship and send it to Weps. Weps, translate it and send it down." She slapped me on the shoulder. "Don't know if they'll be able to do anything with it, but props to them for being willing to give it a try. Let me know if they've got anything else to say."

"Will do, ma'am," I said to her back; she was already on her way over to Burble. The data packet hit my console, and I ran it through my algorithm. There was a lot of data to be crunched, which made me wonder about their reception ability. Should I try to stream it to them in the clear, or compress it and hope they could unpack it all in time?

Unpack. Of course.

Once the data packet had gone through the first time, I encrypted it and sent it away, followed by the decryption key in the clear. We *wanted* them to access the information, after all. Then I set my console to translating the information into each of the other supra-dialects and broadcasting it to the planet below. Each of the encrypted packets would open to the same key, a short string of numeric values.

By the time I had that set up, the ride was getting very bumpy indeed. Looking at the screens, I wasn't surprised when I found out why. Every time the Xan'thuilli ship decided to swoop toward one city or another,

Captain Ja'kara was right there, crowding them from *underneath*, Guns hammering their shields with plasma fire, and Burble doing an absolutely magnificent job of tuning and retuning our shields so that their return fire didn't do more than ring our bell a few times.

Still, we might not have been losing, but we weren't *winning*. The Worm ship had shields that were (for want of a better descriptive phrase) both slippery and bouncy. If our weapons hit them from anywhere but dead on, they'd skid off to the side, pushing the ship away. Even a direct hit only bled a little energy through, as the shields themselves rebounded with the plasma influx.

We were both good *and* lucky, so we were able to keep up the fight for a little while yet, but not forever. Xan'thuilli were not known for their easy-going nature (they didn't *have* a nature that could be described as anything but 'rapacious') and they would keep attacking until they made the perfect move, or we made a mistake. And every shot that Burble collected on the shields strained the projectors just a little more.

Something was going to give, and probably sooner rather than later. But Captain Ja'kara was never the type to just surrender, and she'd decided the Xan'thuilli were not going to have this world. So we, as her crew, backed her in this a full sixteen-sixteenths (as Burble would say). It was just the way things were. And besides, *they* might make a mistake. It had happened before.

Another barrage hit the *Promise Upheld*, and I felt something shudder. "Three projectors just went!" sang out Burble. "Rerouting power now!" I thought I smelled a trickle of smoke, probably from a blown breaker.

And then a message popped up on my screen. It was the locals again. "Captain!" I yelled. "You need to see this now!" She materialized at my shoulder before I'd finished speaking, and scanned the message.

It consisted of a map with a cross marked on it, and thirteen words. **LURE THE SHIP THERE SOONEST. STAY LOW. BE READY TO GET OUT FAST.**

She stared at the map. "Do you know where that is?"

I was already sending it to Pishka. "No, but I wager he does."

"But why 'stay low'?" She frowned, then made her decision. "Helm!" she bellowed without turning her head. "Sensors is sending you coordinates to take us to! The instructions are 'stay low'! If we have to scrape our belly-plates on the ground, that's what we're going to do!"

"But how do we lure them with us?" I asked. "If we run away, they'll go find a city and subsume it."

There was only one real answer, but it required a hard decision. Captain Ja'kara proved her mettle yet again. "Shields! Let the next one through! We need real damage that doesn't disable us! We need to look on our last legs! *We need them chasing us!*"

Any other shields tech, on any other ship, would've protested the order, stared at the captain, or refused to believe the order had been given. Burble merely set to work adjusting the shields yet again. When the next plasma burst hit us, the shield flickered for just a moment and part of the burst got through. I had to give it to that little amphibian, it was a pure artist at its craft. The entire ship jolted and Captain Ja'kara was thrown halfway across the bridge, the handgrip she was holding torn free of its mount.

"Never mind me!" she shouted, as half of us went to unbuckle and go to help her. "Carry out your orders, space you!"

Burble had done its job perfectly. We'd been legitimately hit, but not as badly as we made it look; smoke billowed out of the hull, about where the backup power cells were stored. Lurching awkwardly, the *Promise Upheld* wobbled away on its new course; wounded and fleeing, or so it seemed. Scenting an easy kill, the Xan'thuilli ship pursued.

Our shields took a few more hits on the way there; we fired back, but weakly. If whatever the locals were planning didn't work out, we were going to have to hit them with everything we had. For now, we made them think 'everything' wasn't much at all.

And then we were there. It was a deep valley, with a stream running down the middle. Our instructions were to keep low, so we kept low.

Just as we descended below local ground level—*never* a place we were comfortable being—I got another message. I had to transmit a particular series of coded dots and dashes on a specific frequency, over and over again. What it meant, I wasn't sure. There was a distinct smell of smoke in the bridge as I complied. I prayed to the Lost Deities that the locals knew what they were doing.

We eased to a halt in the middle of the valley, with rock walls towering on either side. The Xan'thuilli ship loomed over the top of us victoriously. To them, it must've seemed as though we'd fled into a trap of our own making.

"Hold …" Captain Ja'kara was on her feet again, staring fiercely at Pishka's screens. "Something's incoming. Hold …"

An epiphany burst in on me, and I threw all my resources into blasting the Xan'thuilli ship's sensors. I made the *Promise Upheld* into a veritable beacon on their screens, to the exclusion of all else.

"*Hold …*" Ja'kara was at my seatback, her vestigial claws punched through the tough fabric into the cushioning beneath. Her eyes blazed as she stared at my screens.

Above us, the Xan'thuilli ship gathered its energy for one final shot, calculated to blast through our shields and render us helpless for their feeding.

And then salvation arrived.

From all points, streaking in fiercely on brilliant flares of high-energy chemical propellant, moving so fast that the naked eye would miss them, tiny cylinders of metal came in over the valley's rim. They were flying so low that they would have had to go *around* hills rather than over them, and they were all aimed at the one target. The Worm ship never had a chance to react.

Since going into space, every species traded out kinetic attacks for energy. Lasers arrive in fractions of a second, and don't require chemical fuels. Plasma is a little more energy intensive, but still works better than a missile that can break down halfway there. So apart from a light meteor guard, nobody ever installed ship-mounted shields that could stop a concentrated kinetic attack.

I learned later that these things were called *'cruise missiles'*. They'd been launched in careful sequence from ships and atmosphere flyers and even ground sites, all timed to reach that particular point at that particular time. The signal I was transmitting was there to tell the missiles that we were an ally, and not to be attacked. That's how dumb their computers were.

But I wasn't arguing with the final result. Of the original fifty-three missiles launched, two went off course and had to be self-destructed, and a third simply missed a turn and flew into the ground. Seventeen blew up on impact with the meteor-guard shield. The other thirty-three smashed into the body of the Xan'thuilli ship at speeds well in excess of the local speed of sound. Chemical high-explosive warheads completed the job that kinetic energy began, and the enemy ship basically disintegrated.

"Now!" screamed Ja'kara. "Go! Go! Go!"

We slammed on the acceleration and whipped out from underneath the descending fireball that had recently been a Worm ship. Picking up speed all the time, we climbed out of the valley, just as the last missile came in. This one was somewhat larger, and I didn't like the look of it at all. "Shields!" I shouted. "Give us everything!"

Burble did just that. I'm not sure exactly what the savvy little amphib did, but our shields snapped up to full for just a few micro-cycles. And behind us, the valley turned into the nearest thing to a star's surface I'd ever seen, short of an actual fission weapon. The shockwave nearly tumbled us into the ground, but we had enough altitude that we recovered in time. Our shields failed for good then, but by that time it was over.

Above the valley, a mushroom cloud climbed into the air.

Repairs were definitely in order. One of the regional groups kindly offered us the use of a remote atmospheric-flyer base, and Captain Ja'kara took them up on it. We spent a couple of sixteen-days dealing with the damage done to the *Promise Upheld* while the locals scoured the area of the blast to ensure no Xan'thuilli had survived.

I talked to a few of them, once we had proper translation equipment. The weapon they'd used at the end was a 'thermobaric device': essentially vaporised fuel, ignited in a cloud. It was usually effective, they explained. 'Effective', I thought, was a severe understatement.

Even apart from that, the more I mixed with the locals, the more I liked them. They had a fairly rough sense of humour, and some of our jokes translated right across without a hitch. With Ja'kara's permission, we invited some of their engineers on board to watch and assist as we fixed the hyperspace engines and other damage. They took lots and lots of pictures.

Ja'kara herself spent a lot of time talking to people with a great deal of decorations on their shoulders. These were from all different 'nations' on the same world; apparently, it was not unusual for neighbouring 'nations' to use a different supra-dialect, despite being separated by only a day's walk. But they all had one thing in common; when Captain Ja'kara spoke about what was going on in the galaxy at large, they *listened*.

Before we lifted off to continue the patrol run, we made sure to give them the full technical specs for the hyperspace drive, the plasma cannon, battleshields and so forth. Basically, everything they'd need to get into space within a few years. Because there was no telling when another Xan'thuilli ship might come through, and we might not be there to get in the way the next time.

Still, I was almighty glad they'd been there to play hammer to our anvil. As we climbed toward space, flanked by ridiculously-flimsy hydrocarbon-burning atmosphere flyers as an honour guard, I suspected that they'd be following in our drive-wake sooner rather than later.

Because if there was one thing I'd learned about humans, it was this: when they decided to do something, they got it done, one way or the other.

Part Two: Scenting Trouble

Over the next ten Galactic Average years, I heard about humans now and again. It seemed they'd made good use of the tech-specs we'd dropped off with them. Every now and again, maybe once in a megacycle, I'd hear a few human-slang terms from fellow travellers, terms that I'd last heard from human tech workers back while we were repairing the *Promise Upheld* in that cobbled-together shipyard.

It was good to hear that the Xan'thuilli hadn't wiped them out. They were a determined lot, as evidenced by their tech. If they didn't know how to do something subtly, they went loud and proud. And when they decided to do war, they didn't mess around. That, at least, was something they'd figured out long before we came along.

The old crew was still mostly together, though with a few changes. Burble had transitioned all the way to female, gotten married, and had holo-pics of her co-mates and hatchlings up on her console. They were still in the swimming stage (the hatchlings, not the co-mates) and they all looked the same to me, but she said she'd named every one of them.

For me, I'd met a nice girl and we were talking about making things official once I got to the end of my current duty rotation. Ja'kara was still our Captain, though she'd gotten a commendation and a promotion out of the skirmish with the Worm ship over Earth. Bringing another sapient species into the Galactic community was worth a few kudos. In fact, we'd all gotten commendations over that one.

Now she was a commodore, with the *Promise Upheld* as her flagship and fifteen others under her command. She'd had each of us serve time in the other ships, bringing their crews up to speed, before she pulled us back into her ship where we belonged. It was an unconventional approach, but it worked; we were a tight, slick fighting group. We were the ones who got sent on probes into Xan'thuilli space, knocking out nests and killing ships.

As a tactic, it seemed to be working. After about the fifth or sixth year, something seemed to give way in the Worm lines, and they stopped taking back the planets we burned clear of them. We amphib-jumped forward into their space, pausing long enough to establish forward bases, then kept pushing.

Their ships opposed us, of course, but our little group could take on a bunch up to twice its size and leave them as chunks of debris floating in space, and we weren't the only strike group of our type out there. At first, I wasn't sure if that was because we'd gotten that much better or if they were slipping. Afterward, I began to suspect it was the latter.

Still, there was a saying about looking a gift animal in the mouth—I think it was something a human said to me back on Earth—so we just kept pushing forward, rolling up their defences. We still encountered ships, but these were barely able to put up a fight. Designed just to get Worms from one place to another. The sort of craft you'd find well back behind the lines.

Which made us all wonder. I wasn't the only one to spot it; Burble, Pishka and Ja'kara also talked about it. For generations, centuries, *millennia*, the Xan'thuilli had held firm, pushing outward where they could.

Their tech, stolen from the races they'd subsumed, had allowed them to face us on a one-for-one (and sometimes better than that) basis. But now it was like we had prodded a fruit long thought hard and ripe, and found it rotten and soft. We were facing Worm ships that were generations out of date, far behind the curve when it came to facing our best and brightest.

We were winning, almost insultingly easily, and we didn't know *why*.

So of course, we had to find out. With Ja'kara commanding, we roved outward into Xan'thuilli space. Part of our loadout included data-gathering probes, and we fired one off every now and again. If we saw a ship, we were to try to kill it *without* reducing it to molten shrapnel, so our tech guys could comb through any computer memory left behind.

And then, one fine day in the middle of the sunless void, we got our chance.

It was a small convoy, but it was burning hard, engines going all out. They were heading somewhere *fast*. Pishka scraped their drive signature out of the background chaff from half a light-year out, and gave us a heading by instinct and eye before his console had finished digesting the information. Ja'kara had the sapient on helm (new transfer from one of our other ships, a Pillan like her called Ga'takka) lay in the course and send it to the rest of the strike force. Then we lit off our hyperspace drives and went to intercept.

Pishka was *good*. We came out on the far side of a star, and were able to swing around it, squarely into their path, before their sensors even registered our existence. There were forty-three of them, but only four were fighting ships. The rest were drudge-haulers, and would be more of a threat through accidental collision than any sort of attack capability.

This was a real possibility, so Ja'kara had the other fifteen start shooting to kill on forty-two of them. The forty-third, a horrifically outdated fighting ship of a type that hadn't been seen on the front lines for more than a century, was ours. We had to capture it, or at least kill it in such a way that we could study its onboard computers.

At FTL speeds, there's no time for a leisurely dogfight. They ran onto our guns before they knew we were there. In the time it took me to wipe my nictitating membranes across my eyes once, the convoy was past us and gone, but we'd vaporised half of them, including two of the escort ships, with our barrage. They couldn't even evade now, because we had their drive signature. We turned and gave chase.

If they'd been any species other than Xan'thuilli, I might have felt pity for them. Ja'kara probably would've given them a chance to surrender. But Worms didn't surrender. They didn't know how.

It was impossible to interrogate a single Worm, as their intelligence only emerged in bulk. They were literally a virus inflicted on the cosmos. So, we had to kill them. And of course, to capture one ship.

We were faster than them, could follow them to the end of Creation and back with Pishka's lock on their drive signature, and I'd gotten a good look at their battleshields on the way through. Single frequency, rotating through three prime-number variables. As good as sitting there naked in the middle of space with a target painted on their vital areas.

I sent the data through to Guns and got back a quick cartoon of a limping prey-beast with a predator strolling up behind it, eating utensils in hand. Knowing the frequency of enemy battleshields can mean the difference between winning and losing, and we had it all.

They couldn't run, they couldn't hide, and they couldn't fight. All they could do was die.

One of their escorts fell back to engage us, while the others kept going. It concentrated its fire on our shields, then accelerated to ram. Burble was on top of her game; her skilful retuning of the shields meant that the incoming energy splashed off our defences like water from her back. Before the escort itself could get close enough to be a problem, the gun crews punched through its shields and converted most of it to undifferentiated plasma.

"Good shooting. Try not to do that to the next one," Ja'kara commented dryly. "We want enough to analyse." There was no censure in her tone; she knew well the demands of war.

As the rest of the strike force closed in on the remaining transports, they tried one last desperation manoeuvre: scattering to every point of the galactic disc. We all knew the order Ja'kara would give, and we were correct. "Pursue and destroy!" she snapped. "The escort's ours!"

It was a calculated risk. The chance of being ambushed was always a factor, but none of the transports had the legs to run away from us. There was nothing in any direction that could hide a force strong enough to challenge us. In any case, the Worms didn't do decoys. It wasn't in their playbook.

We didn't need to waste time deciding who was to go after which transport. Ja'kara had always fostered an independent mindset in her captains, so when it was time to take the initiative, they sorted it out between themselves with a flurry of messages. This left us free to concentrate on the escort, which was redlining its engines in an attempt to get away.

Destroying it would've been easy, but Ja'kara's orders were to capture it as close to intact as we could manage. That made the job somewhat more problematic. Fortunately, we'd been doing this for a long time; 'problematic' just meant we had to take a little more care.

As we got closer, both Pishka and I scanned that ship down almost to the molecular level. We'd been working together long enough that I kept a screen clear he could throw interesting data onto, and he did the same with me. I found the frequency of its sensor spoofing relatively quickly and shared it; a micro-cycle or two later, he reciprocated with a scan map of the resonances within the hull. A little collaboration between us located weak spots in its battleshields directly over what we agreed were its engine nacelles, and we sent the data over to Guns. Three extremely precise shots later, it dropped back into realspace.

"Well done," Ja'kara noted. "Now all we have to do is hit the life support—" As she spoke, another shot punched through the ship, and I watched the life support begin to wind back to zero as atmosphere vented into space. Without missing a beat, she continued. "—and the main power core, *without* blowing it up …"

Guns took another couple of micro-cycles waiting to fire, while Pishka and I firmed up the data. A single shot, and everything died on it: lights, battleshields, the lot.

"Well *done*," she murmured. "Keep scanning for secondary life support. We don't want our boarding party to get any nasty surprises."

This was true. Nobody wanted *any* live Worms on board, or eggs for that matter. Everything coming back on board would be scanned to a fare-thee-well as it was.

I maintained a watch on the Xan'thuilli ship while Pishka kept a lookout all around. Even before the extraction crew got to the drifting hulk, we were greeted with hails from our returning ships. Fifteen for fifteen, and all transports accounted for.

They formed up around us, sensors scanning local hyperspace as well as realspace, and Pishka and I were able to concentrate on watching for any surprises in the dead ship we were looting. A few systems were still sparking and sputtering on backup power, and we steered the exploratory team around those. The ship was open to vacuum, and Worms were as vulnerable to that as any other biological organism.

It had been thought at first that they could use the once-living bodies of their victims as organic space suits, right up until we exposed one to vacuum and watched the writhing tangles of the Worms get ejected out the same orifices they'd used to get into the body. The sight was disgusting, yet somehow deeply satisfying.

Still, that was no excuse to slack off. Along with Pishka, I maintained a steady watch while they located the computers, dismounted everything they could carry, and re-boarded the shuttle they'd gone over by. Neither of us budged, checking and rechecking every reading, until the shuttle was safely back in the bay and everything (and everyone) had been checked over for a sneaky Worm or any eggs. In triplicate.

Once we were squared away, Ja'kara gave the order to back off from the Xan'thuilli ship and dispose of it. Several shots into the right places did the job, breaking up the large sections and causing a series of explosions within. Then it was time to investigate what the front-line troops had recovered.

Xan'thuilli never invented anything themselves. They always made use of the technological advancements of the races they ate the brains of, most of which we already knew. In addition, this was an old ship with outdated tech. It took us more time to set up the correct power supply along with input and output than it did to actually crack the datafiles.

When Pishka and I started to swear, Ja'kara was somehow waiting just inside the hatchway. I suppose when I learned to be exactly where I needed to be, I'd be ready for my own command as well. She stepped forward, getting our attention. "Report."

"Yes, ma'am." I paused for a micro-cycle to get my thoughts into line. "We found out why there's nothing on this side of Wormspace. If these astro-charts line up with ours the way I think they do …"

"They do," Pishka interrupted without taking his eyes off the holo-display.

I gestured in agreement with him. "… then the Worms have found something really big and really tasty out in the Indigo quadrant. You know, behind the Rift. Right about where we found that planet with the humans. Earth, I think the name was?"

"And it's so big and tasty, they're putting out the word for everyone to come and join in?" Her voice was low and dangerous. I recalled she'd been given a case of a local ethanol derivative called 'vodka' before we left Earth. Not to my taste; I much preferred something called 'cocoa'.

"That's our best interpretation of what they're saying," I said. "We could be wrong. That glyph almost certainly says 'come', that one means 'urgent' and that one there is 'plenty to eat'. The rest, we're not so sure about."

"But you *are* sure about the location?" Her nostrils flared as she inhaled, as though trying to get the scent of her prey through the holoscreen. "They're referring to Earth?"

I looked her in the eye. "Yes, ma'am. That much, we're sure of."

"Very well. Back to your duty stations." She stepped back out of the hatch and vanished along the corridor, calling out orders. Pishka and I glanced at each other, then we started shutting down the captured computer.

"Straight burn to Earth?" he surmised.

"Looks like it." I grimaced. They'd been nice people, and they'd shown willing. I hated the idea that they might've been overrun by the Xan'thuilli. If that had happened, we'd have to sterilise the planet down to the bedrock.

"But are we going there to save it or destroy it?" We'd been working together for so long he could almost read my thoughts.

I took a deep breath. "I guess we'll find that out when we get there."

Part Three: Holding Action

"Attention." Ja'kara kept her voice level, the microphone on her shipsuit transmitting her voice shipwide. Hyperspace comms squirted it to the rest of our battlegroup as we ran at flank speed toward a certain location in the galaxy: to save or destroy, we didn't know yet.

"Those of you who were on the *Promise Upheld* when we encountered the Earth humans last time, you will know what I'm talking about. For those who don't, I will be circulating an information packet. Briefly speaking, Earth is a moderate-G world with a dominant sapient species called 'human'. Bipedal, my height, mammalian, dimorphic, highly social, adventurous, technologically adept. They helped us kill a Worm ship the last time we were there, *despite* the fact that their space travel was still based on chemical propellants. So, I made the executive decision to hand over engineering specs for hyperdrives, sensors and all the other technology that would give them FTL capability before the Xan'thuilli came calling a second time."

She paused to let her words sink in. I listened with one tympanic membrane while focusing the rest of my attention on my screens. We didn't *think* the Worms were setting any ambushes in this region of space, but assumptions by definition didn't have all the data in hand. If there was the slightest emanation from a lurking ship, even in hyper, Pishka and I were going to spot them before they spotted us.

"The computer equipment we just captured from that Worm ship yielded some information about why the Worms aren't reinforcing this region of space anymore," she went on, clearly not liking what she had to say but saying it anyway. "They've found Earth again, and they're sending out messages that translate to 'big and tasty' and 'come quick'. Earth and its humans are our allies. It is our duty to go to their aid. I've sent away a message probe to inform High Command of our findings and our intent, and now we're heading to Earth to render aid." She paused. "Or, if it's too late, to render honours and give them their final rest. Ja'kara, out."

Cutting the comms, she dropped into her command chair. It was only ever used when she had absolutely nothing else to do; she preferred to be on her feet, looking over our shoulders as we worked. With other officers, I may have found this irritating and intrusive, but not Ja'kara.

With her, it was reassuring to know she was at my back. She drove us no harder than she drove herself. Every one of us on the *Promise Upheld* would've set course into the heart of a supernova at her command, with absolute faith that she could get us out the other side.

Even if it wasn't her giving the orders to head for Earth, I would've gone anyway. I'd only had the chance to associate with humans for a short while, ten GA years ago, but they'd made an impression on all of us. They were the scrappy newcomers to the Galactic scene, and I personally liked them.

Enough of them seemed to be out and about that they wouldn't be driven extinct if Earth was destroyed, but it would be a huge blow to the species as a whole. I'd heard of some species that had declined and let themselves die out once that sort of thing had happened to their birth world. While I didn't *think* humans would go down that same path—the fact that one of their favourite insults invited the listener to go and copulate with themselves told me that—it still wouldn't be good for them.

Ship cycles came and went as we bored a hole through hyperspace, heading for our goal: Earth, still hopefully untouched. We took the time to prep the ships for imminent combat. Every system that could be maintained while in hyperspace was checked over and tested. The grunts in engineering hovered over the hyperdrive engines, twitching at every flicker of a gauge away from the norm.

When *Remember Panares* called in that their hyperdrives were starting to show problematic oscillations, Ja'kara didn't hesitate to tell them to drop into realspace until they had it fixed. She detailed *They Also Serve* to stay with them; the last thing anyone wanted was to be stuck in the middle of interstellar space with a busted hyperdrive. In that situation, all a crew could do was set out for home and hope their descendants—or remains—got there eventually.

My second was a flightless avian, a Gallan called Lileel; she was adept enough on my board for the most part, but this was not a normal situation. I took to only sleeping while Pishka was on shift so that he could back her up on the Weps board, and I did the same for him when he had to take a mandatory rest cycle. When we were both up, I ran her through drills, trying to get her to the point where she could spot a problem by instinct rather than thinking about it.

Overall, it was a tense time. This was not helped when we got a signal from one of the probes we'd sent out, returning with data. We briefly dropped back to realspace to take it on board, then resumed our onward dash. Ja'kara accessed the onboard data herself, then threw it up on the main display for all to see. Behind me, I heard Pishka mutter something about 'excrement of the sun god' but I wasn't listening, because I was swearing too.

The first star system where we'd fought the Worm ship, one hyperspace jump away from Earth, had a binary pair plus a third a little way away. Humans had evidently colonised the system, with domed settlements on one of the planets as well as orbital habitats. These were in the process of being evacuated, with ships of all sizes and shapes swarming around them. Despite the fact that we'd warned them that the Xan'thuilli were able to detect EM emissions via hyperspace, and quite often homed in on such emissions, the installations were all blaring out audio and video signals even while they were prepping to bolt.

But that wasn't the bad part.

The bad part was the other half of the data the probe had returned with. It had locked onto a Xan'thuilli fleet and gotten a heading as well as approximate numbers. They were bearing down on the colony system with literally thousands of ships, and there was no way of knowing if the humans would all be evacuated by then.

I glanced around the command deck. A Xan'thuilli fleet that big was unheard of, or at least I'd never seen or heard of one like it myself. Pishka met my eyes and gestured a negative to my unspoken question. Ja'kara was staring at the display like she could change the facts there by sheer force of will. We were all right there with her.

"Orders, Captain?" asked Burble.

That broke the spell. "Yes." Ja'kara turned to face us. "I want a course change. How fast can we get to that colony system?"

Pishka was ready with the answer, because he'd known she was going to ask that question. "Half a cycle to a cycle ahead of that fleet, ma'am."

It wasn't a huge amount of time, but at least it would allow us to get set up in the system before the Worms arrived. "Very good. Lay in the course. Send it to Helm. Make it happen. When they show, I want the first and last thing they see to be our guns."

The shapeless anxiety that had been laying over us up until that point dissipated, to be replaced by a laser-focused purpose. When we hit that system, we'd be setting up for a fighting retreat. There was no way our fourteen-strong strike group could hold out against a fleet of that size, but we didn't have to. All we had to do was slow them down long enough for the humans to hit hyperspace, and then we could jump out too. If they had sense, they'd go anywhere other than Earth, but we couldn't depend on that.

Our strategy was already laid out before us, just awaiting the tactical finesse that Ja'kara could bring to it. Once the last human was out of the colony system, we'd jump back to the Earth system and hope that whatever defensive capability they had was able to at least hold off the oncoming invasion until a relieving fleet came in from High Command. *If* a relieving fleet got there in time.

In the best case, the fleet we were facing would be of the same quality as the ones we'd been routinely smearing across spacetime for the last couple of years. But even then, with thousands in play, it would be a matter of quantity overcoming quality. If they were of the better quality, we were going to be in for a hellish fight.

I had no illusions about the end result; we were probably going to go down no matter what, but if that happened, we were going to go down fighting. Ja'kara had made it clear to all of us that she was prepared to blow the ship if we were boarded and looked like losing to the invaders. We might die, but they weren't going to get anything out of us.

Only Pishka and I were able to detect our course change. At this distance, it was barely noticeable. We still had cycles to go before we got there, and the two star systems were only about four light-years apart. I found my attention wandering, and logged off shift to refresh myself and get some sleep before the biowaste storage inevitably suffered catastrophic containment failure.

When I rose, we were close. Pishka immediately sent me the faint traces he'd raised of the passage of the fleet, still light-years hence. One ship wouldn't be detectable at this range, but thousands left a considerable drive-wake. He left his console to his second while I took over the vigil. There was only a cycle or so before we were due to get there, but his species were able to get by on minimal sleep at short notice.

I let Lileel run my console, while I shadowed Pishka's second on his. The invasion fleet hadn't changed heading or speed, though it seemed to have spread out a little. They wouldn't arrive in one huge mass, which would be to our benefit. If we could disable or kill the front-runners, that would buy the humans a little more time. The one good thing seemed to be that they were all coming from roughly the same direction.

With only a few demi-cycles to go before arrival, Ja'kara put a sharp tone over the shipwide annunciators to get everyone's attention. Pishka arrived at a run and dropped into his seat as she began to speak.

"Attention. Attention. All ships, secure for combat. We will not be seeking to hold the system. This will be a fighting retreat. Watch each other's backs, and be ready to enter hyperspace on my order. There are eight billion sapients in the next system over, and it's our job to make sure they don't become eight billion incubators. I'm not going to tell you to do your duty, because I know damn well you'll do it. I couldn't be prouder of you than I am today. Ja'kara, out."

While on normal running, we only went with lapstraps. I secured my full restraints, and made sure Lileel did hers as well. The only one not fastening in was Ja'kara, because she liked to be up and keeping an eye on how things were going.

"Transitioning out of hyperspace in four!" called out Ga'takka. "Three! Two! One! Drop!"

The hyperdrive engines spooled back as we slid down into realspace. There was hardly even a jar; Ga'takka was that good. Pishka had analysed the system traffic from the drone data and placed us above the ecliptic so we wouldn't be in anyone's way.

Which turned out to be a good thing; there were still a lot of ships milling around. Had they been caught unawares? Whoever had organised this evacuation had botched it badly, given that there seemed to still be almost as many ships in-system as there had been when the probe came through.

A couple of larger ships with what I recognised as military lines came nosing out of the pack toward us. It didn't take long for us to receive their hail. My Human-to-Trade translator software deciphered the audio immediately.

*"Patrol ship **Promise Upheld**, welcome back to our corner of the galaxy. This is Captain Peterson, of the **Leeroy Jenkins**. Is Captain Ja'kara still commanding that vessel?"*

"I am indeed," Ja'kara responded, sounding briefly pleased before she got back to business. "But this isn't a social call, Captain Peterson. Xan'thuilli are on the way in overwhelming numbers. They'll be arriving here in …" She paused, possibly doing math in her head. "… about one and a half of your 'hours'. You need to get these people out of here."

"Yes, we know." Peterson didn't sound very concerned. *"We've got it all under control. You'll see."*

With a *huff* of strained patience, Ja'kara tried again. "Captain, I've been fighting these things my entire adult life. So has all my crew. We have *never* faced a fleet this big before. Believe me when I say you do *not* have it under control."

While they talked, Pishka and I were probing them with our sensors. They were allies, certainly. But they were also people who had taken the technology we'd given them ten years earlier and gone their own way with it. We knew Ja'kara would want to see their performance statistics for herself. The last thing any of us wanted was for the newest star-faring sapients in the galaxy to get overconfident when dealing with the perpetual menace that was the Xan'thuilli.

The first thing that popped up on the screen I kept reserved for Pishka was a layout of the weapons on the craft we were talking to. Four holes opened around the nose, being the muzzle openings for tubes leading back into the craft, parallel to the long axis. It could only be a weapon, but whoever it got fired at, the entire ship would have to be pointing at them.

Around the four enigmatic shafts, I saw eight laser turrets, far smaller than the ones we mounted. They'd damage an unshielded Worm ship, but wouldn't do anything against even the most basic battleshield.

Farther back on the ship, there were many other turrets, each one much larger than the laser emplacements, containing paired weapons that didn't look like either laser or plasma weaponry. I did a quick analysis and came up with the conclusion that nothing could come close without being targeted by at least three of the turrets. What they were, I couldn't be sure. They didn't fit the profile of either plasma or laser weapons, and simple chemical-kinetic weaponry would be prohibitively short-ranged for any sort of space engagement.

Over and above that, their acceleration was horrifically slow. This wasn't due to underpowered engines, as I'd first assumed, but the sheer mass of each craft. Looking deeper, it seemed that part of it was a series of mechanisms surrounding the four mystery shafts, and part of it seemed to be high-end capacitor banks, while another component showed up as a secondary set of battleshields, separate from the first. And, apparently, actual metal armour plating on the outer hulls.

By the time Pishka and I had finished our analysis of the Earth craft and finished tossing notes back and forth, we'd come up with half a dozen unsatisfactory explanations for exactly why those ships had been designed that way. Our best guess was that humans had to deal with design-by-committee as well, and we silently commiserated with them.

There were four defending ships in all; they were called *Leeroy Jenkins*, *Murphy's Law*, *Hold My Beer* and *Invading Russia*. I wasn't quite sure of the cultural background behind any of them; two seemed to be relatively standard human names, one referenced a beverage and the other a nation. Or perhaps they were intended to invoke obscure human references I didn't understand. I made a note to ask someone later, if we survived, and if there was anyone left to answer.

Moving slowly to allow for their atrocious acceleration, we arranged ourselves in wall-of-battle, facing the direction where Pishka's sensors told us the Xan'thuilli fleet would be emerging from hyperspace. It didn't take much of a rearrangement to slot the Earth ships in among ours, then we all ran our battleshields up to full as a standard test.

With those massive engines behind them, the human ships had suitably impressive battleshields, though they were oddly tuned, not to mention hugging closer to the massive hulls than I was used to seeing. Of course, the smaller the overall surface area of the shield, the less power needed to keep it up, but it still seemed an odd choice to me. And they hadn't even energised the second set of shields, which made me wonder what they were for.

The micro-cycles ticked downward. Behind us, the refugee ships almost reluctantly lifted off from the planet and pulled away from the orbital habitats before engaging their hyperdrives and fleeing the system. Briefly, I met Pishka's eyes, and he made a gesture of resigned negation. Every single one of them was heading straight back to the Earth system. Their drive wakes, which would normally have dissipated in less than a cycle, would leave the Xan'thuilli a nice clear trail to follow.

There would be no hiding from the Worms. This was going to be a fight. And given that we had the only vessels capable of manoeuvring fast enough to engage in decisive ship-to-ship combat, I had the unpleasant feeling that it was going to be very one-sided, and not in our favour.

"Incoming!" sang out Pishka. "Three demi-cycles, maybe four."

Well, that nailed it down neatly. Even though we were in realspace, Pishka could read a hyperspace ripple out to beyond the point where most of us (me included) would doubt there was anything there to see. The leading edge of the invading fleet was going to pop up in no more than four demi-cycles, probably three and a half.

The information went out to the rest of the blockading fleet, all eighteen vessels that we had. Behind us, more and more civilian ships lined up their trajectories, spooled up their hyperspace drives, and jumped away. A query popped up on my screen, sent from Captain Peterson of the *Leeroy Jenkins.*

"The humans want to know where they'll start coming out," I called across to him.

Three micro-cycles later I had the answer: a box of space about two planet-diameters in front of us. How Pishka managed to calculate that, I only had the vaguest of ideas. I did know he could track and trace the easing down of hyperspace engines as they came close to the dropping-off point, but like all the best showmasters, he never revealed his deepest secrets. Burble once confided to me that she was convinced he used those big cup-like mammal ears to listen to hyperspace directly. I couldn't say she was wrong.

I sent the information back. We only had about two demi-cycles before they were going to emerge. Ja'kara was directly behind Pishka's station, her eyes devouring every twitch and ripple in his readouts.

All weapon crews were ready, their firing solutions trained in on that box. They weren't going to fire until Ja'kara gave the word, to ensure the most destruction in the shortest time. It was clear that eighteen of us were not going to make a huge dent in a thousands-strong invasion fleet, but we wanted to sting them and give them at least a brief pause before falling back.

And then, on both Pishka's screens and mine, the four Earth ships literally jolted sternward a good quarter of their lengths. Their realspace drives flared, slowing the rearward movement and pushing them forward again, but Ja'kara was already on it.

"What was that?" she demanded. "What happened?"

"Magnetic burst, ma'am." Pishka was at his most terse in these situations. "Metallic objects have been ejected from those ships."

The enlightenment burst on me all at once. "Those long shafts! They're for magnetic acceleration! I *wondered* what they were for!"

Just then, all four ships jolted backward once more, despite the forward impulse of their drives. They'd fired again, while we had yet to shoot even once. Of course, we didn't have any targets to shoot *at* as yet.

"Why are they firing?" Ja'kara wasn't asking the question of anyone so much as sounding it out loud. "The enemy isn't in sight yet."

"The Earth ships know where they're going to be, and when they're going to be there," I said slowly. "Those projectiles are still on the way. If they've calculated the velocity correctly ..." I didn't have to say any more. Slowly, I began to revise my initial judgement of the thought process behind the four ships. Humans had already shown themselves to be extremely adept at war. Maybe they weren't as wrong-footed as we'd thought.

"Sixteen micro-cycles!" called out Pishka, after the Earth ships had belted out two more salvos. The projectiles were simple dumb munitions, of a type that I'd only read about in old manuals. Simpler still than the 'cruise missiles' that had so thoroughly destroyed the Xan'thuilli ship when we'd last visited Earth. No warhead, no drive, no guidance, no emissions. Nothing that could be spoofed, and a huge amount of kinetic energy. I didn't know the exact mass of the projectiles, but the fact that firing all four acceleration tubes at once jolted the *whole ship* backward told me that whatever those projectiles hit was in for a galaxy's worth of pain.

And then, right where Pishka had predicted, the fabric of space rippled and bulged, then the Xan'thuilli ships began to emerge. One after the other, then eight, then sixteen, then hundreds. All lighting off their realspace drives and hurtling toward us.

"Now!" shouted Ja'kara.

In the infinitesimal interval between her giving the command and every single ship in the strike group activating their lasers ... the Worm ships began to explode. The front-runners were spared for a few micro-cycles, but the larger bunch, farther back, detonated in a long line coring out the middle of the pack, all the way back to where their fellows were still sliding out of hyperspace.

Then, while I was still blinking over the destruction caused by that first salvo, *we* fired.

The front-runners died then, targeted by fourteen ships' worth of high-end lasers. We began to work our way back down the pack, while I spoofed their sensors and Pishka called out useful targets. Our shields hadn't taken any hits yet, but Burble was tensely ready to make sure *not one Worm* got through our defences.

When the second salvo hit, it was less of a surprise to us, but far more Xan'thuilli ships had poured out of hyperspace by then, so the projectiles had a lot more meat to bite into. Even as I worked to distort the sensor signals going back to the Worms, I had to admire the sheer devastation the four Earth ships were wreaking on the fleet. It was a mere claw-puncture to the main mass, of course, but still very satisfying to watch.

"Fall back," Ja'kara ordered. "Keep firing but fall back." She glanced at the main display, now featuring a view of the colony world. The last of the transport ships was just staggering into orbit and orienting itself to leave the system. It would be woefully sluggish in hyperspace. "We need to keep them slowed down."

The human ships were tied into our battlenet, so they moved back with us; or rather, they ceased using their drives to keep station. Slow though their rate of fire was, each shot drove a horrific weight of metal through the massed droves of the oncoming Xan'thuilli invasion, every projectile causing huge damage to whatever it hit. And they just kept firing.

But even that tremendous weight of metal, aided and abetted by our constant barrage, was not enough to kill the nearest Worm ships before they could start firing back. Spread over eighteen of us, it was bearable, but the intensity was rapidly growing to the point where something would have to give. *Unity is Strength* reported battleshield fluctuations, threatening to send its shields entirely out of calibration.

"Pull back," Ja'kara ordered. "Those of you with stronger shields, cover those without. Captain Peterson, do your ships require covering fire?"

"We'll be fine," Peterson replied. A transmission came through, popping up on Pishka's screen. *"Head for those coordinates. Follow the refugee ships in-system. Thanks for the assist, by the way. You really helped sell it. Now get the hell out of here before we're all surrounded.* **Leeroy Jenkins,** *out."*

A shot punched through *Unity's* wavering shields and scored a molten line along its flank. That decided Ja'kara. "All ships. Jump for Earth using these coordinates, on my mark."

As we turned and prepped for the jump, more shots flashed across the void. I saw the *Hold My Beer* slide into place behind the wounded *Unity is Strength*; the Earth ship's beefed-up shields took the fresh barrage and barely showed any change.

We were fleeing across the system now, the Earth ships falling farther and farther behind with every micro-cycle. Were they planning to engage the entire Xan'thuilli fleet with their four ships? I hoped not; as brutally effective as those magnetic-propulsion weapons had shown themselves to be, any ship could still be swarmed and disabled.

Just as the hyperspace engines spooled up and we jumped out of the system, I wondered: *what did he mean, we really helped sell it?*

Part Four: Striking Sparks

It was a mystery that I worried at on the short transit to the Earth system. Our ships, including the damaged *Unity is Strength*, were holding formation even in hyperspace. With Pishka keeping a keen eye out for potential ambushes, we were as secure as we were going to get.

Once we got to Earth system, that was going to change. Unlike with the colony system, this time it would not be a holding action. We were going to have to dig in and repel a determined invasion. While we'd managed to shred maybe one-sixteenth of the attacking force, that still left far more Worm ships than I'd ever seen before in one place. I could only hope that the humans hadn't put all their faith in those oddly named guard ships.

Ja'kara was talking to *Unity's* captain, with Burble cut in on the link. I overheard a few words that suggested they were going over ways to get their battleshields back up to full capacity before we got neck-deep in it again. Shields weren't my speciality, and I didn't have enough esoteric knowledge to bypass the limitations of physics, so I didn't try to add anything to the discussion.

Pishka's head came up and he flattened his ears in relief. "They got out," he said.

"Who got out?" I asked. "The Earth ships?"

He gestured confirmation. "They're coming along now. I'd be very interested in seeing what they've done to their hyperdrives. It's got a strange harmonic to it. But fast; very fast. Better than the Worm ships, which is good."

"Slow in realspace, fast in hyper?" I wiped my nictitating membranes across my eyes a few times in bemusement. "They must have monster hyperdrives."

"Well, all that weight didn't come from oversized lasers, that's for sure," he pointed out, twitching his whiskers in amusement. Then he got serious again. "Captain, we'll be there in a demi-cycle. The Earth ships are in transit. They'll get here about three demi-cycles before the Worm ships."

"Good to hear." Ja'kara stood up straight, her eyes on the display. On it was the hyperspace imagery of the oncoming Earth system. "Attention. Attention. We've done very well indeed. The enemy came at us, and we bit their nose off. Our allies are following on. We're all still in the fight, and they've lost a chunk of their forces. But this is no time to congratulate ourselves. We're coming up on the Earth system in half a demi-cycle, so assume battle order when we get there. *Finding Hope* and

Lighting the Void, I'm going to need you to buddy-shield *Unity is Strength* until they get their battleshields up and running again. Remember: we're here to kill Worms. Anything extra is a bonus. Ja'kara, out."

Just before we slid out of hyperspace again, I set all my systems to max gain. I needed to know the emissions in this system, and how to hide the *Promise Upheld* against the background noise if necessary. There was a good chance that this battle would devolve into hunt-the-prey, with us cast as the prey.

When the blare of signals blasted out of my console and lit up the command deck, I nearly went over backward. The only thing that saved me was that the chair was literally designed not to do that. Hastily, with my eyes watering and my tympanic membranes ringing, I reduced everything to a saner level. Then I began to look at what I was seeing.

There was electronic noise *everywhere.* The gas giants seemed to emit it as a slow, rhythmic hum. Earth radiated it like the local sun radiated light and heat. Even the fourth planet out was blaring into the void. And finally, there were point-sources spaced in a vast circle around the local star, between the fourth and fifth orbital regions. I wasn't quite sure what those were about. "Apologies, all," I said. "I underestimated the amount of noise in the system."

"That's fine. Don't do it again." Ja'kara's tone was barely censorious. "I'm not surprised the Worms found this place. Between the noise the colony was putting out and this one, they're probably listening in from sixteen light-years away."

"Ships coming out from Earth orbit," Pishka reported. "More of the same type. Many more."

Oh, good, I thought. *We might have a chance at surviving this.*

One of the oncoming ships hailed us as we shook ourselves into formation. *"Outsider group, this is Admiral Holloway commanding the* **Ackbar Was Right***, overseeing Battlefleet Anvil, callsign Anvil Actual. Identify immediately, over."*

Ja'kara rose to the occasion. "Admiral, this is Commodore Ja'kara, captain of *Promise Upheld.* This strike group is under my command. I need to inform you that there's a sizeable fleet of Xan'thuilli due in this system in … about sixteen of your minutes. The ships you had guarding the colony are right ahead of them. Over."

Admiral Holloway's voice changed tone slightly; still crisp, it became almost friendly. *"So noted, Commodore Ja'kara. It's good to have you back. I attended several of your lectures when you were last here. Also, congratulations on your promotion. I see at least one of your ships is damaged. We're going to need you to follow the refugee ships inward, at least until you get through our screen. Over."*

"Admiral Holloway, this is an extremely substantial fleet," Ja'kara tried again. "There are thousands in it. Perhaps as many as seven or eight thousand. You're going to need every ship that can fly and fire a weapon." She stared at the display, where Pishka had helpfully placed up a graphic of the ships that were coming out to meet us. "You have fewer than a hundred ships. They will surround you and bring you down with numbers. Over."

"Commodore Ja'kara, I appreciate the concern, but there are facts that you do not know about this situation. Number one: you need to clear our line of fire. Now." The human's voice took on the snap of authority.

It didn't take Ja'kara any time at all to take note of how the ships were gradually forming up into a wall of battle like we'd done back at the colony, with all those gaping muzzles pointing directly at us. We had a robust hull and a powerful battleshield, but one of those magnetically-propelled projectiles would tear through us like a plasma blast through a snowbank. There was still a gap in the middle, where the refugee ships had gone. Perhaps deliberately, it had been left open for us.

"Understood, Admiral." She touched the collar of her shipsuit. "Helm, take us through that gap. All ships, follow in line astern. Once we're through, form up behind the Earth ships. Let's get out of the way of those big scary guns, people."

As if we'd practised the manoeuvre a thousand times, we swooped through the gap and took up station behind the Earth ships. But not too close; we'd all seen the other ones jolt backward when firing those massive main guns. One by one, the other ships fell into place. I could tell Ja'kara was trying to puzzle out the strategy at work here; with the sixty-something ships before us, it would be like our holding action in the colony system, only taking a little longer to overwhelm us.

"Thank you, Commodore Ja'kara. Now, did you have any questions?"

"Two," she said at once. "First, how do you expect to stop so large a fleet with so few ships? Second, how are you going to prevent the majority of them from simply hyper-jumping straight past you?"

"To answer your first question, this isn't all the ships we have. And for the second, we've seeded interdictor satellites through the asteroid belt. Nothing can reach hyperspace inward of there."

Pishka was already working to update the image on the display. On it, we could see the relative locations of the local star, the Earth, and the other planets. In between the fourth and fifth was a band of planetesimals; the asteroid belt Anvil Actual was talking about. Along with the refugee ships, we'd come out of hyperspace just outside that band, and we'd travelled inward on our realspace drives, so we were now inside the indicated volume of space.

"Interdictor satellites?" she asked. I sent an update to the display, to show the unusual point-sources that I'd detected before. She studied them and made a gesture of understanding.

"Captain Ja'kara, one of the things you probably noticed about us humans is that we can't stop poking at things. When we got the specs for your hyperdrive, we built test rigs and played around with them, until we came up with some interesting effects. The hyperdrive interdictor field is one of those effects."

"I know it's possible to create an … interdictor effect." The slight flare of Ja'kara's nostrils betrayed her irritation, even though it didn't show in her voice. "My question is: why? Why would you deny all ships in your system the ease of rapid transit?"

"Because sometimes you want to be able force ships to go from point A to point B the hard way," replied Holloway. *"On that note, if you could go out and flank the battlefleet and help deal with any spillage, that would be greatly appreciated. Anvil Actual, out."*

The dismissal was clear. Also, the timer Pishka had running in the corner of the display showed that we didn't have long before the Xan'thuilli ships showed up. The interdictor satellites were welcome news, but again I was worried that the humans might be attempting to ingest a bug larger than their head, as the saying went.

If Ja'kara had similar worries, she wasn't showing them. Crisply, she gave orders for *Unity is Strength* to withdraw and effect repairs to their battleshields, while the rest of the strike group moved out and around the slowly-assembling battlefleet. Three ships were placed on each 'side' of the fleet, while the *Promise Upheld* waited behind, ready to dash out and reinforce whichever side needed help the most.

The next arrivals in the system were the four guard ships. I listened in on their communication chatter while I scanned them for damage. There was only a little scorching on their outer paintwork, while their shields were still radiating the remnants of the energy that had been flung their way by the Worm ships. The banter was light and contained many cultural references that I did not comprehend, but I was glad to see more reinforcements. We were a tiny guard force trying to throw back an overwhelming weight of attackers; the only good thing in all this was that they couldn't simply opt to hyper-jump straight past us.

I didn't know humans as well as I would've liked to, but they didn't seem to be showing the grim fatalism of people who had chosen a suicidal last stand and know they're going to fail anyway. I knew that mindset well, having held it myself from the moment that Ja'kara had made the decision to defend Earth no matter what. They seemed upbeat, optimistic. Making plans for the future.

I envied them their ability to ignore the inevitable.

The four newcomers were still moving into place on the outer fringes of the battlefleet, alongside our ships, when the timer ticked down to the last demi-cycle. As if this had tripped a remote trigger, all ships in the main battlefleet simultaneously jolted backward. I knew what that meant, as did everyone on the command deck. Literally hundreds of solid metal projectiles, each one the size of a groundcar, were now hurtling toward the edge of the hyperspace interdiction field. It would be like getting caught in the type of meteor swarm that only existed in the extreme training exercises intended to teach arrogant young officer cadets that it is indeed possible to be in a no-win situation.

Still, no matter how I ran the numbers in my head, there seemed to be no way to reduce the incoming fleet below half before the remainder surrounded each and every ship and overwhelmed their shields with massed fire. Once breached, they could be boarded; if not, destroyed in place. After that, Earth and its in-system colonies would be open to the incoming invasion. If even one-sixteenth of the fleet survived to reach the surface and disperse its squirming cargo, the only way to be absolutely sure of cleansing the planet would be to burn it down to the bedrock with nuclear fire, along with any of the eight billion inhabitants who had been infected along the way.

Harsh methods, but failing to carry them out stringently would only lead to outbreaks flaring up behind our backs. We'd learned that lesson the hard way.

Again and again, the battlefleet fired off its hail of death. Unaimed, unguided, they were devoid of any electronics and barely visible on sensors. There had to be a limit on how many projectiles the Earth ships held, and they were only really good for a surprise attack. A ship with any kind of manoeuvrability would be able to stay out of line of fire while raining its own return fire on their battleshields.

"Incoming!" warned Pishka. "They're not slowing!" This meant, of course, that the Xan'thuilli had detected the mass of metal in the Anvil battlefleet and were timing their drop-out to get much closer. It appeared they could learn from what the four guard-ships had done to them back at the colony system.

Unfortunately for them, what they wanted was not what they were going to get.

They came out of hyperspace abruptly, the transition a lot rougher than normal. Even a smooth drop-out could knock a ship around if the drive wasn't tuned just right; an unplanned one could blow out entire ship systems and leave crewmembers wondering which way was up. Their slower reactions showed the effects as they worked out which way to go and activated their realspace drives.

There were a *lot* of them. Worse, the battlefleet had set itself up somewhat farther back from the interdictor field boundary than we had from the drop-out point in the colony system. As ship after ship appeared from hyperspace and oriented themselves toward us, I found myself wondering what had happened to the salvos fired by the battlefleet. They jolted backward again, reminding me that it was still going on.

And then, after about one hand of the Worm fleet had poured into realspace, the first salvos arrived. Not all rounds hit the front wave, but the benefit of firing into a crowd was that the shot was going to hit *something*. Xan'thuilli ships began exploding, the destruction spreading back into the fleet as projectiles punched clean through their targets, the sheer transferred kinetic energy ripping them apart on the way. I estimated that any one shot was able to destroy five ships or damage ten before it ceased to be effective.

If any ships had any intention of fleeing, they didn't show it. Inside the interdiction field, they would have to literally turn around and fly away, and none of them were doing that. Instead, they were doing what the Xan'thuilli had done ever since we'd first encountered them, millennia ago. They pressed the attack, seeking to swamp our weapons until one of theirs got in a telling strike. Once they overcame us, they could use us or the countless people behind us as fodder to continue their expansion.

I had a very definite opinion about that, as did every member of the crew of every ship facing them.

Not on my watch.

More and yet more Xan'thuilli raged out of hyperspace and joined the charge toward us. The battlefleet continued its steady firing, even as the leading wave of the surviving Worm ships loomed ever closer. One shot would kill five ships, but between reloading the Xan'thuilli ships would get that much closer. The first few shots hit the battlefleet shields, fired by the Worm ships. Unsurprisingly, they glanced off, but that fire would only become more intense as the enemy got closer.

"That's it," Pishka said abruptly. "That's the last Worm ship out of hyperspace."

It wasn't exactly a comforting thought. The display said it all; our seventy-plus ship array was drawn up before an oncoming mass still comprised of thousands upon thousands of ravening enemy vessels, all bearing down on us faster than the magnetic-acceleration weapons could smash them. It was an uncomfortable trade-off; a weapon that could single-shot kill any Worm ship plus his four friends, but it was horrifically slow on the reload.

We must have still had the channel open, because Admiral Holloway answered. *"Good to have confirmation, **Promise**. Initiating stage two: Hammer Down."* Signals flared out from the *Ackbar Was Right* on the hyperspace band.

"What …?" I asked. "What *is* that?"

Pishka stiffened in his seat, his ears going straight up. "Hyperspace traces!" he reported. "Numerous hyperspace traces from the gas giants! Hundreds of them!"

I stared at my own screen, my nictitating membranes flickering back and forth three or four times. Probes had been shot into place alongside the Xan'thuilli fleet, bracketing it on three sides. These were showing up on the hyperspace bandwidth, blinking steadily. "Beacons," I said. "They've put beacons around the fleet."

Micro-cycles later, as the intensity of laser-fire against the battleshields of Fleet Anvil began to ramp up in earnest, the first ships arrived. As bulky as the others, they should still have been climbing out of the gravity well of whatever world they were waiting on. But they weren't. Inside the hyperspace interdiction field, they simply showed up … out of hyperspace.

"How is that even possible?" demanded Pishka, jolted out of his normal reserve. "Hyperspace travel should be impossible inside a field like that."

"Humans," Ja'kara said flatly. "Do you honestly think they'd come up with something like that and then not figure out a work-around?" She waved one arm, the other occupied with a hand-hold. "All of this did not arise out of nothing. They've put *thought* into this trap."

And trap it was. The onrushing Xan'thuilli fleet was now surrounded on four sides by the heavy Earth ships, which began to open fire with yet more of the horrifically powerful projectiles. Hammered from the front, smashed on all sides, the previously-overwhelming fleet evaporated faster than an ice planet in a supernova. I watched as the looming bulk lost cohesion and broke apart under the unyielding fire, shedding more and more ships as it went.

Then the Anvil battlefleet ceased fire, possibly because they were out of ammunition, or perhaps because they didn't want to inadvertently target their fellow ships, which were pressing ever closer to the fleet. Igniting their realspace drives, they pushed forward to meet the remnants of the Xan'thuilli fleet, which numbered fewer than a thousand by now. As they did so, I saw them activate their extra battleshields. But there was something very unusual about the tuning of those shields, not to mention the fact that the main shields of those ships had proved perfectly adequate to this point.

Burble, when I shot the data to her, scratched the back of her head in confusion. "That doesn't make sense," she stated.

"What doesn't make sense?" asked Ja'kara.

"They've got their outer shields tuned wrongly. Inverted. Those won't stop a drought-stricken thing."

"Well, they've got to be useful for *something*," I decided. "They've been playing it by the numbers so far."

Half a demi-cycle later, I saw what it was all about. Some of the shredded Worm fleet tried to turn and go around the battlefleet, but our ships and the guard-ships from the colony were ready for them. Explosions lit the void all around.

The rest seemed to be trying to slip through the array in front of them and get to Earth that way. If that happened, we'd be the only thing standing in their path. We were all on high alert, Guns dialled in, Pishka and me prepped to send them data. If they got through, we'd be ready.

Except that not one managed to get through. As the array of Earth ships surged forward, the Xan'thulli hit the expanded battleshields, which were nearly touching one another, and kept going ... until they tried to exit out the far side.

"They're not battleshields!" I shouted, just ahead of Pishka.

"They're nets!" he agreed.

"They're *insane*," Burble added, but she didn't disagree with our assessment. Neither did we disagree with hers.

Pushing forward, the Earth ships collected the fleeing ships in their own battleshields, inverted to prevent them from going anywhere. And then, within the shields, the captured ships began to explode. I zoomed closer with my sensors, not sure as to the reason why ... until I saw the turrets.

Chemical-kinetic weapons were far too short-ranged for serious space combat, but when the targets were literally only a few ship-diameters away, there was no missing. Each ship became the focus of multiple twin-barrelled turrets—I later got to handle one of the projectiles, as long and thick as my forearm—which hammered rapid-fire high-powered explosive rounds into it.

It was all over within sixteen demi-cycles. The human ships began sweeping the drifting debris out of the region, while the *Ackbar Was Right* approached us.

"*Well, that's done,*" Admiral Holloway said by way of greeting. Pishka managed to get an image of him up on the display. "*Want to come down for the celebration? I'm pretty sure we can throw in free dry-dock facilities for your damaged ship. We'll go and reset the honey trap on Alpha Centauri in a week or so.*"

That was one of the few times I would ever see Commodore Ja'kara taken totally and thoroughly off balance. "Wait, you mean to say you *deliberately* attracted them here?"

"Well, yes," Holloway said off-handedly. *"We've been doing it for years. They won't come in if we have a huge mass of ships waiting, but if we hide out in gas giants, we can usually trap them and wipe them all out. Sometimes we even board and capture the ships."*

I met Pishka's eyes, and saw in his gaze the beginning of the revelation that was dawning in my own mind.

"Board?" demanded Ja'kara. "Do you have any idea how stupidly dangerous that is? If a single Worm gets into your nervous system, you're as good as dead."

The human admiral made a gesture with his mouth that came across as amused. *"Sure I know. I've done it half a dozen times. But we had a secret weapon. So did you, though neither of us knew it at the time."*

"Excuse me," I said, just ahead of Pishka, "but how long have you been drawing them in and killing them?"

Holloway looked thoughtful. *"About six years or so."*

From the glance Ja'kara gave me, I knew she'd figured out the same thing Pishka and I had. It was the humans, casually trapping and destroying the Xan'thuilli, that had given us the reprieve we had so badly needed, five years ago.

Unaware of our revelation, Admiral Holloway was still talking. *"We've been getting some very nice tech off the captured ships. Also, it's amazing what you can find out from live Worms in captivity."*

"Unless you're mind-readers, there's no way you're going to interrogate one." Ja'kara narrowed her eyes. "Wait. *Are* you mind-readers?"

"Heh. No, we're not." Admiral Holloway made the mouth gesture again. *"But we did a lot of tests and we found out what they're unable to tolerate. And it turns out ethanol is one of those things."*

Ja'kara may have been confused, but she could connect data-points as fast as anyone. "So … being drunk kills them?"

I tried to imagine forcing alcohol down the throat of a Worm, but my brain rejected the whole idea. Holloway's next words cleared it up.

"If you've got enough in your system to register over about zero point zero one percent blood alcohol capacity when a Worm tries to get into your nervous system, it dies in convulsions." He held up his hand. Around the wrist were several puckered scars. *"I'm living proof of that."*

Amid the stunned silence on our command deck, Ja'kara was the only one able to speak. "So, when you said we had a secret weapon, you meant the vodka your people gave me the last time we were here?"

Holloway made a bobbing motion with his head that I recognised as a 'nod' of agreement. *"That's correct, Commodore. So, if you wanted to bring your crew down, we could get started on another case. What do you say?"*

"Admiral," declared Ja'kara, "that would be my genuine pleasure."

Humans, I decided, were *full* of surprises.

The End

Beware the Anger of a Quiet Man

Part One: Loss

He knew he was dreaming, but he couldn't break free. This made it all the worse.

"Contact left! Contact left!"

"KILL IT KILL IT KILL IT!"

"Dallas! Heads up!"

Battle buddy implant slamming extra adrenaline into his system. Everything gaining an aura of unreality as his rifle comes up. The Prask warrior-caste looming out of the dust and smoke, two and a half metres tall, all gangly limbs and razor chitin. Compound eyes glowing red in the gloom. The jolt as he fires. He knows he's missed the vital areas. The Prask is on top of him, a battle-blade lancing in for the kill.

He's on his back, the chitin weapon buried in his chest. Endorphins are pushing the pain away, but something's wrong with his battle buddy. The Prask is over the top of him, its other battle-blade slicing down toward his neck. Block with rifle, twitch of finger on trigger. The burst takes out one of its compound eyes, but it's still trying to kill him.

Other men come out of nowhere. Multiple shots hit the Prask, punch through the hardened chitin, shred the protected organs. It falls, on top of him. He can't breathe, doesn't know if that's the wound or the weight of the dead alien soldier. There's blood in his mouth. It's the wound. The Prask battle-blade went straight through his body armour. Must have sliced a lung. There's no strength in his arms. He's drowning on dry land.

I'm going to die here.

There's a cessation of weight as the others heave it off him. Someone feels at his neck, going for a pulse. They pull open his body armour. A dressing goes on.

"Dallas, can you hear me? Squeeze my hand if you can hear me!"

He squeezes as hard as he can.

"He's alive! Call in evac! That thing went deep, messed up his lungs!"

Battle buddy's trying to pump more endorphins into his system, but something's wrong. Pain is ongoing. He tries to scream, gargles blood instead. He can feel it trying to fix him, patch him up so he can get back into the fight. Little fixes are happening, but not big ones. It's draining the blood from what's left of his lungs, and feeding extra oxygen into his bloodstream so he doesn't go braindead, but nothing's getting stitched back together.

He can't move. Can hardly breathe. Hangs on.

Eternity passes.

There's more gunfire nearby, a series of deep THUMPs that says someone's using grenades. Then he hears the shriek of a dropship decelerating. It's coming in hard and fast. The shriek builds and builds, until he wonders how late the pilot left it.

It's a hard landing, hard enough that he feels it through the ground. A knife-edge landing, the type that threatens to break landing gear but exposes the dropship to the least amount of interdiction fire. A hot-zone landing.

Running steps, heavy boots. A female voice, out of breath. "Okay, there's more stretchers on the dropship. Get them and load these guys on board."

"The hell?" someone asks. "Where's the rest of the medic crew?"

*"And how old **are** you, honey?" asks another.*

"No medic crews to spare, no pilots to spare," she says crisply. "I'm it. I'm a backup trainee pilot, and right now I'm your buddies' best chance for survival. Now get the goddamn stretchers and help me load them on the dropship."

There's silence for a second, broken only by distant gunfire.

"Okay." It's one of the guys. "Let's do what the lady says."

He's rolled onto a stretcher, then moved a short distance. A needle stabs into his wrist and an IV line gets started. He can feel his battle buddy greedily grabbing the drugs and sending them where they'll do the most good. The straps barely make an impression as they lock into place.

As the rear hatch whines closed, he can hear the gunfire getting louder again. The engines start with a roar, and he can hardly breathe again, this time from G-forces.

"Okay, guys." It's the pilot's voice, on intercom. She's breathing hard, and he doesn't think it's from exertion. "This is gonna get a bit hairy, but stick with me and I'll get us through." She pauses for a second. "I hope." He doesn't think they're supposed to hear that bit.

Dropships have two modes of flight; normal and emergency thrust. Normally, evacuating wounded specifies normal thrust only. Don't want them to die before they get to the docs, after all. But she slams it into emergency thrust barely thirty seconds off the ground. He experiences the roar of the rockets along with the jolt of acceleration. Half a second later, he feels the almighty THUMP of an explosion that rams the whole dropship sideways. If she hadn't punched it, they'd be debris about then.

"Come on … come on … come on …" She's almost sobbing into her headset. He doesn't think she knows it's still live. With a grunt of exertion, she wrenches the dropship into a turn that he's pretty sure it's not rated for. Another explosion verifies that someone is very definitely trying to kill him and everyone else on board. The dropship creaks and groans, but it stays intact.

A second later, she cuts the engines altogether. They're in a ballistic arc, hanging in the sky between heaven and hell. He thinks he can hear the wind outside whistling past the fuselage. Then she kicks them over again and pulls *the dropship through a corkscrew spiral—which it absolutely is **not** rated for—just ahead of another explosion that rattles everything on board. Something shatters; he's not sure what it is, but the ship's still flying.*

"Mayday. Mayday. Mayday," she says. "This is Drop Zero One coming out of Sector Alpha Three Niner, need air cover. I say again, need air cover urgentmost. I have bogeys swarming on me, and I've got eight, I say again eight, wounded on board. Mayday. Mayday. Mayday. Over."

The voice that comes over the radio sounds determined to be the coolest thing on the airwaves. ***"Ahh, Drop Zero One, this is Ravage Actual. There were no evacs authorised for Alpha Thirty-Nine. You sure that's where you are, over?"***

"This is Drop Zero One, you can court-martial me later, Ravage. They were screaming for dustoff, so I took a ship down. Now are you gonna send me some cover or do you wanna hang back and count the falling bodies after we explode? Over!"

*Damn, he thinks. She sounds pissed. I **like** her.*

When Ravage Actual replies, he sounds conciliatory. ***"Hey, don't get your panties in a wad, Drop Zero One. We're coming in on your seven, and we'll brush the bugs off your windshield. Ravage Actual, out."***

"I copy, Ravage. And thanks. Drop Zero One, out."

After a brief series of far-away explosions, the aerobatics stop, and the pilot takes it out of emergency thrust. The ride gets a lot smoother, and he feels like he could almost go to sleep, if it wasn't for the stabbing pain that just won't go away.

By the time they get to orbit, he's starting to drift anyway. He doesn't pay much attention to the pilot's dialogue with the hospital ship, though the CLANK of docking rouses him a little. The corpsmen come and take him away. Painkillers flood into his bloodstream, and he can finally get some rest. The last thought he has before he slides away altogether is a hope that the pilot won't get into too much trouble for coming and getting him.

He wishes he knew her name. She sounds nice.

He sat up in bed abruptly as he always did after that dream, feeling over his torso for the wound. The scar was still there, but it was well-healed by now. Ten years had a habit of doing that. For the next few moments, he breathed deeply, enjoying the sensation of the night air going all the way to the bottom of both lungs.

Beside him, Kerra stirred. "Bad dream, honey?"

"Sorry. Didn't mean to wake you."

She rolled up onto her elbow. Her face was shadowed, but he knew she was looking up at him. "You're not the only one with bad memories, mister. Which one was it?"

"The dropship evac." He lay back down and reached over for her hand. She returned the clasp. "You were the baddest thing in the sky, that day."

She chuckled wryly. "I got in *so* much shit for that."

"And you got a medal, too," he reminded her with an answering smirk. "Talk about your mixed messages."

She stretched out onto her back, staring at the ceiling. "That's the only thing that got me back into the pilot program after the court-martial. I had to start over from scratch. Every instructor had it out for me. I nearly shitcanned the whole thing. Until you tracked me down to say thank you."

"Hey." He pulled her over toward himself, and delivered a kiss, which she returned with interest. "Someone had to."

"Yeah, well, seems everyone else forgot to." She climbed astride him, which he didn't mind at all. Another kiss was deposited on his lips. "Which is how I knew *exactly* who to celebrate with when I finally got my wings."

His hands slid up her torso, under her loose top. Their lips came together again, and took some time to part afterward. Clothing was becoming very much an optional thing at that moment. So was sleep.

Afterward, they slept entangled in the wreckage of the sheets. He didn't have any more bad dreams.

One Week Later

"And so, following the latest breakdown of diplomatic talks with the Prask, the Confederation of Earth Nations has reluctantly confirmed that a state of war exists once more between humanity and the Prask species, after an uneasy eight-year ceasefire. Prask forces have already been spotted building up on the periphery of the post-war border. We have here in the studio retired General McLean of the United States Marine Corps and—"

He shut off the tri-V; the holographic bubble flickered then went out. Even before he turned to look at Kerra, he knew what she was going to say.

"It's starting again, isn't it?"

"Yeah." It wasn't like he could deny the truth.

"You gonna go back in?"

He shrugged. "Not like I'm good at much else." Life as a drill instructor was fulfilling when he got a good cadre but for the most part, it involved breaking recruits of the same dumb habits, over and over again. All the skills were still there. He'd maintained his standards of fitness. But it just wasn't the same as combat ops.

"I hear they've got new and improved battle buddies." She cuddled up alongside him and traced her finger down the outside of his shirt, where she knew the scar was. "You can finally get an upgrade. Maybe just yank the old one, put a new one in."

"Not quite as easy as that, honey." He put his arm around her, pulling her close. "When they implant those things, they get tied into basically everything. It keeps me running, does self-repair, the lot. Downside, they can't pull it out without causing a *lot* of problems. To upgrade it, a military surgeon has to physically snake a probe in to access the plug and give it upgrade instructions. They're pretty flexible, though. It's usually a routine op."

"Well, it kept *you* alive, so I've got no complaints." She leaned her head against his, rubbing their cheeks together. "You know, I've got my drop wings now, so …"

He'd been expecting something like this. And since he'd encouraged her to follow her dreams, he couldn't exactly complain. Except that he *wanted* to. So, he fell back on the last resort: say nothing, as positively as possible.

"Well, you're definitely *good* at it." He tapped himself on the chest. "Living proof, here."

She could always see through his bullshit. "You don't want me to go out there, do you?"

It never failed. No other person, of any species, could put him on the defensive so fast. "It's not about you, honey. It's about the job. The danger. That last time? You were specifically evacuating the wounded, and they *still* tried to shoot you down. The Prask don't respect the Geneva Convention. Never have."

"They don't respect it on the ground, either," she shot back. "They'll torture, murder or *eat* one of our guys, doesn't matter if he's surrendering or wounded or whatever. There is absolutely no way I'm gonna sit at home safe and sound in the knowledge that you might be lying out there somewhere waiting for evac, with Prask coming over the hill looking for you."

He couldn't argue with that. Didn't want to argue with her at all, in all honesty. "Okay, fine. Just promise me that you'll fly as good as you did the day you reached down through the gates of Hell and pulled me out of there, okay? Don't ever let those bastards get a lock on you."

She reached across and clasped his hand with hers, interlacing their fingers as she enjoyed doing. Metal clicked on metal, and he looked down. Twin gold bands encircled her finger and his alike. "Shit," he muttered.

"What?" she asked. "The rings?"

"No jewellery going into combat," he explained tonelessly. "If they hit you with a microwave beam, it'll spark everywhere and surge your electronics before it ever starts to cook you. Any metal's gotta be approved." He nodded at her ring finger. "I bet dropship pilots will have similar rules. Nothing to get in the way of handling the controls."

She blinked. "God damn it, you're right. I never even thought about the regs when we were getting married." A look akin to pain crossed her face as she stared at her wedding ring. "I don't want to take it off. But I'm gonna have to."

That was when he had the idea. "Does it have to be these rings, specifically, or just rings in general?"

"What, were you thinking of getting plastic replicas?" She tilted her head quizzically. "If it's not metal, it'll break, or get in the way, or both."

"No, no, no." He grinned. "I know a guy who knows a guy."

Eight hours later, they sat in a small clinic that seemed to be a cross between a tattoo parlour and a back-street liposuction dive. Dallas kept these thoughts to himself; Kerra didn't need to be any more nervous than she already was. They were both armed, of course. This was a part of the city, in a part of the country, where *not* going openly armed was an invitation to get mugged or worse.

His 'friend of a friend' was almost a parody of someone who'd lost their medical credentials through overindulgence in prescription medications: pasty skin, reddened eyes, uncombed hair that couldn't decide what length it should be. Dallas had just been given the name "Blosh" as an introduction, with no indication as to whether it was a first or last name. His buddy, someone he'd known back during the last Prask war, had said Blosh was the finest in the business, but hadn't specified exactly which business.

"So, correct me if I'm wrong, but what you want me to do is to *implant* wedding rings on each of you," Blosh said. He had a nervous twitch and a whiny voice, but Dallas didn't care if he spontaneously broke into showtunes so long as he did what they needed first. "Something non-metallic but durable, yeah?"

"That's right," confirmed Dallas. "Gold coloured, for preference."

Blosh twitched, then snorted derisively. "It'll be under the skin. Nobody will see. Nobody will *care*."

"We'll care," Kerra said. She kept her voice level but firm, one step short of don't-mess-with-me.

The red eyes stared at each of them in turn, then Blosh nodded convulsively. "Fine by me." He twitched again. "Fourth proximal phalanx it is." A pause as they both looked at him expectantly, then he sighed. "Ring finger. Left hands, yeah? Yellow ceramic around the finger, bonded in place. Just remember, you won't be able to wear your regular rings on those fingers 'til you get the ceramic ones off. There'll be a bump under the skin. Capisce?"

"Got it." Dallas wondered briefly what they'd gotten into, then he pushed the thought away. So long as the guy did what he said he was going to do, they'd be fine.

In the end, the price wasn't too exorbitant. Dallas eyed the neat dressing on his finger—it was already starting to itch—but paid up. Both he and Kerra had gone with a local anaesthetic so they could stay awake and alert, and Kerra had enough paramedic training that she could spot if Blosh decided to pull a fast one. Either the not-quite-doctor had always planned to keep things on the straight and level or her careful observation put him off, because nothing untoward happened, either during the implant process or afterward during their exfiltration from what he privately thought of as enemy territory.

The incisions took a week to heal. Just as Blosh had told them, there was a palpable bump on the bone beneath the skin, one that went all the way around. Dallas caught Kerra nudging it with her thumb from time to time and grinning. It felt kind of cool to him too; wedding rings the military couldn't order them to remove.

Her updated orders arrived in due time, and she prepared to report for active duty. But his never came. So, he went in to see what was going on. Sure, they needed DIs, but he was still young and fit enough to go back into combat.

Where he ended up was in an office where a medical officer with the rank of Major pointed out details on a slowly revolving hologram that hung in the middle of the room. He'd never actually seen it before, but it was something that had been a part of his life for more than a decade. His 'battle buddy'; more officially, the Autonomous Battlefield Combat Enhancement Unit. This one looked a little battered. Considering what it—and he—had been through, he wasn't altogether surprised.

"The injury you suffered in your last deployment came close to severing your spine," Major Kanto explained. She was in her sixties, with a smoker's cough and grey hair. "In fact, your implant was all that stopped the battle-blade from punching all the way through. It took damage from that, and had to perform essential self-repairs before it could devote all its attention to keeping you alive. Unfortunately, the damage included part of the self-repair module as well as the upgrade plug. It fixed itself, but it used parts of the plug to do it, and the self-repair module had to rewrite its map of the implant accordingly."

"So … it wrote the implant plug *out*?" Dallas had never heard of that happening. "You can't, you know, tell it to write it back in?"

"Only with direct surgical intervention." Major Kanto indicated a point on the implant. "Technically, we could go in through there. Realistically, it would be stitching up any incisions and directly attacking our probes if we tried. It can't even conceive of the idea that it *can* be upgraded, now."

Dallas shrugged. "Send me back in anyway. It works well enough. I'll survive."

"I'm sorry, sergeant." The Major sounded genuinely regretful. "Your implant is … fifty-three iterations behind the ones we're fielding now. You'd be as far behind our men out there in the field as a pre-FTL Marine would be behind you. It's a pity—I've seen your jacket, and we could truly use you out there—but without an up-to-date implant, you'd be throwing your life away, trying to keep up."

"So, I stay a DI." It wasn't a question.

Major Kanto spread her hands in a what-can-I-do gesture. "I've heard good things. Someone's got to train them. You would appear to have a talent at it."

It didn't take him long to decide what he was going to do. He couldn't go out and fight, and he wasn't about to sit at home and worry. "Fine. I'll train 'em."

"Good." Her smile didn't quite reach her eyes. "Someone's got to teach the new kids how not to die out there. Dismissed."

He stood up and saluted. "Ma'am." Turning, he marched from the room.

"Well, there's a good side to this," she said, as they sat side by side on the sofa, hands entwined.

"Let me guess." He'd already been over this a hundred times before. "I won't be out there on the battlefield, so you won't have to worry about whether you're too late to pick me up?"

"Well … yes." She sounded a little put out that he'd forestalled her line. "You *know* I'd be keeping tabs on what area you were in, and either watching for casualty reports or trying to get myself transferred to those areas, just in case. With you training up the new recruits, that's one less worry on my plate."

"I can take care of myself." He hadn't meant for the words to come out so harsh, but it was too late to walk them back.

"Well, *duh*." She leaned over and rubbed her newly shorn scalp against his. "You lived long enough the last time against the Prask for me to get you to medical attention. With you on the back lines, teaching all those wet-behind-the-ears kids how to take care of themselves, it's like the Prask will be having to face dozens of you at a time."

He knew she was just trying to make him feel better, but he didn't want to admit that it was working. "You just take care of yourself, okay? Dropships don't have guns."

"I'll be *fine*." She held him close. "Since the Prask started going after us the last time around, they've arranged for each dropship to have a fighter escort. Make us less of a target."

That made him feel better. Not much, but some.

Two Months Later

Dallas paced along the rows of panting recruits. His discerning eye picked out where one was faltering, and another was trying to cheat by not quite going all the way to the ground. "Hernandez! Tighten it up there! Lawrence! I want to see your nose touch the dust!"

They were good kids, he could tell. Every one of them had heart, and once they had their battle buddies installed and integrated with them, they'd be damn near unstoppable with the right set of skills. It was his job to give them those skills.

"Sergeant Dallas!" It was Ramirez, one of his corporals. Dallas turned to see the young woman marching toward him. She stopped and came to attention in front of him. "Call for you, sergeant."

"Understood. Carry on here, corporal."

He stepped around her and headed for the shack he called his 'office' at quick-march. Phone calls only came through if he absolutely needed to know something *right now*. Otherwise, it was an enlisted runner, bearing physical orders.

Once inside the office, he picked up the phone. "Dallas."

"*Sergeant.*" It was Major Kanto, of the pack-a-day rasp.

She was so far up his chain of command he'd never normally be speaking to her. A chill ran down his back. "Major. What's happened?"

"*You'll be getting official notification, but I thought you needed to know as soon as possible. It's your wife, sergeant. Her dropship was shot down. There were no survivors. I'm very sorry, sergeant.*"

"What?" He could barely hear anything for the ringing in his ears. Blindly, he groped for a chair and sat down. It didn't help much. "How? They were supposed to have fighter escorts. This shit wasn't supposed to *happen!*"

"*The Prask threw an entire squadron at them,*" Major Kanto explained quietly. "*For some reason, they really wanted to knock that dropship out of the sky. They paid for it in blood, but they succeeded.*"

His hand, where it gripped the receiver, squeezed tightly until the plastic began to crack under his fingers. "So, what happens now? We just let them do this shit? Kill my wife, just because she was pulling wounded out of a warzone?"

"No, sergeant." Kanto's voice was firm. *"The brass are sending a message. Every possible high-value target is getting hit, all at once. They're going to learn that they can't pull that crap and just expect to go back to status quo."*

"But that doesn't bring Kerra back." Just saying her name brought tears to his eyes.

"No, it doesn't. Again, I'm very sorry."

"Me, too." He looked up at the squeal of brakes. A military vehicle had pulled up alongside the shack, and he was sure he knew what it was for. "Gotta go. They're here."

"If you need anything, anything at all …"

"What I want, you can't give me." He put the phone down, then stood up and opened the door.

At least they'd sent another sergeant. "Dallas? Radcliffe. I'm sorry to say, I'm the bearer of bad news."

Dallas glanced over at the recruits, then hooked his head back into the shack. "Come on in."

One Month Later

He stood alongside the aluminium coffin. Major Kanto stood on the other side of it. It was fresh back from the previously contested warzone. "Major, why did they take her body? Why did we only get it back now, after hostilities were over?"

Kanto grimaced. "Short version? The Prask are assholes. Long version? Maybe they're pissed off that we forced them to back down, so they're making us ask for every last KIA back. But I read the report. I wouldn't look at the body if I were you. Not if you wanted to remember her the way she was."

His head came up at that. "Did they mutilate her body?" At his sides, his fists clenched. Abruptly, he knelt beside the coffin and undid the clasps holding it shut.

"Sergeant, you really don't want—"

The look he gave Kanto made her take a step back. "All through this, it's never been what I wanted. Well, now *this* is what I want." He lifted the lid and looked at what lay within.

It was a skeleton, fully assembled, the bones kept in place with packing material. Here and there he could see the scoring mark of some kind of blade. The eyeholes stared back at him accusingly.

"I tried to warn you." Kanto's voice was soft.

"They *skeletonised* her?" His voice was rough with disbelief, but he knew all too well what the Prask were capable of. "They *ate* her?"

Her hand fell on his shoulder. "I'm very sorry, sergeant."

Closing his eyes tightly, he felt the hot tears leaking out from between the lids. "And why aren't we bombing them all the way back to cockroach status for this? They *murdered and ate her*! She was a *noncombatant*!"

"The brass decided that surrender and disarmament was an acceptable compromise." There was a faint tinge of disgust in her voice.

He shook his head. "Well, that's me. I'm done. I'll just take …"

His voice slowed and stopped, because he'd been looking down at her left hand for the first time. At the fourth proximal phalanx, where the ceramic ring should have been residing … there was only bare bone.

Disbelievingly, he stared over at the other hand, just in case they'd somehow mixed them up.

No ring there, either. Not even a discolouration to show where it had been.

Nothing.

His heart stopped, then restarted with a hammer-blow of hope.

"You'll just take what?" Kanto's voice was curious.

"Son … of … a … *bitch.*" The truth was unfolding before him. He knew what had been done, and what needed to be done.

"Sergeant, are you alright?" Now, Kanto was concerned.

He stood up and turned to her, his face alight with a fierce joy. "Major, you said once that if I needed anything, I should come to you."

"I did, yes." Her voice was guarded. "Why? What do you need?"

"Access to every single piece of intel on the Prask, especially on the asshole who shot Kerra's dropship down."

"Sergeant, the war's over." She was retreating into her role as an officer. "You can't just—"

"No, it's not." He pointed at the coffin, and its macabre contents. "That's not Kerra. They didn't stop the war because they got hit too hard. They stopped the war because they had what they wanted. *My wife.* Now, I don't know exactly which Prask did all this, or why, but so long as they've got her, then the war's not over."

She blinked. "How—"

"Do I know?" He grabbed her hand, squeezed her fingers around his ceramic ring. "Kerra and I got this done, just before hostilities opened again. Do you see anything like that on that skeleton?"

She pulled her hand free, then looked down into the coffin. "… no, I don't."

"Exactly. *My wife* is the prisoner of some asshole Prask, for reasons I don't even understand, and I need your help to get her back. Can you do that for me?"

She looked at him, considering. "This can't be a sanctioned military op. If we let too many people know she's alive, they'll just kill her."

"I know."

"You'll be going alone, into what's technically the territory of a friendly nation, without overwatch or diplomatic cover."

"I know."

"Once you're in there, I will officially be unaware of your existence."

"I know."

Decisively, she nodded. "Then sure, I can get you that information."

When he bared his teeth, it was in no way a smile. "Good."

Part Two: Investigation

N ow:

"Attention, all passengers ..."

The announcement was warm and friendly. Dallas would've bet a large amount of his salary that it was computer-generated or pre-recorded; there was no way in hell someone could sound that perky, cheerful and downright *human* after the three-day flight.

"... we are now in orbit around Prask;Charra, one of the seven worlds controlled by the Prask. While it was never a major contributor to the war effort, it still lost its capital city to a bombing raid in the last days of the conflict. This, along with other such attacks, is credited with the speedy end to the ..."

He tuned the announcement out. This was stuff he already knew, so it was time to get his head in the game. This was an insertion into enemy territory, whether or not the other side was carrying guns and shooting at him. And, considering his goal and intent, he fully expected there to be shooting at *some* point during the mission.

It would be nice if he could get the wherewithal to shoot back, at some point before that happened. Of course, there was always the age-old creed of the Marine Corps to fall back on.

Adapt. Improvise. Overcome.

Which reminded him of the one problem he'd been unable to overcome; the fact that there were two more people on the mission than he'd planned for. Corporal Ramirez was a good troop and would've been one of his first picks if he'd been looking for volunteers, but the fact remained that he *hadn't.* And the second, a Spec-4 Paulson, was someone he'd never even met before this point. Both NCOs were nominally on leave; neither had served with each other, and the only connection Ramirez had with Dallas was via their DI duties.

Ramirez was nearly as good as Dallas at hand to hand and with firearms, and was a qualified first-aid instructor to boot. Paulson, a pale weedy sort, was reportedly cross-trained in the infiltration of computer systems and the explosive deconstruction of enemy structures. On the other hand, he wasn't very good at the close-in killing aspect.

But that was okay. Dallas was happy to fill that role quite adequately.

Then:

"Absolutely *not!*" Dallas folded his arms and glowered.

This had been known to intimidate more than one importunate

officer before now, but Major Kanto was unmoved. "This is not your call, Sergeant. We both know that a team of three has more chance of surviving a mission like this into hostile territory than a lone operator. Also, having Paulson along will raise your chances of getting in, and Ramirez will improve your odds of everyone getting out alive; including your wife, if she's already injured."

Dallas bit back the retort he wanted to make. Taking a deep breath to calm himself, he eyed Kanto suspiciously. "You're not just medical corps, are you, ma'am?"

She raised an eyebrow. "I would dispute using the word 'just' to describe medical personnel, Sergeant. But yes, I've been known to wear more than one hat at a time. When you first hit our radar, I had ideas of sounding you out about leading a team into Prask space for sabotage and assassination. However, we shelved the idea because your psych profile didn't quite fit the bill at the time."

"And now it does," he said, trying not to sound too sarcastic. "Who do you want me to kill?"

She gave him a direct look. "The Prask officer who considered it was a good idea to restart hostilities just to get his grabby little hands on your wife, along with any of his like-minded friends. Also, to find out *why*. We'd really rather this not start up all over again."

"Killing him, I'll do for free," Dallas said grimly. "I'll do my best to ask him why first, but no promises."

"There are no promises in this business," she agreed blandly.

Now:

They'd done a good job with reconstructing the main city, Dallas mused as he strolled down the shuttle's exit ramp. Following the initial reports of Kerra's death, every major city in Prask space had been hit hard, leaving anything that looked important a smoking ruin. While the scars of the attack were still visible, replacement buildings were already on the rise. The air smelled of scorched earth, overlaid with the sterile tang of new construction.

Prask;Charra was a garden world, home to estates belonging to the higher-ranking members of the Prask nobility and military (who were often one and the same). This meant that the money to rebuild the city was far easier to come by than on planets where it had to be requisitioned via the normal channels. In this regard, Dallas had to admit, Prask were unpleasantly similar to humans.

But that was okay. He didn't like some humans very much either.

Then:

"This is your primary target," Kanto said, bringing up an image of a high-caste Prask on the screen. "The name we have for him is Hakoren k'Fariz. He's as rich as they come and, to the surprise of nobody at all, is currently resident on Prask;Charra. During the second Prask war, he was the equivalent of an Admiral, and had no business flying a fighter. Like every other Prask of his rank, he was commanding a capital ship. But on that one day, he took over from the squadron leader and threw his men at the fighter escort around that one specific dropship. We have recordings of them literally doing kamikaze runs to give their boss a clear shot at the dropship."

"k'Fariz." Dallas let the name roll off his tongue. Now he knew his enemy's face and his name. He still didn't like being railroaded into taking along Ramirez and Paulson, but he was realistic enough to accept that without the assistance he was being given, he wouldn't get anywhere near his goal. "Did he try to pull the same stunt in the first Prask war?"

Kanto shook her head. "That's a negative. He was an Admiral then too, and he commanded a minor battlegroup that never got close enough to the front lines to make a difference. All the information we have suggests that this was deliberate; he had enough influence over the powers that be to get the postings that he wanted."

Ramirez scratched the back of her neck. "That doesn't make any sense. Unless keeping himself out of the action like that reflected badly on him the first time around, and he wanted a chance to make his name?"

"That's *possible*," allowed Kanto, her tone indicating that she didn't think it overly probable. "Prask high society has subtle undertones and overtones that we're still unravelling."

"I'm no kind of expert," Paulson interjected, "but if the Prask were so concerned with 'face', wouldn't the whole aspect of getting them *back* into the war, then pulling something so egregious that they have to surrender just to survive, make him lose ridiculous amounts of prestige?"

"As I said, Specialist, subtle undertones and overtones," Kanto observed. "Much higher-ranked people than you have asked that same question. The best answer we've been able to come up with is that our reaction to the shoot-down of the dropship is so overwrought in the eyes of the Prask that they're claiming some kind of twisted moral victory, even *after* we beat the pants off them."

"Or maybe downing an unarmed, guarded ship is akin to counting coup with them?" suggested Ramirez. "And capturing the Sergeant's wife alive and keeping her prisoner is an extended version of that? All the while they're doing the peace treaty negotiations, they're laughing at us because they know damn well we'll go above and beyond to bring every man back. I mean, maybe it's a spite thing? *We're keeping this one?*"

Paulson shook his head. "Still doesn't make sense to me. I keep thinking there's something we're missing. But like I said, I'm no expert."

"If we truly understood the Prask," Kanto said, "this mission wouldn't be necessary. We'd be able to order them to hand her back unharmed in a way they couldn't ignore. But we don't have perfect understanding. So, we're going with imperfect understanding and a certain amount of brute force."

Dallas nodded. He was *perfectly comfortable* with visiting brute force on the Prask until he got his wife back.

Now:

They moved through the crowd of tourists in a loose group; not obviously together, but keeping tabs on one another via the occasional glance. It was a foregone conclusion that the Prask had the arrivals building under surveillance, so they had to get out into the world before they regrouped. The location of the k'Fariz compound was already known to them, but tours of Prask;Charra didn't include private estates. So the second thing they had to figure out was how to get there and gain entry without alerting the enemy.

The *first* thing was how to acquire sufficiently heavy weaponry (and other equipment) to carry out their mission in full.

But that was okay. The compound wasn't going anywhere.

Inside the k'Fariz Compound

Panting, Kerra spun and stabbed the sharpened rib-bone deep into the eye-socket of the pseudo-panther as it lunged at her. It let out an agonized yowl; razor claws raked across her arm, but didn't do more than draw blood before it went into convulsions. She forced herself to ignore the injury. It wasn't the first scar, or even the tenth, that she'd gained since she woke up here.

She knew she only had a small window of opportunity, so she grabbed the rib and yanked it out before the creature had stopped twitching. With quick strokes, she began to dress out the pseudo-panther, peeling the skin back and slicing cuts of meat from its flanks.

Not as much as she would've liked; there was still some good meat left when the robotic claw descended from the ceiling and closed over the carcass of her adversary.

There was no use in trying to fight the claw, but she'd learned that if she unbalanced its load, it would pause to recalibrate. So, she gave the corpse a yank, then started gouging away at the creature's lower jaw. The robotic arm retracted into the ceiling, along with the body of the pseudo-panther, but she'd managed to pry the jawbone loose. The rib bone was starting to lose its edge, but she could definitely make use of the panther's teeth …

"So quickly do you humans devolve into savagery." The sneering voice of the Prask—speaking English directly rather than using a translator— sounded from the speakers. *"I wonder what your husband would say if he could see you now. Crouching in the dirt like a beast, tearing at raw meat with your teeth. He would turn from you in disgust, if he even knew you were alive."*

"Bullshit." She sneered right back. "A human, unlike a Prask, will do anything we have to, to survive. He knows that. And he does know I'm alive. I don't care *what* you sent back to him. One DNA check would tell him it's not me. And that means he's coming for me."

"We anticipated that." If anything, the sneer grew more pronounced. *"For such a martial species, you are surprisingly yellow-backed about creating clones. We are not. It is how we replicate our best warriors. Forced growth is a thing, after all. We enjoyed our ritual feasting upon our enemy and returned the skeleton to him intact. All the testing in the world would only tell him that it was yours."*

Kerra forced a derisive laugh to hide the swell of hope in her chest. "For starters, asshole, it's yellow-*bellied*. And you are so wrong about us. There are very few things humanity won't do if it gets us what we need."

Unseen by the hidden cameras, her left thumb ran over her ring finger, feeling the lump under the skin. If they'd sent the skeleton of her clone to Dallas, there was no way in *hell* he'd be fooled.

He's coming for me.

All I have to do is stay alive until then.

Part Three: Infiltration

They convened once they were well away from the spaceport, converging naturally on a sidewalk café that advertised human-style refreshments. Dallas fronted up first, despite his distaste at the idea of ingesting anything that had been near a Prask. In his heart of hearts, they would always be the enemy until he got Kerra back and ensured that the asshole who took her *could never do it again*. And even then, he'd be wary of them.

"One medium coffee, please," he said to the juvenile Prask behind the counter. "Plain black, no milk, no sugar." His eyes automatically scanned the attendant for signs of modification into a warrior-caste, but came up with nothing.

While he wasn't conversant with the entire life-cycle of the Prask species, his understanding was that they were hatched genderless and sexless. Unmodified, they would live out their lives as basic drones unless they were fed the correct substances in the egg (raising them to become a male or female of the appropriate level of nobility) or exposed to pheromones after hatching, modifying them to become worker or warrior-caste. Workers were relatively slow and strong, but had minimal aggression. Warriors were fast, aggressive, short-lived and sported battle-blades on their secondary arms that could punch through body armour like a knife through butter.

There were nuances beyond that, but the truth was, he didn't care. He knew what even a nascent warrior-caste Prask looked like, and this one didn't tick any of the boxes. No twitchy movements, no battle-blades, no aggression toward a stranger.

"Medium coffee, black, yes, sir or madam, that will be five *chiraka*," the Prask recited back. Just as humans had trouble telling a male Prask from a female or a drone, it seemed they had equal difficulty with humans.

Fortunately, he didn't have to worry about whatever it was they actually used for money; a handy touch-card had been included in his tourism pack, made out to his faked identity. He tapped it on the reader, which chittered at him with such a lifelike sound that he nearly reached for the gun he wasn't wearing. The Prask youngster didn't seem to notice his involuntary almost-movement, instead tapping an instruction into its console.

Hot liquid gurgled into a paper cup, and he took it from the Prask with a nod approximating thanks. Cautiously, he sniffed at it as he carried it away to an unoccupied table and sat down. It smelled like hot coffee, but he still didn't feel inclined to drink it. For all he knew, he'd been marked from the moment he walked off the ship and the Prask attendant was secretly an assassin with his name on its list.

Sitting there in the sunlight, he pretended to sip at the coffee as he looked around, every inch the human tourist visiting his first alien world. While it was his first time as a tourist—that part was true, at least—he'd visited several worlds already. Usually involving airdrops, explosions and a remarkable amount of carnage.

His boots were already on the ground, so the airdrop aspect was out, but explosions and carnage were still a distinct possibility. All he had to do was find the means to carry them out, then get to the target of his displeasure. The exact amount of carnage would then depend on what shape Kerra was in, and who he had to kill to get her *off* the damn planet.

"Excuse me?" It was Ramirez, bearing something that vaguely resembled a latte and addressing him as a polite stranger rather than a corporal to a sergeant. "Do you mind if I sit here?"

"Be my guest." He made an expansive gesture at the other chairs spaced around the small table.

"Thanks." Pulling out one of them, she seated herself, then held out her hand. "Hi, I'm Carla. First time here?"

He shook it with the feeling of an actor taking part in a play, but knowing they had to look natural. "I'm Don. Yes, I just got in half an hour ago."

The phrasing was as important as the faux introduction itself. She'd used the code phrases which meant she hadn't spotted any electronic surveillance specifically aimed at them, or any Prask paying them particular attention. His reply verified her conclusions, and added the observation that he had yet to see any warrior-caste Prask at all.

Ramirez nodded and sat back in her chair. She didn't seem to be as paranoid about her perhaps-latte as Dallas was about his coffee, as she took a sip and made a noise of pleased surprise. "Hey, this isn't bad at all."

"Um, sorry to bother you," Paulson said as he showed up at the table with a couple of muffins in his hands. "But are these seats taken?"

Ramirez glanced at Dallas, who shook his head, then turned back to Paulson. "Nope; go right ahead."

"Thanks." Paulson pulled a chair out and plonked himself into it. Of the three of them, he fitted the role they were playing best of all. For all that he was within fitness regs, he had a babyish face and sported a slight pudge. Over and above that, he wore an offensively loud Hawaiian shirt (what *was* it about Hawaiian shirts that shouted '*tourist!*'?), and a camera around his neck.

As he sat at the table and ate one of the muffins, he fiddled with the camera, calling up pictures he'd already taken. "My gear's not registering any sound pickups within range," he murmured, just loudly enough for the other two to hear. "We can talk."

"Good." Dallas pretended to take another sip of his coffee. "We need to locate weapons for acquisition. Now that we're on the ground, how are we going to do that?"

"This is the richest city on the richest planet the Prask own," Ramirez replied, then sipped again at her latte. "There will absolutely be buildings they want to guard. And the guards ..."

"... will be warrior-caste, with weapons." Paulson half-turned in his seat, and took a snap-shot of a building across the way. "Of course, then we have the problem that we're trying to mug an armed warrior-caste Prask, without weapons of our own."

Dallas rose from the table, tipping his untouched coffee into what he hoped was a planter. "Less of a problem than you might think."

Finishing off her latte, Ramirez got up as well. "Absolutely, but I'm thinking we scout the terrain *before* we draw attention by kicking the shit out of the locals. Paulson, get a picture of us. You just met us, and you think we're cool."

Dallas could see the sense in what she was saying. As he posed for the camera, he reconsidered his irritation in having others along. An infiltration expert, he wasn't.

The tour bus hummed along its route, superconducting magnets holding them a steady half-metre above the roadway. Dallas sat at one window, scrutinising the terrain. Ramirez, opposite him, did the same on her side. A little way forward of them, Paulson apparently drank in every word the tour guide uttered, and took photos of *everything.*

It appeared to be flat farmland, though he didn't recognise the crops being grown or the beasts being herded. Insectoid like the Prask, they resembled gigantic beetles, though he wasn't sure how their biology worked. That didn't matter; he didn't know exactly how Prask anatomy worked either, but he for damn sure knew how to kill them.

They hummed past a field where a bunch of what he presumed were drones picking ... fruit? It certainly looked that way. A single Prask oversaw them, wearing a sash of some dull-coloured cloth. He doubted very much that it was a noble of any kind. Neither could it choose to rise above its allotted station. From what he'd been told, such aspirations were nigh-impossible for the lower castes; they literally couldn't conceive of defying their place in life like that.

This rigid caste system irritated him on some deep level, but he wasn't on this planet to push societal change on them, even if their biology would allow for it. He had a beef with exactly one Prask noble: the asshole who had Kerra. The rest could sit in their cosy little estates and lord it over the lowborn peasantry for the rest of their misbegotten lives, for all he cared.

"Coming up on the left," announced the tour guide, "we have the truly magnificent estate belonging to the most illustrious of our noble families, the k'Fariz. With a lineage reaching back into antiquity, the k'Fariz dynasty can be truly said to represent the best of us."

Dallas was willing to believe it, but what that said about the Prask was probably best left unaired in any kind of polite company. He didn't want to draw attention to himself, after all. Instead, he studied the massive walled compound that sat in the middle of the huge estate.

If I wanted to get in there quietly, how would I do it?

"Okay," said Ramirez, after examining the image that Paulson's camera was projecting on the wall. The pixel density was astounding, even blown up that large, and the overlays showing infrared, ultraviolet and several other imagery options were pretty good too. "These look like entrances. Here, here and here." The laser pointer in her fingers flicked a tiny red dot from point to point.

Paulson cleared his throat. "Those will be locked or guarded at night. Or both."

"Which is why we won't be going in that way." Dallas gestured at the image. "We find the widest area without entrances, and we go over the wall there. Once we're inside, we go to k'Fariz's private chambers, subduing any Prask we find on the way as quietly as possible. We'll also be setting charges on the way in. Paulson?"

"All ready to roll," the Spec-4 assured him. "I got lucky with my shopping. They use stuff with a lot higher nitrate content than we do. Their version of ANFO is going to go *bang*."

"Good. Ramirez?"

"Next shift change for those guards I scoped out is in about three hours. Looks like we'll get two Prask laser carbines out of it. And I found a vehicle we can 'borrow'. It's a bit decrepit but it should get us out there, or close enough."

Dallas nodded. "I don't care if we have to pedal. Good work, both of you. Now, get your heads down for a couple of hours. We've got a long night ahead of us."

"Sergeant."

"Sergeant."

One of the good things about this mission, Dallas mused as he sidled into position, was that the Prask didn't conscript citizen soldiers. Any guards were going to be drawn from the warrior-caste, and thus by definition created to murder their enemies. Most people wouldn't consider this to be a *good* thing, but he found that it assuaged any potential feelings of guilt about what he was planning to do. Warriors were hatched to die in battle. It was as simple as that.

"Hey!" That was Ramirez, putting the plan into action. She would be staggering as though drunk, supporting an equally unsteady Paulson. "You! Bug-features! Where'za, where'za, hotel?"

Dallas came around the corner, holding the length of dowel he'd broken off a broom handle—some tools were universal—and fashioned into a crude stabbing spear. With fast, silent strides, he moved up behind the closest guard. Still holding their carbines, they weren't pointing them at Ramirez, as they had no doubt been firmly ordered not to threaten anyone who wasn't threatening them.

That was the other good thing about fighting Prask. If they were faced with a situation outside of their biologically programmed role, they had no way of judging what to do, and would always fall back on whatever they'd been told. A worker could be handed a plasma rifle and told that the enemy were coming, but unless they were specifically instructed to point the emitter toward the foe and squeeze the trigger, they would simply stand there holding the rifle.

His chosen target, with its wide angle of view, spotted his movement and began to turn but it was far too late. Closing fast, Dallas stabbed upward with the sharpened dowel, going for the vulnerable seam just under where a human's jawbone would be. Most of a warrior's exoskeleton had sliding plates to prevent this sort of attack, but there were places where it just wasn't possible.

Even as the guard's battle-blades unfolded for combat, the dowel punched through the weak spot, stabbing up into the warrior's hindbrain. He wrenched it free as the warrior stumbled and fell, then jumped back as its fellow guard came at him, battle-blades bared. These looked no less sharp than the one that had messed up his battle buddy more than ten years ago, and he parried the slashes with his makeshift spear. The edges of the chitin blades carved away at the wood, slicing chunks out of it with ease.

Looking up into its blood-red eyes, he found himself irresistibly recalling that fateful day. He'd been armoured, and armed with more than a pitiful length of wood, and the warrior had still skewered him like a lamb chop at a barbecue. *This might not have been a good idea.*

And then the warrior shuddered and fell face-first onto the ground. Ramirez stood over it, the carving knife she'd stolen from the hotel sideboard protruding from the same seam, but this time on the back of its neck. From the looks of it, she'd severed its ventral nerve cord: the equivalent of the spinal cord in humans.

"You okay there?" she asked, nodding down at where his hands still gripped the remnants of his spear, white-knuckled.

"I am now. Thanks." He poured lighter fluid over the broom handle and set it alight, then dropped it to let it burn out. Ramirez retrieved her carving knife and gave it the same treatment. The more they could confuse later forensic analysis, the better.

They dragged the corpses into a patch of shadow nearby, then stripped them of their weapons and reloads. Dallas wasn't familiar with Prask energy weapons, but it seemed Paulson had done a course on them recently. Major Kanto, Dallas gathered, left nothing to chance.

"Okay, then." Dallas looked at Ramirez. "Lead the way to your vehicle, corporal. It's time to go explain to Hakoren k'Fariz the error of his ways."

Ramirez smiled. "Copy that, sergeant."

Part Four: Combat Rescue

When Dallas saw the vehicle for the first time, he wondered if pedalling was going to be a requirement after all. Unlike every other Prask vehicle he'd seen to that point, this one didn't get around by magnetic levitation, but by plain old wheels on the road. Dented, rusted here and there, and with half the paint missing—he suspected that had happened because of a nearby explosion, from when the place was bombarded into submission—it looked as unappealing as something with wheels could look.

Still, he was determined to get to Kerra, so if this was what it took, he'd go with it. Looking it over carefully, he tried what he figured must be a door handle. It clicked, and the door hinged open. Apparently, it either couldn't be locked or the owner didn't bother securing it at night.

Unfortunately, the seats inside weren't very high off the floor—despite being bipedal, the Prask body plan differed markedly from the human one—and the controls made no sense at all. Dallas got a sinking feeling all over again, realising this was one more time he hadn't thought ahead. "Do either of you know how to even drive one of these things?"

Ramirez shrugged. "Sorry, sergeant. I don't drive 'em, I just find 'em."

Dallas glanced at the other member of the team. "Paulson?"

The Spec-4 frowned, peering into the vehicle with the assistance of a hand-light. "I watched the bus driver today, so I think I might be able to figure something out. Ramirez, hold my pack and loan me your knife?"

"Sure. Just to be clear, this is the pack full of your overpowered IEDs, right?"

"Correct." He shrugged the pack off, using two hands, and passed it back to her. "Should be safe, so long as we don't drop it, set it on fire or shoot at it."

"Jesus wept. And you were walking around with it on your *back*? Man, this job's getting too dangerous for my taste." But she slung the Prask carbine over her shoulder and accepted the pack anyway, then dug out her folding blade and passed it over. Dallas knew it would be razor-sharp, but would've been too short to do the job on the warrior-caste Prask that they'd taken the laser carbines from.

"Working with explosives is the least problematic aspect of being in the Corps," Paulson explained as he attacked the back seat cushion with the knife. The fabric cover gave way easily, and he carved out a rough square of the seat-back, which he folded forward to act as extra cushioning on the seat. Thus boosted, he climbed into the driver's seat. "If you screw up, you'll never know about it."

Ramirez shook her head. "There is something deeply, deeply wrong with you, Paulson."

"Sure there is. I volunteered for this mission, remember? Just like you did. Aha." Paulson sounded pleased with himself. "Top controls are levers for steering, plus acceleration and brakes. Mid controls are for incidental stuff like wipers, radio, anything that you'd only find in civvy vehicles. No foot controls. Their leg structure doesn't allow it."

"So, can you drive it?" asked Dallas, in the same low tone the other two had used to carry on their banter.

"In theory, yes. In practice, we'll see." But Paulson sounded cautiously optimistic.

"I'm not asking for Driver of the Year. I just need you to be driver of the next half-hour." But Dallas was already heading around to the other side of the vehicle. Instead of wasting time destroying the back seat cushion, he opted to sit down low, pulling his knees up to his chest.

Ramirez removed her own pack before she climbed into the back seat, carefully placing Paulson's backpack on the seat beside her and resting her own pack across her knees. "Wait, there's no seatbelts in this thing."

"Are we surprised, Ramirez?" Dallas hadn't even looked for one, and wouldn't have put it on if he'd found it. Carefully, he pulled his door closed. "The Prask don't strike me as fanatics for OSHA."

"Well, given that their carapaces protect them significantly better than our endoskeletons …" Paulson began using the knife to lever a panel off the dash. "… it makes sense—"

"I don't give a shit about them protecting themselves," Ramirez interrupted. "I was just going to strap our little bag of death in place. And if you break that knife, I *will* put my boot up your ass."

The panel popped off, and Paulson looked inside. "Relax. I know the exact fracture point of that kind of steel. If I wanted to break it, it would already be broken." He frowned as he examined the wiring. "It can't be this easy … can it?"

Dallas cleared his throat, cutting off Ramirez' incipient outburst. "Normally I'd agree that nothing is 'that easy', but you need to clarify."

Paulson pushed the panel back into place, then jabbed a square button set into the dash. There was a burst of noise, then the entire vehicle shook with the sound of a running engine. "No ignition lock. And I was going to be the first person in history to hotwire an alien car, too." He folded the knife and handed it back to Ramirez. "Thanks for the loan."

Dallas looked around as a light came on in a nearby building. "We'd better get moving if we don't want to be arrested for trying to steal this damn thing."

"Roger that." Grabbing the levers, Paulson twisted one and pushed the other. The vehicle lurched forward, then stopped as the engine cut out.

"Shit," Ramirez muttered from the back seat. "You stalled it, you idiot."

"Hey, it's my first time." Paulson jabbed the starter button again, and worked the levers more carefully. This time, the vehicle rolled forward, turning as Paulson gingerly pulled on one lever and pushed on the other, then trundled out of the small courtyard it had been stored in.

They turned on to the road, and Paulson cautiously accelerated. They still weren't travelling anywhere near as fast as even the maglev bus had—Dallas hadn't seen what passed for cop cars in this town, though he suspected they were faster than this—but at least they were on the move.

Kerra, I'm coming. Just hold on.

k'Fariz Compound
Kerra

She had no idea what time it was—kept down in the depths of wherever this place was, she hadn't seen the sun in *forever*—but it felt far too early when the lights came on, flooding her tiny cell. *"Wake up, human!"* the speakers blared. *"It is time for you to once more earn your lodging!"*

"That's *'earn my keep'*, you self-righteous, pretentious prick," she muttered, climbing to her feet. The sharpened rib bone was ready to hand for stabbing, and she'd fashioned a slashing weapon with the pseudo-panther's jawbone. She didn't know what he was going to have her fight this time, but she was going to go all-in with what she had.

What she *wanted* was a warrior-caste's battle-blade. Those things grew to a near-molecular edge and could cut through ceramal armour; Dallas' career-defining injury was proof of that. With one of those suckers, she could murder anything Hakoren threw at her.

Of course, getting one away from a warrior-caste would be quite the trick. The tattered remains of her Dropship Corps uniform, good against low-end weapons, would do nothing against a stab from a battle-blade. It would go in through her sternum and out through her spine without even slowing down. Not that she'd ever get the chance to be that close to one. Mainly because the Prask also used *ranged* weaponry.

She emerged into the artificially grown shrubbery and low trees that populated the arena. These were probably supposed to give camouflage and concealment to the critters that Hakoren had been sending into the arena after her. She'd learned fast and dug deep into the survival training that everyone got in boot; by now, she was just as good at hiding and sneaking as the best of her current opponents.

The trouble was, in an ordinary situation after the first half-dozen predators died, the others would decide it was too much trouble and move away. Hakoren, the prick, just kept on sending them at her. She was good, but she was still only human, and he hadn't offered medical assistance for any of the (thankfully shallow) wounds she'd received so far. If he kept upping the ante, sooner or later something was going to hurt her badly, and she doubted she'd get any time off to heal.

She just had to hold on long enough for Dallas to find her. Because she *knew* he was on the way. It was the only thing keeping her going.

"I'm here," she called out as she topped the low hillock in the middle of the arena. "What've you got for me this time, bug-features?"

She'd seen enough of him that she was able to recognise a sneer even thirty feet up the side of the arena, in the glassed-in viewing gallery. *"Always the defiance. Not that it will serve you any favours. Today you have a new opponent. Rather, two opponents."*

"I've killed everything else you've sent at me." She flexed her hands on her makeshift weapons. "Bring it."

"Oh, I will, as you say, bring it. Today you face the Prask. A warrior and a worker. I am sure that you will kill the worker, but while you are doing that, the warrior will carve out your human organs." He broke into what passed for laughter among the Prask, though only the nobility used it. *"And I will enjoy your screams before you die, for what you have done to me."*

Kerra blinked. That part was new. "What? What'd I ever do to *you*?"

But he'd either turned off the microphone or was deliberately ignoring her, because no answer was forthcoming. She heard the door across the other side of the arena rumbling open, though it was out of sight due to the plant life. This meant she had less than a minute to do something about her new opponents.

Fortunately, she still had a few tricks that the Prask hadn't seen yet.

The Prask vehicle chuntered along at its best speed, though at times Dallas thought he could get out and run faster than that. Ramirez kept an eye on their backtrail, while Dallas monitored the local equivalent of the police band on one of Paulson's useful devices. There was a little activity on it, but nothing to make him worry quite yet. Nobody had mentioned the k'Fariz estate, anyway.

They'd just passed one of the landmarks that told him they were getting close to their target location when the steady burble of the engine missed a beat. A few seconds later, it did it again.

"Tell me that was your shitty driving and not this piece of crap," Ramirez said, not turning around.

"It's not my driving." Paulson let go one of the levers to tap a dial with his finger; just then, the engine choked and sputtered, then staggered on. "I think I might've misread the fuel gauge. Or this thing's a gas hog."

The vehicle chose that moment to give up the ghost; it rolled on a few more yards, then stuttered to a halt.

"Okay, that's it." Dallas opened his door and climbed out. "Everyone on your feet."

"We're not that far away," Paulson noted as he exited the dead vehicle. "At least it got us close."

"So does an airdrop." Ramirez hefted Paulson's pack as she got out, then passed it over to him. "You can have your little bundle of joy back. I could swear I heard that thing ticking."

"Couldn't have." He slid his arms through the straps. "I used strictly digital timers. I ran out of the Prask-time digital watches I bought coming out of the spaceport, but there were timers in some of the devices in the room, so I adapted them to the purpose. The staff of that hotel are gonna be *so* pissed."

"That's a *'then'* problem," Dallas observed. "Finding out where Kerra is and getting to her, that's a *'now'* problem. Let's get this thing into the ditch, so nobody sees it and starts wondering."

"Goddamn right." Ramirez set her shoulder to the rear corner of the Prask vehicle, with Dallas on the other side. Paulson reached in on the driver's side and steered, allowing them to run the thing straight off the road. Once over the edge of the embankment, it jolted down about ten feet before swerving and tumbling onto its roof. It lay there forlornly, wheels in the air, while the three Marines looked down at it and dusted their hands off.

"Okay, let's move." Dallas led the way, setting the pace at a steady jog.

He could've gone much faster on his own, but Paulson didn't strike him as being particularly physically capable. A brain of the highest order, definitely, but no athlete. Ramirez brought up the rear, both maintaining a watch on their six and keeping an eye on Paulson.

All the same, it only took them ten minutes to get to the entrance to the k'Fariz grounds, and another fifteen to sneak past the obvious (and less obvious) intruder scanners. Once again, Paulson's tech proved its worth, mapping out the route they had to take in order to dodge the invisible scanner beams.

At the base of the wall where he'd picked out the entry point, they paused to regroup. "How you doing, Paulson?" He looked the Spec-4 over.

Paulson was breathing hard, with sweat running down his face, but he faced up to Dallas all the same. "Ready to do it all over again, sergeant."

"Copy that. Ramirez, up and over?"

Ramirez smiled. "Up and over, sarge. Let's do this."

Removing her pack and purloined carbine, she placed them at the base of the wall, then took several steps back. Dallas clasped his hands together as he bent his knees, then crouched to bring his hands even lower. A mental signal woke up his battle buddy and brought it to full capacity. "Call it, Ramirez."

She took several deep breaths, flushing her lungs with oxygen. "Three. Two. One. Go."

At the instant of saying, '*go*', she sprang forward, running straight toward Dallas. Within a stride of him, she leaped into the air, her foot coming down into his clasped hands. His battle buddy surged power through his limbs and he heaved her upward as she jumped. She rocketed upward a good three metres, catching the upper edge of the wall then swarming on top in the best confidence-course style.

The wall was flat, so she lay prone along it, reaching downward. "Rope. Weapon."

"Roger that." Opening the top of her pack, he took out the coil of rope—not military issue, but a well-known brand among hobby climbers—and tossed one end up to her.

She caught it, stuck it between her teeth, then caught the laser carbine when he tossed it next. Slinging the carbine over her shoulder, she took hold of the rope with both hands and rolled off the far side of the wall. Dallas already had his end of the rope braced, and let it pay out in steady increments.

When it went slack, he tugged on it twice, and got three tugs in reply. A single tug could be a mistake, but the two-three code was '*go ahead*'. Two tugs would've been '*I have a gun pointed at me*', but only if she couldn't get her own weapon into action first.

He slapped Paulson on the shoulder, then unslung his carbine and took up a guard position, facing outward. Behind him he could hear Paulson's soft grunts as he made his way up the wall. On the other side, Ramirez would be hauling on the rope for all she was worth. Fortunately, Paulson wasn't particularly bulky.

"I'm up." Paulson's quiet words got Dallas' attention.

Slinging the carbine again, he grabbed the trailing end of the rope and tugged a length of it back over. Paulson took hold of it again, and

Dallas lowered him on the other side, much as he'd done with Ramirez. Finally, he fastened the top of Ramirez' pack, donned it, and laid hold of the rope.

As Ramirez and Paulson braced it with their weight on the far side of the wall, he activated his battle buddy again. Power surged through his arms, and he hauled himself up and over the wall in just a few seconds. There was no way to rappel down, so he let himself drop; his legs and then his arms took the impact, collapsing like a metal spring.

"Right," he said, standing up and dusting his hands off. "Let's go find Kerra."

Hakoren k'Fariz glowered at the interior of the arena that had been set up under his family compound. With his understanding that humans were a civilised, urban species, he had planted various species of trees and shrub to take his prisoner out of her element. Unfortunately, those same plants made it almost impossible for his sensors to view what was going on anywhere but the central hillock.

Worker-caste Prask were slow but strong. The one that had been placed in the arena had been given firm orders to pursue the human and drag her out into the central area so that the warrior could kill her at its leisure, once she was in plain view of the observation platform. Likewise, the warrior had been ordered to chase her into the worker's arms so that she could be captured and then killed for all to see.

There was just one flaw with this situation: they couldn't find her.

As soon as she'd been informed of her pursuers, the human had ducked back into the trees, vanishing like she'd been born among them instead of in a city environment. Hakoren felt aggrieved; someone, somewhere in the chain of information gathering, had dropped the egg sac. A non-feral species should not take so easily to the wilderness.

Four times, the warrior and worker had circled the arena, even going in opposite directions in case she was simply moving ahead of them. They had caught neither sight nor hearing of her. It was both puzzling and irritating.

He activated the speakers and ordered the pair to sweep the arena again, more carefully. There was no way she could have escaped, and he knew she wasn't back in her cell. Which only left the arena.

But they had searched the arena, several times.

Where could she be?

Kerra lay utterly still under the pile of leaves she'd painstakingly gathered in the hollow next to one of the larger trees. Her arm was across her nose and mouth, and she exhaled through the cloth in case they were using heat sensors to look for her breath plume. Her hands gripped the rib and jawbone; not tightly, but just lightly enough to know they were there.

She needed the warrior to come past her in a particular direction, without the worker nearby. If she could get the drop on the little bastard—her only blessing so far was that the warrior seemed to be a young and inexperienced specimen—she could kill it. But if the worker interfered, that would spoil the whole plan.

Unfortunately, although they hadn't yet thought to look under the innocuous pile of leaves just off the path, neither had they cooperated with her plan of action. Every time the warrior had come past in the right direction, the worker had been with it, or within line of sight. It was more than a little frustrating.

But she could wait.

Right now, she had nothing *but* time on her side.

Standing watch as Paulson planted one of his IEDs next to the exhaust port of what was possibly a power generator, Dallas looked around as Ramirez nudged him. With a tilt of her head, she indicated a largish building. As he looked at it, he frowned as he noted certain mechanisms up near the top of the roof. The entire roof was intended to open outward, giving whatever was inside access to the open air.

"Private aircraft, do you think?" His voice was just a murmur.

"Something like that." So was hers. "But whatever it is, it's a VTOL."

"True." He rubbed his chin in thought.

"Get Paulson to blow it up?" Her teeth gleamed briefly in a grin.

"No. Got a better idea." With their vehicle dead, they'd need *some* way of getting out with Kerra, when they found her. It would be better than walking, anyway.

He was running his battle buddy constantly now, which was what allowed him to hear the scrape of the sentry's foot just before it came around the corner. Moving faster than humanly possible, he jammed the muzzle of his liberated carbine in between its mandibles and into its mouth, then pulled the trigger. The soft, mushy sound of the back of its head exploding outward was louder than the shot itself, and it collapsed to the ground.

In the distance, he heard a voice call out interrogatively. It was in Prask, but he judged that they didn't quite know for a fact there was something wrong yet.

This, of course, would change.

"Done," Paulson reported. "Where to now?"

"Main building," Dallas decided. "What are the timers looking like?"

"First one's due to go off in thirty seconds," the specialist replied. "Staggered after that."

"Perfect. While they're running around looking for us, we'll already be inside their perimeter." He indicated the main building with a knife-hand. "Lead the way, Ramirez."

"Roger that, sarge." The corporal moved off, with Paulson following along. Dallas trailed Paulson, checking six and making sure nothing jumped either of his comrades.

Just as they reached a shadowed doorway in the side of the main building, Paulson held up three fingers. Then two. Then one.

As Paulson folded the last one over, Dallas drove his boot into the latch of the door. The **THBOOM** that lit up the night behind them drowned out the impact and the screech of tearing metal as he ripped the lock clear out of its housing. Flying open, the door rebounded from a wall, but he stopped it from closing all the way. "Go!"

They followed him in, Ramirez pushing the door shut behind them. Dallas was riding the surge generated by his battle buddy; at some point in the future, he'd have to slow down and let it repair the damage he was doing to his body, but right now was not the time. He moved through the building fast, senses flaring and carbine barrel tracking where his eyes went.

Two warriors appeared at the top of a set of stairs; he fired twice, before he was even really aware of their presence. Laser holes burned through their chests, they tumbled down the steps. If either one had been a worker or a noble, he would've spared it for interrogation, but warriors didn't submit to interrogation. For them it was victory or death, with nothing in between.

Paulson tapped him on the shoulder and showed him an electronic map. He scanned it, picked out likely locations, and moved on as more explosions sounded from outside. The window for finding Kerra (and possibly Hakoren) was getting narrower, but he still had time.

He *would* find her and get her out. The only variable would be how many Prask died on the way.

When the distant explosion sounded, rumbling through the ground, Kerra wasn't sure what to think. Then the second one came, a bit closer, and she grinned savagely. *He's here. He came to get me out.*

Hakoren's hectoring voice came over the speakers, ordering the worker and warrior to leave the arena and attend him at once; or rather, that was what her imperfect understanding of Prask told her he was saying. Through a gap in the leaves, she saw the worker tromping ahead, going out of sight. Then the warrior came past ... precisely where she needed him to be.

Gathering herself, she burst up from under the covering of leaves, leaping on the warrior's back. It hesitated before turning toward the sound, she realised belatedly, because it had been given strict orders to leave the arena, superseding the orders to find and kill her. Her legs wrapped around the middle of its thorax, and the jawbone in her left hand hooked on its mandibles, pulling its head back.

Its lack of experience told in her favour as it staggered from the sudden assault, waving its manipulator-arms and battle-blades in an attempt to regain its balance. Had it been a veteran, it would've allowed itself to go down, and taken the fight to its attacker while on the ground. But by the time it actually started responding correctly, it was far too late; Kerra had punched the sharpened rib up under where its jaw would've been on a human.

One battle-blade sliced her arm briefly before it staggered and went down. She rode it to the ground, working the rib around in the wound to maximise the damage she was doing to its brain. Once, twice, three times, it spasmed, then it went still.

She knelt there over its corpse, breathing heavily, keeping a lookout for the worker. There was no sign of it, or any other Prask, which told her that nobody had witnessed the kill. This didn't surprise her, given that there were still explosions sounding nearby.

She tore off the remains of her sleeve to bind the shallow cut, then studied the joint connecting the limb to the Prask. Thoughtfully, she pulled the rib out from the thing's head and pried at the joint with the sharp end. There was a little play there, so she smashed the jawbone into it a few times machete-style, then tried again. This time, she was able to wedge the tip of the rib into the gap and exert some force as a lever.

The rib promptly snapped.

Undeterred, she pulled out the broken bit, wedged the rest of it into the hole, and tried again. The leverage was less, but she could feel connective tissue giving way. Pulling the rib from the gap again, she twisted the limb as hard as she could, trying to recall the last time she'd dismantled a lobster.

With a combination of twisting, brute force, and using the sharp teeth on the jawbone to cut the last shreds of flesh, she separated the limb and hefted the battle-blade. The next part of her escape plan was to get out of the arena; fortunately, she had an idea for that, too.

Grabbing the dead warrior by one arm, she dragged him through the trees to the open area, then stepped back. If she was correct, the automated system would drop from the ceiling to grab up anything that was showing zero life signs. After all, it always had before.

Down it came, the chain rumbling through its pulleys. She watched as the massive metal grabber-claw opened to scoop up the warrior's corpse ... then dashed forward and swung the battle-blade at the cable alongside the chain. It sliced through with a shower of sparks, but she only felt a faint tingle. The claw juddered to a halt, then began to retract.

"Nope," she growled, leaping up and snagging the empty claw, then climbing higher while awkwardly hanging on to the battle-blade. She hung on for dear life as the cable and chain retracted into the opening in the ceiling of the chamber.

There was a conveyor belt, she saw, as the claw cleared the opening. The claw was evidently designed to swing over and deposit its burden on the belt, which would then convey it elsewhere. To her moderate surprise—she really would've thought they'd have a computer running this aspect—there was a worker-caste at a control panel, operating the claw.

Dropping to the floor as soon as there was a floor for her to drop onto, she headed for the worker. It watched her approach, apparently having never been instructed what to do if someone hijacked the grabber-claw. To be fair, she figured, there were probably guards in here to handle that aspect. Usually, anyway. When people started blowing up Hakoren's shit—some of those explosions had sounded *vicious*—he'd called all of them away, without considering that she might accidentally take advantage of their absence.

"You," she said, delving into her rudimentary understanding of the Prask language. "Where Hakoren?"

Obediently, it replied ... and she had no idea what it was saying. Or rather, she knew a few words here and there, but not enough to make sense of it. She levelled the battle-blade at it, and it shrank back. It knew danger, at least.

"Take ... uh, go Hakoren," she ordered. "Go Hakoren now!"

It looked at her then at the battle-blade, and turned toward the exit. She'd been quite prepared to kill it if it became uncooperative, but it seemed that a sharp enough tone backed by a battle-blade superseded previous orders.

Unless, of course, it had been given specific orders to '*lead the human into a trap if she escapes from the arena*', but she was betting against that.

Battle-blade at the ready, she followed the worker-caste as it found its way unerringly through the building. Staying in the arena might've been the least hazardous bet, but she'd never been one to play it safe.

"What is happening?" Hakoren k'Fariz was having a bad day. He'd been looking forward to seeing the human dragged from whatever hiding place she'd manufactured, but now his main and backup generators had been damaged by explosions, and several of his storage buildings were on fire. "Someone get me a report! Someone tell me where the enemy is! Someone tell me *something*!"

He'd initially thought that the compound had been bombed from the air, but the computer records hadn't shown any craft approaching before the air-detection systems went down to the power loss. Currently, he was working on the theory that an assault force was bombarding the compound from a distance, using lobbed explosive devices. It would explain why none of the operating sensors were picking anything up; that sort of thing was horribly low-tech, and the Prask had never really developed it much.

Humans had, though, which made him wonder if they were behind this. Or perhaps a rival Prask noble faction had copied human weapons to throw the suspicion off themselves. Either way, they hadn't broken in through any of the gates, so he had his warriors lining the walls and guarding the gates, so that if (and when) they tried to actually breach the compound, he could repel them with ease.

The door to his secure command facility beeped as the key code to open the lock was entered. He looked around with annoyance, ready to berate whichever worker had decided to bother him with a trivial matter. The worker entered, and he recognised it as the one working the hoist over the arena, which made no sense at all.

And then the human burst in through the doorway and charged across the room at him, and he stopped worrying about anything making sense. She was filthy and ragged and there was fresh blood seeping through a cloth bound around her arm, but the really important part was the hacked-off battle-blade she had touching his thorax as he pressed up against the wall.

"Go," she growled over her shoulder at the worker — in *Prask*. "Close door."

It did as she said, which surprised Hakoren considerably. Who knew humans could hit just the right tone to command menials? What was even more surprising was her presence, and the blade she wielded.

"Surrender now," he attempted. "Lay down your blade. I will release you at once."

"Haha, no, asshole," she said, and applied a little pressure to the blade. He could feel it beginning to penetrate his thorax: a surpassingly unpleasant sensation. "I don't trust you any further than I could shit you."

"Then what do you want?" he demanded, trying not to sound like he was pleading for his life, while doing exactly that.

"Two things," she said. "First, tell me exactly what I'm supposed to have done to you. Second, show me how to operate the in-house cameras. You can do both at the same time."

"You don't know why?" He was honestly surprised. Surely he'd told her at some point.

"Assume I have no idea." She let off on the pressure from the blade, allowing him to walk over to the console.

Using his upper arms, he activated the screens for the house security cameras, gesturing to the controls she would need to manipulate them. "You see here the button to switch to the next screen, and this one controls the microphone ..." At the same time, he eased his lower left hand under the edge of the desk to where a plasma pistol awaited in its holdout holster—

The battle-blade sliced downward, and he shrieked as blazing agony tore through his lower left arm. Ichor pulsed from the shorn-off end as the severed hand, holding the pistol, landed on the floor. Lurching backward, he clutched the truncated limb, staring at her as she raised the blade again.

"What part of *'I don't trust you'* didn't you get the first time, you back-stabbing piece of shit?" Crouching, she scooped up the pistol. "Okay, now I know how to use the cameras. Stand over there and don't move, or I *will* see how many shots it takes to kill you."

He stumbled back to the wall, wondering how things could have gone badly wrong so quickly. Holding the pistol trained on him, apparently alternating her attention between himself and the screens, the human laid the battle-blade down on the top of the console and started looking through the cameras.

About four screens in, she paused and pressed the button for the microphone. "Dallas? Hey, yeah, it's me. I've got you on camera ..."

"*Dallas?*" Kerra's voice came out of a nearby speaker. "*Hey, yeah, it's me. I've got you on camera. Head up those stairs to your right, along the corridor, then take a left. I'm in the safe room at the end.*"

The interior of the house had been bigger and harder to clear than he'd initially thought. They'd checked Hakoren's bedchamber, but he hadn't been there, but there were a few guards inside the house that he and Ramirez had ended up killing. One had cut Paulson but not too badly, and Ramirez was patching him up.

"That's her?" asked Ramirez, looking up as she finished.

"The one and only." Dallas felt a grin spreading across his face. Kerra was the smartest, toughest, most tenacious woman he'd ever met, and she'd just proven it all over again. "Paulson, you good?"

"Get it for me." She watched as tiny dots swept toward the shuttle on the screen. "Hold on!" she called out, then cut the main drive and hit the manoeuvring thrusters. The massive shuttle spun like a ballerina, then creaked and strained as she engaged the mains once more. Gravity seemed to go every which way, but she was used to that.

Two of the missiles went wide and self-destructed, but the third was more persistent, swinging around in a wide turn to follow her. But she'd aimed *at* the interceptors, boring up through the pack, so they had to scatter. One turned to follow her but got into the way of the third missile; the explosion was far astern.

The console beeped again, and Kerra swore. A dozen more interceptors were climbing into view. This was going to get very hairy indeed, and she didn't know how long the shuttle's fuel would last.

"Guard is open!" Paulson sang out.

"You're a goddamn genius." Kerra pressed the radio button on the controls, even as she manoeuvred to present the smallest possible cross-section to the new interceptors. "Mayday. Mayday. Mayday. This is Flight Lieutenant Kerra Dallas, escaping from Prask captivity." She rattled off her service number. "Will squawk triple seven, am under attack, require cover urgentmost. I say again, Mayday. Mayday. Mayday."

There would be no faking out the new interceptors by flying at them. They'd surround her and shred the shuttle. She had to go for orbit, and hope to outpace them with the oversized engines Hakoren had evidently paid out the big money for.

Gritting her teeth, she shoved the throttles all the way to their stops, but the interceptors still came on. First one, then another, achieved target lock. She tried corkscrewing to break the locks, but it only gave them a few seconds' respite.

"Mayday. Mayday. Mayday," she tried again. Was there nobody listening out there? "This is—" And then, the most glorious sight in the world happened. Half a dozen interceptors, squawking human ident codes, appeared ahead of the shuttle, coming on fast.

"*Prask shuttle piloted by Flight Lieutenant Kerra Dallas,*" came the voice of the element leader. "*This is Peacekeeper Actual. Please confirm that you are escaping from Prask captivity in a captured shuttle. How many souls, over?*"

"That is a solid confirm, Peacekeeper Actual." She took a deep breath. "Four souls plus one Prask prisoner, over."

"*Copy that.*" The interceptors flashed past in an instant. "*Steer one five three point five to rendezvous with our carrier. We'll brush the bugs off your windshield. Peacekeeper Actual, out.*"

"Roger and out." Kerra angled the shuttle onto the new heading, helpfully pointed out by Paulson.

As the carrier swam into view far ahead, and explosions bloomed far behind, she allowed herself to begin relaxing at long last.

It was over.

She was going home.

Epilogue

They sat on the beach, watching the sunset over the ocean: a proper sunset, in Dallas' opinion. Best seen from Earth, in other words.

Kerra was quiet, leaning up against him, inside the circle of his arms. These days she was like that, rarely demonstrative but always finding excuses to touch him. To reassure herself that his presence wasn't a dream.

Not that he was complaining, or that he was any less starved for her nearness.

"Ramirez called earlier," he said idly. "She says she's just about got the latest bunch of recruits ready for me to come and put the finishing touches on them."

"Good." He heard the smile in her voice. "She's a good troop. They both are. I'm glad they didn't get in too much trouble."

He chuckled. "I'm pretty sure Major Kanto has strings to pull that go into some pretty dark places. *Nobody* wants to see what she can come up with if they really decide to cross her. Also, she got a *ton* of intel out of Hakoren before they gave him back, which made everyone very happy indeed."

"I still think they should've kicked him out halfway and made him walk the rest of the way." She'd just about gotten to the point by now that she could talk about the Prask noble without shivering. However, her tone was deadly serious.

"No argument here. But Kanto told me something when I asked her about it." He shifted his weight and settled his arms more securely about her. "He was mutilated in his own house by his own prisoner, then taken prisoner himself, dragged off the planet, and then later freely given back. Every one of those things is another smack in the face, honour-wise. He was *begging* not to be returned. According to her, they had to literally kick him out of the airlock at the other end."

"Oh. Oh, I *see*." She began chuckling. "And from what I've heard about how much backbiting goes on at the nobility level, any sign of weakness at all gets *hammered*."

"Got it in one. And there's another reason we didn't get more than a slap on the wrist." He captured her hand in his and ran his thumb and forefinger over her ring finger. "They learned about our implants, and now it's the next big idea for IDing KIAs. Not rings, but coded bumps on the long bones. A dogtag you can't lose."

She snuggled against his chest, curling her fingers around his. "And all because you didn't want to take off your wedding ring."

"No." He kissed the top of her head. "All because one particular Prask asshole's kid played stupid games and won stupid prizes with your dropship."

"True."

They went back to watching the sunset, while waves lapped gently on the sand and a light onshore breeze brought the smell of salt and seaweed to their noses.

It really was very pretty.

The End

Acknowledgements

I wish to thank my friend Karen (Angel466) for beta-reading these stories and improving them measurably.

I also want to express my appreciation for all my Reddit readers who upvoted and commented on the stories.

And if you've bought this book and read it all the way through, you're pretty awesome too.

Cheers until next time.